IF YOU MUST RUN AWAY

Judith F. Kennedy

For M.

A few infinities
and this woman's work

all
at sea

Chloe Marsden was lost. After walking hours through the failing light and oncoming weather of a late November day, she thought, maybe, she neared the wharfs of Seoul. Maybe. Four ports into a twenty-one-day cruise out from Shanghai, hemmed in by fog and jumbled streets with few views of the iconic skyline – any iconic skyline – she did occasionally wonder if she was wrong about the Seoul part.

"But I'm not lost," she reassured herself, *"I've just misplaced the Yellow Sea."*

Even an intrepid pedestrian cannot lose an ocean in a country that is all peninsula – everybody knows that – and having fled to Asia on the premise that if her doctor's receptionist couldn't find her, they couldn't schedule her heart surgery, she lacked the mileage commitment of one of "those" tourists. Yes, it had been a sad waste of defiance spending the day trying to find the bottom of a hill, where all civilized countries keep "sea level" and their cruise ship terminals. She wasn't so cuckoo for cocoa puffs, though, that she climbed up and over Bukhasan Mountain without noticing and was now halfway to Pyongyang.

Doc might not see any distinction, but you do, right?

Burying her chin deeper into her infinity scarf, Chloe continued her trudge down the crooked road full of the scent of low tide, yet mysteriously lacking salt-water, salt flats or an eleven-story, ocean-going vessel setting up for Taco Thursday on the Lido deck. Jostled along by her fellow travelers, black-haired persons dressed in the international urban winter couture of black coats, black puffer jackets, the occasional rebel black hoodie and a man four paces ahead in a black wool trench who looked like he was going places, her flaming hair, teal pea coat and chartreuse daypack slung crosswise across her chest remained the sole splotch of holiday color.

She and the gang finally got held up by a red light at the corner of Wasn't This Supposed to Be Avenue and Whichway Now Road. That was exciting. One never knows what seventeen seconds access to tiptoes and a new axis to stare down might bring into one's life. Shipping containers. Twinkle lights. In a pinch, Taipei 101.

The remaining fifteen seconds she used to make faces at another wall of anonymous concrete apartment blocks, small restaurants and smaller shops vying for space and her attention. In every direction, hanging signs and for-rent banners creaked and flapped overhead in the wind. Sandwich boards crowded the narrow sidewalks. Bold calligraphy emblazoned steaming windows. The whole landscape burst with news and information as to what was "right here, right now!", "today only!", "pick me!". People wearing black outer garments appeared to find this knowledge useful. They participated. They cared. Perhaps, they could read Hangul. Chloe watched them jerk open glass doors with decision and disappear around corners with takeaway containers and somewhere else to be, all seemingly unaware, or unconcerned, that nowhere and tacked to nothing was a picture of a ship with a helpful arrow pointing dockward.

The cold seeped up from the pavement, and the crowd on the corner shuffled restlessly waiting for the light's *plink plink* to turn go. Chloe wiggled her toes on the downbeat, ever more aware that watching the horizon and not watching out for puddles had left her canvas sneakers all squelchy, and began to fall prey to the inevitable questioning of one's life choices that one does in November when turned around in the back alleys of Southeast Asia with night descending.

Her original plan had not been to flee the jurisdiction. Of course not. It was to hide under the bed and just not answer the phone. But then she remembered she was 34. And had credit cards. And that Holland America loves a last-minute traveler. So, maybe Plan B – run, run away – wasn't wise or affordable, but it was a much more mature and interesting way of ignoring someone. The ending up, somehow, at a random intersection, 6,842 miles from the couch where one was supposed to be resting and looking behind three-story apartment buildings for the lee side of the Pacific Ocean, that part, well, those things can happen to anybody.

Skipping the pilgrimage from her gate in Terminal E to Hudson News in Terminal B, now that was a bad decision with long-term consequence. Life on the road is hard. Navigating the risk of going through security twice and the temptation of buying gum at a 200% markup is how we do hard. Everybody knows that running away from home – successfully – requires the legitimacy of purpose, essential reads and laminated cartography that only comes from visiting one's airport newsstand. If that takes buying a $7.00 pack of Wrigley's, oh well. She left town in such a rush, some might say mad panic, she hadn't even remembered that by 4:37 in the afternoon gum becomes a snack, so technically, it's only a 175% markup.

The last, hurried cross-current of black backpacks clipping her shoulders and white shopping bags taking out her knees buffeted Chloe out of her musings on the joys of wintergreen and a *Lonely Planet* map insert. Yanking the strap of her daypack back into position, the contents bumped and rattled a gentle reminder. She did not lack all the necessities of a wandering life. The soft lump poking her spine must be the dog-eared, small print paperback of *The Hobbit* in case she got stuck in line anywhere. The tinny clink, a cheerful umbrella covered in Monet's flowers yet to be of any use in the misty moisty air that surrounded rather than fell. And last she checked, the zippered pocket held enough local currency to buy an extra fancy cup of coffee and drink it indoors. This random, nameless, useless intersection couldn't be the end of the road, that was just the wet socks talking.

"And just because we don't see an eleven-story, ocean-going vessel setting up for Taco Thursday on the Lido deck, doesn't mean it isn't there. Fog brings out the inner lurk in everybody."

The light plinked back to green, and once more Chloe stepped off the curb into the unknown. Somewhere along this road her larger geographic principles would be vindicated. Even if the Yellow Sea she sailed in on was really the South China Sea, and therefore on the wrong side of the street from where she thought she left it, and even if adrenaline and curiosity had taken her a remarkable distance that day, she steadfastly maintained that oceans had to be somewhere. Some things are too big to stay lost forever.

Chloe trudged on.

W HEN DISEMBARKING FROM *MS WESTERDAM* between the hours of breakfast buffet and first brunch seating, the navigational aids Chloe thought would get her home in time for Tex Mex included a smart phone that maybe might work in Asia, a cheerful sense of adventure, and the basics of spoken Hangul familiar to any self-respecting lover of the K-drama – the ability to distinguish nuanced variations on "I like you", "I love you" and "I'm...*sniff*...sorry" and a firm grasp on how to address new friends, random elders, and that ubiquitous figure in any Korean adventure worth having, a grumpy CEO. She was only going three blocks. Maybe six. The ship's Shore Excursion Manager, though, preferred his passengers slightly better equipped before walking the gangplank. Prior to the ship making port, he noticed Chloe's name missing from the sign-up sheets for day trips and stopped her as she passed his kiosk heading for the Wednesday evening pasta bar.

"Chloe, I really think you'd get more out of our all-day, hop-on hop-off bus tour," he said, laying the glossy brochure on the dark, walnut countertop for her to peruse.

"Uh-huh," she responded, staring where he wanted her to stare and listening politely to his sales pitch.

"See, look, it has six stops and that includes Changdeokgung Palace."

"Uh-huh."

"You'd like Changdeokgung," he continued, pointing to the relevant beauty shots of the throne room's elaborate painted and coffered ceiling, and a tea house surrounded by Japanese maples. "They have excellent gardens, even in winter."

"Uh-huh."

"It's only $249, and for that you get lunch, entry tickets and translators."

"Uh-huh."

"So, should I sign you up? They leave at 8:00 AM," he asked, reaching for his clipboard.

"Nuh-uh," she replied, neatly refolding the brochure and replacing it in the display rack so he wouldn't have to. "I'm gonna try the docks this stop, going more with an *On the Waterfront* vibe. Thank you, though! When it is time for Tokyo, you and me, Damien, I'm all in. Tomorrow isn't Tokyo, is it?"

"It's Seoul."

"That's what I thought. Have a great night!"

With a friendly wave, Chloe walked off to meet her friends for second seating.

The Excursion Manager watched her red head bobbing away in the crowd, his brow furrowed in the same worried expression he used when a guest opted for tours off the Internet that promised to be twice as exciting and half as expensive as his carefully curated and vetted offerings. Calling over his shoulder to his subordinate working on the other side of the counter, he asked,

"What time do we sail tomorrow?"

"2 AM," the Assistant Manager replied, looking up from his end-of-day paperwork.

"We can't put a LoJack on her, I suppose?"

"Where can she go?"

"It's a city of ten million people."

"Actually, it's twenty-five million, if you count the suburbs," the Assistant Manager corrected him with a yawn, reaching behind his head to scratch his back with the eraser end of his pencil.

"We are never going to see her again. Do we have missing person forms for Korea?"

"Oh, come on," the younger man protested, watching his boss jerk open file drawers. "There's nowhere to go and nothing to see if you are on foot. We're docked in the back beyond. If she takes a hard right, she might see an eco-tourism rice paddy and some newer high-rises, but other than that, warehouses and shipping container storage lots ring the harbor, like, four blocks deep. Who wants to look at that in November?"

"Until you get up the hill."

The Assistant Manager shook his head.

"She's never going to walk up that hill. Don't worry! She'll go buy a bubble tea, take in the view from the pedestrian bridge over the highway, and by the time the ice in her cup melts, it will have started raining and she'll head back. If she orders an *Americano* or likes staring at industrial cranes and other people's cargo ships, maybe she'll hang on for fifteen more minutes. We wish we had some nearby options for the people who show up at the desk at 8:30 AM hoping when we said the tour starts at 8:00, we really meant 9:15, but we don't."

"Maybe you're right," the Manager conceded, closing the last drawer with a rolling clang. "There is only the one street that crosses over the highway. Maybe she'll never find it?"

"That's the spirit."

The Excursion Manager sighed in resignation, resettled his striped tie, and returned to sorting flyers for helicopter tours over Jeju Island.

As Chloe left the kiosk, navigating her way against the tide of people leaving first seating for the early shows on the Promenade deck, she too sighed over her decision. She appreciated the Excursion Manager's effort to connect her with both an Imperial landscape frequently used as a television backdrop for Korean period dramas, and an extraction team. His superior wisdom in Shanghai guided her towards the Yu Garden/Huangpu River cruise combo instead of the walking tour of the Bund and cemented her faith that here was a man who knew his stuff and his people. Now one of her closest shipboard friends, she often sat on the wooden stool he kept under the counter, helping with small kiosk tasks, vouching for his authority with new customers and listening to dispatches on the great war between the blues band and housekeeping over those missing guitar strings with all the partisanship of a crew member.

A man so right about Yu Garden, and about how failing to restock the musician staterooms with mini shampoos was a deliberate escalation of hostilities, must be equally correct regarding all things Changdeokgung. She was simply far more cognizant of her doctor's view of reality than she let on. Or let anyone else know about. Through machination, luck, faith and raw willpower she had yet to collapse in public, but her tiny cabin witnessed one, maybe several, alarming crumplings and thuds. Taking her broken heart on a tourist blitz of the massive, sprawling city on a hill with all the stairs of Monaco and none of the handy escalators would not end well.

She therefore decided, almost as if it was prudent, and reasonable, and just as interesting, to explore only along the water's edge, and aggressively distill her Korean bucket list down to two items. Item One, find very, very old buildings, the older the better, and how hard could that be in a port city continuously occupied since 2,000 BC? Item Two presented a slightly greater challenge. To intently eavesdrop anywhere people wearing suits gathered, so that like Jane Goodall stalking the business community of Korea, she might achieve her dream of...*sniff*...hearing *"Depunim!"* used in the wild.

It seemed like a good idea at the time. Doc would strongly disagree, but ha ha ha, he probably thought she had run off to Paris and was yelling in the wrong direction.

the kindness of local wind

Wandering off that dreary Thursday, Chloe found the port of Incheon as described by the Assistant Manager, had she risked asking him. She toiled several blocks along a busy, four-lane road that served the wholesale businesses and low warehouses lining the harbor, trying to marvel at a landscape painted in a Crayon box rainbow of gunmetal grey, rusty nails, November sky and cold water.

Stumbling upon a pedestrian bridge, she crossed over the heavy morning traffic, hoping it would dump her down onto the flat, quiet, orderly grid behind the industrial corridor. Instead, she found herself red-faced and a little short of breath slowly climbing up into an older neighborhood being redeveloped in the "just put it anywhere" modern school of rapid design. Apartments, businesses, parks, shops and the occasional detached house appeared in the most unexpected places and combinations all along its aggressively vertical hillside.

Enough pockets and corners of history did remain to cross Item One off her bucket list by lunchtime. The thrill of victory temporarily demoted her uncertainty as to where o' where the one path back down to *Westerdam* might be to a non-issue. It was probably somewhere over her right shoulder, and given that it had been missing for about three hours, likely...a block and a half away.

What was far more important was what was in front of her.

Sitting on a handy wooden bench, munching the croissant unlawfully snagged off *Westerdam's* breakfast buffet that tumbled around in her bag all morning wrapped in two napkins, she spent a near-noon snack pause contemplating ye very olde...something grand and wonderful. It had a swoopy roof with curly, terra cotta tiles and heavy carved beams under the eaves, surely what she gazed upon had a story and cultural significance to the Korean people. It had its own bench. A steady stream of visitors passed in and out of the olde building's large, brightly painted wooden doors suggesting the structure was a temple, but she would try not to judge if it had been resurrected as the other neighborhood Starbucks. Its permanence, continued relevance, and elevation to bench-status in a vast sea of newly poured concrete made her own problems seem as temporary and insubstantial as the crumbs rapidly collecting down the front of her jacket.

Eking out the last bites of laminated, buttery goodness and the larger flakes caught by the inside napkin, Chloe did wish she put more thought into her own continued survival. If she only more fully committed to defrauding the cruise line, she could have at least walked off with two additional pastries and a tangerine. Or, if she wanted to be a non-criminal about it, if only she was brave enough to venture into one the neighborhood's ubiquitous 7-Eleven's. From the vantage point of the bench, two familiar green and red neon signs glowed out of the fog, each asking the same, age-old question: in a city of twenty-five million people, was blindly poking one's nose down mysterious, dockside alleyways any less scary than wandering a foreign snack aisle in search of chocolate chip cookies and a Gatorade? Really? Was it?

...Yes, she decided. Yes, it was.

Despite watching endless reruns of Lee Joon-gi acting out how convenience store transactions work in-country, making it look easy, solving every customer service problem with a beautifully choreographed martial arts scene, he never ate cookies. Nor did any episode cover whether triangle *gimbab* came in "plain" flavor. Her idea of "spice" was basil, not *gochujang*. Ok Taek-yeon playing a Joseon chef, not even Lee Dong-wook interviewing a Buddhist chef could entice her to explore foods that lived outside American flavor profiles or known snack packaging.

"This parochial stomach is definitely a character flaw abroad," she admonished herself, and folded her napkin into a funnel to convey the last, itty-bitty crumbs into her mouth.

Such fatalistic thoughts – however true – were still unsuitable after a tasty alfresco lunch contemplating a people's architectural genius. This nation invented the swoopy roof. Who was she to pre-decide the power of a well-dressed local demonstrating how *tteokbboki* worked? Scrambling to her feet and de-crumbing her person, she recommitted another hour to CEO hunting. The road to the left of the bench looked narrowest and most winding, and therefore the most interesting, so despite it being the only one without a 7-Eleven, she gave herself a small fist pump of encouragement and struck out in that direction.

Yeah.

Of course, anyone who has eaten more than butter and a sugar rush for lunch knows that a street too small to support a convenience store does not house a business district. She did augment Item One on her bucket list with the temple's domestic counterpart, an old but not quite olde traditional home with a less ornate but still swoopy roof. Tucked into an odd bend, clinging on like the stubborn bits in a post-Thanksgiving roasting pan, it, too, was having an exciting time. Its original side gardens were hosting a yet-to-be-resolved contest between at least two surveyors, the Streets Department and a developer who clearly didn't own the last needed five feet for its apartment project and built it anyway. Lacking a bench to take in the Escher-ness of it all, Chloe slowed her steps to admire the remnant of a high brick wall topped by a hefty vine. Both had outlived at least four wars, kudos there, and weren't going to fold over some zoning issue. Peeping through the wall's pretty wrought iron gate into a courtyard, she also glimpsed an actual, live, working kimchi jar, and felt like a better person for it.

Encouraged by a sharp, impatient honk to stop trying to add a chalk outline to the property's storied history just to stare at condiments fermenting, Chloe followed the brick wall around its last two corners to find combat and modernity had mowed down the back garden in favor of a bustling high street. Back on track with Item Two, she lurked hopefully along behind a trio exiting a sushi restaurant dressed in casual Friday attire until the local residents' need for a "Beer Cream" establishment over mature peony beds again left her blinking and scrunching her forehead and waiting to get run over.

People who invest in huge, black, permanent English letters stapled to a brick wall know what to call a thing, and they don't need to explain themselves to Americans with a peony bias. Scanning the shelves visible through the unglazed openings, though, Chloe couldn't work out what that thing...was. A giant, pink, plastic, soft-serve ice cream cone guarded the front entrance, that felt...suggestive, but inconsistent with the giant banners announcing a blowout, 50-70% sale on something...not ice cream? Really? Blinking even harder, she wondered if said persons were having trouble finding their target customer. Despite the liberal splashes of English words and numbers, it might not be her.

"Oh no! Look away!" she admonished herself, belatedly spotting the cashier trying to catch her eye to come in and...participate. Her compelling need to uncover the mission behind the moniker that was Beer Cream was just nosiness, though, it had no cash value, not before she mastered 7-Eleven's. With a quick bow and bright smile of encouragement, she passed on, missing out on the Beer Cream culinary adventure and the young man's informed opinion about people eavesdropping around the port, prying into what strangers do with their court-yards and small business loans. The latter, though, likely dovetailed with the 114 episodes of *Peter Gunn* she was also ignoring.

For her, that research strategy yielded two students quizzing each other for a vocabulary test and a middle-aged woman buying perilla leaves from a street vendor. The designated hour stretched into two-and-a-half as she unsuccess-fully pinballed between interesting nooks and local landmarks and rounded many a few corners without paying much attention. It was time to want her ship back. Promptly, before the tide went out.

"Looking this hard down by the docks for a man in black calling himself "The Chairman"...was that ever wise?" she consoled herself. *"Would he want that? Let's head back to the excursion kiosk and get the Assistant Manager to hand over those macrons he bet me over the missing guitar strings. I so knew it was Felipe."*

Accepting the sad truth that solving shipboard mysteries was just easier than finding men wearing Armani in real life, Chloe took the next two right-hand turns as a good-faith effort to reverse course and started home for dinner.

ALAS, WITHOUT A HANDY *FODER'S* pocket edition, some people may be unaware that just above the harbor Surely This Is the Right Road dead-ends into Oh Rats It Ain't Street. A *Rough Guide* might also mention that small, white delivery vans who try to thread a path through the crush of parked cars and an awkwardly placed dumpster often get their angles wrong there, and a bit stuck. And so will hapless travelers. Forever.

Like many before her, Chloe found herself pinned up against a corner real estate office to allow the day's contestant room to jump the curb, listening to the endlessly repeated screech of metal against metal that did not belong to the driver as he refused to take the easy way out. Abandoning her life at sea for the available one-bedroom unit listed on the flyer in the window appeared to be the only way forward. At least Doc's receptionist would never think to look for her in a Korean second floor walk-up.

Guesstimating where ₩1.5 million rent falls on a scale between swankytown and affordable housing, however, takes effort and *DK Travel* never recommends that street corner to do mental arithmetic with so many zeros. Wonky and a death trap, it also catches the wind as the temperature drops with the afternoon sun. After a damp day had hovering between misty, sleety and snow, a blast of cold, early night air carried the four snowflakes that had made a decision. They swirled around the van and plinked against Chloe's right cheek with a dark, arctic-explorer-going-the-wrong-way insistence that she was nowhere near home.

"Four snowflakes do not make a weather event," she chided herself, glancing up to read the clouds.

"Said Shackleton, who also thought he knew where he was going," her tired, cold feet grumbled back.

"But in a pinch, this unit looks available now. Shackleton didn't have rental options."

When one's back is up against a landlord on the side of a mountain, what is also true is that the wind and weather usually come off the sea. Even Shackleton knew that much. Trusting to ancestral wisdom, Chloe turned her red nose and blue ears into the next gust, and waited for a slight pause in the grinding gears. Dodging recklessly across the road, she turned her back on the van, driver, and any chance of discovering the Hangul pictograph for "washer/dryer", and headed up Let's See Who's Right Alley.

ELDERS, THEY KNOW STUFF. WITH a little more Rudolph and a little less Yukon Cornelius it took eleven seconds to finally locate the spine of the hidden restaurant paved in cobblestones that led down to the pedestrian bridge. With one sniffle and a tired "Hallelu!", Chloe turned left into a light cold breeze, still following the wind.

Threading a path through the early rush of diners, insatiable curiosity and one last attempt to complete her bucket list again won out over gloom and blisters. Strolling along she peeked into windows, trying to guess what the grill patrons were grilling, and whether the metal funnels over each table required grill skills to properly draw the smoke off the individual braziers. She peered over the shoulders of customers sitting at the open-air stalls to see what was being plunked in front of them, distinguishing from random wafts the differing smells of fried, brown, and red dishes. She walked extra slow past noodle shops, hoping to see people stirring things with their chopsticks the way they always did in K-dramas before they said something interesting. Alas, not one of the patrons appeared to be saying anything to their boss.

At the fruit shop, the vendor being temporarily absent from his upside-down milk crate, she risked one last pause in front of a box of apples she had no intention of buying to double extra check her memory that this steep incline was not another one of those dead-end, lying liar, staircase fakeouts down to the highway retaining wall that made people cry. Another gust rattled down the alley with a sleety milieu and teared her up instead. Snow without a hat was moderately romantic, but misplaced in an ice storm, in a restaurant district that could only supply her with healthy snacks not worth the trouble of stealing from a buffet line, somehow that felt extra Edwardian gone wrong.

"You can't lose out to Shackleton," she insisted, trying to rally herself down the home stretch. *"He made it safely back, and without Taco Night Buffet waiting for him."*

"Yeah, but Scott didn't. Doomed to a low-rent, Terra Nova exit for lack of a pencil and notebook to commit one's last thoughts."

"Debby Downer, the Yellow Sea is a wee harder to miss than an invisible magnetic confluence. Our fruit seller is practically almost next to the gift shop in the ship's lobby, we must be near on top of it by now."

One more time the weather interrupted her internal debate regarding meteorology, travelogues, the signs of imminent demise, and how far one had to go to get decent Tex Mex in Asia. It caught at her coat and pulled her feet into taking the left-hand turn. One more push and she stumbled against a lighted shop window under a small striped awning just down from the corner.

Beyond the plate glass, a familiar and dearly beloved sight appeared. She blinked several times in case it was snow blindness, but the welcome display remained. A pastry case, a real, live, lighted pastry case full of cream and sugar and possibly, that there was a *tart tartin* on the second shelf.

Indecision seized her. Did the natural impulse one had whenever passing the new gourmet donut shop back home remain viable and correct across thirteen time zones? For this unique culinary challenge, she thought she could maybe just cobble together enough courage and language skills to point and pay, and with the ₩50,000 bill in her pocket, they might even believe she could count. No quibbling was required in a pastry shop. No matter how inaccurately she gestured in Hangul, it took an investment of time and relationship to discern between a chef's item of greatness, the thing next to greatness but still best thing ever, and the not quite best thing ever, let's try the jumbo eclair next time.

Chloe glanced behind her at the gloom and damp, calculated the risk of frostbite, and looked back into the lighted room. It was an equally unassailable travel maxim that when someone makes something you love, when found, wherever found, it is one's duty to buy it. It was that final, altruistic argument that propelled her over the threshold. She pushed open the door, heard the comforting tinkle of the bell required for all pastry shop doors everywhere, and stepped inside.

CHAPTER THREE

the first port in a storm

Crossing the shop threshold, Chloe's immediate impression was that of warmth and kindness, of things loved and well-used. Avidly scanning the pastry case, she also felt certain that someone nearby was very good at his job.

For this was surely a man's shop. A bijou, utilitarian establishment, the counter and pastry case ran along the left side, and on the right, some battered tables clustered around a tiny stove. Except for a few plants, and the occasional picture on the plaster walls distempered in pale green, there was little extraneous ornamentation, and none of the fluffy clutter that comes with grandmother's recipes and grandmother somewhere about the place.

The spareness only highlighted the star and point of the enterprise. Displayed in the well-lit, industry-standard glass cabinet, Chloe's expert eye recognized the selection and its regimental aspect indicated that this unknown man was French-trained. Like the space itself, his desserts combined restraint with a *je ne sais quoi* promising that the cakes, pastries, and yes, that was a *tart tartin* on the second shelf, included an equal measure of proper technique and sugar-butter good time.

Before committing her mind to the selection process, Chloe glanced around to ensure she hadn't unconsciously shoved anyone out of the way in her beeline across the worn, wooden floor. She found the shop dead empty. Gratitude to have the queue to herself was quickly replaced by a skosh of resentment towards the local population. A legion of customers ought to be blocking her path, dithering between the surefire classic *du jour* or the experimental joy *du moment*. He had baked it, they should come.

"They must not know," Chloe chose to believe, preferring to disparage his marketing efforts rather than the taste of the nation that birthed her favorite television actors. Considering her own journey to his door, she also conceded that his neighbors were far less susceptible to being pushed around by local wind.

As she began her own ritual dither, her disdain for the missing hordes turned to pity.

"They just don't know," she concluded with a great deal of compassion. *"Poor things."*

She bent down to look closer into the case and stepped back to get the full experience, twice, yet a hard choice remained between the blue *entremets*, a bold choice in pastry, blue, or the yellowy, maybe lemony, cake with lots of mysterious, perfectly equal layers, or the chocolate *canelé*, how could that be left on the shelf, it had a 3-D chocolate butterfly. No dessert on the ship came with a 3-D butterfly, and as she could see, now, perhaps it should.

A hesitant, disembodied voice broke the silence. The first five syllables spoken comprised the standard Korean greeting. Maybe. Not hearing near enough unknown syllables tacked on afterward to suggest the shop wasn't empty, it was closed and to get out, Chloe guessed with a 62% certainty she was being requested to stop flip-flopping around and order something.

A little reconnaissance helped spot a young woman with heavy bangs and dark-rimmed glasses peering anxiously at her from behind a row of cellophane-wrapped madeleines. The stark contrast between her expensive canvas work apron and the cheap yellow blouse sold in the night market three blocks away, and her effort to blend in with the cookie display rather than distinguish herself from it, suggested both a new employee and one with language skills on par with her customer.

Chloe returned the greeting and bowed once to demonstrate her understanding of rudimentary Hangul, pointed to the blue dessert and managed a (surely) near native, "this one, thank you". With a subsequent glow of pride, she watched the woman's hand reach for the correct item, and when half of a glass lens reappeared among the cookies with a slight questioning air, answered it with another bow.

"Hangul isn't so hard after all," she told herself with triumph as her selection was removed for plating.

Idly listening to cake plates nervously fumbled and clattered, doubt suddenly assailed Chloe. This *entremets* sat alone in a man's shop, a shop without customers. It was blue. It was the dessert that went best with the sleety gloom and the jazz playing over the shop's loudspeaker, the bluesy kind of jazz, the kind with trumpets, but was this really a French chef's house or a wannabe Francophile with good house music trying to push the boundaries of sugar with ghost peppers and blue food?

"Well, Plan B was death by sleet anyway," she reminded herself, and turned to deciding whether to forgo the table by the window with the view of the darkening alley as more suited for "Spring seating" and opt for the one closest to the heater.

The counter person spoke again. Chloe listened intently to the low sound of syllables, syllables, *"ca-fé"*, more syllables, many of them getting lost among the cookies, and all of them standing between her and her last hope of sustenance before she re-found her ship. She kept the hand clutching her ₩50,000 inside her bag and took a leap of faith that the woman was not asking for money but rather making a timid offer for a companion beverage. Thankfully, they weren't having this exchange in a 7-Eleven, where anything could happen. Watching unskilled hands require six tries and three head ducks to line up the grooves on the portafilter and a misguided elbow scatter a full measure of espresso across the counter was more than enough drama for someone who suddenly realized she had very limited funds and only knew the Korean word for "yes".

The woman's two-handed gesture used by every TV secretary was far less ambiguous. Politely ordered to stop staring and go wait somewhere else, Chloe bowed one last time and a few short steps away from the counter, reached her journey's end. Dropping down into a wooden chair, she took advantage of the solitude to flop back in a sprawling attitude anathema to most Korean woman in public.

"This may be my favorite café in the world," she thought, wriggling her toes in time with the jazz and feeling the heater steaming away her damp sneakers and the lower third of her jeans until one last fumbling clink announced the safe arrival of her order.

"Gamsahamida," she said quietly.

Taking a minute to gather her strength, and let the counter person scurry away, Chloe opened her eyes, picked up her fork, and took her first bite.

And sighed.

Not the sigh she made coming ashore acknowledging the expected fall weather. Or the intermittent loud sighs of needing a hat or a map or a tangerine. Or even the quiet one she made when she forced herself to be reasonable and turn down the Imperial gardens.

No, this sigh was for being right the first time. Here was a man who did not require one to manage one's expectations. The difference between other people's culinary best and his offering was all the wide world between the reliable satisfaction of hearing *Sinner's Prayer* on a Motown jukebox versus experiencing Ray Charles perform it live, balanced on one leg of his piano bench. You don't know until it hits you in the face and then, then you know. The blue in the dessert was blueberry, not squid ink, no gochu peppers, and the mousse was lemon, not vanilla pudding. Sweet, tart, creamy, crumbly bits, she even got her citrus on without having to buy the cake because like all well-managed shops, the chef reused components across multiple dishes.

After weeks of wandering untethered, awash in endless, meaningless decisions that might equally have found her watching Netflix reruns on her couch, or counting out *pesos*, or *colóns*, or on safari in Zimbabwe, always running away not toward anything, Chloe realized with a start that crossing this random threshold somehow brought her back to a world she understood, where even small choices mattered. Like a newly awoken sleepwalker, her eyes darted around the room with confusion and fresh awareness, once again taking in the harmony of the pleasing shade of green on the walls, the well-watered plants, and the shabby chic dinged and mismatched furniture that invoked a balance of functionality and comfort, all while continuing to savor her host's superior *entremets*.

"You, sir, are a genius and deserve good things and happiness for showing up to work today," she silently directed towards where she guessed the back premises must be. She hoped he wasn't taking the lack of customers to heart, and that he knew that all artists suck at marketing their own product.

"It takes a village!" she added, enjoying another, larger mouthful of lemon blueberry sunshine and happiness, *"that's why God invented museum gift shop managers!"*

CHAPTER FOUR

one enchanted evening

Somewhere around the fifth bite of *entremets*, and third sip of an acceptably decent cup of coffee for a novice barista, an eruption of very unhappy Korean issuing from a very unhappy Korean man shattered Chloe's reverie. It also brought home with immediacy the full bijou-ness of the shop. Despite being mere feet away from this violent happening, though, Chloe remained unbothered. She lolled her head in the direction of the disturbance to see her new best friend at the counter quail, eyes lowered, as the source of the commotion burst through the inner doorway waving a piece of paper and clearly having a feeling.

At just over six feet tall, with close-cropped hair, vigorous gestures, strong, sure hands, and the muscular forearms of a man who rolls his own dough, the angry newcomer towered over and effaced the petite and shy shop assistant. Watching the two mismatched combatants with mild curiosity, Chloe assessed the volume, hand waving and partially visible documentation, and narrowed down the issue to somebody ordered too much or not enough. Or maybe forgot to pay something. She craned her neck slightly to get a better glimpse of the paper.

Her nosiness, even unto other people's business correspondence, made Chloe laugh to herself, but alas, flapping Korean paperwork read sideways did not make it more decipherable. She settled for proving her ability to recognize written Hangul in any form or font.

Suddenly, with a frisson of joy that almost made her sit up properly, Chloe realized to whom this noisome catastrophe had happened. Here, she was certain, was the elusive CEO. He was even grumpy, how on brand for the genre. Clamping her lips to hold back a cry of *"depunim!"* and a triumphant laugh that Item Two had at long last been achieved, Chloe settled for scrunching up her shoulders in satisfaction that the gentleman met, at least in profile, a CEO standard worthy of both a TV show and her grossly truncated bucket list. It was also true that he wasn't wearing a suit, and the second toggle on his chef coat was buttoned wrong, he hadn't shaved, and his hair was a little wonky as if someone had sat at a desk for a moment clutching his head, but still, these were minor considerations this side of trying his mousse.

As a former boss, she also recognized the exasperation of a reluctant delegator proved right. Her business mind rapidly assessed the empty shop, the price point of his product, the stray twitch that sent her order's entire profit margin onto the floor while the bulk of his talent lay unregarded on the lighted tiers and easily determined what had gone so wrong with this man's dream that made him yell over clerical issues. Her intuition also knew he would soon regret what he could not stop himself doing. The Zen of the establishment was inconsistent with a man who harangued junior staff not allowed to harangue back, and his outburst would only add another small, shameful indignity to what looked like a very bad day.

Roused into action by camaraderie, and as his only other equal in the room, possibly in the enterprise, Chloe felt a sudden duty to intervene. Perhaps because she was so far from home, or too tired to think, or think it through as both rude and highly inappropriate, but almost before realizing it she slipped up out of her chair and over to the gap in the counter and touched his arm.

JUST THAT SMALL SOUND AND light pressure interrupted the chef, as he became informed the shop, his shop, was not empty. He turned to face this new crisis head-on. Alas, the combination of the disaster in his hand and the disaster before his eyes was greater than his front-of-house skills. Instead of smoothly transforming into an apologetic and conciliatory café owner and bowing his way out of the situation, he froze in front of his target customer and now worst nightmare – a Western tourist. The paper he held crackled as his hand suddenly clenched into a fist.

Part of his shock, however, was that this person did not look like an affronted patron, and the hand on his arm did not feel like the unpardonable liberty of a stranger. Her clear-eyed gaze held a mixture of kindness and empathy and remonstrance, her touch the authority of an old friend. He felt understood and commiserated with, and also that he was being asked to stop now and to make a different decision.

"My poor boy, you've had a hard time, haven't you?" said Chloe in English, patting the man's arm soothingly. "Express yourself at me, instead. Having experienced the sugar butter happiness of your food and establishment, I am entirely on your side."

It took remarkably little force for her to draw him away to the other side of the counter where he no longer loomed over his staff. Removing the paper from his hand with a low, self-deprecating laugh that even up close and right side up it still conveyed nothing, she put it safely on the counter. Turning a more serious face towards him and holding his arm with an added firmness, she said,

"*Miannada,* I can't converse in Korean. *Je ne parle pas bien le francais,* either, but I hope by doing something completely American, I'm not doing something unforgivably *irrespecteuese* in this country."

She continued with a quiet earnestness.

"Whatever this calamity, whoever in marketing is letting you down, and whatever contingency plan, or Plan B, or disaster emergency preparedness you are being asked to do or forced to do, know that it isn't to give up making this food. You are a genius pastry chef, and God is on your side on this one. That I guarantee, and I hope the 20,000-foot perspective from a stranger that you didn't ask for at least provides some supporting clarity on what is or is not the next right action."

The man knew enough English to follow 80% of her speech. His French was better, and much better than hers, but he understood English pretty well. He wasn't listening to her words, however, so much as tracking their import by how she looked at him. He even read the flash of humor as she took the unpaid bill out of his hand and found her self-communing as transparent as her idiosyncratic words and manner ought not to be, yet was.

He should have shaken off her hand immediately. He should have bowed politely and refunded her order. He should have been confused and terrified to watch the birth of an Internet troll come to document for all of social media his rare loss of temper. Instead, he listened and was comforted. He did bring his right hand up to disengage hers, but even that act made it only as far as covering her cold fingers with his warm clasp before the impetus burned itself out.

They looked at each other for a moment in friendly silence before Chloe continued.

"Meanwhile…"

She gestured with her chin towards his counter person still standing with eyes lowered, waiting for her portion of the event to recommence. After a pause, Chloe added a questioning look that asked what he was going to do, first, about that.

Reading this stranger's career advice and ethical reminders with such ease felt remarkable. Ceding the authority to interfere, however, was a privilege he did not accord his longtime girlfriend, or to this extent, even his business partner. But the woman was right. He found himself nodding back with resigned and rueful agreement to both unspoken requests – to stop and to make things right.

"Thank you," Chloe said with a squeeze to his arm, watching him silently relent. "And don't let anyone worry you after I'm gone that your business is about to get torpedoed online. I shall remember your *entremets* forever. Respect."

Her face suddenly clouded with her own association of ideas.

"Not that my forever is a very long time, but even though my dreams are over, yours are just beginning. Truly. Don't give up. Until people try your food, they can't possibly know someone like you exists, now can they? They may not be here, but that doesn't mean they're happy about it. Poor things."

Midway through this pep talk, the man noticed the woman's vitality waver. It was like watching an image go in and out of focus on old TV set when the rabbit ears lost the incoming signal. He felt an unaccountable desire, mirroring her earlier one, to step forward, step up, to find out why all was not right with this stranger. To do something. But he did not, a thing he never forgave himself for.

Chloe's mind had long since caught up with her mouth and come down on the side of exit stage right, right quick, rude person, but now her body began to make its similar protest known. Her heart disliked it most when she stood up unexpectedly to do something interesting, and was insisting that she immediately rethink that decision, or it would do it for her. With a final squeeze to the man's arm, she started her wobbly and belated tactical retreat back to her chair.

Suddenly, the bell on the shop door tinkled forcefully. They both turned towards the new person entering the café.

"*Oh my goodness, it's a Bond Villain,*" thought Chloe, taking in the woman's very high, very fashionable heels (with an inward sigh of acknowledged inferiority for wandering about in sensible shoes), the tight, short, very fashionable black suit and severe but very becoming hairstyle.

"*Oppa!*" the woman called out.

Chloe turned back to the man with a look of surprise and indifferently concealed disapproval. She didn't mean to, it just came from her soul. The incongruity of this beautiful, high-style creature – Chloe readily acknowledged, BV was all that – with that grating, nasal, look-at-me voice, and the greater discordance of both with this warm and comfortable shop...well. No one could approve of this woman calling this man *Oppa*. No.

Catching the shop owner's startled response, Chloe immediately turned her head farther out of view of the other woman and shmushed up her face in somewhat of a silent apology. Not for what she said, but for saying it out loud. Turning back with a perfectly smoothed, neutral expression, she made a polite, colorless bow towards the stranger, stepped away from the man and returned to her seat. She heard the man cough suddenly, which might have been a laugh, but she chose not to look and refused to find out.

"Who is that, *Oppa?*" the newcomer asked, coming to a standstill in front of him. "Kyung-ho *shi?*"

Chloe peered into her coffee cup as if something in the dregs required her immediate and all-consuming attention, and made a newly formed, even-if-it-killed-her commitment between herself and the last two fingers of her cappuccino to hereafter not roll her eyes at people just because they were cursed with an unpleasant speaking voice. Jealousy, she decided, that's what that was. Well, if she invested more time onboard the ship participating in the milder fitness offerings, and less on the general stampede for the 11 PM chocolate buffet, perhaps she, too, would have the hamstrings needed to walk the mountainous city in 4" heels like a native. That wasn't the Bond Villain's fault. Meanwhile, if he, they, really it was they, if they found her business advice useful, great, she was moving on with her life. And if only that man, person, owner-guy-boyfriend, if he would start cooperating, how hard could it be?

The owner's first effort to let her go back to her place in the universe and his dessert, however, was an abject failure. In response to his girlfriend's sharp inquiry, he turned to introduce her before lack of information, purpose and one brief, humorous, mocking glance, caused him to falter.

"This is...a customer," he answered abruptly instead.

"*Humph,*" the woman flounced. At least, that's what Chloe assumed from the sounds she wasn't listening to, happening in a world she was no longer a part of, as she turned her head, again, bit her lip, held her breath, and tried very hard not to laugh. She thought she succeeded rather nicely. Why she thought the situation funny at all, she really couldn't say.

Her impolite and unaccountable mirth subdued, Chloe put down her cup and exchanged it for her fork. Then changed back. What a shame if his, a, this here dessert was to become a choking hazard before she figured out which nuts he, someone, used in the crust, and she really couldn't enjoy the discovery process with so much noise and commotion. Her former contemplative view of the window now unavailable, she turned to stare at the stove, and resolved to pretend the shop was empty until it became so again.

"*Oppa*, I have come to talk to you," said the Bond Villain into the waiting silence, linking her arm with his and causing him to start.

He realized he had been waiting, intently, for his customer to take a bite of the new *entremets* to gauge her reaction. His attention recalled, and reading the woman's body language to indicate she would resume eating only after certain persons were removed from the vicinity, he allowed himself to be pulled unresistingly into the back premises.

As the sound of the woman's voice and the click of her heels on the floor receded, Chloe smiled faintly at her temporary madness and the strange, brief encounter with the shop owner before the incident faded out of her mind. Her illness did that when she was tired. It became very loud and all-consuming, even after the remarkable past ten minutes.

Now that the greater part of her mind was no longer occupied with staying upright or calculating and recalculating how long she needed to remain so before she could regain her stateroom, and revived by a little food and having warm toes again, the futility and stupidity and danger of her flight to Asia, and her reckless day's itinerary, washed over her. It blotted out even the magic of the shop. Or perhaps, the magic and comfort of the man's shop, and his food, and communing with a like mind facing equal catastrophe made it possible to face what drove her head-on to do it.

forks, branches...

A few weeks earlier, and about the same time in the afternoon, Chloe sat in the patient's chair of her doctor's left-hand side exam room, the one with the blue upholstery and counters, not the tan ones. Scientifically wedged into an upright position, her elbow on the small work desk and her hand propping up her head, she half-listened to Doc flip through her thick, overstuffed chart, as he incorporated her most recent test results and made determinations and updates on her prognosis.

Grey-haired and earnest, both Doc and his litany bristled with technical terms and bad news. It all mattered little to Chloe in the immediate, however, which is why she wasn't really listening. As much as she refused to collapse in public, collapsing and/or bursting into tears in Doc's exam room was even more unacceptable. She couldn't afford to internalize his words, not yet, not until she made the three-hour drive back over the mountains and returned to her couch, but she did hear him out.

"We've tried everything else," is what he said, leaning back in his chair, the thickness of the chart a mute witness to how long and how many other ways they had fought and tried. The collective medical knowledge of the planet lay wrapped in that scuffed manila folder – the latest clinical trials out of Johns Hopkins and Harvard, the latest research papers out of Europe, the best traditional therapies from Asia. Even half-listening, Chloe's brain fully realized that Doc running out of ideas was a very bad sign. She tried harder not to care, not yet.

He laid two paths before her. A year to live, and a calm, but unpredictable and sudden end, or one final experimental trial that started with shutting off half of half her broken heart, followed by a course of medicine so strong she would wish she was dead. The last part was how Chloe shorthanded it for later reference, but it was based on a widely held belief that 67 pills a day sucked for everybody.

"It just might work," posited Doc, "it's worth a try."

He also prepared her for the last twenty minutes of her life, if it didn't.

"It will feel like a panic attack," he explained, describing the warning signs if her heart and lungs failed, "but it isn't one. You can't breathe, and your body is panicking. That's a different thing. Fighting it won't do you any good, though, it will just waste energy you don't have. And need."

"With luck it can pass, but until you need to be intubated," he warned, "there is nothing we can do, so don't push it. Or push yourself over the line."

"Keep calm and carry on?"

"Stay calm, don't overexert yourself, and carry on, yes."

"Intubation...," she repeated, trying to remember if she had seen that word done on *House*, or maybe *Hospital Playlist*. "That sounds unpleasant."

"Dying is worse," he replied, "so we're not skipping that part. We want you off the couch, but while we still don't understand the underlying cause, find a middle way. Let's start with the surgery and see where that gets us."

Chloe raised her head enough to give him a disapproving side-eye for any plan where she had to pay with her heart, today, for a little breathing space tomorrow, when she was fairly certain she could cling on and turn a year into eighteen months. Eighteen months was a long time to give John Hopkins to invent a better idea.

She then moved on to an equally pressing, equally unpleasant consideration.

"I'm not saying you're not right, but insurance companies expect to be paid either way. Heart surgery will cost thousands and thousands."

"So, pay them."

"I already sold the house to settle my first round of medical debts, and then the smaller, cheaper one I replaced it with, and then my car. That shiny one out parked next to yours is a rental. Now you're asking me to risk a quiet, lamentably early death in the comfort of my own apartment for the likely possibility of living under a bridge. That would kill me with or without your long shot."

"Or it might work," he insisted, "and you can have your life back and job back, pay off the debt, and get out of my hair."

"I'll think it over, I promise," she dissembled, hoping to slink out of the exam room with vague commitments that sounded like she had agreed to something when she hadn't. She discovered some time past that the medical establishment does not accept "but I don't wanna" as an argument, or a decision, when one is thirty-something and dying and there is still one last Plan B. Even when success might involve living heartless and under a bridge. It was always possible she and Doc were both right. The rest of the year was going to suck beyond measure, and she was giving up five minutes before the miracle.

"Don't worry," she reassured him, "if I choose wrong, which I do all the time, God will send his angels. Backup, it does a body good."

"*Pffft,*" he responded with annoyance. Doc was equally against her practical reliance on the Divine intruding on their treatment plan. "What if He doesn't?"

"He sent you, didn't He?"

Doc had his usual overfull docket of other patients to fight for and with that day, so after he typed her updated prescriptions into the computer, she slipped away without a referral. Just to be on the safe side, once she settled her bill at the receptionist desk, and caught up on the latest back-office gossip regarding Doc's new intern, she ran away. Home, first, but the soft, low, rolling peaks of the Appalachians didn't seem a good enough barrier to stop people from making her do unpleasant things. So, she raided a third of her credit line allocated for the surgery and ran the other way, putting the Rockies, the Sierras, the Pacific Ocean, and some volcanoes between them.

It wasn't wise, this last hurrah of a trip, but it's amazing how far one can get on fear, denial, willpower and Mastercard when one really doesn't want to hear what someone has to say.

Now sitting in this small café at twilight on the dockside of the other side of the world, Chloe put her fork down on her empty plate and pushed it away, warmed, sated, and oddly, temporarily invigorated. She briefly wondered if the chef used medicinal ingredients in his food, like secret kale, and fervently hoped it wasn't alcohol. She also remembered exactly where she was now. She passed the shop's awning that morning. Down the corner, from the foot of that road, she would be able to see the Starbucks, a real for sure one, not the temple she lunched in front of, and it marked the entrance to the wharf where *Westerdam* lay docked.

Plotting out her final steps back to the ship, Chloe again acknowledged the foolishness of spending the day so far away from it and all its accoutrements that she was beyond help or assistance. No one on the ship knew of her condition, but they would notice if she was dead and know what to do with the body. Wrenching her mind away from past false steps, Chloe relaxed once more into the quiet comfort and stillness of that place. Then finally chose her next right action.

"We have to go back and fight one last time," she told herself. *"We have to face up to this."*

"Don't wanna."

"We've been over that. It's just one more block of time being incapacitated. Take your medicine, binge watch K-dramas and pretend Jung Hae-in's characters exist in real life. He does, even if you don't. That has to count for something."

"It's gonna suck."

"Probably."

"I'm not going to survive it."

"Probably not."

"Can't I stay here?"

"No, you cannot die in this man's shop," she told herself firmly. *"Koreans consider that bad luck times infinity, the whole block would freak the freak out. You have seen a handsome, grumpy CEO in the wild, yelling AND glaring, what more do you want from your bucket list? Maybe you will live on here as that one nice American who let people make fatal customer service errors without destroying their business online. That's definitely going out on a high note."*

Ji Kyung-ho came back just in time to watch the tail end of this silent debate.

WHEN HE LEFT HIS CUSTOMER to finish her dessert, Kyung-ho ushered his girlfriend into his scruffy back office.

"Can I get you a coffee?" he asked, standing hesitatingly by the door as she took off her coat and settled herself on the worn, plaid couch with her usual sigh of distaste.

She shook her head.

"Are you hungry?"

"No."

"Well, I'll just...," he began, walking over to his desk and pushing some loose papers around. He then walked back over to the door.

"...Actually, if you can give me one second to check something, I will be right back. We had an incident right before you came in. I...I'll just...I want to double-check the situation, make sure everything is fine," he said disjointedly before beetling out the door.

He made it as far as the opening to the shop. Cautiously peeking his head out, he saw the lower half of the stranger's outstretched legs, a third of the table, and the empty plate. The latter gave him a flush of professional satisfaction. She hadn't even left the base of the dessert or eaten around the glaze. He wasn't sure he got either component exactly right, yet, but seeing they worked well enough to be wholly consumed was encouraging.

Peeking his head a little further, he caught the woman's face in profile as she sat, cup in hand, looking out into the dusk. The change in her demeanor startled him. Her face no longer shone with happiness, or kindness, or contentment. It was now the face of a woman girding herself for a long and difficult journey.

"She is saying goodbye," he thought.

As Kyung-ho drew back into the doorway, Chloe tilted her head to consider the waning light outside and saw with it the risk of getting lost again in the darkness. Shaking herself out of her reverie and into action, she reached forward to collect her bag off the opposite chair. Giving herself an internal *"one, two, three, go!"*, she stood up and moved purposefully towards the door.

Passing the counter, the little rack holding the shop's business cards caught her eye. On impulse she took one, leaving a blueberry thumbprint on its pristine surface. She laughed softly and looked down at her hand to see the transfer from when she shoved her plate away. Rubbing the edge of her thumb against her jeans, Chloe regretted that basic hygiene abroad required wasting the last, the very last morsel on unappreciative but fortunately like-colored denim.

Tucking the card safely into her wallet, she also noticed her emergency ₩100,000 bill. It wouldn't do her any good taking it on to Japan, especially not if it meant leaving so many orphaned desserts behind. She considered how big a sample box her friends back on ship needed to get the full experience, while weighing the risk and potential heartbreak of the chef's genius ending up in Custom's trash bin by a quick mental review of relevant episodes of *Border*

Patrol: US, Nothing to Declare: Canada, and *Border Security: Britain, New Zealand,* and *Columbia.*

Her cost benefit analysis coming out at eight items without nuts, she looked over at the frightened-to-the-end counter person, valiantly holding her post while trying to look busy and so avoid further contact. Chloe couldn't ask the girl to do any more that day, not after being yelled at, so instead, glanced around for a tip jar. Not seeing one, she quietly left the money on the counter.

With one last smiling bow in the young woman's general direction, and a short goodbye in English – unintelligible words the recipient fervently hoped was not the start of something new – Chloe left the shop. Turning to the right, then left at the corner with confidence, she made her way back down to the waiting ship.

Leaning against the wall out of sight, Kyung-ho heard his customer say something in a low voice to Soon-yi, then her footsteps, and then the sound of the bell announcing her passing. As the door closed, he suddenly straightened up and came back out into the shop just in time to see the woman cross in front of the window. Walking over to look outside, he watched her head west toward the docks. It was Thursday, he guessed she must have come in on the ship.

"Is there something wrong?" asked Soon-yi, venturing out from behind the counter to clear the table.

"No, just checking the weather."

Kyung-ho stood in the window, watching and waiting, long enough for Soon-yi to return with the empty plate and cup and discover the windfall on the counter.

"Oh, my goodness!" she exclaimed and brought the money over to him.

"Where'd that come from?" he asked.

"That foreign lady left it. Did she order something from you? I can deliver it when we close up, if you want."

Soon-yi was painfully timid, and more than content to sit in an empty shop unlikely to attract rowdy patrons and study for her C-SAT. Kyung-ho often thought of getting rid of her. Ninety-nine other part-timers, however, would have shoved the bill in their pocket and said no more about it, thought no more about it, especially after getting reprimanded. Her unexpected honesty suddenly showed him the person beyond her shyness, and her potential as a valuable, trusted asset. He made a mental commitment to keep her on and see if they could help her gain confidence. In the meantime, he shook his head as she tried to hand him the money.

"It's not for me. She left that for you."

"Me? Why?"

"She does things like that," he replied with certainty, however unjustified. "She probably thought you needed a little boost after getting yelled at. How much did she give you?"

"₩100,000! Why would she do that?"

Kyung-ho smiled and shrugged. He then reached into his back pocket and pulled out his wallet. He, too, had one, lonely ₩100,000 bill. He took it out and gave that to Soon-yi as well.

"Here, this one's from me. I'm really sorry I lost my temper earlier. I shouldn't have done that or asked you to do the reordering without supervision. Oh, and thanks for the upsell today. You did great with a foreign tourist. I'm proud of you."

Soon-yi looked at her hand in wonder. Breakfast, breakfast for almost two months, and it even came with praise from her employer.

"Thanks, boss!" she replied. Chloe would have been slightly disappointed to hear her use *boseu* rather than *depunim*, as a title far more suitable to the owner of a bijou enterprise, but thankfully, by then Chloe was almost to the pedestrian bridge and well out of hearing. Soon-yi shoved the two – two! – unexpected bills into her pocket.

"This is the luckiest day I have ever had."

"Mine too."

Kyung-ho smiled and returned to his office. The happiness on Soon-yi's face made him feel his house, however bereft of custom, was back in order.

CHAPTER SIX

...and leavings

Kyung-ho and his now completely empty wallet walked back into his office where Gong Min-a sat impatiently on the couch, just as he had left her. Supportive, decorative, a shrewd business mind, an old friend, all of that true and well-known, but suddenly seen through the added lens of those mocking blue eyes. Eyes that Kyung-ho trusted could see both the why and the no and decidedly did not approve.

"Where are you taking me tonight, *Oppa?*" Min-a asked, standing up to refasten the top of his chef coat and smooth his hair before sitting down again.

"Nowhere, I'm afraid. We didn't get many customers today, and I just gave Soon-yi my last ₩100,000. But I can make you some ramen, and of course, we have excellent dessert to go with it. You should try my new blueberry and lemon *entremets.*"

"Instant noodles and blue pastry? Who will order blue food? And you never think of my diet. Or me. Why are you paying your staff first? You should pay them last."

"Soon-yi needs to eat, too."

Min-a shrugged, looked down at her hands and started settling her rings and rotating her watch back into the correct position.

"She's young, it's the risk you take working part-time. If your business fails, you can't pay anyone."

Kyung-ho was equally familiar with Min-a's detached views on money and who gets to have it but confronting it mere minutes after experiencing the stranger's generosity felt as if he had turned and walked into a wall. His unprofitable blue food, and the irrelevant and importune needs of little people was unlikely the real source of her annoyance, however. He guessed his change of plans interfered with her engineering a meeting between himself and the new investor she found. She had threatened to facilitate a sit down for two weeks running.

He guessed right.

"I thought we could stop by L'impasse 81 for drinks after dinner," Min-a suggested. "Mr. Park said he would make a window in his evening just for me. If you assured him you will bring Choi Jae-soo on as your business manager, I know that would give him confidence in his investment and speed up the contract process."

"Shouldn't that window be for me?" Kyung-ho asked dryly, taking a seat at his desk and pretending to fuss once more with the papers left scattered about after discovering the invoice. "And I have a business partner. Wallace has been with me since the beginning. He left his job at the Westin to join the enterprise, I can't throw him out like that."

Min-a sighed with impatience at Kyung-ho's continued, stubborn resistance to how the business world works. He traded a secure and prestigious job at the five-star Josun Palace Hotel for this dumpy, nowhereville start-up that didn't even cover the cost of a proper meal and yet seemed unwilling to do anything to make it a success. The sooner this shop, a walking anecdote about "new owner errors", ceased to exist the better.

"Wallace Yan will understand more than anyone," she advised with some heat. She stood up to indicate there was nothing more to discuss, and that it was time to leave for the restaurant. "You can't survive without an influx of capital, and you need it immediately. I told you not to take this backwater shop. He should have stopped you, which just goes to show he isn't a good fit."

Min-a was nearly correct, as usual. Her proposal was logical, desperately needed, and probably could be negotiated to allow Wallace staying on in a subsidiary position. Accepting it also meant permanent compromise on producing his ideal food and required marriage to her. The ordinary costs of doing business. Kyung-ho enjoyed his artistry, but not enough to starve for it, and on paper he and Min-a were a perfect match. They had known each other since Kyunggi High School. He could offer no legitimate explanation for his hesitation to either arrangement, not to her, or Wallace, or even himself.

As he remembered the stranger's visceral reaction to his future wife with a smile that got him in trouble even as he made it, suddenly that point of view clarified his own. Le Cordon Bleu, and later his work at Hotel Le Meurice honed his mind and muscle memory on how to bake with precision and order, which is why the plans he made with Gong Min-a – safe, conservative, and always sound on paper – felt so comfortable and correct. And she was right. Leaving his shiny, well-appointed hotel kitchens to coax the same quality out of dinged and mismatched secondhand equipment in a poky dark space, that was a little crazy. After four months, the shop hadn't attracted enough patrons to know yet even whether he was a bad chef-owner, or just the wrong chef for his chosen location. He received even less feedback on his specialty items, desserts with too little margin for a hotel kitchen or a high-rent district, the soul of his art that would live or die in this back alley.

But he who started his career on the Rue de Rivoli loved his poky storefront tucked into an alley down by the docks. And his knowingly foolish blueberry dessert, which is why he worked so hard on perfecting it. Maybe, he suddenly realized, he needed to trust that he loved them for good reason, and that it mattered. He doubted he would ever learn why either had such an impact on that woman today, but as an experienced, professional chef, he saw that they had.

He also now had the market research to prove the profitable food Min-a thought good enough for the masses would make his customer demographic with delicate jawlines and like palates disappointed if they ever came back for seconds. His work risked making such people fat and diabetic. It should at least make them truly happy. He had forgotten how it felt to bring his customers an unexpected joy.

In the time it took Min-a to put on her coat and adjust it in the mirror behind the door, Kyung-ho shook off the confusion of the last two years. Slowly, he pushed his way up out his chair, turned to face her, and braced himself for something very unpleasant and stupid he might be about to do.

"I can't go," he announced, surprised but relieved to hear the words coming out of his mouth. Once he began, it felt much easier to go on. "Min-a, you're a beautiful woman and a good friend, but...I don't think we are right for each other. I can't do this deal. I can't be...the kind of man who would make you proud, and I don't want to make you unhappy trying and failing."

The look she gave him cleared away all his doubts. Loss, disdain, chagrin, they were all present, but she was not heartbroken. She also was not surprised. That was information. He hoped his words were political enough to salve her pride and fend off her need for casual revenge, especially for the crime of saying it first, but he was certain that once his imminent bankruptcy occurred, she would not need consolation.

"Is there another woman?" she asked.

"Absolutely not," he said.

"No, my woman is sailing with the tide," he thought, before quickly squashing such a ridiculous idea and the equally absurd, sharp, internal protest that it was true.

"Who can compare to you?" he continued, gambling that assuaging her ego would blind her to any sign of duplicity. "I doubt I will date anyone again until I have something stable and established to offer, so, that's probably never."

"Who was that woman grabbing your arm just now?"

"Just a customer. I was yelling at Soon-yi. She did it to get my attention. You know Americans, they touch strangers. I couldn't be rude or just shove her away. She might give the shop a bad review. She might be a somebody."

Min-a continued to eye him with suspicion.

"We met about two and a half minutes before you arrived. This has nothing to do with anyone or anything else, Min-a, it's just for the best."

"Well, you will regret this."

"Probably," he agreed, "but you won't. And that's what matters."

With a final *"humph"*, which had greatly lost its impact now that Kyung-ho associated it with one American finding it hysterically funny, Min-a banged the office door back into place against the wall, collected her purse off the couch, and stalked out of the room. Kyung-ho listened to another set of retreating footsteps, another jangling door opening and shutting in his life.

He sat down again in his old desk chair with the duct tape patch on the seat and familiar squeak whenever he leaned back, and put his hands behind his head. There he sat until Soon-yi looked in to say the shop was closed up and she was leaving for the night. There he sat for a long while after, wondering what he had done.

CHAPTER SEVEN

all aboard

The *Westerdam* Excursion Manager was more than relieved to see Chloe walking through the lobby that evening. Looking at his watch, he noted she had been gone far longer than it took to drink a bubble tea and watch some traffic. Once again, he called out to her as she passed.

"Hey, Chloe! Did you have fun on the docks?"

"I did, thank you for inquiring," she answered, stopping at his counter. "Just for you, know that I resolutely ignored strangers offering day trips to Mount Seorak and Nami Island. The Nami people even hawked their tours in English, but I stayed strong. Getting off our ship to get on someone else's boat without telling anyone, well now, that might have suggested I didn't want dinner. Or my luggage back."

The manager blenched a little at the narrowly avoided hazard. He would have never thought of looking for her in another part of the country. Or Japan. He made a mental note to stop relying on keeping track of her ashore merely because she had red hair and was wearing one of the only bright blue coats in Asia.

Chloe continued.

"I had such a good time, I even found a thing I need you to tell me what it is," she said, reaching for her phone. "If it's a Starbucks, though, I need you to lie to me."

He looked at the picture she pulled up on the screen.

"This is...a temple. Did you get around alright?"

"Oh, thank God, it really is a thing. Get around alright? I got all the way to the 15th century and back in time for Taco Night, navigating solely by my expertise in urban planning, all things nautical, and a fortuitous love of pastry that did not let me down. There's even an apartment I am seriously considering, I'm so native. Is ₩1,500,000 a lot for a one-bedroom?"

"You have to pay three years rent in advance. It's too late in the day, though, to explain the complexities of the Korean rental market. You got lost without a proper guide, didn't you?" he asked, returning to switching the brochures in the display racks from Korean to Japanese excursions. "Is that why you're late?"

"Misplaced. That neighborhood has a shocking lack of signage. It's not my fault the tourist board is letting everybody down. But I was misplaced in a blizzard. That led to some moments. There was a weather event involved."

"Did it snow?"

"Four whole flakes, I was deeply concerned for my personal safety."

"Did you get lunch?" asked the not-concerned manager, not looking up from his sorting.

After a stricken pause, Chloe blurted out,

"I stole a croissant off the breakfast buffet."

"Busted," she added with a sigh.

Her confession, too, left the manager nonplussed.

"They don't recommend that. It leaves crumbs all over the ship. Did you get lunch, though?"

"You mean table food? Alone? You want me to approach haphazardly, without guidance or companions, a thousand-year tradition steeped in nose to tail cooking, where the simplest meal is accompanied by a cornucopia of side dishes laced with unexpected offal, seafood and gochu peppers? Yeah, no. No."

"That neighborhood has American franchises on every block. Why didn't you stop into a Subway, or have some fried chicken? You must have seen enough signage to know the Korean word for "chicken" is chicken."

Chloe traded the manager the next stack of flyers off the counter for the discards in his hand, and started tidying up his leftover piles so they didn't get crumpled.

"Yes, I can say chicken, but I don't know the Korean hand signal for "not the red-colored one". Duh-uh. I also don't know what "one" of something means. A piece, a bucket, a flock? I only had $20 to make a mistake with. Don't judge me, but I wasn't even brave enough to venture into a 7-Eleven."

"A foreign 7-Eleven is a culinary bridge too far? Really?" he asked, stepping back to eyeball the display and look for anything that didn't belong.

"I'm not proud of that," she said, "I know I have let Lee Joon-Gi down. I know that."

The manager picked up the empty carton and moved back behind the counter to refill it with the neat stacks Chloe had made.

"You need a Hallyu star to explain how a Korean 7-Eleven works?"

"What choice can't Mr. Lee provide clarity on? And you and I both know that selling salted orange snacks in an American franchise abroad does not make them Cheetos. Odds are they're Szechuan-flavored, powdered squid bits because Frito-Lay will give the people what they want. A person needs to be informed. Now, if you all would stop encouraging me to eat land meals in chairs and just take the time to teach me the pictograph for a smiley-faced potato vs a smiley-faced shellfish, maybe Mr. Lee and I could move on to other topics."

"You're right," he conceded, "it's our fault."

"Thank you," she said, taking advantage of the newly open space on the counter to drop into a more comfortable lean with her chin in her hand. "Don't think I abandoned the lovely tour you wanted me to take to spend the day huddled in and around an airport-esque food court, though. I did find a very happening district full of local restaurants and local people eating. I just wasn't one of them."

"How far did you walk?"

"It's just up the street. You know, that one, up there."

She pointed vaguely over her left shoulder to indicate "towards the city" but was in fact pointing to a large floral arrangement and beyond that, Qingdao, China. Her surprise intel caused him to add two extra zeros to his refill request form.

"There's a happening food neighborhood near the docks?" he asked, hunting for his eraser.

"Oh, yeah. Barbecue, noodle shops, those outdoor places with the white tents, they were all crowded to the gills by the time I passed through around 5:30. It's a whole culinary world, and no tourists so that there is the international sign of "good food".

"Have you been to this café?" she asked, fishing the business card out of her bag and handing it to him while replacing her phone. "This is the beating heart of it."

The Excursion Manager looked down at the name and street address.

"Nope."

"You can keep the card, if you want to try it. On my way back the wind knocked me about, and I ended up right in front of it, inclemency does have its benefits, so I took the hint and had an afternoon tea pastry break. Wow. Truly. You know in *Wuxia* when they randomly bump into the extra, super, ninth-level master in a back alley?"

"No."

Chloe tried her description again, with more of the literal seriousness his food deserved.

"The owner is French-trained. His 3-D chocolate butterfly garnishes are worthy, I think, of the *Meilleur Ouvrier de France*, but my guess is he's too much of a rebel to win. Like Van Gogh trying to get a show at the *Academie*. And now he's come home. He's definitely Korean. I was going to bring some of that genius back to share, but I wasn't sure if dessert could come through Customs. Can one get arrested in Korea for smuggling sugar butter?"

"I wouldn't put it past you."

"Hey, did I get to Japan ahead of the ship today? No, I am a trouble avoider. Anyway, I'm sure *Westerdam* fed the tour the best it could with the information it had, but this shop is exactly what is missing in the schedule – a familiar option in a sea of picturesque and mysterious Korean restaurants. If you guaranteed him for dessert, you could get even someone like me to sign up for a culinary tour. I mean, I'd only look at the tripe and squid and chicken feet, not eat it, I'd wait for dessert, but I'd be there for the moral support of others. Like when Marilyn wanted to go base jumping. It takes a village."

"Also, anyone can find a good pastry shop on any old main street anywhere," she concluded, "but a secret, high-end pastry shop hidden near the wharves is the tourist tale legends are made of. Happy stories make happy, repeat customers, and happy people have big mouths."

The Excursion Manager immediately grasped the wisdom of her précis. Chloe was already his favorite passenger, which is why he regretted the possibility of leaving her behind anywhere. She never complained about lines and waiting for other people, and treated both he and his staff as valued experts, not lower-class servants. She even took his side on internecine wars among the crew. With this act, however, she was elevated to shrewd, helpful professional. He received the business card with gratitude and intended to forward it for immediate follow-up to the local tour leader, due back in another half-hour with the last excursion group.

With a heroism tempered by regret, Chloe relinquished her memento. She consoled herself with unpleasant facts, like that she couldn't actually read anything on the card, and stalking a man with a girlfriend from abroad was so gauche, nothing good would come from that. Better it go where it might do some good, if it wasn't thrown away.

"Where will we be tomorrow?" she asked, distracting herself with the promise of new horizons on the East China Sea.

"Osaka."

"I can't do the Go-Karts with Costumes Tour, I just can't," she said, pointing to the offending brochure.

"I know."

"It is one flavor of full-on, Japanese immersion – dressing up as a giant chicken and driving through the streets on an ATV, very cosplay, very webtoon – but please don't make me."

"We won't. For you we recommend this tour," he said, selecting a different flyer from the new display and handing it to her. "Look, it includes the Kinkakuji Temple, a shrine and a bamboo forest."

"*Ooooh, bammmbbooo.* I feel so known. Sign me up! Well, I'm off for tacos. See you tomorrow, bright and early."

"Good night! I'm glad you had a nice time and got back safely."

When the Excursion Manager returned from the storeroom after putting away the carton of Korean brochures, his tie once more askew, he found the local guide sitting behind the counter filling out his time sheet and post-tour paperwork.

"Hey, I was hoping to catch you," the manager said. "How did it go?

"We needed three buses this time," answered the guide, counting up participant numbers on his fingers, "and they're all back aboard ship with five hours to spare. You're welcome."

"You're the best! Your team is getting great comments on the evaluation sheets. Hey, check this out," he said, handing him the business card he received from Chloe.

"Little Paris Café?" the guide read out loud. "What's this? What do you want me to do with it?"

"Chloe brought that back with her."

"Who's she?"

"Your new best friend. Instead of going on your tour, she took a stroll around the docks."

"Why?" interrupted the guide.

"We don't ask Chloe "why", we ask her "and then what happened?", she's one of those people. She found this place in the heart of a popular, local food district. There's one hiding right up the street, apparently."

"Oh. Would she know if it's any good?"

"For the restaurants, you're on your own, she is also one of "those people" who think Brie is an exotic cheese. She's extremely knowledgeable when it comes to our dessert buffet, though. Just check it out this weekend, if you have a chance. It might be the perfect cornerstone for that culinary tour you've been wanting to create. As Chloe pointed out, Westerners are very open to a food adventure when they're guaranteed dessert."

"Huh, she might be right. Great, I'll check it out."

"Well, I'm off ashore," the guide said, shoving his completed forms into the correct slots behind the counter. "If the café works out, I'll email a proposal to you, and we can talk about it the next Thursday you're in port."

"Great," echoed the manager. "Have a good week! Thanks for not losing any of my passengers!"

CHAPTER EIGHT

those we leave behind

About the time Chloe was halfway through her third taco, and the Excursion Manager was locking up his kiosk for the night, Kyung-ho's business partner, Wallace Yan, stopped into the Little Paris Café. By then Kyung-ho had moved his wondering from the office to sitting out in the dark shop with his feet up on a chair, sipping an espresso and watching out the window the people passing by the entrance to his alleyway.

"I see not much happened here today," Wallace said, turning on the light before walking over to the counter and checking the cash register tape.

"Actually, a lot happened."

"Did it make us money?"

"Uh, it lost us a huge investment."

"What did you do?" Wallace asked, pulling down a chair off an adjoining table to join Kyung-ho at the window.

"Well, the investor was very interested. If he could embed his own manager to manage his investment."

"I figured that. He wanted Choi in, didn't he? What did you decide to do?"

"Well...," Kyung-ho paused to take another sip of espresso. "Do you want a coffee? I can make you one?"

"What did you do?" Wallace repeated.

"Well, Choi sounded like he was going to be very bossy and have a lot of opinions, that wasn't going to work, and I couldn't fire you, so...I...I fired her."

"Min-a?"

"Yeah."

"You broke up? With Gong Min-a? The only woman who doesn't mind how grumpy and poor you are?"

"Uh, yeah."

Wallace ran his hand through what was left of his hair.

"Why? She was your biggest support. She's been by your side ever since you got back from France. She brought this investor herself, too. She put the whole deal together."

"Yeah."

"Yeah, he says. Is there a why?"

Kyung-ho laughed and took another sip of coffee.

"Just doing what I was told."

"Why are you giggling like a crazy person, and since when have you started listening to other people? Other than Min-a, whom you randomly just declared your independence from."

"I don't giggle, I am recalling a humorous incident. A customer came in late in the day, an American. She was here when Min-a stopped by. She made this face..."

Wallace crossed his arms and waited.

"...okay, a face, is she Helen of Troy? Medusa? So what, and then what happened?"

"She wasn't trying to be rude, but she had this...reaction to Min-a...it was..."

"Try forming a sentence with a verb and object, maybe an adjective. Something. All I know is an American came in. What did she order, by the way?"

"The new *entremets*."

"Did she like it?"

"A lot."

"Oh, that's information."

"I know, I'm going to keep developing that one. There are a few tweaks that would really bring it to its full potential. Anyway, what I'm trying to say is, the person who instantly understood the blueberry, instantly and viscerally understood – and disliked – Min-a."

"Was she jealous? Min-a is a lot. You know...women...She's a lot."

"Don't know. She just looked at me like...actually very similar to how you are right now and went back to her own business. I very nearly laughed out loud."

"Laughed? A woman made you laugh, and at your own girlfriend? I certainly hope you weren't caught, and/or we're up to date on our fire insurance."

"Oh, I was very nearly caught. Strike that, I was caught, the American had her hand on my arm when Min-a walked in."

"Wait a minute...No," said Wallace, pushing back his chair and standing up. "I'm just going to check the CCTV."

"But I'm telling you..."

"You aren't telling me anything. I want my CCTV and will make my own decisions, thank you very much."

Together the two men walked back into Kyung-ho's office and re-grouped around his desk to watch the security tape Kyung-ho pulled up on his computer.

"Wow, she really likes the blueberry," said Wallace.

"Wow, she does. She told me how much she liked it, but even blurred and grainy – is this supposed to stop a crime? – even with this thing, you can tell she really meant it."

"Why are you yelling at Soon-yi?" Wallace asked, pointing at the screen.

"Oh, I forgot that part. She ordered us twelve cases of gold leaf."

"Twelve...cases?"

"Twelve."

Wallace moved over to the couch and plunked down with a sigh.

"Isn't that enough for the dome of a smaller temple?"

"We are sorted for gold leaf for the millennia," Kyung-ho answered, rotating his chair to face him.

"Can we...?"

"We cannot."

"What goes with gold leaf? Blueberries?"

"That isn't a bad idea. I had thought...no, yes, that's where we'll dump our leaf. With any luck, it will be a bestseller. Otherwise, we're going to be pushing some extra gaudy wedding cakes."

"Would they sell?"

"They would, but purposely crafting an abomination to start a trend I really don't support, well, I will if we have to, but I hope I can unload our surplus mother lode on something a little more Renaissance and a little less Vegas."

"Make an Elvis dessert! I can hire a..."

"Now you're just hurting me. We will start with Starry Night and see how that goes."

"Am I supposed to know what that is?"

"The blueberry dessert, but with a marble glaze and gold leaf moon. It will look really good in the case."

"No Elvis?"

"Do you need an Elvis?"

"Yes."

"Then I will make you an Elvis to celebrate you staying on."

"Great," Wallace responded, stretching his arms over his head with satisfaction, "now explain why you were holding hands with that woman."

"I wasn't!"

"Hello! What was that?" Wallace pointed back at the computer screen. "I have eyes, even if you think my taste is tacky. Why were you holding that woman's hand, and why on earth did you keep me on and kick Min-a out?"

"Well, just look!" Kyung-ho said, rolling the tape forward. "See! That's our target customer, and she won't even eat while Min-a is there. That can't be good for business."

Wallace leaned forward to see the monitor, and then sat back shaking his head more from disbelief than disagreement.

"Are you going to tell me the real reason you turned down the investment that would have saved your business?"

Kyung-ho tried again to explain.

"Did you ever have a sign taped to your back in school? You can't understand what's happening until someone comes by and takes it off and shows it to you? That is what this woman did. In about a minute and a half she got me to stop yelling at the world and focus on the real problem. Min-a thinks I left the hotel because I just wanted all the money and all the credit. She doesn't think you make me enough money."

"I don't," Wallace admitted. "Isn't that my job?"

"No. Your job is to understand the cost of making our food our way, and the choices we have to make to keep doing it. You run the Informed Compromise Department. Like this shop. A tiny, backwater shop that we can afford is not the Gangham high street one Min-a wanted me to rent. That woman today, she saw it from our perspective. That the shop was right, the food was right, the real question is how to get customers to us, not for us to change to get customers."

Wallace was surprised, and moved, to be so explicitly identified as part of the business model, not just the reliable adding machine. He also grudgingly appreciated that at least one person didn't think they were nuts, or that he should be fired.

"All that in a minute and a half?"

"A happy Westerner is not a subtle thing, and she seemed to really zero in what we are doing wrong."

"Do you have any ideas yet?"

"Nope." Kyung-ho said, turning back to the monitor. "But it's easier to think of them now that I no longer doubt moving here in the first place, or whether I need to put all my creativity into changing out all the products. If we have to close, I feel a lot better about it now that I know it won't be over the things we know how to do. It was the things we didn't that was the sticking point, the things that took luck."

"All that in a minute and a half?"

"All that."

"Oh look, there she goes. Bye, stranger!" Wallace said, waving at the security monitor. "Happy trails!"

"Now what are you doing?" he asked Kyung-ho.

"I just want to rewind it for a second."

"Why?"

"I just want to see something."

"It's a stranger sitting in your shop drinking coffee and poking at sugar. Can we get back to what really matters here? What are we going to do in a post-Choi, cash-free universe?"

"I don't know. How long do we have to do it, again?"

"Did you sell that kidney like I asked you to?"

"No. I thought we could try robbing a bitcoin bank first."

"You get on that. I would say we have through the end of the year, and then you have to make a decision."

"And if nothing changes?"

"Then the decision is made for you. If you go to a loan shark, though, know I'm taking that kidney out myself before they do."

"I'd better get on your Elvis dessert, then. It won't be the same if you see the watered down, cost-effective version I'd sell in someone else's shop. They don't have our gold reserves."

"You do that. And you still haven't explained why you were holding that woman's hand," Wallace said pointing again at the image from where Kyung-ho had again rewound the tape.

"I would if I could, Wallace. It was one of those days. I'll go get you a blueberry," he said, pushing up out of his chair with another squeak. "I'm sure we will feel more aligned when we have all eaten the same food."

famous last words

That night Kyung-ho stayed late at the shop long after Wallace departed for the suburbs, rethinking his plans for it, calculating how much serendipity was needed to replace Min-a's investment strategy and tweaking his blueberry dessert, all over three bottles of soju. At 2:07 AM, he finally heard what his ears had been straining for, the horn of the great ship as she pulled out of her moorings.

"Goodbye my lady, I think I made you proud today," he said holding his shot glass up in a toast before finishing the last of the last bottle. He realized how long it had been since he could say that. Just a few decisions done right, but he felt solid ground beneath him again. He rinsed out the empties and put them in the recycling bin, locked up his shop, and went home for a few hours rest.

Walking along the silent street, Kyung-ho told himself the day's run-in was a chance encounter with a kind patron A nice, helpful, fellow businessperson who was extra nice about what could have been a social media disaster. That was all it was, and more than enough. He found he could convince himself of that argument eight times between the shop and his apartment. Coming back in the morning, the distance had shrunk to six, which was either progress, or that the argument was losing. One or the other. You know.

By the time Kyung-ho returned home again the next night, however, his internal debate over whether it was dumb or not dumb to expect "that American" to ever return – she did take such an interest the business – was subsumed by his wondering not whether she would, but whether she could. The more consideration he gave to what he read in her face right before Min-a's arrival interrupted them, the more times he re-watched the security tape – for market research purposes – and saw her leave, the less he could unsee.

Each time he watched her gather her purse and turn to face the cold, grey street, he wished he had stopped her. Or encouraged her. Something to change the way she stared down the road back home. It comforted him to witness how much his shop and his food briefly made her happy, but it was oddly unsatisfying given his profession.

Before she left, though, the security tape showed that she turned and said something to Soon-yi. From his side of the doorway, he hadn't caught the words, but it was one mystery he thought could still be solved, and definitively. He pressed Soon-yi on it when she came in for her shift. Market research, it was important to have all the facts.

"Good nice...*ummm*...seep-pence," was Soon-yi's recollection.

"I don't think that's a word. Are you sure? It's important."

In an effort to be helpful, Soon-yi acted out Chloe's last moments in the shop to assist her memory, and in case it offered context to the inexplicable words and actions of the enigma that was a foreign tourist.

"She stood here and took one of your business cards. Then she kinda turned towards the back and said "good nice, seep-pence", and then smiled and left."

"Seep-pence?"

Soon-yi just shrugged with the complacent certainty that whatever the woman said, it wouldn't be on the English section of the C-SAT. She went back to folding napkins with cutlery for set-ups.

A couple of weeks later, Kyung-ho asked his business manager for a second opinion. Not that it mattered, he was simply curious and it had bothered him. Waiting eleven days felt like he was giving it the right level of importance.

"Wallace, your English is better than mine," he said, bringing over a second espresso order to Wallace's table where he sat cataloging receipts. "What does "good nice, seep-pence" mean? I think she meant "good night" but she might not have."

"It means nothing."

"What does it sound like it means?"

"I have no idea."

"If it was a goodbye. If that's what somebody heard, in Korean, when somebody was saying goodbye, in English, maybe, what did they actually hear?"

"Where?"

"Here. Soon-yi heard somebody talking, and that's as close as she could get to it."

Wallace sighed and paused his ten-key inputting.

"In English? Uh...seep-pence, seep, goodnight, seeeep...seep? Sweet? Goodnight sweet...oh, prince. Goodnight, sweet prince. It's Shakespeare. If it was anything, that is. It was said in a pastry shop."

"Oh," Kyung-ho said with a breaking smile.

"Are you the prince?"

Kyung-ho shrugged and looked out the window.

"Shakespeare said it, not me."

"Oh God, who are you dating now? Does she have money?"

"No one! And don't even whisper that."

"If you were going to break up with Gong Min-a, we should have rented the concrete building. You're the one who wanted to go wood. Don't blame me."

"You're safe on that front for some time. It took me thirty-seven years to find one woman I will let tell me what to do, what are the odds there are two, and with blue eyes?"

"In Korea? I think we are set for life. Is this why you are obsessed with making blue dessert?"

"Two is not "obsessed". Just eat your Blue Suede Shoes, be grateful, and tell me about our quarterly taxes."

"Well," Wallace replied before pausing to take another bite of banana cake layered with blueberry jam and smile in appreciation, "stop staring out the window and tell me what you want me to do about the filing."

"I was thinking. This is me thinking."

"Since when has your thinking involved standing at that stupid window counting the people walking by? Every time I come in these days you are at the window. It's winter, I would rather be sitting closer to the heater. I'm only using this table so we don't have to yell fiduciary secrets across the room. You're getting weird since you've been single."

"You have your own dessert, and a job, because I got weird."

"You're right. I love the new you. Sit down, at least, and tell me what you think next quarter will look like."

Kyung-ho took a seat.

"Is that from *Romeo and Juliet?*" he asked instead, smiling a little as he watched Wallace lick his fork.

"No, it's from the big death scene in Hamlet," Wallace answered, putting down the utensil and moving the plate away from his papers. "Are we done? Can we get back to your own 21st century empire?"

Kyung-ho suddenly pushed back his chair and stood up. He took a half-step towards the door before stopping himself.

"Now where are you going?" asked Wallace.

"I'll be right back. I have to check something," Kyung-ho replied. With that he yanked open the door and rushed out of the shop.

"You're not wearing...," Wallace called after him before getting up to properly close the door, "...*ugh*, he's gotten so weird."

Wallace was not wrong. It was mad and foolish to be dashing through a seaside community in December, without a coat and for no reason, but Kyung-ho's feet would not be stayed. He half-ran, half-walked to the bottom of the street and up over the pedestrian bridge. From the top of the bridge, he could see the Starbucks and down to the harbor. The empty harbor. It was Tuesday and the ship was not there.

Even if it was, that woman surely disembarked in Tokyo or Hong Kong or gone on to ports south. It was absurd to come all the way down to the waterfront to see for himself that she was really gone. It was even more absurd to stand there shivering for several long minutes while he willed her ship to return. Slowly, he turned around, and hugging his arms to his chest, made his way back to the shop, pushed and buffeted along from behind by the sharp ocean breeze.

He wondered as he climbed back up the hill if his American would ever find out what her momentary presence and small kindnesses had wrought. The second and last pebble she cast, triggering what was quickly becoming an avalanche in his life, arrived the very first Saturday after she had gone to sea and had already swept them away.

CHAPTER TEN

the waiting years

Kyung-ho was standing at his shop window, day three of his journey to weird, looking out towards the main road where people seemed to continually seek out pig's feet and chicken gizzards rather than French Korean dessert. Gong Min-a had been painfully accurate about his location's lack of foot traffic and chance customers.

Watching the street offered no solution to his lack of custom, so instead, Kyung-ho watched the street while reassessing "that American's" response to his new *entremets*. A risk, blueberry, a fruit with the least appealing color of all, and hard to source from the suppliers. Gong Min-a often questioned whether it was worth it. Kyung-ho had to cobble together the American's reaction from what he experienced and from the grainy, grey surveillance video, but he thought he achieved the response almost unhoped for in his target demographic – perfect contentment and satisfaction – and it wasn't yet fully refined.

As Kyung-ho mused over whether the dessert needed a full moon or crescent moon component, he heard the shop door rattle and the bell give a sharp ring. Turning to his left, he watched a brisk, bright, young Korean enter. The man looked around appraisingly, bowed to Kyung-ho, and moved up to pastry case.

"She was right," the man said, scanning the contents of the case, and taking another look around the café.

Very glad to hear it, whoever "she" was, Kyung-ho asked,

"Can I help you?"

"I need one of this whole shelf," the man replied. "Can the staff here speak English?"

Kyung-ho nodded.

"Pretty well."

"Great. I'm considering bringing my tour group in a week from Thursday. We expect about 20-30 people, mostly Westerners. Can you accommodate them?"

Kyung-ho again nodded, startled but outwardly calm.

"No problem. We have additional seating out back."

The man reached in his pocket for a business card, and mistakenly handed Kyung-ho back one of his own, one marked with a blueberry thumbprint.

Kyung-ho looked down at the card with a smile, shaking his head slightly in wonder. He then asked,

"You work for the cruise ships?"

Glancing over at the card in Kyung-ho's hand to see if corporate changed the tag line, the man realized he had given the shop owner the wrong one.

"Oh sorry, that's yours that Chloe gave us."

He reached back into his pocket and sifted through the top few cards for the correct one.

"Yes, I handle excursions for the Holland line. This is a great location. It's near the terminal, but far enough away from the tourist strip to have a local feel. That's important with our clientele."

Kyung-ho nodded his understanding.

"We're a relatively new community. The City has been helping us redevelop this area. Let me give you a clean card of mine."

Kyung-ho walked over to pull a fresh card from the rack and tucked the stained one along with the man's into his own breast pocket.

"Koi?" he asked, imperfectly catching at the name as he began to construct the pastry box for the order. "Koi recommended you?"

"Kk-low-ee," the man sounded out phonetically. "An American. One of our customers who ate here in the past week. She recommended your shop as one that would appeal to our tour demographic."

"I remember her," Kyung-ho said, also recognizing such a French name on the man's second try pronouncing it. "She really liked my new dessert. I'll put one in for you."

Kyung-ho carefully squeezed the extra dessert into the box along with a few more cards, and the brisk young man paid for his order and went on his way. The whole interaction took less than twelve minutes. Kyung-ho marveled how the most remarkable events happened in the shortest amount of time around that woman, who now had a name.

"Chloe," he repeated softly to himself in the empty shop, "Chloe."

He then took out his phone and texted Wallace about their new opportunity.

While Wallace rushed over for a planning session, the tour guide made a few more stops in the neighborhood and then carried his parcel of treats back to his office for final approval. Passing out the items and hearing a cascade of inarticulate variations on "yum" in his wake, he considered he received it in full. The need for even more pastry, or the insatiable desire for a field trip, or perhaps the supplemental report that the shop owner was handsome and not wearing a wedding ring, sent his colleague in charge of day trips to Busan, and the one handling Sokcho, and the one for Jeju Island back for seconds the following day.

Torn between keeping Little Paris a trade secret, and the desire to broadcast the newest best thing, fortunately for Kyung-ho the tour office came down on the side of publicity. And just as Chloe predicted, publicity was the only missing ingredient in his success. Three weeks after becoming the marquee destination on the Holland America culinary tour, the shop had its first marriage proposal moment, and two months later the Eternal Love dessert – the Winter Wedding version, the one with the ginger biscuit base – was a regular menu item after going viral on Instagram.

The positive impact of Chloe's business acumen rolled outward as the rising tide lifted all boats. Thursdays quickly became a thing in the restaurant district, with a regularly appearing sea of non-locals and Western faces pointing, clicking and eventually acclimating the small shops to using pidgin English and butchered Hangul. It anchored the pastry newcomer into the community as a good luck charm, revenue generator and useful resource on the ways of foreigners. It elevated the status of the formerly invisible, and unprofitable, horde of hungry students who now lingered over their a la carte items on what was colloquially known as "invasion day" to be on hand to serve as interpreters, picking up tips or a free side dish for their assistance. It even increased the district's popularity on other days as times when locals could dine in peace.

It even led to Kyung-ho being discovered by his own people. The tourists talked to the hotels, and the press, and the travel blogs, and eventually even the cool kids in the next town over heard about him. Ably assisted by Wallace, he opened a second shop in Seoul, then a third, and within a year a central kitchen to better service catering jobs and commercial contracts. He won accolades, and awards, and soon a steady stream of true believers were returning from Paris lamenting that Le Meurice was not quite quite without him. It was still excellent, the in-crowd would tell each other, it just, well, you know, it was good to be home.

Through all these changes in his outrageous fortunes, Kyung-ho continued to carry in his breast pocket a blueberry-stained card from his first encounter with success as an independent chef-owner. In times of celebration, and challenge and decision, gazing at it centered his mind on how his success was achieved, and how it was not. It helped him avoid the temptation to sell a more "cost-effective" napoleon during a cash crunch, and softened the blow after the failed, unwise venture in bread. "That American" wasn't really his target customer, those he learned, as he had suspected all along, universally disapproved of unpleasantness erupting in public view, but she was a reliable reference point in differentiating what was a necessary leap of faith in order to progress, and what was just jumping off a cliff. In honor of his happenstance angel, or perhaps in memoriam, he tweaked and renamed his signature blueberry as Chloe's Starry Night.

"Are you really going to call it that?" Wallace asked.

"Yes. It's not done, though, it needs a gastro molecular element."

"Why be an expensive pain in the ass for no reason? Isn't the gold enough?"

"No. If I use the right technique for the right purpose, it will turn basic chemistry into magic. Her business advice was exactly the same. One on level all she did was tell the truth and go out of her way to be kind, but because it was the right truth to the right people at the right moment, look at the chain reaction. The least I can do is name my best dessert after her and make it my best. She was, after all, the first person to love...it."

After a great deal of experimentation and thought, Kyung-ho turned the blueberry glaze into a marbled night sky, added a gold leaf sphere for a moon that released a little puff of lemon-scented fog when cracked open, and covered the glaze with a scattering of tiny stars his staff cursed him over when there was a large order. He never told the press who this Chloe person was, though, which was unexpectedly media savvy and sneaky of him. He found them much more likely to print the whole title of the dish in the hopes of scooping the mystery, and the more social media called her out by name, the easier it might be for her to remember, or to find the shop if she ever returned to Korea. He was certain she would want to try the new version of his (her) *entremets*.

Months passed, and everything continued to change for Kyung-ho, and he continued to grow and to change everything. Everything except that one tiny corner of his life, quite unimportant really. For no reason Wallace could discern, every evening he would stand in the window of whichever shop he was working out of that day, and he waited.

auditioning for the second act

Five months after the opening of Seoul's much anticipated *keikeu ga-gye,* Jogeum Parri, or what tourists called the Little Paris Café, the new Gangham one not the Yonghyeon one, and eleven days before Little Paris' contract with The Westin New York hit Wallace's desk, a scant 6,173 miles away Chloe Marsden waited in the semidarkness backstage at the final audition for Season 14 of *Yes, Chef! America.* Leaning with both hands on the handle of the metal cart holding her signature chicken Milanese with arugula salad, she nervously rocked it back and forth, listening to the wheels squeak with each push, and bitterly regretting she had ever set foot in Kyung-ho's shop.

In Chloe's infinite wisdom, and in an attempt to find a new normal and a new job opportunity after her successful heart surgery – that is, she survived it, that was something – Chloe applied to the show. Eating at "that Korean place" had been a uniquely memorable and life-changing moment on a journey spanning five countries and four seas taken with three thousand strangers. That was information. She thought, perhaps, it also might be a sign the food industry was the right milieu for a second act career. Unlike her previous work as a historian, food certainly had a more established tradition that once people ordered it, they were expected to pay for it when it came out.

Also, in the long, slow recovery spent collapsed on her chintz-covered couch, watching the top two-thirds of her television screen through the fluffy haze of the grey cat curled up on her chest, purring life back into her broken heart, it occurred to Chloe that since reality wasn't working out for her, maybe she should try reality TV. Welding, fashion, construction, glassblowing, extreme survival, these shows were obviously spectator sports and she knew she wasn't an *Iron Chef* or a *Great Baker*, but after binge-watching twelve seasons of *Yes, Chef! America* in broadcast order, then six seasons of *Yes, Chef! UK*, then two seasons of *Yes, Chef! Canada*, then eight seasons of *Yes, Chef! Australia*, which had triple the episodes of any other franchise and therefore much more screen time for contestant backstories, she thought she found her forum.

Even if she didn't get selected for the show, filling out forms, meeting small deadlines and getting rejected was good practice for rejoining the business world. So, she carefully answered the questionnaire to appear like an interesting person, searched her old phone for a decent photo of herself sitting upright, and re-watched her favorite Season 8, the one where she wanted both finalists to win, for pro tips.

Now having made it to the stage where the fictional character she created in her paperwork had to at least prove she knew chicken tartar was not a thing, and awash with stage fright, Chloe could see, now, the error of seeking career advice from handsome strangers. With another ten minutes to wait for her turn in front of the judges, there was just time to admit she had been led astray by trauma, limerence and a common bond with a fellow sugar addict, surreptitiously pocket her Himalayan finishing salt, and run for the exits pretending she left it in the car.

Reminding herself she was on film already demonstrating her grinding technique, Chloe made a strenuous effort to distract her mind – and body – from taking such an extreme measure. She looked around the holding area for her new best friend, Al, the *Yes, Chef!* cameraman. Al was equally exotic and interesting as a backstreet pastry chef, with his dark, rockabilly hair and tattoo of a dragon on his forearm. His own professionalism and skill documenting her knowledge of salt mill settings for all of America was undeniable, despite her current regret she hadn't chosen instead to demonstrate tossing greens using the correct utensils.

She and Al met after a culinary disaster made the floor temporarily impassible for union people carrying expensive equipment. It took a surprising amount of time for the crew to find a mop, and she let him rest his camera on her station to wait for the all-clear. Making small talk while she dredged chicken brought Chloe back to the days when she had the energy to stand and have friends. To a surprising extent, it also neutralized the tense, competition atmosphere. Al told her stories about learning to walk backwards for his job, and the funny things he bumped into as part of the learning process. He also gave her a few solid tips about what made food look delicious on television. She, in turn, offered her top-line impression on whether he should sign on to do the nature documentary next, or his buddy's low-budget movie.

"It's not my field, Al," Chloe said between bangs, as she crushed cloves of garlic with the side of her chef knife, "but you kinda light up talking about horror. Could be a great fit. Your day job is filming what real people look like when they're really scared, and reacting to a CGI killer zombie dolphin, that can get a little abstract for the actors. You add multi-layered experience."

Al nodded his agreement as he blocked a stray clove from flying off the bench.

"It's about the money, isn't it?" he asked taking the wedge of lemon she held out and thoughtfully rubbing it over his callused fingers to neutralize the garlic oils.

"Going with the job that pays always looks like the wise choice," Chloe replied with the sympathy of a fellow starving artist, "but even I can tell you're not excited about Mongolian yak migration, Al, and I'm busy toasting off spices. What will the IMAX audience think?"

Receiving the signal that the floor was finally safe, at least for IATSE members in good standing, Al hoisted his camera back up onto to his shoulders, and Chloe gave him a friendly thumbs up as a goodbye.

From her vantage point in the holding area, Chloe finally spotted him across the room, expertly capturing a competitor flambé buttered toast. A great guy, an interesting guy, helpful and talented their Al, and he had those huge biceps from carrying all that equipment, but even with her mind fully occupied with alternately cursing the OG dark-haired stranger, counting the components of her dish to ensure that everything had made it onto the plate, and looking for the exits not already blocked by a kitchen fire, she knew...not her guy, Al. It was information.

Chloe recalled her thoughts with a start and took her hands away from her cart before the wheels locked up, or she twitched wrong and the whole thing careened off in a rogue direction. A runaway cart sent her competitor's full plate of chicken cutlets skittering across the floor that morning. A second cart incident, and from the same audition group, would make Season 14 the Go-Kart Season, just like when Bobby from Season 11 started dropping servingware and it became their thing. Steeped in *Yes! Chef* history, Chloe knew that nobody ever remembered how "Butterfinger", formerly known as Bobby from Memphis, had a way with ribs. Or won the Falling for Flavor! Week team challenge, and bungee jumping for dibs on the protein, that took doing.

"I don't want to be the Go-Kart Girl of the food world," Chloe thought with despair, *"why can't I just stay home and talk back to the TV like a normal person? Stupid pastry chef with his stupid chocolate butterflies."*

Whether she ended the day a food star, a byword, a friend of the show, or another ghost among the vague "thousands" of unselected applicants, at least she knew who to blame. She made one last survey of the contents on her cart, and risked a few more wheel squeaks to relieve her feelings about her relentless bad habit of being nice to people who make blue food and look handsome with wonky hair, until interrupted by the production assistant tasked with coordinating the contestants' entrances.

The tall, calm woman with brown hair cut in a short back and sides and the unexpected flair of a black tuxedo jacket worn over her regulation black tee shirt stopped next to Chloe's cart to check her name and dish against what was written on her clipboard.

"You're...Chloe, right?"

Chloe nodded back, oddly comforted to be still correctly labeled and identified among the dozens of competitors being processed that day.

"When I give you the signal," the PA instructed, "push your cart down between the row of lights to the big, masking tape "x" in front of the judges. There you'll present your dish, and after the judging just bring your cart back out and leave it over there. Simple. Did you get everything done for your cook?"

Chloe nodded again.

"Great. Joe here will take your picture with you and your dish."

Chloe obediently turned and smiled for the young, gangly man holding the Polaroid camera.

"Great," said the PA, taking the undeveloped snap from Joe and attaching it to her clipboard, "They'll be ready for you...should be in about 30 seconds."

"Thanks, Rachel," Chloe said, reading the PA's name tag. "How's your own day going?"

"It's my third season," Rachel replied, surprised at being asked the first question about herself from any applicant in all four rounds of final auditions. "I've already seen it all."

"Wow, go team. If I've just jinxed you, I apologize ahead of time if any contestant suddenly has a melt down because you won't let us serve marshmallow, oysters, or anything hotter than a jalapeno," Chloe replied, listing off the three well-known taboos of the regular weekly panel.

"You're up!" Rachel said with a smile, getting a signal from a counterpart wearing a headset standing further along the makeshift corridor. "Good luck!"

CHAPTER TWELVE

who forgot to make the donuts?

Chloe trundled her heavy cart down the aisle marked by regularly spaced stand lights, and successfully came to a rolling stop in front of the three restaurateurs sitting in a row in front of a giant blue screen emblazoned with "*Yes, Chef! America, Season 14!*" in silver gilt.

"Good morning, Judges," she said politely. Recognizing a familiar, thankfully unsinged, tattooed forearm off to her right, she added a friendly, "hey, Al."

"Don't speak to the crew," she was admonished by the stout chef in the red jacket sitting on the left-handed stool.

"Sorry, Chef," she replied with the tiniest inner laugh for falling afoul of the Mean Judge so soon. At least she hadn't run over his foot with the cart. While Rachel handed the panel her paperwork, she glanced around again at the lights, and at the various, black-clothed people holding reflectors and boom mikes doing mysterious stuff that Al was trying to keep out of frame.

"So...*uhhhh*...Chloe...," said the *Yes, Chef!* Head Judge referring to his clipboard, before looking up at the cheerful hopeful paying attention to all the wrong things. "Are you here to be the next *Yes, Chef!* Master?"

Chloe blinked a few times and froze.

Many other "home Italian cooks" had done the same when first confronted by that international superstar in Sicilian cuisine, Chef Matteo Amato. The grape leaf logo on his crisp, white chef coat was almost as famous as his salt and pepper elegance or his red gravy. It wasn't the reason Chloe became suddenly tongue-tied, but she was darn glad for the cover.

The only right response to his expected opening question was a loud, enthusiastic "Yes, Chef!" that would be later jump-cut in with twenty-four other "Yes, Chefs!" to make the show intro. It was Season 14, everybody knew that. She did try to give the rote answer. Twice. Alas, an untimely conviction rose up in her throat. There was no way could she win this competition. She didn't even like sushi. Some seasons they had to make it. What crazypants thinks they can be a *Yes, Chef!* Master without having an opinion on *maki?* And now, the second thing they had asked her to do was lie, and apparently, she couldn't even get that right.

Having wheeled her cart into the room, however, it was her responsibility to wheel the cart out, Rachel said so. It made her signature Plan B, run run away, a wee problematic. She refused to draw Al further into controversy and ask him to give her a hand turning her cart around, but it was as near as a whisker she went full B anyway, and God only knew what steering capability the carts had at speed.

"You can't knock over light poles and electrocute new friends and enemies just because you suck at decision-making," she told herself firmly, taking another second to get her breath back from pushing the cart, and her mind in the game. Now was also not the time to decide whether anyone would look for an amateur Italian chef in the Amazon headwaters, or if it was safer to be just another fork in the cutlery drawer in Genoa. If she could avoid poisoning the esteemed panel in the next three minutes, she wouldn't even make the highlight reel and just vanish from their memory. That was so doable, and a much better exit strategy.

The judges, used to persons with no experience being on television panicking a little at the start of their segment, took advantage of the awkward silence to flip through her dossier and readjust themselves into a more comfortable position on their high metal stools.

"You seem nervous," said Chef Juan Navarro, restarting the interview. Chef Juan had leveraged his strategically disheveled hair and knowledge of Mexican street food into a franchise of casual, fast casual and fine dining experiences, and was the *Yes, Chef!* audience's favorite Friendly Judge.

"Is this your first time in a cooking competition?" he asked, his deep, accented voice sounding genuinely interested. "Tell us why you are here."

"Yes, Chef. Sorry, Chef. And Chefs."

Chloe refocused and started again.

"I cook Italian, but don't even know what I don't know about what you know about acquiring a commercial amount of tomatoes. So, I'm going full open hands, and see if it takes me to a place where making food "people" like, that is, my people, intersects with making food pay."

Chloe paused.

"Is that remotely what they asked? Why are you talking in air quotes?" she asked herself and rocked her cart a tiny bit to retest its maneuverability. She re-concluded it would require a good three TikTok's worth of film to make the turn needed, more than enough for editing purposes and immortality.

"Do you think you can get a decent Parmesan in Manaus?" she accidentally asked out loud.

Chef Matteo looked at Chef Juan with a shrug, which might have meant, "I don't know, do you?"

Maybe. It might have.

"Who cooks with open hands?" asked Chef Parker Stanley in a sneering undertone, hoping to get an answering snort from his fellow chefs for the camera, not a response from her.

Chef Parker's notoriously snarky comments had elevated him as the meanest Mean Judge across all the franchises. Setting aside his signature devil outfit, and his holding one's life in his cantankerous hands, witnessing his shtick in person Chloe could see the effort required to act out his role, and felt it must be tedious to have one's brand be relentlessly impolite, unkind, and uninterested. Not that he cared about her competition philosophy, or her chicken, but there was probably lots of other stuff during the long day he did want to know.

Having already failed the easy questions, though, she chose to respond to Chef Parker's rhetorical one. She held up her hands palms up, fingers spread wide.

"See, open, that's all. Open to making food for people, not for what I get out of it. Open to receiving advice and critiques, and ready to let go of what is not working. When the fear of losing or looking stupid on TV gets loud..." she turned and waved to the camera, "...hi America!"

"...or in your world," she continued, "it might be the loudness of price points and margins and critics..."

As she talked Chloe's hands slowly contracted into fists.

"See. It's natural to do this, and this doesn't allow me to receive anything, or offer anything, I can only hold on to what I already have. Plus, it's hard to cook the best food using my fists."

Chloe knocked them together to emphasize her point.

"Oh gosh, I hope I didn't just invent a twist," she added with a slight alarm. "Anyway, that's all I meant. Open hands."

"How do you expect to win with such a laid-back attitude and weird gestures? This is a competition," responded Chef Parker.

"I'm holding up your schedule with my *Mosquito Coast* fantasia and memory devices, aren't I? I apologize. It's just my practical way to remember that my job is to do my best, listen well, and wait to find out how proximate that gets me to the money ball. Deciding if my best is the best is entirely your job."

"Did you bring your signature dish?" asked Chef Matteo, choosing to sidestep whether she understood how reality shows worked, and move the segment along.

"I cooked something I hope you find memorable, appropriate, and makes you glad you ate it."

This time Al's camera was in position waiting to catch Chef Parker's flash of signature annoyance for the audience at home.

"That was not the question," he snarled. "You're really difficult, you know."

"I get that," Chloe replied, wondering if her three minutes of unfortunate choices was up yet, and wishing she didn't babble when she got nervous. "If I only had one signature dish that I would make regardless, I would consider my repertoire too small to even audition. I chose a dish I love, that's light and palate cleansing, in case you're inundated with salt and spice bombs, and also a dish I make a lot, so I could adapt to ground conditions, nerves and catastrophes."

"What's the food dream?" asked Chef Matteo, moving the segment forward again. As the Head Judge, it was his responsibility to ask all the "tough" questions, and ensure each Q&A happened in its proper place and time, so the editors wouldn't have to go looking for it. Chloe immediately recognized another *Yes, Chef!* standard, but again stumbled between the truth, nervous ramblings, and providing a usable soundbite, which is all they wanted.

"I want to develop a line of mid-range products that give food a little...," Chloe twitched her shoulder in lieu of using an actual word. "You know, a little higher than ketchup, lower than the acquired taste of mushrooms picked under the quarter moon on a secret, eight-hectare farm in Belgium. I love the wonderful alchemy that happens when people are gathered around a really good meal, and I'm interested in supporting a Sunday dinner-level table magic for the people without grandmothers."

"You mean creating a line of grocery store product?" asked Chef Matteo.

"More farmstand, but I realize selling in the grocery store refrigerator case moves far more units. My stepsister's husband Glenn's family is Cider Hill Farm, that's my target customer."

"Are we supposed to know what that is?" Chef Parker asked, again rhetorically, but this time for his fans at home.

"All the cool kids know Cider Hill Farm," Chloe responded. "Glenn's a whiz at growing stuff, he's a farmer *and* a thinker, we're very proud of him, but they also have a lovely farmstand where he sells cider donuts. Who doesn't love a farmstand, and cider donut season is America's happy time, but Glenn makes it artisanal. Because he makes their cider, which is super cider. Everybody knows that."

"*Tch*, like you know everybody," Chef Parker mumbled on cue.

"No really, everybody," Chloe echoed with conviction. "They stopped into this small Italian town once, just passing through, and t for truth, this random fellow tourist said, "I know your farm. You guys make the BEST cider donuts." That's our Glenn. And Karen, but she married into the family, she would have made a success of wherever she went. Anyway, my goal is to make a line of condiments and sides worthy of being sold alongside Glenn's donuts. Right next to the cider, which is a-ma-zing."

"Did any of that really happen?" asked Chef Juan.

"Oh, yeah. It's Karen and Glenn's second favorite travel story. That's how successful their farm is. They get to leave it."

"What's their first?" Chef Juan asked, causing Chef Parker to sigh loudly, even though he started the entire exchange. Chef Juan's role was to bring out the color commentary behind the dishes and cooks, continually dragging out the taping schedule as he pursued tangential lines of questioning. Chef Parker was rarely interested in the backstory or opinions of anyone who wasn't already nominated for a James Beard award, and Chef Matteo, as the only judge tasked with reading the contestants' audition paperwork, was equally uninterested to hear belated, supplemental data.

Responding to Chef Juan's prompt, while furthering her education about what really happened among the judges in all the places Al wasn't pointing his camera, she answered,

"According to Karen, it's telling me that story when I was coming back from Paris, and they were connecting through Charles de Gaulle coming back from

South Africa. Shocking shocker, we ended up seated next to each other on the plane. We laughed, we cried, if only Glenn had brought donuts. They've started shipping them now, though, how dangerous is that?"

"Did that really happen?" Chef Juan asked again.

"Gosh, the fun train doesn't stop in your town very often, does it? It happens all the time. And who makes stuff up on national TV?" Chloe asked, finally confused into silence.

"Really, Al?" she responded in surprise, catching Al's expression of disbelief at her naivete, as he turned the camera to pan the judges.

"It's me?" she asked looking around at the crew who nodded along with Al. "Really? Huh."

"She's right about that Cider Hill cider," Chef Matteo commented to the other judges. "It got Best in Show at, *ummm*, you know, the national farmer one, that one. You should get some for that pork dish you've been developing, Parker."

Chef Parker, now extra grumpy because Chloe hadn't brought them any of this world's best cider, or donuts, and instead just pushed off his lunch break talking about them, while again violating the first rule of filming by addressing members of the crew, interjected another snarky swipe to get the segment back on track, and amuse his fans.

"How is this dish worthy of *Yes, Chef!*, Chloe?" he asked gesturing to her simple preparation. "It's chicken salad."

"But it's tasty chicken salad," she responded calmly.

Chef Matteo refocused the interview by asking the final standard question.

"So, how did the cook go for you today?"

"Well, there was a little chaos backstage when another contestant's protein got knocked onto the floor. Thankfully, I had extra, but it made us all cook jumpy and do the meerkat head-swivel afterward whenever we heard that squeaky sound."

Chloe rocked her cart a bit to demonstrate the sound of a runaway cart and acted out the head fake, while Chef Matteo put out a restraining arm as Chef Parker sputtered and twitched on his stool. Chef Juan asked for more information.

"You gave away your ingredient to a competitor? What if they cook better than you?"

"Then it would be a shame if they didn't get a chance to shine because of someone else's carelessness. I brought extra in case of catastrophe, and that is what it got used for, so it was all good. That Rachel person said it was okay."

"But that catastrophe didn't happen to you," explained Chef Juan, while Al continued to film what would become Season 14's go-to reaction shots of Chef Parker objecting, with feeling, to a contestant's spectacularly bad competition strategy.

"I know, and I'm so grateful," responded Chloe to Chef Juan, letting Chef Parker do Parker for Parker Nation. "That poor woman. It must've really thrown her off her game to see her primary component on the floor. They looked so well-cooked, too, with those really nice char lines, you know, those. Thankfully, she could refocus and start again."

"Well, let's taste it," said Chef Matteo, again moving the segment along before Chef Parker's head exploded.

The three men got down off their high metal stools and moved towards Chloe's cart. With one last rueful shake of his tousled locks over her helping the enemy, Chef Juan picked up his fork and made eye contact with Chloe, a gesture many women before her welcomed with a simper. She scrunched up her face and shoulders, and stared back at him sideways.

Surprised, he responded,

"You look like somebody is about to throw a bucket of water on you."

"Good. Because that's what I'm braced for. Glad I am in position."

With another shake of his head, Chef Juan joined the other judges poking, pulling apart, and then tasting her dish. Telegraphing their assessment to each other, they put down their forks and returned to their stools. Chef Matteo led off the critique.

"The dish is good. It's not outstanding, and the plating is rudimentary, but for a home cook, it's good."

"*Hmmmm*," Chloe said tilting her head as she evaluated his input. "Does the sauce add dimension to the chicken seasoning? Is it at least balanced?"

Chef Parker responded instead of Chef Matteo with a grudging shrug, eliciting a spurt of laughter from Chloe before she wisely squelched it.

"A contestant is supposed to be crushed if we don't like their food," instructed Chef Juan.

"*Ahem*. Yes, but that's not Chef Parker's "I hate this" face. It's Season 14, everybody knows that."

"It isn't praise, either."

"Heard. I recently overcame a medical crisis, and recalibrating one's fear response takes some doing. Plus, you all got me thinking about Glenn's donuts, and they come with their own inherent happiness that kinda blankets everything, like the cinnamon sugar they're rolled in. So good. Although my dish won't win Best Plate of my group, knowing that even Chef Parker liked it, it's still a great day for me."

"That's not what I said," Chef Parker snarled.

"You're mad I didn't make anything with the cider. I know, I get it. That's fair. I should have. Or at least brought donuts."

"Well, she's got you there," said Chef Juan looking down the row.

"Thank you, Chef Juan, now he's mad at you," Chloe said watching Chef Parker give him a signature, malevolent, side-eye. "Here's hoping we can keep the focus in that direction, so by Judge's Deliberation he will concede I did not purposely withhold the greatness that is all things made with Glenn's cider. It's just pressed in late summer, which is not now. Now is BA time on the farm, you know, Before Apples."

In response to Chef Parker's extra loud sigh that Chef Juan was opening another black hole time suck with a confirmed rambler, Chef Matteo closed her segment.

"Well, thank you Chloe, you may go," he said, dismissing her.

"Thank you, Judges," Chloe replied, as she lurched and squeaked her cart around trying to make a three-point turn and get the wheels in the right direction. "Thanks for trying my food! I hope you have a great day of taping."

"Bye, All!" she whispered, rebel to the end, as with one more back and forth she got the angle right and trundled away.

wallace gets the last yes

Hours later, the judges stood over a folding table set up in the now otherwise empty room, sorting and re-sorting the Polaroids and looking for the most promising hopefuls. Out of the three hundred that made it to the live round, they needed twenty-five to put through to the competition.

"So, which one of the contestants will be this year's winner?" Chef Juan asked the others, fanning out the pile to get to those seen earlier in the schedule.

"Can you guess?" responded Chef Matteo, who already knew.

"This one," Juan said. He flipped the picture over to find the name written on the back, "...Fran Malinowski. She got the emergency chicken from that hands girl, didn't she? Lucky for her and us."

He pushed her photo over to the "yes" pile.

"Who helps a competitor using the same protein?" replied Matteo. "Nope, you guessed wrong. It's this one."

Chef Parker picked up the indicated Polaroid and tossed it back on the yeses with zero enthusiasm.

"Her food is competent, but she will never get nominated for an *Emerging Chef Award.* Not ever."

"She's good at *mise en place,* and will make good TV," Matteo countered. "Look, the camera loves her."

"You mean Al?"

"There's a problem we don't need. Camera, camera," Matteo insisted, "not cameraman."

"Anyway, she's our girl. This one, this one, and this one should go through as well," he added, pulling out the photos of a few more standouts. "Oh, and here is...Felix...our token pastry chef for the season."

Juan nodded enthusiastically.

"That lemon lavender meringue pie was amazing, I'm behind that one."

"Who's our homemaker cook?" asked Parker, flipping over Polaroids to find the abbreviated biographies pasted on the back.

Matteo pointed out the photo with the coconut curry.

"We're going with a stay-at-home dad this year, Ajiz."

"How inclusive. Hey, should I ask why moderate knife skills make this Vivian woman the destined star?" he asked, moving his own selections over to the growing pile of yeses. "Can't we shove her off onto *Supermodel New Now*? Aren't they filming over the mountain in Vail? I want someone who knows what a gyutou is."

"Stop threatening to leave us for *The Next Iron Chef*," Matteo answered pushing a whole swathe of discards over in front of him. "No, we can't, are they really, and funding, what else? You want to get paid, don't you? Is that our "no" pile? All these can go."

"Well, if you get her, I get this one," Juan said, pushing another photo into the "yes" pile.

"Is that the hands chick?" Parker asked. "She can't even chop onions as good as our winner."

"Get over the donuts, she'll make much better TV. Says here she survived a near-death illness. That's good backstory. Didn't she bring that up today? Or am I thinking about the cancer lady?"

"Cancer lady. Magic Brussels sprouts," added Parker to jog his memory. "Sprout lady is a definite no."

"Leave it to you to cut a cancer survivor," responded Juan. "Anyway, under my guidance, I can improve the knife skills of cancer-free, hands girl by a mile."

"Guidance, huh, is that what you are calling it? I thought you were into brunettes?"

"Makes a nice change. And Navarro Streetshop is always in need of entry-level cooks, so when she gets cut, I can console her with an internship. Getting to work for me as a consolation prize makes even better TV."

"I don't think your plan will work out quite like you want," said Matteo absentmindedly, as he debated between two hopefuls with similar pork dishes. "She doesn't look like the type."

"She told us she has open hands. I'm just offering to fill them. Let's go with this one," Juan said choosing the photo in Matteo's left hand and moving it to the top of the pile.

"Fill them for now," said Parker, switching Juan's selection out for the photo in Matteo's right hand.

"All we have is now."

"Well, good luck with that," said Matteo, agreeing with Parker's choice, and laying out the yeses into five rows of five to see how many slots were still open. "So, Juan has his wild card/new girlfriend/intern, I have the winner, is there anyone you really want, Parker?"

"What about this one?" Parker suggested, picking up the photo with a lobster bisque.

"I know you love properly cooked seafood, but actually, hands girl was right...," began Matteo.

Parker interjected.

"If Juan insists on putting her through, you better start calling her by her right name or that nickname will pop up when it's least convenient."

"I suppose. What is it?" asked Matteo.

Juan scanned the rows to find her photo.

"*Uhhh*, which one was she again?" Turning over two Polaroids, he finally located the right one. "It's...Chloe."

"Chloe, then. I think we should listen to her about the lobster guy," Matteo continued. "A great signature, this...Oliver. I get why you liked it Parker, but I think he will crash and burn outside his comfort zone. He admitted to being a pescatarian. Meat Week is week one this year."

"See, my girl's already adding value," said Juan, "none of us want to see what he does with a steak, and now we don't have to."

"He's a fishmonger, though," Parker argued back. "Remember two years ago? When we didn't have anyone left who could fish for the fishing challenge?"

Disaster. We had to let one whole team haggle with that sport fishing group who did not want to give up their trophies."

"You're right. How late did we film that night?"

"You slept the whole time the kids were out, so what did you care?"

"This year we are sending them fly fishing on a mountain. Alone," Matteo interrupted. "We'll definitely need a fisherman. Is he a fishmonger, or does he fish?"

"Oliver caught his own fish," said Parker.

"Lobsters walk into a trap. You're thinking of flounder guy. Says here, lobster guy has a family boat. I am fine with him after all," conceded Matteo, rechecking each man's background.

"Thanks," said Parker pushing the bisque in place to start filling out the last row. "I want this signature dish, too...Paul...those short ribs were awesome."

"And the Executive Producer also wants this guy," Matteo said, flipping over another photo. "...*uhhhh*...Mr. Pedestrian Turkey Piccata. For some reason, he and our winner are a one, two deal."

"Should we know why?" asked Juan.

"Does it matter? I hear he's a player, though. Be careful he doesn't try to cut you out with your hands. I mean, your Chloe."

"Let him. That will give me two things to console her about."

"Okay, out of these twenty-five are there any that can't cook?" Matteo asked, as they did one last review of the skills and backgrounds of the finalists. "We got lawyer, nurse, CPA, HR administrator, craft store owner, *ooooh*, a plumber martial artist, that'll be a fun person to see get mad."

"That IT guy with the remedial souvlaki, he really can't cook," answered Juan, pulling him out of the third row. "I know you wanted a few more white-collar professionals turning to food, Matteo, but no. No."

"What about under your great tutelage?" asked Parker.

"No. Besides I already have my project. Hands, I mean Chloe, will keep me busy until at least episode five. How about this guy...Travis?" he replied, pulling a "rustic" meatball dish from the top of the discards, and moving it into place. "It says his family owns a pumpkin farm. That's interesting. Audiences love a farmer."

Matteo nodded.

"Okay, yes to farmer Travis, no to IT, everybody has a wildcard, we didn't leave out the winner, and Juan has a new girlfriend. Are we ready? Can we live with these?"

"And," he paused before sweeping the other photos away, "live without all these?"

"I don't think we missed anyone important," Parker replied. "If we did, they just won't air their audition."

"Alright, let's go tell them."

"I want a donut," complained Parker. "If hands girl doesn't bring any to the show, I'm cutting her Week 1."

CHLOE SPENT THE WINDOW OF time between the shocking conclusion of her *Yes, Chef!* audition and the start of filming managing her confusion at getting selected for the show, organizing how to leave her apartment for some unknown amount of time, including how the rent check...checks?...check? would get to her landlord, and memorizing her recipes. It was a lot.

Choosing to say yes to *Yes, Chef!* was a decision that perhaps, once again, ignored the distinction between still being alive and being actually restored to health. Her willful blindness was even less explicable after witnessing what the latter was supposed to look like while in the hospital. The grey and listless man wheeled off into surgery from the recovery bay directly across from hers returned a completely different person. Pink, smiling, he sprang out of bed and hustled away with his relieved wife long before it came Chloe's turn to prove she, too, was at least ambulatory again.

Chloe relied on her pride, and her commitment to the *Project Runway* ethos, for her discharge paperwork. Clad in a hospital gown, hospital gore and a hospital blanket draped over her shoulders like a child's superhero cape, she faced down the daunting challenge to walk unassisted from her bed to the bathroom five bays away like a model assigned a dud designer Week 1 fighting to survive through to the Week 2 selection process. The ER nurses pronounced she had the best post-op walk they had ever seen as they signed her release forms. It wasn't the same as being recalled to life like her fellow patient, but it got her out of there, and as for rocking the zombie chic, it was a triumph, a key superpower for a reality television gig that might require running around doing zany challenges.

If she wasn't so busy looking under the bed for the best shoes to stand up in for long periods of time, and packing television-worthy, yet kitchen-appropriate clothing ensembles, she might, maybe, have acknowledged she was still a zombie chick trying to keep up with normal people. Maybe. Sitting down on her bed to catch her breath after successfully locating the Mary Janes under her bed, the boots in the back of the closet, and her green, canvas sneakers out by the front door and ranging them on the floor by her suitcase for a final decision, her one salve to her conscience was that all legitimate places of employment have liability insurance, and don't want to see dead people. It was essential, therefore, to practice how long and how well she could hide her illness. She passed the brief inspection of nine countries' Customs and Border Patrol agents, and they were trained observers, so a three-month taping schedule with 24/7 cameras felt like a reasonable next goal.

Participating on *Yes, Chef!* was also almost, kinda, less risky than staying home to explore the limits of her new normal. If she turned blue all alone in her apartment, she had zero chance of successfully calling 911, opening multiple sets of doors, and then communicating the issue to whomever came through those doors. Whereas, if she failed to be mindful of her limitations in the *Yes, Chef!* kitchen, not that she would, collapsing on TV was twelve times worse than doing it in Doc's office, but if she did, well, it was the only temp job she could think of with a medical crew on standby. That would be new and handy.

"Nothing like finding out," she told herself, and committed to her black Mary Janes as both indestructible and a cute shoe, and rejected her favorite, but overly loose and floaty blouse she usually wore with them as openly courting fifteen minutes of television fame from self-immolation. Death was one thing. Stupid death was another.

On the other side of the planet, Wallace Yan was working strenuously to get a far more reluctant person attached to the *Yes, Chef! America* project ready for showtime. Time Wallace knew would be a good marketing investment for the Little Paris brand, and career-forwarding to their celebrity chef. Unless it wasn't.

"No," Kyung-ho said when Wallace first tentatively broached the possibility of maybe doing the show, and he kept saying it, even after Wallace signed him on as guest judge for Pastry Week.

Kyung-ho understood that savory chefs had an important societal function, he ate food, he got it, but he didn't really understand them, and he didn't want to go anywhere they outnumbered him twenty-eight to one. Not only did they, as a species, not grasp the value-add of sugar work, but they used measurements like "a dash" and "a sprinkle", amounts anathema to the precise chemistry required in a pastry kitchen.

Wallace conceded Kyung-ho's point and agreed that a French show offered much less of a language barrier, and more mutual cultural understanding about what really mattered in life. He just didn't care.

"Well, you should have thought about that when you decided to expand to New York and not Paris," he told Kyung-ho, cornering him at his old desk in his original office where Kyung-ho still liked to do his serious thinking and most of his paperwork. "The Pastry Week is halfway through the competition this season, most of the contestants will be gone by then."

"Go away."

"I am going. I'm going to America, and I'm taking you with me."

"Marketing is your problem, leave me alone. I'm trying to design a blinged-out wedding cake for the Hu's. It'll be expensive. What more do you want from me?"

"Establishing the legitimacy of your brand in a foreign market is your job," Wallace countered, "that's why I am making it your problem. Nothing says "I'm a somebody" like showing up as a guest judge on a reality show. All you have to do is hold up one of the fancier items out of our case, let a handful of people clap while cursing you under their breath, have a few opinions, and come home. You have to be in New York anyway, what's a few extra days in Denver on the way back? It's like an extended layover, and if we fly back in that direction we don't have to transit through Qatar."

"I don't wanna. I like sand and touristy camel rides."

"You are not tanking our marketing plan to play Lawrence of Arabia. What's the issue here? The media loves you, surprisingly, o grumpy one, it's time to expand your horizons. Have you seen the rent on our new shop? We need all the customers we can get. Let's take advantage of how most Americans like to go to New York City and all of them love to eat sugar."

Kyung-ho stopped impatiently tapping his pencil on the desk to ask,

"Who watches the show?"

"Everybody, it's very popular. I'm not shoving you out onto a low-rent, start-up, cable access morning show. *Yes, Chef!* is in Season 14. They now have franchises all over the world. World people are your people."

"Fine," Kyung-ho conceded, refusing to give Wallace the satisfaction of knowing which, if any, of his arguments prevailed. It was only one, after all, and Wallace didn't need to know. "Now can I get back to preparing for the Hu wedding? We're running out of gold leaf. Can you believe it?"

"Wow, really? Has hell frozen over as well? And thank you," said Wallace. "Especially since you are already under contract, and they expect you there in another month or so. But thank you."

welcome to the big time

Day 1 filming of the new season of *Yes, Chef! America* began, as usual, with the lucky twenty-five finalists gathered in the judging area of the show's large warehouse kitchen, waiting to hear Chef Matteo, Chef Parker and Chef Juan welcome them to the competition, explain the weekly challenges, and enumerate this year's prizes. This segment was largely for the benefit of audience members at home unfamiliar with the series. The contestants well knew what they had to do, and what it would get them, but everyone was quite happy to listen to the judge's annual spiel, cheer on cue, and put off actual cooking for as long as possible.

Before bringing in the judges, the production assistants in their anonymous black outfits got busy sorting the contestants into three, visually attractive rows, while the tech crew, also wearing anonymous black outfits, made their last lighting and sound checks. The contestants themselves, wearing their best amateur cook couture under new white aprons with their names embroidered in blue, stood on their masking tape x's, as directed, and looked around at their fellow competitors and the space where they would be competing.

The basic layout of the main hall was easily recognizable to any fan of the show, but for the cooks seeing it in person, and set up for the full complement of contestants, what an entirely different experience. Row after row of workstations, one whole wall of shelving holding a dazzling variety of kitchen gadgets and equipment, the well-stocked mini grocery store in the corner, the lounge area off to the side with enough yellow couches and chairs for everyone to sit down on something – they felt like elves in an enormous food workshop.

As the wait for the judges stretched on, the silent nodding and smiling to each other whenever their roving eyes crossed paths gradually shifted to pointing out landmarks and recalling associated events of past seasons. None of them could yet believe they were standing feet from right there, in the gulf between their nervous rows and the lone small table the judges stood behind when evaluating their plates, right there was where the winners each year were decided.

"Remember Season 8?" several whispered to their neighbors, receiving a chorus of nods. Who hadn't watched the epic and still hotly contested finale showdown between Adam and Emily?

"That's where I'll be standing soon," announced the confident, dark-haired woman dressed in an elaborately embroidered peasant blouse and distressed jeans cuffed to accentuate her sandals with a 4" cork heel. She seemed to direct her comment across the ranks to the blond, surfer guy with the aggressively unbuttoned Hawaiian shirt. Many of the other women turned towards her as she spoke, wondering if she was right, and if they packed wrong, and whether they could send home for real pants.

"Is she going to cook in that?" wondered Tammy the ER nurse to her fellow second row competitors, looking down at her own worn Camopop UGGs, which she had thought causally chic footgear for working late-night triage and matched all four of her jeggings.

"Are we cooking today?" she asked directly to Paul the lawyer standing next to her. "I would set those sleeves on fire if I cooked in them."

A vision of responsible know-how in his best casual Friday, blue Brooks Brother button-down, properly buttoned up and ready to go, Paul believed the woman about her sleeves, but didn't believe that was the shirt either of them was actually interested in. He just smiled politely and went back to trying to glimpse what the show stocked in the five-bay dairy case.

The tall, weatherbeaten man in the orange tee-shirt emblazoned across the back with "I'm Beet" promoting some farm implement, suddenly interjected, "I still think Adam...," into the general conversation, causing the people around him to move off their marks to give him a little space. Wherever he was going with that, them there were fightin' words. Thankfully, the woman with elaborate cornrows and a no-nonsense demeanor standing on the "x" to his right turned her back at that moment and shut it down, but it took several minutes for the others to stop nervously eying him, wondering if he was this season's troublemaker. Even if his height got him continuously shoved into the back row, with that shirt, and that kinda talk, they could all tell, he wasn't going to stay there.

Not that Janiva, who owned her own yarn shop but had a heart for Kobe beef preparations, had meant anything by cutting off Travis' unwise and unfiltered opinion. She planned to compete for Team Switzerland. She simply turned with everyone else as Ashley, the mousey-blonde woman with the nasally twang, triangulated that over there, right there by the shelving with the mixing bowls, that must be where Butterfinger Bobby from Season 11 dropped four sets of ceramic ramekins in four successive episodes. A memorable achievement for Bobby, and a timely warning to the contestants to stand out for the right reasons.

"Now, that *won't* be me," pronounced the supremely confident Vivian, again inviting the group to eavesdrop on her private conversation with surfer Jake. Again, the others all hoped she was wrong. Except Ashley, who knew a star when she saw one, and was already jostling her way against PA orders to maneuver a spot next to her in the front row and hopefully, onto her team for the first Group Challenge.

Chloe remained staring at the gleaming stack of white servingware, sighing for poor Bobby, and her own lack of planning that left only the bits and edges of the cheerful logo on her purple tee shirt proclaiming "this is my happy place" visible under her apron. A "hey! I know you" from the person with Harry Potter glasses that Rachel the PA shoved into Ashley's abandoned mark interrupted such unproductive musings and regrets. It was Fran, the former recipient of her replacement chicken. The two women gave each other a hug and exchanged congratulations and introductions, while everyone else turned back around and started craning their necks to see into the adjoining restaurant area where the formal judging segments took place.

Stay-at-home dad, Ajiz, unkempt and roly-poly and confident his professional eye for small squabbles about to erupt would take him far in the competition, pointed out where Alberto (now Chef Alberto, his hero) had presented his Spaghetti Five Ways for the first time. Ajiz then broke into a rendition of *My Way* as a tribute to Alberto's signature song in the competition kitchen, and the subsequent name of his first restaurant. Ajiz hoped to carry on both Alberto's food luck and musical traditions for Season 14. Several contestants joined him for the chorus, including Chloe who dragged her hesitant, new friend Fran with her via an encouraging elbow, giving Ajiz a boost of confidence he was on the right path, and walking it out among his kinda people.

Those not singing along noted that, from what they could smell, somewhere out of view craft services was already working on their lunch.

"Is that lunch? I think it's our mid-morning snack break," said the sunburnt fisherman, his feet firmly planted in a wide stance in case the floor suddenly rolled away, countering the prevailing whispers through the crowd that if it was lunch, it was probably just for the judges.

"I heard they feed us a lot here," Oliver continued to insist, "I think it's our snack."

"I thought we just ate what we made," responded Felix, the weedy, wannabe pastry chef who looked sixteen but was really twenty-seven, animated by the sailor's confidence with a dawning hope that for the next however many hours, days or weeks he would be fed properly. He paid his way through electrical engineering college by baking cakes and living mostly off the discards.

Owen the roadie and Troy the plumber, both union men, were just starting to explain to the unaffiliated the rules regarding employee meals and break times in a shop governed by collective bargaining when the judges came in.

"I'll tell you later," was the last loud whisper heard before both the chatter, and Ajiz's musical interlude, faded into a quiet shuffling, as they all turned the right way around, adjusted their collars and resettled their aprons, and double-checked they were on their marks.

Chef Matteo, and his bright white chef's jacket, looked even more imposing in a tricked-out kitchen than either had in front of the blue screen at the auditions. Flanked by his two fellow judges, one in his devil coat, the other in the latest in funky chef pants, Matteo took his accustomed place at the head of the nervous rows of this year's hopefuls. Receiving a signal from the crew that they were ready, he officially started the show.

"Congratulations to our top twenty-five contestants! Welcome to Season 14!" he announced in his cultured and refined style of enthusiasm.

The contestants responded with enthusiastic applause and a few high-fives.

Chef Matteo continued.

"We have some *great* prizes for you this year. The winner gets...a guest contributor slot at Food & Leisure Magazine...a full set of professional cookware and appliances from Kitchen Aid...a cookbook opportunity from Random House, and I'm sure the last reason any of you signed up...a quarter of a million dollars!"

He paused for another round of loud clapping and variations on "Mine!" and "No, Mine!".

"Well, in order to get to the finale, you will need to survive three tough challenges every week. Are you ready?"

"Ready, chef!"

"As you know, Round One of every week is the Imitation Challenge set by our weekly guest judge, because why?"

"Imitation is the sincerest form of flattery!" they said, yelling back in unison that well-known *Yes! Chef* catch phrase.

"That's right! Using the instructions provided by each week's guest judge, your job is to recreate their signature dish. The winner of that round gets a special advantage going into the first elimination round of the week, the dreaded Reinvention Challenge. There contestants must use some, or all, of the ingredient list from the Imitation Round, along with anything they like out of the pantry, plus the wildcard, to make a brand-new dish. And remember, contestants are allowed to set aside any components from their Imitation Round, prior to judging, they think came out exceptionally well. But you must use it in the new dish, so be sure you are confident about it before you turn it into leftovers. The loser of this round will...go...home.

"*Booooo...!*"

"The winner of the Reinvention Challenge, of course, will be a captain for Round Three, the Group Challenge, and gets to pick his or her opposing captain. I think you will have a lot of fun cooking out and around the Denver area. As you know, teams will go head-to-head, and the winner will be chosen with the help of our guests. The winning team of the Group Challenge gets a special reward, you'll really want to win them this year, and the cook who performs the weakest on the losing team will...go...home."

This elicited another spirited response from the contestants, including various groans, and a few exchanges of "not me!" and "yes, you!".

"So, are you ready to kick off Season 14?"

"*Yaayyyyyyy!!!*"

"Then welcome to Week 1: Meat and Greet!"

"*Yaayyyyyy!!!* Meat and Greet!!!"

"Our guest judge for Meat and Greet! Week is from over the border in Oklahoma City, executive chef and owner of the Cattle Baron Steakhouse, longtime friend of the show, please welcome back, Jimmy *Bobbbbbb* McIntyre. Jimmy Bob!"

From the mention of "Meat", certainly by "Oklahoma", the contestants were already whispering "it's Jimmy Bob, right? Gotta be." among themselves. A regular guest judge, several contestants visited his restaurant to prepare prior to the start of filming on the off chance he was back for Season 14. All were relieved to see him mosey through the entrance doors in his well-known brown leather vest and Oklahoma-shaped belt buckle, carrying his cloche.

Jimmy Bob's appearance signaled Season 14 would follow the "standard" opening week formula, rather than the "unexpected twist" formula thrown in every few years. Standard Week 1 evaluated their mastery of the basics and gave everyone a chance to calm their nerves and settle into the new kitchen environment. Season 4 contestants started with Yokohama Yabbadoo! Week making sushi, a week Chloe and all fans of the show remembered vividly. The Reunion episodes occasionally checked in with that Season's scarred-for-life eliminated contestants. While neither one from Yokohama! Week had returned to the kitchen, the Season 12 audience learned Mackenzie was about to bring tuna back into her life again, so, progress. Cooking Jimmy Bob's food had never, yet, made anybody cry. Not like sushi.

For Chef Jimmy Bob's eighth appearance on the show, he brought his restaurant's latest signature dish, The Lord Done Down Dirty, a Flintstone-sized porterhouse steak and dirty rice. After lifting the cloche to a round of applause, a small, lucky contingent was invited up to taste the dish. The next ten minutes were then spent by the more media savvy contestants vying to get their testimonial on camera, while Jimmy Bob offered the group at large some general tips, peppered with ranch colloquialisms, regarding beef preparations and what pitfalls to expect in preparing this dish. Finally, an excessive 150 minutes was put on the time clock, and the contestants raced to find their workstations and start the first challenge.

CHAPTER FIFTEEN

meat, two veg, and the great pumpkin

The crew assigned Chloe a fourth-row cooking station on the stage-left side of the warehouse. It was a long way from the mini grocery store, but relatively close to the rack holding stand mixers. As she took her place, she looked down with trepidation at Jimmy Bob's recipe printed out on an 8"x11" sheet of paper that lay on her section of butcherblock countertop. Chloe knew the basics of cooking steak, naturally, and her father would have loved Jimmy Bob's food, but she almost never made rice, had never eaten dirty rice, had never even seen it on a menu. Taking advantage of the surfeit time, she slowly and painstakingly checked and rechecked the instructions for every scrap of information on that component.

The surrounding contestants seemed much more confident. The young, skinny kid assigned the bench next to her appeared unfazed by the first challenge and he was rumored to be this year's baker, what did he know for steak. Catching her wandering glance, Felix gave her a friendly thumbs up and began expertly organizing his cast iron pans. Chloe could also see Fran's curly light brown hair two rows ahead and watched her steadily and methodically tackle her hunk of red meat. Up front, that Vivian was surprisingly cool and practiced, as well. No wonder she sounded so confident earlier, she moved from task to task with just a glancing reference at the recipe, almost as if she had seen it before. Chloe remembered the three of them had been assigned the same prep timeslot in the audition kitchen, and it was Vivian's cart that had gone rogue. Their group must be extra lucky seeing how many of them had made it onto the show despite all that audition drama.

"*Let's do this!*" Chloe said to herself and got to work.

The smoke from twenty-five grills filled up the room as the contestants banged and clattered and occasionally swore their way through their first cook. Oliver the fishmonger complained, or rather posited, and only when Chef Jimmy Bob wasn't nearby, that grouper would be a better protein with the rice. Paul, whose husband never let him cook fish at home, took that under advisement and asked him several questions about grouper pairings while he competently deglazed his pan for the *au jus*. Ajiz announced he thought dirty rice was groovy, and whistled his way through selections from *Les Mis*, until Fran asked him to switch to *The Lion King*. He happily obliged, and agreed it went better with Jimmy Bob's food.

The first real surprise of the challenge, except to Paul, who was waiting for it, was when the ER nurse set her oven mitt on fire. Twice. Tammy insisted she wasn't alone in trying to burn down the kitchen, what with all the dripping fat flareups everywhere, but even though the contestants were still a disparate group of strangers, somehow everyone else was of one mind that it was different if you set equipment on fire not actually needed for the challenge.

While the amateur chefs cooked, the judges circulated warily among them filming the floor interview segments, stopping at each station to taste, guide and ask questions. The contestants were ready for the spotlight. Years of holiday dinners, and generations of family know-it-alls had prepared them for maintaining the required grace under pressure. Specifically, cooking while other people told them they were doing it all wrong. Battle-hardened Oliver, the frequent preparer of what his tired family wrested that day from the cold sea, Ajiz's smiling clashes with a mother-in-law who was not a fan of curry, Fran's discouraging boss who was also her cousin and wanted her to remain his assistant forever and just eat her food at Thanksgiving, everyone had their training regimen.

And yet, as the judges slowly progressed up and down the rows, one after another contestant discovered that this, the "easy" part of the competition, well...they sucked at it. The path of the judges could be traced in the crowded, noisy room by either a sudden increase of clattering as utensils were dropped or wielded with over-aggressiveness, or the odd pockets of silence and char as contestants froze upon their approach. The cameras caught Janiva vigorously chopping her garlic with a spoon as she expounded on her wish to own a Japanese steakhouse and captured all four creaky bangs it took for Felix to remember how oven doors opened, although the show only aired the last two, and of course, Ajiz's outburst became part of that episode's commercial.

"What do you mean you don't like my pan sauce?" he exclaimed, almost as if he had never heard such a thing in his life. Ajiz was so startled by this revelation it took him two lines to join in with Felix's low, sympathetic, "*I can't makkkkke you love meeeee, ifff you donnnn'ttt...*" after the judges had moved on.

"Where's my *Lion King*?" interrupted Fran. "You can't have us crying into our dirty rice all morning."

"I may need a minute," answered Ajiz as he poured out his sauce and started again.

"Don't gotta worry," encouraged Jimmy Bob, temporarily stranded and left behind at Ajiz's station when the cameraman following the judges paused to get a long shot of the room. "Just 'cause trouble comes visitin', don't mean you gotta give it a place to sit down. Plenty of time for fixin' this here wrong."

Of course, it wasn't Jimmy Bob's job, or brand, to be honest with amateur cooks who were also his customers.

The walk-through did re-cement Chef Juan's reputation as the "friendly" judge, or more accurately, the "good cop" by his moderate interest in where each contestant learned the wrong method they chose to cook the steak. The other two main judges stuck to variations on "what taught you to think you could cook?" and "why come on the show to prove you couldn't?". No matter how many times Chef Parker said, "you're burning that", though, it never seemed to get old for him.

Vivian alone had a standout comfort level and performance in front of the judges and the television audience. She managed to slowly, but competently, prepare a uniform mirepoix while plugging her family business. It was even her actual family business. Oliver stumbled and bumbled into giving the impression he worked at a hardware store.

"Wow, she really puts her whole heart into her camera work," Chef Juan whispered with admiration to Chef Parker, as Vivian expertly tipped her pinch bowl to display her *mise en place* to the folks at home.

"Yeah," Parker agreed, "maybe that's why there is none in her food."

Travis the farmer also garnered the judge's general respect for his calm and steady presentation style, belied by his excessively orange outfit, despite them arriving at his station just as he was questioning the doneness of his beef. He fielded a Q&A about bone-in versus bone-out preparations with so little drama the cameraman didn't bother to film it – wouldn't have even if all that Day-Glo wasn't throwing off his light levels – before the cavalcade moved on, to the dismay of Jake who had no warning the judges were so nearby and heading his way.

Chloe both froze and clattered when it was her turn to be interviewed, stopping and starting like a blender as she alternated between pausing to listen to the judges' questions, and pushing on wildly with her cook while she thought about how to answer them. She hoped practice would make her presentation a little smoother over time, but throughout Day 1 her nerves only became more pronounced.

The general chaos of such a full kitchen may have also contributed to Chloe et al's jumpiness, failures and snafus. The spacing between the rows of cooking stations was noticeably tight, crammed as they were with cooks, crew members, film equipment, oven doors opening, and the occasional mixing bowl left on the floor, which some, marked-for-early-elimination amateurs thought of as overflow space. There were also the occasional pileups from twenty-five contestants trying to learn the kitchen habit of saying "behind, chef, behind" when threading their way to the equipment wall or elsewhere in the kitchen. Not everyone was good at it.

This might explain Chloe's cry of alarm when Chef Juan, passing by to interview the row behind her, suddenly crushed up against her as he tried to get out of the way of the boom mike operator. He apologized immediately, and while they waited for the log jam to clear, kindly used his free hand to demonstrate a better technique for wielding a chef knife. The other he kept on her shoulder where it first landed, you know, to be out of the way.

Chloe found it even harder to listen while cooking while also instinctively making her body more convex than nature intended to keep her contact with a judge to just those two points, but she tried her best to absorb his valuable tip on using more of a rocking motion. The interaction was brief, and for Chloe, soon forgotten as she scraped her now-charred rice into the bin to start again. Mostly, she was just grateful he criticized her for a skill she knew she didn't possess, and that she avoided singeing her apron.

For Chef Juan, he had already commented on Jake's carrot dice, the firmness of Paul's rice, and Felix's over-use of finishing butter before he moved far enough down the row to be out of earshot, so it was possible he didn't long remember the incident, either. There was no reason to, since it didn't work.

Eventually, mercifully, time was called for the first challenge. Rachel the PA even moved the countdown clock up twelve minutes because everyone finished early. The contestants weren't all certain they had completed "the" dish, but all were relieved they put up a dish.

WHILE AL AND HIS ASSISTANTS got shots of each plate before judging, the cooks milled around checking out their competitors' final products, and forming into tentative cliques based on their first impression of each other's kitchen skills. Across the room from Tammy Firestarter – Paul said it first, but they were all thinking it – one cluster of contestants bonded over her disruptive cooking style. The general consensus was that a nice long rest from the ER was perhaps wise and necessary, but transitioning to food, maybe not today.

"Should we encourage her to try something in the Raw Food Movement?" asked Chloe, hating to see anyone's dream crash and burn on Day 1.

Fran, contemplating her own career shift from the soul-destroying grind of Human Resources, understood how work troubles could get into one's food. She suggested,

"Or work for an ashram? Meditate all day before she touches fire, that kind of thing. Until she can put the past behind her."

"As long as, you know, at the end of the day there was still an ashram," said engineer Felix, aware the fire suppression systems in less-regulated industries were a bit iffy. "It's a shame she keeps spontaneously combusting like that."

"Let's ask Ajiz what he thinks of our plan," said Fran. "Hey Ajiz! How soon do you think it would take Tammy to burn down an ashram?"

Ajiz had been too focused on admiring his beautiful grill marks to listen in before hearing his name invoked. Confused by Fran's question, he responded,

"Why do you think I know anything about ashrams? I'm a stay-at-home dad, not an interesting person."

"But you use the word "groovy" a lot. Don't groovy people know about ashrams? Don't they have to?"

"I have an eight-year-old and a two-year-old at home. You can't swear if you use groovy in the same sentence."

"Really?" asked Felix, a sponge for new information.

"Yeah, you try it. I mean you can, of course you can, but it doesn't roll off the tongue quite the same."

"Trouble at home, Ajiz?" inquired lawyer Paul, far more interested in learning about a potential client with a beautiful char technique than discussing Tammy issues. She already had shown him everything he needed to know about her. Hearing Paul's ask, Vivian and Ashley lingered as they passed by, hoped he would elicit something juicy and unflattering they could leverage during their interview booth segment.

"Mud," was Ajiz's surprise answer.

The two women made a collective sigh of disappointment. Ajiz continued undaunted.

"We thought the countryside would be a great environment for the kids. What was I thinking? Do you know in the city sometimes people don't even know it rained? I can't water a hanging basket without finding muddy footprints in the attic."

"Sounds like a raccoon problem," offered Paul, ingratiating himself further with sympathy and useful insight. "You're right about the city, though, especially if you're at the office all the time. God, I spend too much time at the office."

"Please take me back with you, to a world without earth," begged Ajiz, "my family can vouch for my goulash. I won't tell you what's in it, but I make it once a week. Our dog is also very friendly. Promise."

"You got a dog? In a world without sidewalks?"

"My wife and I were very committed to the process."

"Well, you're safe here, Ajiz. Even the garden area is graveled to the...Oh my God, is that a bloody footprint? Is that from the steaks?"

"Wow, that looks like somebody lost something they needed," said Ajiz as they all turned to look at the stained floor where Paul was pointing.

"Oliver," Fran reported, "the fisherman. You would think a person used to chopping live things while bobbing around on the ocean could aim properly at something dead and stationary."

"Probably thought it would move, threw him off his game," posited Paul.

"Is he gone from the competition?" asked Vivian, breaking into the conversation now that it might contain useful information. "Did somebody already go home?"

"No, to the hospital," said Chloe.

"Oh," Vivian responded, no longer interested. "Well."

After a pause, she then added, since she was standing there anyway,

"Did I hear right, Chloe, were you really terminally ill? Isn't this show too much for you? Are you going home?"

"Wow, when did that happen?" Fran asked with the dual concern of a fellow human being and the grateful, former recipient of some timely replacement chicken. "Are you okay, now?"

Startled and flustered to learn her medical condition was somehow common knowledge, Chloe stuttered a vague response.

"Oh, it was a wee bit ago."

"Obviously you were misdiagnosed," pronounced Vivian, disappointed once again.

She was quickly echoed by Ashley, as everyone already knew she would be, with a twangy, toady,

"You're probably right."

Their words piqued Chloe into speaking with more exactness and less wisdom.

"No, when you have died for a while, you can tell the difference between that and just being super sick."

"It's awful boring," she added belatedly, trying make the subject not worth pursuing.

"What is?" asked Fran.

"Probably the story," whispered Ashley to Vivian.

"Oh, dying," answered Chloe casually, turning to straighten up the cannisters on her bench and put her dirty utensils in the prep sink she shared with Felix. "You can't make plans. And did you know the *Law & Order* franchise doesn't actually last forever? Thank goodness for *Yes! Chef* going international. Gotta say, though, the subtitles for *Yes, Chef! India* leave a lot to be desired."

Her deflection didn't work.

"What was wrong, if I may ask?" said Paul. "Was it cancer?"

"Oh, no, that applicant cured herself with Brussels sprouts. My heart is broken, that's all. It's too depressing to think about right before judging, though. We need a garden!" Chloe said abruptly, running out of tasks to fuss with on her station, and again trying to change the subject. "Wouldn't it be soothing to sit in a garden after we cook? Anybody have one? Ajiz, you're our natural man, you must have a market garden."

"My children are my garden." Ajiz said.

"Wow, you really don't get the country living concept."

"We started with keeping a dog alive, and seriously, that was all the mud I needed."

"It's not sanitary to cook with dirt under one's fingernails," said Vivian.

"I live in an apartment," volunteered Fran.

Paul sighed and admitted,

"I only have a patio with an unwatered moonflower."

Travis, the otherwise large and largely silent presence in orange – by now everyone privately acknowledged they had misjudged him – spoke up unexpectedly.

"I have a farm."

"Travis, how eminently reliable as a man and fellow contestant," responded Chloe. "What kind? Where? Tell us everything. Soothe us before our first Judge's Table with tales of your garden farm thing place."

"It's just an ordinary farm, you don't really want to know," he replied, reluctant to be drawn into further conversation.

"I do," she said, grateful to talk about anything other than lying about her health status. "Trust me. What do you grow?"

"Pumpkins."

"That's no excuse for dressing like one," said Vivian in a carrying whisper eliciting a few awkward sniggers from her fellow front row contestants. Except Janiva, who once again refused to be drawn into controversy.

"Big pumpkins?" Chloe asked hopefully, talking over the rude disturbance.

"Yes, we grow the mammoths."

"Oh my God, you grow county fair pumpkins? You're that guy? They aren't made by forest elves or trolls or unicorns, but rather someone we know?"

"It's not that exciting. We supply local States for city displays and festivals. We also grow regular sized jack-o-lanterns, plus cooking gourds, but the mammoths are our specialty."

"It's the coolest side hustle, ever. Isn't it?" Chloe asked, looking around at the other contestants and garnering a general nodding agreement from everyone except the fashion police.

"We all know how to grow a tomato," said Ajiz in support of Chloe's enthusiasm, "well, I only think I know, but giant pumpkins are pretty cool."

"See?" said Chloe, "We are totally calling you Linus from now on."

"How is farming my grandfather's property a side hustle?" Travis asked.

"You're a chef who happens to have inherited arable land, Linus, not a farmer. We can all see you plated the rice dirt component thing better than even Jimmy Bob."

"Is it hard?" asked Felix, open to other career paths in case sugar didn't work out either. "Do giant pumpkins grow themselves?"

"That's a trade secret."

"*Tch*, Linus," said Chloe, "So not a sharer. Young Felix is here to learn. Still, coolest side hustle ever."

With that Chloe fell silent, content to listen to the others shift the focus to pestering Linus née Travis with pumpkin farm questions, and enjoy the warm, burgeoning camaraderie and emerging personalities among at least one segment of contestants.

Suddenly, they were all interrupted by Rachel the PA.

"Back to your benches, everybody, back to your benches! Thank you!" she said walking down the center aisle clapping her hands. "That's not your plate, Tammy! Thank you! Places!"

Borrowing Oliver's abandoned dish as the one nearest to her, Rachel began to briefly demonstrate how to carry a full plate up to be judged without outrunning the camera or bumping against the woman holding the boom mike. A short Q&A followed responding to the contestants more acute concerns, like what happened if they dropped anything, until Rachel saw the cameramen re-hoist their equipment back onto their shoulders and she moved out of the shot to allow taping to continue.

CHAPTER SIXTEEN

friendly dogs and unfriendly men

The first Judge's Table was as uneventful as a meal at the Cattle Baron Steakhouse. Everyone slowly and carefully transported their plate from their station up to the front table without sloshing anything on themselves or the floor, and the walk-throughs already previewed and prepared them for what they heard once they arrived. In the end, or as was expected from the beginning, Vivian won. Her perfectly timed, 30-second tip for the home viewer on how to turn carrots into tiny orange squares apparently tipping the scale among a dozen relatively equal gravies. Travis received special mention in the form of an extended discussion with Jimmy Bob over rice preparation, and Janiva lost, but it was a toss-up between Tammy's black steak and her blue steak with mushed garlic. Unlike Tammy, though, Janiva was shocked at her performance, and insisted someone must have turned off her oven. The judges were unswayed. A contestant that put up raw meat with that much time on the clock was not a keeper. Both women were warned to raise their game or one – or both – would be sent home the next day.

Fleeing the threat of an early double elimination, the Season 14 cohort left the warehouse quickly once dismissed for the day. Shoving a little in their effort to get out the massive double doors of the warehouse, they spilled onto the gravel sweep to find three utilitarian, grey vans waiting to take them to their accommodations. This year the contestants were to be housed in a pleasant, over-sized log cabin usually rented out to the larger ski parties. It had rooms full of bunk beds, a generous kitchen, comfortably furnished common spaces, and a well-landscaped terrace with a view across a forested range of hills.

As they climbed into the vans, Rachel handed them a sheet with their room assignments. The list had Chloe in a triple with Fran and Tammy. All three were relieved. That is, if one of them hadn't brought any aromatherapy candles, incense, or other flame-associated items. The list also showed that someone thought rooming farmer Travis in with surfer Jake a good idea. Oliver, Paul, Ajiz and Felix together in the loft seemed a much more harmonious grouping. Vivian, of course, snagged the master bedroom with the en suite bath.

"That woman just can't lose, can she," commented Fran.

"And she has Ashley in with her who laughs at all her jokes, and from the look of her steak today, shan't be with us long," added Ajiz, "they'll have a whale of time."

Arriving at the house, Chloe's trio joined the contingent who discovered the pile of takeout menus on the sideboard in the dining area and ordered in Mexican for dinner. Some contestants just raided the fridge, and the shelves of the house's cookbook library, and retreated to their bedrooms to brush up on meat preparations with ad hoc sandwiches, frozen pizza, and cereal. The Chinese takeout group gathered in the common room to eat scattered across the woodsy, mix and match couches and lounge chairs, and watch sitcoms.

Unused to being around so many people and for such extended periods, once her burrito platter arrived, Chloe went outside to find a quieter place to dine. Poking around a bit, she discovered the seating area on the terrace. By daylight it probably had a nice, green view of the mountains, but in the dusk, it looked out on vague, grey humps. Taking a spot on the wicker loveseat, she schlumped down into the cushions with a crunching squeak, put her feet up on the glass and wicker coffee table, and balancing her paper plate on her chest to catch the crumbs, ate her meal staring at the twilight sky and the thin slice of bumps and shadows visible above the parapet wall.

As she finished the last of her tortilla chips, she heard the slider to the living room open. Looking over she saw the tall, rectangular silhouette that must be Linus come out onto the terrace. He appeared to hesitate whether to join her or move to the picnic table further down the terrace.

"Hey, Linus," she called out. "If you don't need to eat at a flat surface, feel free to come enjoy the view. It's very pleasant, even the short-people option."

"Hi," he replied without moving.

The slanting light showed that he continued to look towards her seating area. After letting him be for a few moments, she added,

"Something on your mind, Linus? Who's your buddy?"

"No...I just...Well, I mean...Jake said..."

He trailed off.

Chloe finished the last chips and waited unhurriedly for him to make a decision, or to finish his thought. Or not. After another pause, he crossed over to her side of the terrace. Standing behind the side chair nearest the door, he toyed for a bit with its striped, blue cushion, then burst out with an abrupt, unexpected warning.

"I think you should be careful around Chef Juan."

"Huh," she responded. "As a man, or as a person?"

"What?" he asked, pushing the cushion away and causing it to flop over onto the chair seat.

"Do you mean as a guy, like a guy to date, guy, or as a judge out for me as a competitor?"

"Both."

"Huh. Sounds like a story, and how did my name get into it? Got a story for me, Li?" she asked, finally turning her head to look directly at him.

Instead of answering, he readjusted the fallen cushion back into place.

Chloe tried a different tack.

"Is it something that has happened, or something that might happen? And how did you find out about it?"

"I don't...I shouldn't..."

"Man code?" she asked. He didn't respond. "Well, thanks for telling me that much, Li. I suppose anyone can start looking attractive if one gets unhappy, overtired or overstressed, and even a "friendly judge" isn't friendly to everybody. It's always good to have a man's perspective on these things ahead of time."

"I don't know if...I...I mean, it's not that I *know*..."

Once more he trailed off.

"No worries, Linus, I'll just believe you. You understood dirty rice in a way I never will, and now I know about the pumpkins. If you can't trust a pumpkin farmer, what is the world coming to?"

"Hey, how big is your pumpkin farm?" she asked, changing the subject to one he was slightly more likely to be forthcoming about. "What's harvest time like? Do you have a corn maze?"

"You're not interested."

"You should believe me when I say things, Linus. Don't we have a farm here, or a garden, or something involving dirt?"

"There's an extensive herb garden at the warehouse, and we have a vegetable patch at the foot of those stairs over there."

"Awesome. Except, I hope Ajiz doesn't find all that loam triggering. Is it worth it? To go down there? I have a broken heart, so I try to avoid meaningless stairs and inclines."

"There are tomatoes and greens and peppers and a strawberry patch."

"*Ooohhh, strawwwwberrries.* Hey, you're the expert, will red berries grow here? Everybody knows proper blueberries grow on mountains out of the rocks, and apples are complicated, which is why we need our Glenn for them, but for some reason cherries need the South of France. Once you've eaten a Mediterranean cherry, the domestic ones are more like a red thing with a stone in the middle."

"I haven't eaten a Mediterranean cherry. France isn't allowed to import produce to the US. Strawberries will do fine here. The soil's been professionally augmented by the same people who did the warehouse garden."

"I suppose it's my duty as an Italian chef to go look at the tomatoes, so I'll have to check out the strawberry beds while I'm at it. Hey, who works on your farm? Is it your people, or do you use migrants? How do migrants know when to migrate? I think Glenn uses international Ag. Schools, or maybe Facebook."

She was equally unsuccessful in her effort to learn what kind of people worked the pumpkin harvest, and how they knew when to show up. This time, perhaps, because the slider opened again. Both turned to see the person coming out to join them.

It was Jake.

"What are you two kids doing out here?" he asked, sauntering over, his largely unfastened shirt fluttering open as he went. Linus had the pleasing, rectangular solidity of a working man, but Jake moved with the added, oozing sensuality of an athlete who often walked around in public half-dressed.

"Oh hi, Jake," Chloe called out with a studied friendliness, refusing the invitation to gawk. "Linus is telling me about harvest time at his family farm."

"Trying to put her to sleep, Travis? That's no way to make a move on a woman."

"Yay. I don't want anyone doing that," was Chloe's forthright response. "And the women here all already know Linus doesn't creep."

"That's a good thing," she added in an aside to him, in case he got confused about such things.

"As if," Jake responded with a derisive snort. "And why are you calling him that?"

"Because I'm living for his pumpkin patch. Duh. No need to try to compete, though, we can't all be as cool as Linus. Right, Linus?"

He agreed with Jake.

"As if."

"Do you want me to compete?" asked Jake, feigning to unbutton the remainder of his shirt.

"Oh, do not get naked in front of me, Jake," she requested, more alarmed than interested. "Don't you have a girlfriend back home?"

This wild, but educated guess elicited a quick, sharp glance towards Travis.

"Saw that," said Chloe. "Girlfriend? Wife? Boyfriend? You do know it's an insult to flirt with someone whom your someone wouldn't be bothered to see you flirting with on national television. That'll dead-end right into a punch in the nose, that's just how that ends."

"And stop giving Linus the stink eye," she added catching him direct another warning glare in that direction. "He refuses to discuss the current pumpkin market, who here has the next level skills to get him to talk about your love life?"

"What about you and Chef Juan?" Jake countered. "Thinking about getting a little sumpin' sumpin' on with a judge?"

"Are you insane?" Chloe sputtered, even more concerned to now be cast as the perpetrator not victim. "I don't even know Chef Juan."

"We all saw his "lesson" on knife skills today. No need to fake surprise. Travis did too."

Chloe's eyes darted back and forth between both men seeking more information, or confirmation.

"I didn't see anything," said Travis, "I was busy with my own cook. Anyway, I'm heading back in. I want to read up on braising techniques."

Releasing the seat cushions, now crushed into divots where his fingers had held them, he made his move towards the slider.

"Right behind you, Li," Chloe said as she collected her detritus, unwilling to be left alone in the dark with yet another man on Day 1, especially a half-naked one.

"Well...'night!" she said to Jake, "and don't think I don't know you're crazy. Chef Juan? That's you just trying to call me a bad slicer who's too chubby to skate past the third challenge on her looks. That's not nice."

Reentering the house, she skirted around the back of the couches in the lounge to catch up with Travis.

"I'm sure you didn't mean to ditch me out in the dark with a Jake," she told him in a low voice.

"Huh?"

"I forgive you for being confused, this one time. Hey, congrats on your performance today. We thought Jimmy Bob might give you your own belt buckle."

"Thanks."

Together they passed through the dining area and out into the hall.

"You're not interested in our farm, you know," he insisted as she paused to throw her trash in the large grey kitchen bin, and brush the crumbs from her shirt into it, "it's boring."

"Okay, Linus, I will believe you have your reasons for saying that. All I'm sayin' is that nobody else agrees with you. It's already true that when you go into a room here, most people think you are knowledgeable, interesting and are glad to see you. It's done already. Don't worry, though, this isn't *me* hitting on *you*, it's just how I talk. Telling people the nice things other people say behind their backs is what I do for fun."

"I've...I've still got research to do," was his only response, and at the foot of the stairs he parted from her and headed towards the library.

"Good night!" she said and began a slow climb to the second floor. Pausing on the third riser she leaned over the banister to address his back retreating down the hall. "Thanks for speaking up, Linus! Scaring is caring."

tricks are for kids, alliances for cool kids

Chloe found Fran sitting cross-legged on her top bunk, working out the plating for her Reinvention Challenge dish with two colored pencils speared though the loose bun of her hair and holding a third.

"Did you bring Tammy back with you?" she asked absentmindedly, tucking the green pencil in her hand behind her ear and picking up an eraser.

"No, Tammy's still watching TV. There's a *Chopped* marathon on, if you want to do any last-minute research."

"Seen 'em," Fran replied with confidence, blowing away the eraser dust before groping again for the green pencil. "I like being informed before I do something on national television. Where did you go? I didn't see you after the food arrived."

Chloe closed the door behind her, and careful not to look in the direction of Fran's notebook, walked over to her own bed and plunked down on the floor by her suitcase.

"I went to hide out on the terrace."

"And then what happened?"

"Heh," said Chloe with a short laugh. Unzipping the main compartment of her bag, she threw back the lid with a small thump and jingle. "You're right. If I wanted to be alone, I should have left the property. Well, the surfer guy came out to be friendly, that was an experience, interrupting Linus, our farmer, who was full of mysterious hints and warnings. The gossip will keep for at least another half-hour, though, if you're still working."

"Are you really going to call him that?" Fran asked, shutting her work, and putting it back into her knapsack.

"Yeah. I like it."

Fran turned on her side, and with one hand propping up her head, idly watched Chloe rooting around in her luggage for overnight things and an outfit for the next day. On the third try, Chloe found the corner where she tucked her electric toothbrush and dislodged it with a few sharp tugs.

"Hey, do you think Vivian and Ashley being mean to Linus earlier made him feel less-than?" Chloe asked, rewinding the cord for the charger, and looking around at their outlet situation. "Chef Jimmy Bob went on and on about his dish, yet the boy seems oddly dour. I think that's weird."

She re-zipped her luggage and began folding tomorrow's clothes into a neat pile onto the top of the lid.

"How can you tell, and why do you care?" asked Fran. "You forgot socks."

"Oh, thanks."

Chloe moved her clothes to dig through the side pockets.

"Earlier, he just kept his mouth shut, but now he seems in a mood," she responded. "And we want him cheerful and on our side, Fran. He's a pumpkin farmer. That automatically makes him part of the cool kids. Plus, he's proven he can cook, and I think under all that looming silence is a nice guy. "I'm Beet", that's funny, especially on someone who has probably never blushed in his life."

"Blushed? Now what are you talking about?"

"Beets turn everything pink. Anyway, now that we the cool kids have given him a nickname, at least he will know he is part of we the cool kids, that's just science. When he picks us for the Group Challenges, you'll thank me then, and when he doesn't need it anymore, I'll give him his name back. Promise."

"We're the cool kids?"

"Duh-uh. That woman Vivian, surfer Jake..."

"They have a thing going," interrupted Fran, "got some intel on that during the second break today. Remind me to tell you."

"*Oooh*. Well. Wish I knew that before I accused him of it to his face. Anyway," Chloe continued, "those two, Troy and Owen who got sucked into their vortex for their talent, Vivian's parrot, Ashley..."

"Call her Echo. When you get busted, you can pretend you mean Zeus' nymph girlfriend."

"Prudent! Well, a clique that includes both Zeus' girlfriend and God's gift to women must be the popular kids. Obviously, that makes us the cool kids. Keep up!"

"How nice for our team," said Fran sitting up again to gather her art supplies and take the stray pencils out of her hair. Looking at Chloe through the gap in her upstretched arms, she asked,

"Speaking of stories, was Vivian right? Were you terminally ill?"

"Well, terminal schmer-minal. It does make interacting with Jake even more depressing, though. After a long spell as a couch potato, I really feel my new dumpiness in the way he talks to me."

"First, you haven't lost your figure, so I don't know what you are talking about, and second, there's always Chef Juan."

"Not you too! Now you're just trying to get me to quit the show."

"Is that what Travis warned you about? And no, you can stay. I need to repay the favor of saving my audition dish before you go home. Seeing how I'm going to win."

Chloe laughed good-naturedly.

"Spoken like a real Vivian. Glad to be a small part of your victory story."

"Now, tell me about Jake. And Travis." Fran asked eagerly, laying back down again on her elbow. "I told you putting that odd couple together would be nothing but drama."

"You did. Jake accused me of having a thing with Chef Juan, and Linus flat out warned me to keep away from him. How am I a femme fatale? I'm not even wearing a vee-neck. Did you spot any weirdness with Chef?"

"Chef Juan was a little "helpful" today regarding how you hold your knife. People saw."

"*Ugh!* Did I fall afoul of that professor that hits on everybody? What if people think my success is from sleeping with him? If I have any."

"I sense trouble, Chloe. Your Linus may just have a suspicious mind, but Jake strikes me as a complete dog himself. If his radar saw people hitting on people, even if it went over your head, that's what went down."

"*Ick-a-yuck-a.* I'll get Oliver to show me the knife cuts from now on."

"Oliver cut off his hand today."

"My knife skills are doomed. Hey, is he alright?"

"He came back to the house, that's information," reported Fran. "He's a commercial fisherman, half his limbs are probably re-sewn on during a rolling sea. Must be thrilled this time they did it with sterile equipment. Anyway, creepy men about the place where there are TV cameras – trouble."

Chloe agreed.

"At least I have been warned, Fran, before I got in a car alone with Chef, or ran errands together, or something happened out at a group reward. I told you Linus would make a great teammate."

"And thankfully you're old enough to skip over the "it couldn't be that guy, it couldn't happen to me" naive window of doom and get down to practical defensive strategies."

Chloe nodded and considered her options.

"Bear spray? Isn't that a mountain thing tool? Do you think a PA has some? Or what thoughts have you about me faking a boyfriend on national television?"

Fran gave the latter serious consideration.

"Would that stop him? I wish we could ask Jake. Why, do you have one?"

"A pastry chef I met abroad would make a credible, imaginary love interest, but he has a girlfriend already. And I don't know his name."

"Screwing with someone's relationship on television for a fake ID might not end well. If she is dating a chef, she probably watches a lot of late-night Netflix. How did you fall in love with someone from abroad?"

"Easy, I've eaten his food. It tastes good and feels good. I think he does something medicinal with his ingredients.

"Booze," suggested Fran. "Not that I know, because I don't really eat sugar, but I knew a Latin chef who could do the same thing with a gazpacho. The only chef who has ever gotten me to eat vegetables."

"Exactly. Same thing, only different. Anyway, now with the Juan thing, instead of just worrying about what's in front of us, we also have to worry about who is standing behind us."

"We see this all the time in HR. That's why I want a small café where I can throw people out when I want to. I tell ya, all day I solve problems that wouldn't exist if everybody just tried my new celery-salted onion rings and stopped being annoying. It's hard to give my all to corporate's less-than solutions."

"Is that your food dream?" asked Chloe with a laugh, glad to turn the conversation to solvable challenges.

"No, hold that thought," she said, standing up with her bundle. "Let me go take my shower, then you can vent about people invading your office making their problems your problems. You don't want all that residual angst to get into your food."

breakfast of champions

The next morning Chloe and Fran came downstairs to find a strainer full of fresh, and freshly washed, strawberries dripping water onto the middle of the kitchen island.

"Are these for us?" Fran asked. "Where'd they come from?"

"They must be out of the garden," Chloe guessed. "We have a garden, somewhere at a lower elevation."

"Travis got up this morning and picked them," said Oliver, entering from the dining room.

Chloe smiled.

"That Linus, such a team player. How's your hand?"

"Fine. I only needed four stitches. I could have done it myself. Are you really going to call him that?"

"Join me, it's fun."

"No, it's not," said Travis, quietly entering the kitchen behind Oliver and walking over to the coffee machine.

"Yes, it is. Does everyone at home call you Linus?"

"No one calls me Linus."

"Good, because that wouldn't be fun at all. Thanks for the ripe fruit," Chloe said, opening the refrigerator door to scan the contents before closing it and pulling open the freezer drawer. "You know, I'm going to have a smoothie, in honor of you going full strawberry patch in hopes I will call you something else. Which I won't. I don't suppose anyone got up extra, extra early and made muffins?"

"Felix is the only pastry person here," reported Oliver, "and he only makes cake."

"And pie!" Felix piped up from the dining table in the adjoining room. "The judges loved my pie."

"Then where is our breakfast pie?" Chloe asked, sticking her head out of the doorway. "Linus brought up these lovely berries, where's our flaky goodness to go with them? Not even some buckle?"

"You're right, I have let you down."

"Thank you, as long as we are clear. Are you doing a Wellington today?" she asked, leaning against the doorframe.

Felix looked up from his looseleaf notebook with surprise.

"How'd you know?"

"Because you have to. Have you designed your design for the top yet?"

"I can't decide which one to use," he said, gesturing to a few crumpled, discarded sheets on the table. "My roommates won't give me an opinion. They say real men don't garnish."

Chloe nodded with sympathy.

"Being a savory chef, it can be so soul-destroying as a profession. Let me finish making my smoothie, we'll talk. I love pastry even though I can't make it, so a bribe at any hour will always find me amenable, and ready to have an opinion."

"But I haven't bribed you, yet."

"And if you go home today, you never will. Think of it as a prudent investment. Fran will help."

"No, I won't," Fran said over the sound of the De'Longhi.

"Fran won't help. More pie for me, that's what I think."

A short while later, Chloe returned to stand in the doorway holding her smoothie to continue her discussion with Felix while she listened for the sound of the toaster.

"The guys do have a point. The judges are savory chefs, too, and likely not as pro-garnish as we who love pastry. Your design should probably be functional, you know, hint at what's in the pastry case."

"I was afraid that was too obvious."

"Obvious and obviously well-made are good things in Week 1. If they say, "what is this" or "I don't get it" they may not trust what's in it, nudging them psychologically towards a bad score or even just a lower score. As a pastry chef, you need all the points you can get to give you the runway to screw up."

"No abstract design, then?" Felix called out as she went back into the kitchen to butter her toast.

"Abstract can be beautiful on a Wellington. You do you," she called back, "I was merely highlighting one element of risk so that you can make the most informed decision. Choosing a random, giant, Linus homage, strawberry cutout because you found a cool cookie cutter might scare them into looking for jam where no jam ought to be. That's my point."

"You shouldn't help him," said Fran as she followed Chloe out of the kitchen with her own coffee and bagel.

"It's not really fair," Oliver agreed, retaking his seat and returning to flipping through the Bobby Flay cookbook he was studying. "Travis, you don't think it's fair, do you?"

They all turned towards their farmer seated at the end of the table, busy making some kind of list in his notebook. He remained stoic and noncommittal without being mean about it, which as they would learn was very Travis in the morning.

"The competition does not rise or fall on the garnish of one pastry case," Chloe responded, glancing over Felix's shoulder at his latest idea before she sat down between him and Oliver. "Stop being a bunch of atheists. Unless you are atheists, of course, in which case I withdraw that. But if you aren't atheists, stop being atheists."

"How is being fair and wanting to win atheistic?" protested Oliver who spent enough time at sea to know there was a God, and he wasn't it.

"Because the Big J, for those of us who follow the Big J, didn't say love your enemies so ha ha ha, I can screw you over in a cooking competition. Be not afraid. Being kind and supportive will not make us weak or vulnerable or lose. I'm not giving Felix *my* Wellington. That, you are right, would be self-sabotage. I am encouraging *him* to give *his* best Wellington. If it's better than mine, he deserves to win."

"Of course, yours wouldn't be better," Chloe said turning to Felix, "if I was making one, which I'm not."

"I know."

Oliver wasn't convinced.

"Why are you here if you don't want to win? Helping everybody cook better than you do is not a good strategy."

"I ain't helping nobody," announced Fran, "I've got enough to think about with my own cook."

Chloe shrugged.

"Do I want to win a quarter of a million dollars? Love me some of that, but anyone can have one of those. What I really want is a meaningful career I can be proud of, and if I have to climb over all your cold, dead bodies to get funding for it, well, we've all seen Poltergeist. In the end, it just doesn't work out. I don't want to see dead people."

"I think you're being naive about how this competition thing works," said Oliver, "and are mixing up your cinematic references."

Chloe acknowledged the latter with another shrug, while vigorously defending the part of her *Yes, Chef!* strategy she was certain was true and correct.

"Listen, we all have different boundaries and limitations in this completely foreign environment. Fran needs full concentration during the cook, so we shouldn't expect her to notice what's happening on someone else's station. I'm the last person to help carry in the nine bags of rock salt needed for anyone's special ice cream, and if I offer, refuse. Giving my opinion about pastry design, though, that's light and easy and fun, at least for me. Linus our Farmer picked extra strawberries to share. That was both kind and teaches us earth-free people what ripe fruit looks like, plus it lets Fran take a step back from scurvy today."

"Will he regret it if Fran does well in the competition? I say no. If the only way you can win is if your competitors are so vitamin deficient their teeth fall out, the responsibilities that come with winning will be your downfall anyway, and someday you'll regret not having taken fourth runner up like you should have and got invited back for a second chance to shine brighter at All-Stars."

"You're talking crazy. If people know you are this nice," Fran countered, "they're just going to take advantage of you. You ought to know this, it's Season 14."

"Bad people are going to bad no matter what we do," Chloe responded between bites of toast, "they'll just adapt their plans to whether we are being nice or sneaky or crafty or stupid, and blame us for their actions. Naturally. Being kind, though, is like that Iron Dome missile defense system they have in the Middle East, you know, where everybody is always shooting off rockets at each other for no good reason. It's not 100% effective, but the one rocket that gets past it is a better outcome than the thousand they shot at you landing on your head, which they were gonna do anyway."

Wiping the corners of her mouth on a paper napkin, she then took a long pull of her smoothie.

"You don't have to believe me, though. Just watch me and see if I'm right."

"I don't believe you," said Oliver, "and I don't know what you are talking about."

"I get that."

Fran asked for additional insider information, which they already knew she would do morning, noon, night and twice on weekends.

"You in the Middle East getting shot at by rockets sounds like a story. Is it a good story?"

"Eh, it's not that interesting, seriously, happens all the time there, but while yes, Lebanon has shot exploding projectiles in my general direction, which I found unfriendly and uncalled for, this invaluable lesson I learned while on a date in Texas."

Fran leant back in her chair with crossed arms, the way she would if presented with a yet-to-be-proven copier incident back at the office.

"Okay, lay that one on us, because I don't believe you, either, that this is a remotely sane competition strategy."

"Alright, but just this one dating story. One."

Fortifying herself with another large bite of toast, washed down with a gulp of smoothie, Chloe began.

"What happened was, a while back I was on this first date once, right, and we were on our way to, well, wherever. Anyway, we stopped for gas. You know. Well, when the guy got back in the car, he handed me a lottery ticket, one of those scratch things. He picked it up when he went inside to pay or something. I haven't played them hardly ever, do you?

Oliver nodded.

"Oh, I have."

"My mother does," said Fran. "She gives them out at Christmas."

Chloe continued.

"I think I have seen, like, three myself. Anyway, I thought it was a cute first date idea. So, we scratched them off, and guess what?"

"You won," said Travis.

"I did, o wise Linus. Guess how much?"

"Twenty dollars," said Oliver.

"Nope."

Fran guessed,

"One hundred?"

"Nope. Ten...thousand...dollars."

"Oh my God," said Fran and Oliver in unison.

"I know, isn't that crazy?" replied Chloe, finishing the last bite of toast, and wiping the butter residue off her fingers.

"What did you do?" asked Fran, eager for even more inside information. "Rub his head for luck every time you left the house? Did you bring him here in your suitcase?"

"I handed the ticket back to him," Chloe mumbled with her mouth full.

Oliver shook his head in disbelief.

"You did what? You're nuts. I ain't listening to you about anything."

"In my...ethical world people land, that's the right thing to do. I didn't know this guy, I didn't pay for the ticket, this wasn't my money. Plus, he had been complaining about his ex-wife walking off with some of "his" cash, I don't know, some married people problem. So, I handed it over to him and said "look! God gave you your money back". The whole thing was a whiz bang, we were still sitting at the pump."

"You're crazy," said Fran.

Oliver agreed.

"I would have kept it. The guy did give the ticket to you. Did he at least split the cash after?"

"Nope. If he had, that I would have kept. But he didn't. Boy, was that a lot o' learning about his character in the first ten minutes of a date."

"Now, I need coffee," Chloe said standing up, "does anyone need another cup?"

"Sit down and finish your story," ordered Fran.

Chloe dropped back into her seat with a sigh.

"The story part is kinda done. Maybe because it was such a lot of money," she continued, toying with her empty plate, "it was easier do the right thing, right quick, than if it was like $500, where I might have thought maybe it didn't matter so much either way. Anyway, I was totally in the greed-free zone that day, thank God, and handed the ticket back to him right off. That was that."

"This is a sucky story. Did you dump him immediately?" asked Fran.

"It indeed colored what was our only time together."

"How does you being nice and losing out on ten grand do anything but prove our point that being nice doesn't work out for you?"

Oliver nodded again in total agreement.

"You're not going to tell us you went back in, bought another lottery ticket, and won Megabucks, are you?"

"Linus?" Chloe asked, turning towards him.

"Why are you asking Travis?" Fran demanded. "It wasn't Travis, was it? Or does Travis know him? Do you guys already know each other?"

"No, Fran, Linus was not present on my date in Texas. But I suspect he got to the punchline from the beginning, and I feel slightly judged about who he thinks I've been dating. Linus, can you bring it home for us, so I can go make my caffeine?"

"The ticket was fake."

"Ding ding ding. I think it was this guy's idea of a joke. And a test, because he had money, and liked to see how a new woman reacted to money. Something like that."

Oliver blinked a little in shock.

"Oh...my...God. What a jerk!"

"He was pretty well off, so he might not get how completely life-changing ten thousand dollars can be. But yeah, he was. I needed heart surgery at the time, too, and had been putting it off because it meant selling my house to pay for it. So, you all totally get how much extra it would have sucked if I had, even for a second, thought I just received a windfall that never was. Instead, the whole incident was me getting a little hurt because somebody I met once was mean. The End."

"Wow, this is an extra sucky story. What happened with the guy?" Fran wanted to know. "Did you knock a plate of food onto his lap? Walk off with the more handsome guy at the next table halfway through dinner? Something?"

"We drove off, and the date rolled on. It was such a short, dumb thing to do, I didn't really think it through for a bit. But, of course, within a few hours he was so dazzled by me, and my practical, ethical standards he was calling me "his woman". Poor thing."

"What about you? Did you actually forgive Mr. Nightmare Life Partner?"

"Forgive him? Yeah. Date him? Hell no, and then wasn't he sorry. That's my point. He showed up that day ready to be a super-duper extra jerk-ola no matter who I was. It was a bullet I couldn't dodge, and only by being kind did it mostly bounce right off me and hit him. Ha ha ha."

Oliver shook his head.

"I don't get it. He played a joke on you, and it worked."

"Yes. He executed his nasty plan flawlessly. He discovered a random woman's view on windfall cash. But, by choosing the sneaky, mean road instead of just talking about money and marital assets over dinner like a normal person, he lost what God brought into his life that exceeded what he even thought possible – a non-greedy woman. He won, he got me good, but what good did it do? Judge-y Linus is right, I shouldn't have been there at all, but that's a different story."

"Anyway, the Iron Dome Mean Dodge is my competition philosophy. There will be saboteurs. There will be sucker punches. We will probably make a gazillion honest mistakes that have bad consequences to ourselves and other people. And playing palace intrigue does get results. Look at Season 5 when Eddie the Weasel got runner up."

"No matter the short-term outcome, though, undermining each other to snatch the one grand prize will just end up undermining our own future. Seriously, who hires rodents to work in a kitchen? Maybe some of us are really here to meet a business partner. Getting cut gracefully in Week 3 is better empire-building than stabbing that person in the back to claw a spot onto Week 4. Or maybe some of us are here just to know we tried our best in food, so we don't have lingering regrets when we go work for our uncle's accounting firm, whose clients turn out to be fans of the show. Maybe God just wanted Oliver here to see mountains for some reason, what a completely new thing for a man of the sea. We none of us know exactly why we are here, but we can know, because it's already true, there are infinite prizes and good outcomes for all of us. God has a much bigger imagination than the producers, more reach, and He actually wants us to succeed. All of us."

"You don't have to believe me, though, or agree with my personal spirituality, or even have one of your own. You can just watch what happens to me and see if I'm right. I think it's a principle like gravity – no matter how you think things fall on your head, they still do. Today, I'm just going to focus on what really matters, pre-extorting Felix for the hope of a later pie. You know I only love you for your pie, right Felix?"

"I know."

"As long as we are clear. Let me get my coffee, and then we'll talk pastry case design. Intimidate me with your interpretation of the perfect Wellington."

"Worst story ever," said Fran to Chloe's retreating back.

"Got that right," echoed Oliver.

Travis just went back to his notebook, but Fran and Oliver could tell by the quality of his silence and the way he turned the next page that he was entirely on their side.

CHAPTER NINETEEN

the cool kids
get shorted

During the opening segment for Day 2, the first Reinvention Challenge, Vivian's hardball gambit regarding her advantage as the winner of the Imitation Challenge would later cause most veteran home viewers to shake their heads as predictable, cliché, and too antagonistic, too soon. It was Season 14. Everybody knew that kind of gameplay backfires by Week 4 at the latest.

She used her right to choose the wildcard ingredient to require everyone to cook with horseradish. This announcement caused Paul to elbow his roommate, Oliver, who shook his head along with everyone later watching from home. The three of them came over in the van together that very morning – it was caught on the van cam, for all the world to judge for themselves – and Oliver happened to mention that the one root vegetable he just couldn't get behind was horseradish. As a fisherman, he ought to embrace it, it was his duty, but he never had.

Facing his kryptonite so early in the competition, and with only one working hand, Oliver's one, minor consolation was that someone saw him as a threat and was trying to get him sent home before he was back to cooking with two opposable thumbs. Janiva, sitting behind him in the same van and determined to have a better cook today than yesterday, was just glad she had not mentioned her peanut allergy. Everyone else wasted valuable Reinvention time whispering about Vivian's strategy first, and what to do with the new ingredient second. The collective opinion was to not talk too freely, or too honestly, in front of her from now on, a policy decision that really could have waited until their lunch break.

With or without Vivian's stratagems, however, the contestants were more than ready to bomb their first chance to "express themselves" in the kitchen through the medium of leftovers. A full thirteen out of the twenty-five actually reused the meat from the previous day to save time cooking another behemoth chunk of beef. Ashley, Troy, and Red Shirt Ronnie (they knew he was doomed for early elimination from the first mixing bowl he placed on the floor) hadn't covered their leftover porterhouse properly the night before, and came in to find cold, dried-out hunks needing rehydration to make anything useful. An hour into the cook, they then learned none of them were skilled in rehydration techniques. Roadie Owen and painfully shy Aaron's Week 1 nerves caused them to reheat their properly covered beef too hard and fast, resulting in a series of hot, dried-out hunks that were poked at and also left untasted at Judge's Table. The other eight learned the technical term for seasoned beef left overnight in the fridge is "marinated", and that it would not change its flavor profile just because they wanted to go in a different direction for Day 2.

As the contestants began to remember, relearn, or not learn, the tips and tricks from thirteen previous seasons of *Yes! Chef*, not every dish ended up as a pile of rocks with a pan sauce. Chloe and Felix delivered solid, upper middle-of-the-pack performances. Felix's beef Wellington with the abstract pastry design did come out better than Chloe's beef Stroganoff with handmade noodles, but she thought that was funny. Oliver just shook his head at her, again.

Called upon for his opinion, Travis said she salted her beef but forgot to salt the mushrooms, which she had. She clapped her hand to her forehead and sighed at her oversight.

"See, you should learn from our Linus," she whispered to Oliver, "when he talks, he offers something real *and* useful. You just overwhelm me with disapproval."

"What did I say?"

"A head shake is worth a thousand words from a sailor used to communicating during hurricane season."

Ajiz, and later the show editors, agreed with Chloe.

"You're a head-shaker, Oliver," he concurred, "you're that guy. Know your power."

Jake's Day 2 strategy involved putting up a perfectly decent beef stew that took a nanosecond of thought and earned him the stink eye from three of the four judges for his obvious intention to skate through to his guaranteed near-miss victory with lazy competence. Jimmy Bob, though, appreciated both his speed and style. Janiva redeemed herself with a second, perfectly cooked and charred porterhouse, reestablishing her career opportunities in Oklahoma, but losing points for letting pride triumph over innovation. Nurse Tammy lit her new oven mitts on fire, again.

The nerves in the kitchen over who was in danger of elimination might have dissipated had the contestants recognized the look that passed between the judges as Tammy's third fire broke out. The conflagration happened just as the cameraman turned away, endangering his very expensive equipment – they always had extra crew on standby – without even getting the shot. With a sharp nod of his chin, Chef Parker gestured to Rachel the PA to snag one of the now-burnt rags off Tammy's station. If a miracle happened and she pulled off a decent dish, then just as miraculously, and oh so sadly, bits of dangerous, carcinogenic, choking hazards could be conveniently "found" among the successful elements of her plate. Al was a veteran crew member, and a victim, he knew what to film and what not to.

AMID THE STEADY EXCELLENCE OF early front runners Travis, Fran, Vivian, the desultory Jake, Chloe, Felix, and Mr. Talking Head Oliver, who despite rarely eating meat surprised everyone what a whiz he was at cooking it one-handed, lawyer Paul had his shining, standout moment on the show. Hiding in a sea of contestants, luxuriating in another day with a ridiculously generous cook time, he set about the task as he would after work on a Tuesday, a day he had been known to make Cornish game hens just because he was in the mood, and they were there. He browned without charring, he added wine, and the right wine, in proper measure, he turned his oven to the right temperatures. Cheerily bustling along, his mother's short ribs came out splendid, as always. The dish had no plating finesse, but neither did the owner of the Cattle Baron Steakhouse, so it was a good week to make them.

If only Paul hadn't reprised his memorable audition dish, perhaps Vivian might not have overtaken him for the victory. You know, maybe. The judges still found Paul's satisfying, if unoriginal, food a welcome palate cleanser after their (pretend) sampling of Tammy's Charred Oven Mitt with Bottled Steak Sauce. His triumph in red meat even eclipsed Jimmy Bob's memorable critique – offering Tammy that old truism from Great Plains hunter families,

"I don't wanna to know what it is, I need to know what it was."

Returning home that night, Paul and his roommates, along with Chloe and Fran, were among those crammed into the third vehicle. During the fifteen-minute drive they celebrated Paul's runner-up victory and chided Chloe for her "loss". Paul was quick to downplay the superiority of his own dish.

"I just browned them and put them in a slow oven," he remonstrated to the group, "Janiva did the same, but with a different cut of meat."

The others had no answer, they just knew he was mistaken.

"I know you think you are communicating culinary information to us," said Chloe, who ate several bites of the leftovers on Paul's station. "Yes, we can, technically, brown things. We, technically, had ovens. Some of us even own super swanky ovens with specialty cooktops back home. And oven-safe pans in multiple sizes. It's still different."

"She's right," agreed Oliver. "A steak is not a fish, it's an inferior product, everybody knows that – and don't get me started on horseradish – but I can grill some landmass when I want to, and I still don't know how you did it."

"How do we get you to embrace alternative proteins?" asked Paul.

"Hey, Fran doesn't really understand the need for green vegetables. A meal without a fish, even during Meat Week, I'm sorry, it isn't really food."

"Jimmy Bob said all onions make you cry," said Fran in defensive of her signature food pyramid, "but no vegetable makes people laugh."

"Then he's a fraud who's never been to a half-decent county fair," responded Travis.

Jake, comfortably situated up in the passenger seat by the driver, offered a different perspective.

"Paul's a dinner party legend back home, haven't you seen his intro package?"

"No," replied Oliver, "why have you?"

"I don't know, one of the PA's must have been playing it. Today was right up his alley, though."

Paul admitted to enjoying the occasional sit-down meal with his husband and select friends, but continued to wonder why the group would marvel over skills they all possessed. He did agree that when they arrived back at the house, he would remake his (mother's) short ribs while they watched to prove it did not require TV magic.

In support of his winning dish making its third appearance, twice in the same day, and inspired by Jake's mention of dinner parties, Chloe added her roasted tomatoes to the night's menu. Travis volunteered to walk back down into the garden and pick some kale. Fran then offered to make her onion rings, Felix his strawberry and basil turnovers, and Oliver some fishcakes as a tapis moment while they waited for the entree. After a cramped but much more relaxed cook in the house kitchen, they piled their dishes on the long glass dining room table, and ate it buffet style, camped about the dining and living room chairs.

Surrounded by good food, some destined to become competition standouts themselves, Paul's (mother's) short ribs should have been as he expected, always a crowd-pleaser but one among many solid dishes. Instead, a legend was born. This may have started from the surprise miracle of Oliver ending the second day in the competition fat and happy and partially agreeing with Chloe that being nice to people sometimes did pay off. No matter how many times Paul insisted he simply knew to use a cheap French wine over an expensive Italian, though, everybody else agreed with Chloe that it couldn't be that simple.

"We need more market research. Maybe if we tried...his roast pork that would be the Rosetta stone?" she asked the others.

"As a pastry chef," seconded Felix, "I definitely need more exposure to the right way of doing things savory. Would something in bacon assist us?"

To scientifically prove that executing Paul's family classics required more than just a sane amount of respect for the *New York Times* food editor, the cool kids agreed to regroup the following night for Round 2, More Paul, and went to their bunks with a new, additional pressure to survive past the first team challenge.

CHAPTER TWENTY

their star is born

For the Meat! Week Group Challenge, the show sent the contestants to Empower Field to prepare a staff picnic for the Denver Broncos. The competition "twist" – and they all agreed they walked right into it, more fool them for being surprised – was they must cook in food trucks with limited space and equipment. A mad scramble ensued to reorganize their menus after several ambitious contestants, led astray by the vast array of equipment available in the competition kitchen, needed to abandon their elaborate beef dishes for ones more suitable to the accoutrements of their first apartments.

The Blue Team under Janiva's leadership might have performed better, possibly, if they hadn't filled up the time gaps during the challenge debating over their own dinner menu, instead of the Bronco's lunch menu. The wrangling started with Oliver overriding Chloe and Felix's original suggestion. Or trying to.

"Pork roast and bacon are the same food," he insisted during the team's *mise en place*, "you can't have both."

"What do you know, fish guy?" retorted Felix.

"Felix let's not get aggressive," admonished Chloe. "Watch me do hands across the sea, watch and learn."

"Well, Oliver dear, how about...bacon cheddar potatoes? Wouldn't they go swell with the lobster I know you embezzled out of our team budget at Whole Foods, and is now taking up an outsized portion of our team cooler?"

She opened up the Coleman and pointed to the offending bag.

"Food truck food that moves, how is that subtle?"

"Paul promised to make me a side seafood, and he only knows how to boil crustaceans. You're not gonna tell…"

"Don't be silly. Just help me to help you. Give the kid his bacon."

"Cheddar bacon potatoes it is," Oliver agreed. "I see your point, and I bet Paul's are amazing."

They finalized the dinner menu of roast pork, cheddar bacon potatoes and applesauce while waiting for the Broncos to vote for the winner by kicking a field goal into the endzone of their preferred team. Travis insisted they also needed green beans, but everyone (minus Fran) understood that as a farmer, he had to say that. Team Paul were team players, though, so if he made it, they (minus Fran) would eat it.

After a long, tough day on the gridiron, Vivian's Red Team won, naturally, and as their leader, naturally, she also took home the individual win. Troy the plumber would have been the actual winner, however, if he had more self-promotion. The blue-collar version of engineer Felix, and therefore someone with much more practical field experience, he was showing himself to be the Season 14 kitchen hack whiz. He adapted his oven-fried steak on the fly to meet the limitation of one fry basket and an iffy flat range in a way that left many contestants open-mouthed and suspecting the presence of a ringer.

The promise of Paul's dinner mysteriously lessened the Blue Team's angst over their loss and their half-decent dishes corrupted by twists invented by a bunch of twentysomethings dressed in black who obviously lived off ramen and cheap beer. Despite the eleventh-hour wrangling from Janiva over whether it was really the week for pot roast not pork roast, which sent Felix scuttling over to the competitor's truck at a key moment during service. It also tempered the general competitiveness and spitefulness at Judge's Table. Anyone exiting the show that day would also lose their seat at the dinner table. Facilitating that tragedy was a heavy responsibility.

Letting the judges decide with minimal input, the second eliminated contestant was considered as predictable and fair as the first, and mollified the devastated Blues. Red Shirt Ronnie – they called it, who in America thinks Chef Parker eats food plated on the floor? – had tried to be clever about the twist. Abandoning his steak fajitas upon learning he would have to make forty orders using one cook surface, not forty clean pans, he insisted on contributing a "refreshing" salad with packaged greens and a Whole Foods dressing. Buh-bye.

THAT NIGHT, THE SURVIVING CONTESTANTS sat down to eat together in the dining room, the glass expanse now augmented by a rickety card table they found in the hall closet. They watched the simple feast come out dish by dish with eyebrows raised and giant grins scrunching their cheeks back to their ears. Then came the furtive sneaking of bits and edges until Paul's sharp "hey!" put their hands back into their laps. The blessing, the passing of plates, it all led up to that first bite when they looked around at each other, mouths full, eyes half-closed and nodded. Nodded with the certainty that regardless of the ongoing, competitive death battle, all was right in the world.

"Have you tried the applesauce?" Chloe asked Troy around bite four of what was his debut at the cool kids table.

"No, I'm still working on my pork."

"Well, you must stop for a second and try the applesauce. Other people only think they can achieve this kind of greatness. Pure simplicity, pure magic. Join me in the place of sunshine and happiness."

Troy obediently rotated his fork around his plate, not yet a believer. As Vivian's new best friend, especially if he continued to shun the spotlight, Troy intended to hold out days and days with his happenstance alliance against the cool kids. Or, at least until the new teams were chosen for next week. His loyalty cracked like a piñata, however, when the rumor that roast pork would be making an appearance that night finally filtered across party lines. For the first ten minutes of dinner, though, he still played it off like he was just a spy.

That next bite, he became one of them.

"*Ohhhh* yeah," he said with his mouth full of apple-y goodness, "oh that really...yeah."

Chloe added another spoonful to his plate.

"Right, uh huh, right? Isn't that exactly what you wanted when I said apple-sauce? You mentally prepared yourself, I know you did, to take a step back in your expectations. It would be fine, it would be apple-esque, and then bam! Applesauce. Welcome, Troy."

She then leaned around him to call down the row.

"We love you, Paul!"

A chorus of happy nods from the table seconded that declaration.

"We really love you."

Sadly, and really more for the judges' sake than anyone else, the future dinner party legend for all of America never shone again in the arena itself. While Paul did make an affirmative choice to participate on a reality television show, he refused to embrace the basic tenets of a reality television show. Perhaps because he didn't need the money. He never allowed random deadlines, competition twists, or the brief to impact his food choices if it ruined his dish, a sin dinged by the judges more and more with each passing week. The cool kids learned quickly his best food came from leaving him to feel his feelings about what was available in the fridge, or the mini grocery store on set, but unlike the judges, they didn't mind except during Group Challenges. Nor did America, watching from home. Even through their TV sets, fans knew the cool kids were right and loved Paul even more for being wrong.

Making one person cook all day every day for the competition, and then every night for the contestants, however, would sap anyone's creativity and energy, and might send that person home early. Nobody wanted that. Well, nobody with a soul. While Jimmy Bob took the Red Team out for the Group Reward dinner at Joker's Wild and introduced them to farm-raised rattlesnake and antelope steaks, Janiva wisely started working out a tentative schedule that rationed out the nights Paul was on supper duty.

As the competition moved forward, often the contestants starved on take-out and cereal between his dinner shifts, but sometimes they, too, met the moment. Travis grilled a steak au poivre they became particularly fond of, and Chloe's simple Italian fare made them feel they were eating up the coast from a Peter Mayle novel. The latter they usually ate out on the terrace for the full experience. Oliver would fry up a fish anytime for anyone, especially Paul, whom he was designated to feed on Paul's days off, while Fran's comfort food took the edge off the worst bad day on set, if also leaving them lethargic and unready to fight again. Even Vivian's competitive edge took the occasional day off, and she would contribute her own competent but heartless "alternative classics". Already by the close of Meat and Greet! Week, most of the Season 14 contestants agreed – they came for the quarter million, but stayed for dinner.

the fellowship of the ribs

T he camaraderie engendered by some of the contestants dining family-style back at the house, both with Paul's food, and enduring the hardships together the nights....*sniff*...without Paul's food, had an odd, unintended consequence in the warehouse kitchen. It countered a large swathe of sneaky. Particularly, the behind-the-scenes machinations the judges and producers inserted to heighten the show's dramatic tension. Eating together created a SEAL Team 6 vibe among the cool kids that they had a job to do, and the mission was hard, and they were gonna go through some things, but what equally mattered was everyone getting home in time to find out what Paul felt like making next. Or again. This mindset continually lowered the emotional temperature, no matter what happened on set.

In prior seasons, Chef Parker was known (to management) as someone especially skilled at inventing plausible rivalries and sustaining faux conflicts with well-aimed barbs and innuendo. Playing on the fears and insecurities of twenty-five people trying to take each other out to achieve their dreams, that part required minimal skill or effort, but it took a certain touch and experience to do so without wholly undermining their ability to complete challenges and avoid all of them imploding at once. Chef Parker found it unusually hard, however, to disrupt or disturb the Season 14 kids.

"What are we, filming in Australia?" he complained to Chef Matteo at the start of Week 2's Imitation Challenge. "When did *Yes! Chef America* become a team sport?"

The judges mistakenly attributed the noticeably kinder, gentler competition atmosphere more often found on their sister franchise with the inadvertent, back-to-back scheduling of two easy-going guest judges. For Playin' Chicken! Week they invited Chef Ari, urban legend and chef-owner of that Indianapolis hot spot, Pluck!. He used rap bars rather than cowboy solecisms to explain his dishes and techniques, and the regular judges didn't quite follow his references any more than they really understood what "when in doubt, let your horse do your thinking" meant, but they sounded encouraging. It was acknowledged, however, that both guest judges were being asked to critique their core demographic, and it was in both men's best interest to grow their brand rather than alienate future customers.

Whatever or whomever was disrupting the ordinary flow and tension of the competition, Chef Ari's arrival did exacerbate the situation. Instead of using his Imitation Challenge cloche moment to introduce Pluck! and it's Indy Cordon Bleu with proper fear and intimidation, he exhorted the contestants to,

"...Lose yourself in the mooooovement, the moment, you better own it, never let it go! You only get ONE shot, do not miss your CHANCE to blow, this op-por-tu-ni-ty comes ONCE in a lifetime..."

For the contestants, Chef Ari's 60-second solo was timely and needed, as all Eminem superhits are, and Oliver surprised everyone by backing him up with the beatboxing. Watching a large proportion of his audience head-bobbing along, Chef Ari knew he was connecting to them as both a chef and artist. The regular judges did not find any of this helpful.

Chef Ari dismissing the contestants back to their benches with an added, *"you can do anything you set your mind to"* was, perhaps, overkill in the face of Pluck!'s signature dish, but the contestants appreciated the sentiment. They thwumped and shuffled their way to their stations in time with Oliver's *"dun dun dun dun dun dun"*. Felix even threw out a twerk on the way, but everyone, including Al the cameraman, pretended they didn't see that.

When Jake one-upped Felix, though, and brought his SexyBack, well now, that made both the day's highlight reel, and Paul stub his toe on the corner of Janiva's station.

"Wow, he's really good at that," commented Fran. Unlike Paul, she took the precaution of pausing prior to gawking.

"Look away, Fran! Quick!" warned Chloe in a whisper. "Don't get sucked into the vortex!"

"I can't. I don't want to, and I can't."

With one hand firmly over her eyes, Chloe made an executive decision to go nuclear.

"Look!" she announced, "Glenn's donuts have arrived!"

"What where?" asked Fran, momentarily distracted by an (almost) competing need for fried carbs versus spicy Timberlake. She turned towards the rear doors.

Clinging to Fran's arm to slow her down as she tried to swing back around, Chloe took a relieved breath before confessing,

"I'm sorry I had to lie to you, Fran. You'll thank me later."

Jake, being Jake, stopped dancing in the middle of a verse the second he lost his audience. He had moved over to his station in the third row by the time the two women looked for him again.

"The show's over," Fran said with disappointment.

"I did it for you Fran, and for us all. Paul just took out his toe," said Chloe. She pointed over to where he was still hopping up and down on one foot and getting his shoulder fool-slapped by Janiva. "Do you want him to go home from gangrene, Fran? Before we know what he can do with chicken? Is that you want?"

Fran took a moment to center her mind on the competition floor and away from the club.

"I was wrong, I see that now. I think we can all agree, though," she added in a low tone to Chloe and a few of the surrounding benches, "we now have the appropriate converse to the Paul Standard."

They all nodded their acknowledgment of her wisdom, and out of that moment of temporary disharmony and power struggle was born the Jake Sexy. When a dish looked so good but tasted so bad, which happened a lot, especially in the early days of the competition, it was Jake Sexy.

"All this chaos over a cordon bleu," Chef Parker complained.

IN THE TIME IT TOOK the giant competition clock to wind down for the Imitation Challenge, Chef Ari further undermined the start of Season 14. He became the first person in the warehouse to recognize Ajiz's habit of falling into a series of jerks and flailings was not a seizure. It didn't look like a twerk with a jazz hand, and by rights, whatever Ajiz was doing ought to have included jazz hands, so the cool kids had been at a total loss. The popular kids had been on team Jimmy Bob, whose cowboyism, "I dunno, that puts flies on me" sounded obscurely snarky, but on the nose. Chef Parker hoped whatever it was would inadvertently knock over someone else's plate.

Chef Ari instantly spotted a fellow fan's homage to hip hop.

"Poppin' John!" he exclaimed passing Ajiz's station, "right on!"

He didn't laugh or anything.

The surrounding contestants turned towards Ajiz with variations on "Really?", "Seriously?", "What's that?", and "no man, you're not actually good at this" (with head shake).

"What? I have kids," Ajiz protested, "this is me staying relevant. Check out my fresh routine to the *Glee Season 2* soundtrack."

The judges' annoyance at Chef Ari clearing up mysteries they wanted unsolved, and that Ajiz still hadn't knocked anyone's plate on the floor, may have led them to be extra testy at Judge's Table when Ashley put up a chicken dish made with beef stock. By the time they critiqued Ajiz's "cordon pinkish" that even Chef Ari agreed wasn't worth a celebratory wormin', their disapproval was palpable, strongly seconded from the ranks by Fran wishing Ajiz would leave crossovers to the real Justin Timberlakes of the world.

"If you start Jake getting down, getting sexy again," warned Chloe, listening to her grumble, "you aren't getting any of Paul's roast chicken tonight. Let the man dance it out."

To Chef Parker's final annoyance of the day, Chloe's nonsensical admonition actually worked. Hearing Fran's grousing transition back to a low, supportive *whoomba*, Chef dismissed the contestants with just one terse, unfriendly,

"Go home."

janiva didn't come to play

Chef Parker returned to the warehouse kitchen for the Reinvention Challenge with renewed focus, ready to start more bad trouble and after a night's consideration, better prepared to counter negative rap influences. He identified the perfect target and watched carefully for the perfect psychological moment to salt the victim's mind with suspicion over lurking, nefarious goings on. It should have worked. It should have been awesome.

Yet, it still failed. Was it Chef Ari's fault? Chef Parker wasn't sure, but it might have been.

What happened was, seconds before the judges arrived at Janiva's bench, her first batch of waffles for her grandmother's, it-better-be-right Chicken and Waffles stuck coming out of the waffle iron. The audience at home would later cheer for Chef Ari stepping in to offer a little Jay-Z wisdom to help her regain some composure. His intervention strongly contrasted with the "insensitive" and "oblivious" bad timing of Chef Parker. Parker warned Janiva to cook with a heat source this time, reminding her that serving the judges "blue" chicken would be the death knell for her hopes and dreams.

Despite such proven and effective floor interview scare tactics, the already flustered and baffled Janiva flat-out refused to credit Chef Parker's further "wondering" if it was Felix that messed with her oven on Day 1. Felix borrowed her flour during the cook, having dropped his on the floor, and therefore was in the vicinity of the crime. It was possible.

Al the cameraman turned with some difficulty in the small space to film Janiva's reaction shot to the allegation, further proof Chef Parker's strategy had merit. A Week 2 contestant trying to cook under the threat of burnt food, salmonella and elimination, and then a judge bringing a stranger danger problem into the mix, even the crew expected that to make good TV, and got into position.

Frantically scraping the divots of her waffle iron, and looking at the clock, and listening to Chef Parker's threats and conjecture, and humming along with Chef Ari's additional bars that we *"can't be too scared to fail, searching for perfection"*, and fielding questions from Chef Juan about her grandmother...Janiva still wasn't having it regarding Felix as an Enemy of the People.

"No, we checked that out already," she replied without any suspicion or paranoia, scanning her bench for the previously forgotten cooking spray. "He got the ratios wrong for his naan at dinner last night, and Chloe was worried how wheat keeps running away from him. Right before Oliver offered to teach him how to bait a lobster trap as a backup option, I joked with him whether he dusted my oven on purpose to douse the pilot light as his only path to victory."

"Well, who would mention...?" Parker vaguely insinuated, casting a wide net for any latent tension.

"It keeps you running," Ari added, surprising everyone by unexpectedly going old school and bringing the Jimmy Bob.

"That's true," Janiva agreed absentmindedly, grooving along with Chef Ari while eyeballing the right amount of batter to pour for Attempt 2, Going to Be Right Waffles. "I'll ask him again. He might have brushed off the knob wrong or something. He's young. He may not know how to come clean. As Chloe would say, that'll get into his food. We don't want that."

Chef Parker didn't even know what to do with such collective illogic that actively desired a competitor to be emotionally centered, but hoped he sowed one small seed of discord. Or at least increased the chance of a raw chicken thigh arriving at Judge's Table. He would have been more displeased and less certain, though, had he overhead Chloe's further contribution to his lecture.

Chloe's bench was situated immediately in front of Janiva's, and after the judges passed on, she turned around with admiration.

"Gurrrrlllll, you rock. All that incoming and you kept on cooking. How can I learn to be you?"

Janiva shrugged.

"It's my grandmother's Chicken and Waffles, it has to be right."

"Well, she's going to have serious swag at the Assisted Living facility once this airs. You go, girl. Now that you're cooking next to Paul, the bad oven luck seems to have ended, as well. Maybe it was a front-row thing? Maybe those plugs get kicked out of the outlets with the added traffic."

Chef Parker's last hope for a Janiva-centered implosion fizzled after time was called. The judges plainly heard Ajiz leading that section in *"Song Sung Blue"* to her chicken. They expected musical noise from Ajiz, but the rest of the contestants ought to have been silent, terrified, and waiting for their critiques, not laughing that Felix didn't know how to snap in rhythm, not even to Neil Diamond. How was this Week 2, Chefs Matteo and Parker silently telegraphed to each other, where was the fear?

Chef Parker fully intended to live up to his devil coat, though. He could send Nigel home for the crime of inventing a better seasoning mix for Pluck!'s cordon bleu, he could damn well scare a bunch of amateurs into turning on each other.

AND HE DID.

During the Playin' Chicken! Group Challenge, his first – successful – salvo began as a whisper campaign laundered through the PA's. "Rumor" had it that "someone" on the Red Team conspired with the Blue Team to throw the team challenge. Chef Ari attempted to diffuse the rising tension by instructing the contestants, *"a loss isn't a loss, it's a lesson"*, but Chef Parker was confident he knew them better than some kid from Brooklyn. He boasted to Chef Matteo the resulting and inevitable war would last weeks. That there rumor was almost mostly true. Kinda. If one didn't know what actually went wrong with the Red Team's dishes.

THE CONTESTANTS WERE SENT OUT to Mount Bear Ski Resort to make lunch for the Rescue Crew Summer Training Camp participants. Well, early in the cook Blue Team Jake tripped Red Team Aaron in the supply shack, because Jake was mean like that. Shy and all-vanilla Aaron had been expected to slip past another full week of eliminations cooking his family's...*yawn*...standbys to go home without being remembered by the judges or viewers or participants, and Jake's bullying went equally unnoticed. Unfortunately, Aaron's added, silent worry that the wild mountain blueberries he was carrying when tripped might have flown into everyone else's components, and the frightening number of people it required he consult to avert a team disaster, overwhelmed his limited ability to speak intelligibly to camera while browning drumsticks. That got his team's attention.

In the frantic push to get lunch on the table between the airlift protocol training and the class on basic ice shelter construction, Aaron's brain couldn't register that even the mini blueberry variety is not an invisible additive. The resulting color change in any contaminated dish would have alerted his teammates without his help. His red-faced, bumbling ineffectualness reached acute levels waiting and watching for one of the Red Team's other eleven dishes to turn fruity, and his disjointed defense at Judge's Table suggested a guilty conscience about something far more than nonexistent berries. The Red Team voted to send him and his not bad blueberry barbecue chicken – the helicopter pilot liked it and said so, on camera – home, largely for the crime of calling attention to himself, and thereby making everybody nervous.

THE PROMISED REWARD FOR THE winning team further inflamed the potential for blame and recrimination and a vague intrigue over the root cause of Aaron's distress. Chef Ari decided to take the winning team on a balloon ride.

"How has that reward got to anything to do with chicken, Ari?" Juan asked at the end of the on-site segment, while the judges waited for their drivers to take them back to the warehouse.

Chef Ari just shrugged.

"How does anything have anything to do with chicken? This isn't Japan, you know. And I want to go on a balloon ride. We'll take KFC with us, how's that?"

"Boston Chicken is our sponsor," Matteo corrected him automatically.

"Whatever," Ari responded, "just know I am not catering it. I'm going on a balloon ride."

"By the way," he added, "do I have to bring this Paul person? I wasn't listening to the rules."

Chef Matteo was confused by the question.

"What do you mean? He's on the wrong team."

"Is he? I thought he was the wildcard playing both sides. They all kept talking about his food during Judge's Table.

"They're weird like that," pronounced Matteo. "He almost won Week 1 and they can't get over it. Just ignore them."

you can't dance, so don't ask me

The continued fallout over Jake's overlooked prank and Aaron's inability as an amateur home cook to track and taste every dish coming out of a busy kitchen, proved Chef Parker's Machiavellian touch was back and fully operational. As he predicted, two large teams intermixed and dispersed across three vans for the ride from Mount Bear back to Judge's Table led to a long drive punctuated by heated, partisan whispers and many a side-eye at one's seatmates. During the critique, confirmation of the challenge winner, loser and the reward, plus a few, well-timed "observations" from the bench and a panegyric from Chef Ari about ballooning sparked open accusations and counter accusations regarding the unfair win and mysterious loss. Once re-sorted and re-crammed together for the ride home, the marquee Season 14 conflict firmly took hold.

Arriving back at the house, most contestants opted for the extreme measure of dining on private stashes of KIND bars in their bedrooms, but that time-out did little to ameliorate the situation. At breakfast the next day, successive knots of warring factions commandeered the coffee machine, daring the enemy to just try to jump in for a refill. No amount of internal discussion, or the work of envoys, spies and double agents could resolve What Really Happened on Mount Bear. Or convince anyone to just let it go.

The first and only break in hostilities came when the challenge winners left to live their *80 Days Around the World* fantasy life with Chef Ari.

"Good luck not slamming into a mountain!" said Oliver, summing up the Red Team's position as he waved them off from the window.

It was then the Lucky Losers, as they later designated themselves *ad nauseam*, decided the only way to cheer up would be to host a meatloaf competition between Paul and Travis. They agreed ahead of time no bets would be placed, and that Paul won, but the production of one perfect and one darn fine loaf did put a song back in their hearts. They surprised even themselves how easily they set aside, yet again, any gloom and gnashing of teeth over yesterday's loss, and just enjoyed eating Paul's food. The discussion gradually turned from the Mount Bear Mysteries to what Travis maybe might have changed in his dish to match Paul's. Not that he could reach that culinary height, or they wanted to put unrealistic expectations on him, but in a good-humored debate over whether if something was different, was it almost just near as good?

Somewhere between a strong wrangle on how to properly mix ground meats by hand, and various anecdotes on the merits of homemade breadcrumbs, the interest in the Red/Blue chicken and bear conflict right-sized itself. Clearly, in the end the Red Team won by losing. They were eating Paul's meatloaf, while the Blue Team dined on frozen-by-the-altitude, take-out chicken. They gained valuable, atavistic insight on toasting bread which might come in handy later in the competition, and could forever twit the Blue Team for being out of the house for the Great Meatloaf Cook-Off. That was a lot, and a lot to look forward to.

At the end of the meal, it no longer being the end of the world, Felix offered to round off the evening with his lemon sponge and took Paul with him to make coffee the right way. The rest of the team waited around the table, fat and happy and picking at leftovers.

"I'm so glad I am wearing my eatin' pants," said Chloe.

The conversation moved from desultory opinions on how many vegetables one could, or should, hide in a meatloaf, back to whether an enemy lurked in their ranks. While they couldn't agree on either subject, the latter lost enough of its earlier heat to be considered objectively.

"Who could have done it?" asked Janiva reaching for one last swipe of Travis's gravy. "This isn't quite Paul's, but it's darn good."

"Cake's coming," Chloe reminded her.

"Right, thanks," she said and resolutely put down her fork with a *twink*. "I still say somebody turned off my oven Day 1. Chef Parker suggested Felix, but come on, the kid is making us dessert."

Chloe agreed, adding,

"You know, Fran's on the Blue Team, and she didn't hear or see anything weird yesterday. I think that's information. I don't know about what, though,"

"Telling Fran would take the secret out any sabotage," said Travis, offering his own, quiet insight on recent events. "I'm not calling you a liar, Janiva, I'm just asking. Are you sure you didn't turn the dial wrong yourself? It was Day 1."

"Wow, bold accusation, Linus, after somebody likes your gravy," said Chloe, shaking her head at him. She lacked Oliver's authority, though, and he stayed firm.

"When I left my station to grab a rice cooker it was a blazing 400 degrees," insisted Janiva, "and when I came back it was stone cold off. I say if it happened to me, and it happened to the Red Team, whatever it is, it's going to keep happening."

Travis didn't agree, but did conclusively rule out their former chief suspect.

"Then it couldn't have been Aaron. He isn't the bumbling but effective Inspector Clouseau-type who knocks into a cooktop at just the right angle. Today he acted guilty, but would a guilty person act like that?"

"We were too mean to him, poor little guy," interjected Troy, taking one more spoonful of mashed potatoes to keep his strength up waiting for dessert. "I was so mad we were going to lose, and I wasn't going home for it, but..."

Chloe reached out to clutch Troy's forearm in mutual contrition regarding the Red Team's defense at Judge's Table.

"We *were* mean, Troy. The dreaded "who should go home?" question. How do you answer that without embarrassing already embarrassed people? I know I'm perfectly capable of humiliating myself, and getting busted by the judges, without anyone's help pointing out what exactly I did wrong."

"I told you this is a competition," said Oliver, "I warned you."

"You should have followed my lead!" yelled Paul from the kitchen. "I kept my mouth shut."

"Well, my Troy is right, he knows things," said Chloe, "and of course, so is Paul. Testimonial."

"Is that the same as Amen?" asked Janiva.

"No...Yes. And, but, I mean the thing when it's a thing. Like in Charles

Dickens, when people get together and write something down and then sign it to make it true."

"You mean an email?" asked Travis.

"Okay, Linus, if you want to be all twentieth century about it. We were wrong, and mean, so we should send Aaron something written down that he can look at in a safe space, or show it to his parents and friends after the episode airs, to make it right. He can't have gotten far yet, although maybe he's already gone. How do we deliver it to him?"

Janiva suggested they use tomorrow's interview segments.

"We were mean on TV, we can be nice on TV to balance things out. He'll at least see us do that. Eventually."

"Doesn't mean they'll air it!" yelled Paul.

Troy assessed the team resources.

"Well, we can't make a TikTok without our phones, but maybe if we talk about him a lot, a whole lot, some of it is bound to slip through. What are we going to say, though? Poor little guy wasn't a very good cook."

"We don't know that," countered Chloe, "we just know he was half your size, and shy, and that made him nervous. None of us can cook our best under those conditions."

"I don't know if you guys missed this, but Jake tripped him," he belatedly confessed witnessing. "Yesterday. I thought Aaron got put off his game because I showed Oliver how to do the *Pu Bu* stance too close to his workstation, but what if..."

Chloe clutched Troy's arm tighter.

"*Tch!* Poor Aaron! We deserve to lose. We let Jake beat up our teammate, and with your *Pu Bu* so close and on the ready for justice. Oh, I feel so bad, and he missed meatloaf."

"Testimonial," agreed Janiva.

Nodding back at her, Chloe left the table to look for a pen and paper, while Travis, still quietly unconvinced that Janiva knew how to work a strange oven, brought the conversation back to the original problem.

"Since we don't know who sabotaged us, do we need to know? Maybe nobody did this time, either."

Everyone looked around the table, pondering these twin radical thoughts.

"Let's wait for cake," said Chloe, coming back to her seat. "We need Paul and Felix on this."

The Red Team was still lingering over the remains of loaf, lemon sponge and coffee, weighing the benefits of cooking with paranoia or oblivion and thinking positive thoughts about Aaron for Chloe to jot down, when the Blue Team came home. Nervous about the resentment they were walking into, yet ready to be envied, a few braver Blues with clearer consciences lingered in the hall to see how the anger management was going for the Red Team. Instead of being glared at and ignored, however, or asked how many feet up it took for Ajiz to drop his mittens overboard, they were called over to the table to try a Felix cake and the strawberry coolie and chocolate ganache that "Paul just whipped up, the man's a magician", invited to opine on glass versus metal loaf pans, and asked whether they thought Troy's kung fu moves gave his team an unfair psychological advantage.

Fran eagerly rejoined the group around the table with relief.

"Wow, this is really good meatloaf," she said, spearing the last corner of the extra-browned outside edge of Paul's dish.

"Don't miss Travis' gravy," said Janiva, offering the official olive branch, although Troy already spoke for them all by silently moving his chair two inches to allow space for her to squeeze in between himself and Chloe.

"You should've tried it when it was still warm," said Chloe, reaching behind her back to pat Troy's shoulder for relenting with such forbearance. "Why go be a midair Popsicle, dodging nasty precipices with limited self-propulsion? Doesn't eating fried chicken in mittens make it fuzzy? Why do all that when Paul had a meatloaf in the oven?"

"They made us?"

"Cruel and unusual punishment, this show. How was the view? Oh, remind me to get you to sign the testimonial for Aaron."

"What's a testimonial?"

"It's a thing. You guys missed so much while you were out."

The next day the judges walked into the competition kitchen for Chef Ari's Masterclass expecting his week to close with snarls and dark undercurrents while he demonstrated various ways to incorporate chicken with broth. It puzzled them to find the cheerful atmosphere of a morning already well spent, and to be met by Oliver with the declaration that it was Aaron Day.

"We're also celebrating Blueberry Barbecue, so, it may come up."

In the Red Team's quest to alert Aaron of the new holiday, and their new certainty he was a victim not a perpetrator on Mount Bear, Felix tricked the youngest PA into admitting all the contestants' cell phone numbers were stored in his contact list sub-folder. Calling Troy over to commandeer his device, they began blowing up Aaron's with texts. Through a series of emoji's, GIF's and odd, obscure references to anyone not present at Meatloaf Madness, they apologized for their obliviousness to his traumatic experience and informed him that Troy kicked Jake in the shins on his behalf, that Oliver gave Jake a devastating head shake, and that everyone looked forward to him proving at the reunion show what a great cook he was when people weren't being mean to him. While they had Jake cornered, the team even made him add his apology before deciding to let the matter, and the violence, drop.

"For now," Troy added.

Listening to the contestants argue whether the karate chop emoji was supportive or triggering bewildered the judges. Over in the lounge, Vivian could also be heard boasting loudly and with proper condescension about the superiority of her Blue Team, and its imperviousness to physical intimidation, but Vivian denigrating other contestant's skills was ordinary background noise. Nobody believed she actually wanted to go on a balloon ride, not in those shoes.

Then Ajiz began teaching his opposing team counterpart, Reid, how to Pop during the taping delay while they waited for Al to locate his spare battery pack. That unfortunate spectacle made no sense at all. At Judge's Table those two sworn enemies repeatedly gave each other the stink eye over the remarkable – and suspicious? – similarities between the Blue Team Chicken Pot Pie and the Red Team Chicken Hand Pie. What could have papered over that schism enough to risk inexpert, tandem side stomps? Fran, thankfully, interrupted Ajiz's lesson, but without any hint of lingering partisan warfare either, or teamwork gone wrong. She simply admonished the party of the second part in her best quiet, authoritative, HR manner,

"Don't, Reid. Seriously. The crazy leg is not the dance move for you."

"What do you know for Poppin'?" Ajiz responded and stuck out his tongue at her. "Poppin' is E for Everyone. It's the blueberry barbecue of the dance world. It's almost Paul's meatloaf."

A welcome difference of opinion, however obscure, but it, too, lacked the expected and desired animosity for the judges. The same incident that now added another set of flailing arms to the competition kitchen had left Ajiz and Fran stuck in an "I told you not to do it" death drop over Ajiz going head-on against a known pot pie master. Also a classic *Yes, Chef!* beginning to a permanent, failed relationship, Fran and Ajiz ought to be glaring and snarking for days without any assist from Chef Parker, waiting to see who would be proven most right and what the other was gonna do 'bout it. Especially given that Fran was right, and like his proselytizing for the P among people better suiting to crumping, so often Ajiz thought he knew best, and thought wrong. And never...admitted...it.

Yet, Chef Parker's tailored, targeted, inflammatory ask – whether Ajiz finally conceded he learned his lesson about competing menu items – only triggered Ajiz to pause his manhandling of Reid's limbs into the proper arm swing position long enough to make the un-hate-filled overture,

"Who brings you the *Hakuna Matata*, Fran?"

It was Fran's reply, though, that really let Chef Parker down.

"I will always prefer a tango, Ajiz, but I still love you almost as much as Paul on a Wednesday with time on his hands. Go Aaron, go Blue," she said, and walked away to find Chloe to act out for her Troy's earlier confrontation with Jake's lower limbs.

With a loud exhale of exasperation to his fellow judges, Chef Parker stormed off the set before Chef Ari could even explain to the contestants the difference between "stock" and "bullion".

CHAPTER TWENTY-FOUR

the unnecessary food group

One chef who did not share the desire of her fellow panelists to walk into a tension-filled competition kitchen was the guest judge for It Ain't Easy Being Green! Week, Chef Bowen Chastayne from that Minneapolis celebration of vegetables, Gaia Restaurant. Blonde, fit, and with a love of tofu that dated back to her early days in college, Chef Bowen hoped to inspire the amateur cooks and home audience with her knowledge of all things chlorophyll. Minutes into her opening segment, however, it became apparent how few contestants knew how to make vegetables the star of their plates, or venerated persons who could. They already appeared far more interested to learn her restaurant was located just north of the Valley of the Jolly Green Giant, than about Gaia itself. Not even Travis knew that was a real place.

Adding to Chef Bowen's stress from being Season 14's "weird food" judge, and possibly now believed to be a fictional character, management scheduled Green! Week as the real start to the competition. They shortened cook times to competitive lengths, and six challenges in, the easy outs like Tammy Firestarter, Red Shirt Ronnie, the tactless Nigel, and that last guy, whatshisname, were identified, and one by one, getting sent home. Those in middle of the pack felt a new pressure to take risks and get noticed that did not always elevate their dishes.

The Imitation Challenge set by Chef Bowen was her signature Happy Veggie Shepherd's Pie. She chose it thinking everyone liked getting creative with piped mashed potatoes and a blowtorch, and that the required technique level was only moderately greater than Jimmy Bob's Week 1 porterhouse. It baffled her when the recipe made four contestants cry mid-cook trying to blanch, parboil, and vaporize ingredients many thought required pressing one button to magically come out of the package done how they were supposed to be done.

Oliver spoke for the majority when he banged down the lid of his steamer to ask,

"Who knew vegetables came in more flavors than "crudité", "microwaved" and "soup"? Who thinks that's a good idea?"

"Preach! brother," echoed Fran.

Three other contestants made independent, yet identical attempts at Judge's Table to pretend they came from a British heritage that claimed mushy peas as part of the culture. Each one gave that as the primary reason they overshot Chef Bowen's meaning of *al dente* on their first dish/first try with a Gaia classic.

"Focus on how much the contestants need you, and the improvement you'll see by the Group Challenge," said Chef Matteo in an undertone, counseling Chef Bowen through her first Judge's Table and yet another train wreck of her dish.

"But why would anyone try an excuse that hasn't worked the first two times?" she whispered back.

"Have you watched the show?"

Chef Juan tried to get to the bottom of this UK culinary phenomenon more directly, as only he could.

"I thought you told us during your audition you were part Norwegian?" he asked Ashley, taking on the heavy lift of walking her through an explanation of her dish.

"I am. That is British, only more so. You remember the Viking invasions? It's my understanding mushy peas come from the Vikings. That's what I heard, anyway. They say."

Everyone looked to Chef Bowen for her view on what "they say" regarding boiled vegetables and migration patterns in the North Atlantic.

"I'm more familiar with the modern farm to table movement than ancient food traditions," she lied, silently wishing her week fell after several more elimination rounds, equally unaware of the show's policy to keep a useful idiot or two around in the kitchen for a piquant element.

"You should have been here during Season 4's Sushi week," Chef Juan mumbled into Chef Bowen's other ear, while Ashley collected her plate and returned to her station, "we'll never do that again."

Chef Bowen's spirits did revive after "that Ajiz person" (she meant Travis) presented. There was someone who really understood how to char kale, and she was able to hope once more that if peas were a bridge too far for the bulk of contestants, maybe somewhere, out there, among the remaining dishes, was a second Ajiz (Travis) who could make a decent swirl using a starch product. Chloe's dish also confirmed Gaia's recipe could be followed, if one wanted to, even if she, too, remained a nonbeliever that shepherd's pie could be made without a good beef broth.

As the contestants came and went with their plates and their excuses and their meat bias, however, Chef Bowen's repeated, whispered questions about "who's Paul?" and "why are they talking about that Paul, again?" did finally alert Chef Parker to the real source of the Season 14 weird problem. Kinda.

As Chef Ari noted the previous week, random, aspirational references to Paul's food repeatedly cropped up at Judge's Table. When Chloe presented her chicken tetrazzini adaptation of Ari's Indy Cordon Bleu, she informed them,

"I was trying to push myself, going for a Day 3, Paul's back!, flavor, effort, thing. You know?"

No, the judges didn't.

The question from Troy, "...but are you feeling the simple taste sensation that even applesauce, done right, can bring?" had been met with silence.

The judges considered such odd, cross-promotion just bad gameplay, echoing Jake's counter narrative that "some people" were encouraging Paul to make food guaranteed to lose. Except, Jake was wrong. The cool kids knew how to throw people under the bus with far greater efficiency. It was Season 14.

No, the meandering interruptions of the judge's "teaching moments" to repeatedly highlight a confirmed also-ran was all Chloe's fault. Duh. Despite her competition strategy not working well yet for her, somehow it still leeched into the cool kids' otherwise cutthroat fight for their lives and careers. Because she was right. It was more fun, and resulted in a better outcome, to let Season 14's dark horse shine, without being afraid, and without needing to take him out the minute he didn't. It was almost as fun as talking about his unique culinary talent. Incessantly.

The judge's response to Felix serving a mini peach tart with Chef Bowen's vegetable pie, however, finally taught the cool kids it was not fun to openly aspire to the Paul Standard in front of the panel. What Felix unwisely said when presenting his dish was,

"You know when you're just this side of full, and then Paul whips up an ad hoc coolie, and you think, "Exactly. That's what it needed, I'll have another slice." You know, that? I thought my dish..."

No, Chef Parker didn't know, and just because half the contestants nodded along didn't mean Felix was right, or making a point, or making good TV. Paul didn't even agree with him, Chef Juan asked. Chef Parker found Felix meddling with the components of a professional's dish additionally frustrating because the token pastry chef could not be eliminated before Pastry Week. Felix should not be relying on that fact, since one hadn't been announced yet. The years Juan was on a diet, they often skipped it.

Only secret immunity allowed Felix to dodge the Bottom Three after his rambling homage to Paul and his added element that wasn't even green. His spot went instead to Fran for what she did to Chef Bowen's shepherd's pie. She blow-torched the peas. Raw peas. Chef Bowen needed a minute after that.

"Who tops a pie with "burnt"? Raw burnt," she asked, covering her face with her hands as she rubbed her third eye. "They were raw and then burnt. Does she think that is how they make parsley? Who does that?"

While Chef Juan tried to rally Chef Bowen's crushed spirit, Chef Parker dismissed them all for the day with a stern warning that encompassed both Felix and everyone else heading down the wrong path with him – focus on their own food and the challenge at hand. All four judges hoped for a better day tomorrow. None of the contestants expected one.

America, though, saw backstage footage the judges did not, and would not be surprised later at what happened during Chef Bowen's tenure in the *Yes, Chef!* kitchen. By this point in the broadcast season, they already had their own, deeply held opinions regarding the Paul Standard, and could follow the contestant's most banana non sequiturs from "thanks, but if we're comparing my biscuits to Paul's (mother's), well...." to "what did I expect, without a Paul Wednesday morning marinade, it could never...". No properly informed witness to the following events failed to credit you-know-who for saving Fran's food dream and, maybe, changing *Yes, Chef!* forever.

CHAPTER TWENTY-FIVE

it ain't easy, it ain't green

Fresh and ready and still violently anti-vegetarian, the cool kids started off the dreaded Reinvention Judge's Table whooping and clapping for Paul and his version of a Navratan Korma. The mood quickly turned to surly, however, to hear their fearless and favorite leader dinged for not highlighting the Green! Week wildcard ingredient, iceberg lettuce.

"We are already at Week 3, Paul, where's the lettuce?" asked Chef Matteo.

"The Mughal empire would not approve. I used kale. You liked Travis' kale."

"You mean Ajiz's," corrected Chef Bowen. (No, he didn't.)

"That was for the Imitation Challenge," barked Chef Parker, "it was in the recipe. Today you needed to add iceberg lettuce."

"He is right about the Mughals, though," said Chef Bowen, goaded into rescinding yesterday's disingenuous ignorance of classic vegetarian dishes in today's defense of the Indian royal house. Or, according to America, falling herself under the magic of Paul doing Paul.

"I like the kale," she concluded.

Chef Bowen had a soul, though. Chef Parker did not, and his opinion was definitive and terse and unchanging.

"The challenge was iceberg lettuce."

A momentary tension gripped the contestants, as always, over what tragedy might result from Paul's deliberate rule breaking. His days were numbered, everybody knew that, and then starvation would pick them off one by one. Ashley went up next, however, and tried to sell a risotto that substituted mushrooms that "looked like lettuce" for lettuce. A collective sigh of relief passed over the cool kids. Especially with Chloe's whispered reminder of "yesterday's peas!" that only a confused, nomadic person on a ship actively engaged in piracy would claim as their own.

Tension in the room reignited and bubbled even higher, though, when both of Season 14's culinary rock stars, Oliver and Fran, underperformed even Ashley. The unthinkable became increasingly possible, that one – or both – would go home.

Oliver proved Week 1 his brain could adapt to a fish-free menu, and he loved him some iceberg lettuce, but he revolted at being asked to make a meal of his own devisement without any animal protein. He spent the bulk of the challenge with his arms folded in protest before throwing together a dish of creamed spinach and mashed lima beans plated using silicone, fish-shaped molds and served in lettuce cups. As if that made them something.

Chef Parker's side-eye at Oliver's "vegetables under the sea" platter led Fran herself to fall against Chloe's shoulder saying,

"Too soon! Too soon!"

No one, of course, realized Oliver also had secret immunity. If he plated empty ring molds, in lettuce cups, some variation on "well, at least he..." would squeak him past the danger of elimination until the fishing challenge, still another two weeks out.

 Fran full-on panicked her way through the battle with her nemesis color. And lost decidedly. A hushed silence fell over the contestants as they watched her walk up to Judge's Table with a plate of all brown food, with lettuce cups, weaving a little on the way hoping someone would accidentally knock the dish out of her hand. The boom mike operator had too much experience to be dragged in as a co-conspirator, but as Fran passed Ajiz's station, she just mistimed a collision with his Poppin' John post-cook routine. It was then she knew, as did the judges who saw enough during walk-through, her last hope was gone.

After three weeks in the cool kids club, however, Fran should have trusted that a fellow member could do the robot and still notice a friend in obvious need of encouragement. She was two steps past Ajiz's outstretched arm when he whispered those now-famous words,

"*Pssst*, Fran! Paul's making fried chicken for dinner. It's his mother's recipe."

Everyone in the warehouse kitchen, and later the fans at home, saw Fran's spine stiffen and chin rise as she received that intel. And how with that as her only carrot, she fought on to vegetable victory. "Conviction like Fran" and "walking up with Fran-level conviction about your food" became competition watchwords for the rest of Season 14, and likely would be for all seasons to come.

Chef Matteo started off that landmark critique by stating the obvious.

"Fran, I don't see anything green about this plate."

"The green is in the essence," she replied with an aggressive, unblinking stare.

"Butter is not essentially green," Chef Bowen gently demurred, trying to walk the line between honesty and not kicking someone who already failed to get themselves tripped, "and it isn't actually a food."

"Butter is a grass byproduct, I don't know what is more green than butter," Fran calmly and brazenly insisted, "but for this dish, the focus is on vegetable oil. Frying vegetables using vegetables, I think, embraces the essence of the challenge without being too literal. You can see, also, how I made iceberg lettuce the star of the plate."

That part was true.

Neither Al's camera, nor the personal and/or public social media accounts of the judges established whether any of them agreed with Fran, beyond this new perspective on vegetarian cuisine having zero impact on Gaia's menu. Anti-Fran fans insisted, however, that three out of the four panelists just pretended she had a point, until the dish Troy carried up next greatly lessened their need to try.

Poor Troy. A plumber trained to make logistical decisions in dark, cramped spaces and often in the presence of spiders, his brilliant, can-do mind could hear a competition twist and make it work at lightning speed. Last week, after the announcement that contestants could no longer use spoons halfway through his transformation of Pluck!'s signature dish into his own Duck Duck Chicken Soup, he invented the Troy spork that some contestants still used as their go-to implement. Apart from his porterhouse cling film fiasco, which he and Janiva were still investigating, the man delivered. Until that one day in Week 3, when he listened to the wrong people telling him he needed to get "creative". Everyone thought the giant stopwatch in the sky would get him, someday, but not gourds. Not their Troy.

"Troy...? What...?" was all Chef Matteo said, standing before his dish, but that was more than enough. Oliver's head shake alone, tinged with relief as it was for his own competition journey, summed it up for those in the kitchen and with the audience at home.

"I know," Troy replied. Because he did.

"Shouldn't we leave all things curcurbi to Travis?" added the snarky red devil. "He's the expert. You're a plumber."

"I know. Spaghetti squash. I just thought it was the right vehicle for gazpacho."

"It wasn't a gluten-free challenge."

"I was mistaken. I see that now."

"It was his time" was the commonly said but thoroughly unsatisfactory explanation for Troy's decision to abandon his popular coleslaw medleys, and eclipse Fran and Oliver's race to the bottom with a gourd soup with iceberg chiffonade. Some thought he should get points for his knife work, and for not serving his soup in lettuce cups, but then, they weren't the ones who had to try the dish.

"Troy and gourds," whispered Janiva to Paul, as Troy collected his bowl and returned to his station, "who let that happen?"

"We failed him," Paul agreed. "He nailed the Jake Sexy, though."

It was the shakeup of the season. Was it sabotage? Troy never would say, not even during the reunion show. Possibly because it wasn't covered during his "where are they now" segment. Felix's advice that the white-collar version of his job paid eight times more than food, and came with dental and without arachnids, sent Troy back to school, and the editors thought that made a much better human-interest storyline than going deep on "why gourd?". Also, as a weekend rugby player, Troy took being piled on by the judges less traumatically than the others, so he didn't go on and on about it and work the information into all non-related interview segments. Unlike some people.

During the elimination segment, however, the mysterious and tragic fail of Troy was summed up for the audience at home by clips of Chloe openly wiping away tears as she watched his chances of a *Yes, Chef!* title die with Chef Matteo's first bite. Not, as she explained during her own interview segment, that she was voting against Fran, or Felix's great career advice, just Troy missing dinner. Anyone who understood applesauce...missing fried chicken...and someone who spent the bulk of his working life contending with darkness and spiders and scrumming, whatever that was, with mean people in striped shirts, the whole thing was just tragic...*sniff*...and hard to accept.

The Judge's Deliberation over whether to eliminate Fran or Troy grew over time to an Adam and Emily level conflict with the general public. It nearly broke the Internet the night the show aired. It was unlikely that Chef Bowen could distinguish between the crime of Fran's tempura'd potatoes on lettuce ("we know these are tater tots, right?" Chef Juan asked his fellow judges off camera, "we can at least admit that among ourselves, right?") and Troy's unwise foray into chilled soup, but the other judges openly credited Fran's strong defense as assisting them in making a (foregone) conclusion. That there was the winning spirit.

So, in the end, Fran did indeed hold on until dinner and the spiritually reviving moment that was Paul's (mother's) fried chicken, as she, too, discovered that Chloe was right. Being nice to other people during the competition really did pay off in wholly unexpected ways.

DURING THE FOLLOWING QUIET EVENING spent listening to Paul stir and brown and bang in their home kitchen while Fran caught them up on the latest show rumors, the cool kids reflected on such a hard, conflicted day. Aaron had been a sad loss, but Troy going home felt like the competition was starting to get real. It certainly didn't help that Paul let someone else do the mashed potatoes that night.

"Who made this starch product?" Chloe whispered to him, after two or three bites could not ease the pain of losing her Troy.

"Ajiz helped out," Paul whispered back. "I think he came into the kitchen about when Fran reported she "happened" to hear Rachel discussing a supply of kettles. There must be a Pioneer or Western week coming up."

"Wow, that woman, if I don't hear it from her, I just don't know. Anyway, back to our more pressing tragedy," Chloe grumbled, lowering her voice further and looking meaningfully down at her plate, "let's cut that experiment off at its knees."

"*Shhhh.* He made them just the same. Everything is in there. I watched him do it."

"It is not the same, it is entirely different, and therefore wrong. Why do you let people touch things? You know we don't like it."

Paul laughed, part gratified, part disbelieving.

"It's a lot of work on my own, you know. Notice the number of people sitting at this table."

"I can't help it if we love you best, Paul."

"Well, you're wasting the best parts of my effort," he said, as he speared the half-eaten and abandoned chicken leg off her plate.

"*Ugh*, dark meat, have at it. I'll finish the rest of your corn muffin, though."

Chloe continued to pick at the potatoes with uncharacteristic dejection, however, prompting Oliver to add his own reassurance from down the other end of the table.

"Troy'll be alright without us," he claimed.

"Will he?" she asked, making a series of clinking sounds as she stabbed her plate with her fork. "Out there, alone, with the spiders and never no Paul's (mother's) short ribs to come home to? What if he hears a ticking sound above him and Fran isn't there to tell him to trust his still small voice? Everybody knows rugby fans riot for no reason, that sounds dangerous."

Suddenly, a voice piped up from the common room to weigh in on Choe's distress.

"You have a crush on Troy, don't you, Chloe?"

"Don't be creepy about my little brother from another mother, Jake," Chloe yelled back. Jake rarely availed himself of the open invitation to dine with them, but they often found him lurking on the periphery of any gathering, ready to make fun of people.

"It was you, wasn't it, telling him to abandon his slaw," she added with deep suspicion. Well, for Chloe.

He pretended he couldn't find the TV remote, and did not answer.

"You bettah not let me catch you," she warned. "Don't forget, Troy has martial arts training. He knows how to kick someone in the shins only just so hard. I don't."

She turned back to the others around the table.

"What if our Troy thinks we don't miss him, or are glad he went home? I know somebody has to, and I was amazed and happy your conviction saved the day, Fran, but..."

"He won't. He'll understand," said Fran. "Rachel promised to give him the Tupperware of leftover frozen meatloaf. He knows we were saving that for an emergency. Trust the meatloaf."

"I suppose. But if I find out for sure whoever told him to go for the gourd, they'll be sorry."

She directed another meaningful glare towards the common room.

"Chloe...what are you gonna do?" asked Paul with concern, hearing a new, uncharacteristic note of dark determination in her voice. He moved a fresh, preemptive drumstick onto her plate.

"Just you wait," she replied. "I'll tell you when it happens. People thinkin' they can be mean to my Troy and get away with it, oh, they'll see. Where's my camera? I'm goin' to go do an interview segment."

She pushed back her chair and stalked down the hall towards the interview booth set up in the library, without even taking her chicken. Glancing around at the table with alarm, Paul asked,

"She wouldn't really sabotage anyone...Fran? Would she? I know the competition is getting to everyone, but...is even Chloe going to crack?"

Fran shrugged.

"Maybe? I guess we'll find out. She's really mad Troy went home before his birthday next week. If he doesn't get cream cheese frosting on his cake out there, oh, heads will roll."

"Gourd soup," Janiva said with her even-keel sympathy about the entire incident, "how did we let that happen?"

CHAPTER TWENTY-SIX

licorice
choo choos

By the opening of Wagons and Trains! Week, most remaining contestants understood how the twists and constraints of the individual challenges worked, and snafus in the kitchen were becoming less dramatic and more on-brand. Ajiz was gonna sing more than he stirred, Felix drop flour all over the floor, and Janiva waste valuable cook time staking out her heat source watching for saboteurs, it was how they rolled. This settling-in period might, maybe, be why Episode 13 was agreed to be the most boring of the season. What with the reintroduction of animal products, and Chef Parker's evil genius taking a week off to recharge and refocus, assembling nineteen versions of Clementine's Table's signature Prairie Schooner was a snooze-fest. America loves Chef Joe, and he can call his dish what he likes, but The Schooner was still just glorified beef stew, and Jake made one of those in his sleep Week 1. This was Week 4.

Ashley did try to work up some camera time excitement by dropping her Imitation recipe into a pot of boiling water, but everyone knew she wasn't going to read it anyway. Despite how much noise she made fishing it out, or how many implements it took, no one paid much attention. Not even Vivian, who might have been splashed. Al the cameraman kept an eye out, but even that drama never materialized.

The boredom even calmed Chloe's ire over the Gourd Incident into an occasional low, mournful, "I miss my Troy" whenever his hack expertise was especially missed. Chef Joe was a fan of "authentic" cooking techniques, probably because otherwise even he would have to admit the Prairie Schooner was just beef stew, and the cool kids knew Troy would have had an easy workaround for being forced to grind their own corn for the polenta side.

Even the twist during the next day's Reinvention Challenge that dishes had to be made entirely in one kettle and served over a can of chafing fuel created no buzz or grumblings or accidents worth filming, almost as if the contestants saw that coming days ago. Chloe taking four unnecessary jabbing clicks to light her fuel can, and her seemingly random references to "people getting hit by lightning" and "won't they know, then" did raise a few eyebrows and cause Al to linger near her station an extra four minutes, but she seemed content to rely on divine forces and not her own active participation in the zapping process. For now.

The unexpected settings and team dynamics of an off-site Group Challenge, however, could still undermine simple dishes and basic kitchen techniques in spectacular ways. Just when the crew thought two extra cases of Red Bull would be required to survive Chef Joe's tenure, Wagon! Week rolled right over Chloe in one moment of distraction.

America's beloved Chef Joe brought the contestants to work the galley of a mining excursion train, which he thought sounded fun, at least when described by Chef Parker. Ten minutes into his Group Challenge, he became thoroughly unbeloved by eighteen people, their family, and their more partisan fans. The cramped quarters and cooking on a serious incline led to more than one reference to the early days of Hollywood when undesirables were simply tied to railroad tracks and left to their fate.

The crew hoped for a similar outcome. They found it hard to see or film in the semidarkness, other than creating the impression of too many arms and heads and knives crammed into such a small space. They did capture some artistic footage of contestants doing vague tasks in bright yellow safety helmets, but those weren't really "action shots".

Alas for Chloe, the most spectacular cause of the Blue Team's grumblings. It was her misfortune to be holding a full spice jar of fennel just as the train entered an unlit portion of tunnel. Startled by the sudden darkness, her arm jerked up and sideways with the rocking car, and a cloud of grey-green dust settled over what was meant to be a lightly scented chicken.

Travis, her partner in the galley, turned surprisingly grim at her moment of carelessness. While the crew rushed in, risking contaminating their black clothes to capture the cloud backlit by the string of tunnel lights outside the train windows, he stepped out onto the coupling to brush off his shirt and jeans and give his head a quick, rough scrub. Removing some portion of anise smell from his person did help reset his normal working affect. A little. Re-entering the train car, he left his pulled pork safely in the warming drawer for an additional three minutes to help Chloe scrape the extra spice off her chicken and re-plate the dish, and they were both able to finish on time despite the interruption.

Chloe tried to be philosophical about her bad luck and worse timing.

"Inclines, they're just not my friend," she told him as they shuffled down the corridor to the passenger car. "Whaddya gonna do? Thanks for your help in there, Linus, and I'm sorry I ruined black Twizzlers for you."

He just looked at her narrowly and said nothing.

"Do you want me to be in charge of strawberries tomorrow morning to make it up to you?" she asked.

"No!"

"Don't worry about it," he added with less vehemence, "it was just unfortunate we got assigned that stretch of tunnel."

All their scraping and dusting, however, didn't much help Chloe's dish. Perhaps it was the dim lighting, but at least the mouthful that made it onto Chef Parker's fork was a licorice chicken only a Dane could love. Some people tried to cause problems at Judge's Table, and later back at the house, suggesting Travis purposely ignored the obvious because he was still mad about his hair, but Chloe guessed that theory originated, as all such things did, with Echo, the two-headed snake. She didn't believe it.

"He's a pumpkin farmer. No matter how crazy the competition gets, he isn't going to turn into *Children of the Corn*. Just because we were in hell, doesn't mean it froze over."

No one delivered an unqualified success that day, but Fran's food was particularly suited to fast casual eaten in a plume of coal smoke in the heart of darkness. She brought the Red Team to victory with a credible Miner 49'ers Chili and (almost Paul's, commercially ground) Cornbread, and was looking forward to the reward. Chef Joe announced he was taking the winners prospecting for gold, and with any luck, Fran planned to augment her future prize money with an advance.

"I'm so proud of you," Chloe told her, putting her own missteps in the dark behind her after their dismissal. "I think this is the beginning of great things for you. You beat out Vivian, and that's really great things beginning right there."

"Do you think she will try to run me over with the van?" Fran asked, pushing open the glass door of the mine's visitor center, and holding it open for Chloe.

"Thanks," said Chloe, following her out into the parking lot. "Where would she get the keys?"

"It's Vivian."

"You are so right, Fran, eyes open. I wouldn't drink anything she casually hands you, that's for sure.

"Communal food only."

"Look alive, stay alive. It will take her at least until the semifinals to work up a tolerance to arsenic, if she goes with a Dorothy Sayers with the punchbowl kinda way thing."

"Unless she started already."

"I so wish we were kidding."

The two paused at the curb of the drop-off zone and looked around for where the grey vans might be parked.

"I think they were over there," said Fran pointing off to the left. "Section C. Isn't that Ashley heading out?"

"Following Vivian's lieutenant into the forest, what could go wrong?"

"That's just a line of maple trees. The forest doesn't start for another hundred feet. We should be fine. Maybe."

The two women strolled down the long line of parked cars following Ashley, slowing their steps so they wouldn't actually catch up with her.

"And, speaking of walking off a cliff, or into traffic, or falling into a snake pit by accident...," Chloe began.

"Oh God, what happened? Did Travis flip out when you dumped a whole jar of fennel on his head? Is it a secret, Scandinavian street drug? Did he pull a "Juan" on you in that dark and tight space?"

"Close, but wrong guy. Juan pulled a Juan and invited to take me back today in his car. You know, so I don't have to listen to Oliver sing Grand Funk Railroad from hell until breakfast. Apparently, our Juan knows a quiet place with good food that would cheer me right up. Since I am currently coated in fennel dust, I sense an intermediary step in that process."

"Oh...my...God."

"I know. Thank you, Jesus, Linus prepared me for this Week 1. I tell ya, if we get lost out there in the trees, I might be okay with that. And out there is bears. Without Linus, do you realize I might have got into a car with a wolf? My brain is so shook up from being bounced around on that train all day, I might have thought Juan was being nice. I might have been that girl."

"The man has skills. He probably had a plan ready for today, and just adapted it to circumstances. A contestant who spent all day in a coal mine...lot of opening there without the fennel."

Chloe stopped to stare up at the sky and shake her head over the trap she almost plummeted down into. Fran continued,

"So, how did you get out it? Have you gotten out of it?"

"I told him all that anise flavor was like getting clove'd when you have your wisdom teeth out, and that I was going home and doing a juice cleanse."

"What???"

"I panicked, Fran. If I was still holding my cast iron skillet, I might have banged him over the head. Please get me out of this 1920's Hollywood talkie. Please, somebody save me. Somebody not Juan."

"Well, perhaps you should consider having your fellow galley slave stand between you and a really bad TV moment."

"Do I want to know what you are talking about, Fran?"

"Travis. Think about it. I think he likes you.

"*Nooooo*, I think he likes how comfortable he is around me as a woman, but that isn't the same thing. I like him just the way he is, and that makes him feel confident."

"Isn't that everything?"

"*Nooooo*. I like him just the way he is, a man I am not sleeping with. I be the buddy, the nice person boosting his confidence, not the *femme fatale* sweeping in for her man."

"Maybe it's time to sweep? What can go wrong? This is just me, but big picture, getting involved with a nice guy never goes wrong, and hey, somebody should like him, his shoulders are amazing. It's like using up left-over heavy cream, you never want to waste that."

"It's all for you, Fran, really."

Both women suddenly stopped in the tracks and watched their "Ashley" get into red Ford 150 and drive off.

"At least we didn't catch up with her," said Chloe, "weird strangers reeking of anise, she might have run us over, too."

"Oh look, there's everybody," she said waving to Ajiz, as they caught sight of the heads and shoulders of a group of contestants off to the left in section D.

"Listen, Chloe," Fran continued, squeezing between a black SUV and a little Chevy Cobalt to get to the correct aisle, "stop trying to dodge. Travis likes you not me, and I say, go for it. In my experience – and you know I work in HR, what haven't I seen? – no matter the wrong, or embarrassing, or just a lame plot twist that divides you forever from a nice guy, every nice guy story ends with a "but he was such a nice guy". That makes it a risk worth taking, even here. Versus no matter how fabu a good time you have dashing off to Paris with a bad boy that story always ends with "I wish had never met you", and if you're never going to think of someone again, it's best to not have thought about them in the first place. Especially when it requires transferring departments. Oh, the paperwork. Honestly."

"I completely trust your HR skills and abilities, Fran, but I'm still not going for the Great Pumpkin," Chloe whispered as they finally reached the waiting vans. "Unlike Paul telling us twelve times he plans to have a burger for dinner when we all know he's gonna eat whatever Oliver smuggled back from the Whole Foods seafood counter, I have already not chosen Linus."

boot camp takes to the hills

Back at their own workstations in the warehouse kitchen, with all the elbow room to elbow people and none of the provocation of coal smoke and semidarkness, the contestants stared with dismay at the whole sturgeon that lay on each of their benches, brought to them by the owner of Big Sky's Riverwalk Café. It was an ominous start to Gone Fishin'! Week.

"What are we supposed to do with this?" Janiva asked the room at large.

"Run?"

"Pray?"

"Who does this to a roomful of amateurs holding giant cleavers?"

"Shouldn't this be a walleye?" complained Oliver. "Why do Montanans need to be an ass about invasive species? And what's with the dinosaur theme this year?"

Even Paul was unexpectedly grumpy, and he rarely cared what other people thought he should cook, even during Imitation Challenges.

"I told you, Chloe, we should have watched *Jurassic Park 3* last night," he said, "but *nooooo*, you wanted to watch *Vincenzo*."

"You're upset I made you watch Song Soong-ki properly attired in an Italian vineyard? Are we having that conversation? These dinosaurs are dead, man, no one calls Jeff Goldblum to supervise a postmortem. See the bigger picture."

"Then who mocked Chef Joe's beef stew during their interview segment?"

he grumbled back, staring over at Ajiz. "I thought we agreed not to point out the simple challenges? Now they've over-compensated."

"It wasn't me. It was Vivian," Ajiz protested.

"Ashley," Fran corrected in a whisper. "Vivian pretended she would, out loud, and little Miss Echo took her seriously."

"Yeah, well," continued Paul, "I bet it means they are taking us out to hunt for the Rocky Mountain Loch Ness for the Group Challenge. You wait."

Fish expert Oliver had a gloomier outlook.

"It's probably a lamprey eel hatchery. Lampreys eat people."

"Well, you got me there, Paul," conceded Chloe. "Unless eels can be fended off with hockey sticks, even Taec-yeon can't help us with this one. But don't think I am not still waiting for you to apologize. Soong-ki, in a landscape, in a suit, if that doesn't work for you, I don't even know who you are anymore."

Highly sensitive to tension among the ranks and drawing a blank on any musical reference involving K-drama, dinosaurs, or giant fish to reset the mood, Ajiz jumped in with a question to Fran instead.

"Hey, isn't Chloe always mumbling something before she cooks? It's a miracle after the Fennel Moment she's still here, maybe it will work for us. Hey Chloe!"

"Yeah?" she responded, looking around to find the section of benches calling out to her.

"What is it you always say when you start?"

"Start what? When?"

"When you start the cook."

"Nothing."

"Yes, you do."

"*Uhhh*...Oh! God, help me to express your will through my work. It gets my head in the game."

"Does that apply to forty-foot sturgeon?"

Thwunk! was heard from Chloe's station followed by a "ha ha *haaaaa*." Craning their necks, the others saw she successfully chopped the head off her fish and was giving herself a small celebratory fist pump with the hand not holding the giant cleaver.

"Apparently, it does," responded Janiva.

Fran was more skeptical.

"Shouldn't we ask Oliver for guidance before relying entirely on divine intervention for today's survival in the competition?"

"No, we can't waste it," said Ajiz. "It's Gone Fishin'! Week. Out there, wherever there ends up being, he'll be our only hope of making it back alive. There's killer lampreys on the loose."

"So right. Well, here goes nothing. You start."

Thwunk!

Thwunk.

Thwink...

"...*Ohhhh*, rats! Chloe!!!"

"What? If you don't know only God can save us from a prehistoric whale, Fran, I can't help you."

"Have you really survived this long on magic?"

"Magic is holding my breath hoping this mammoth interloper turns into a pesto. My way is to leave room for the universe to say back "actually, what would be most helpful in the situation is for you to put up a well-cooked sturgeon, allow Me to guide you". We all know I don't listen to anyone, but it can't hurt to start off a project pretending I might. That's all I'm saying."

"Plus, the thing started out four feet long. What, your chop was so bad you can't get six servings out of what's left? Ask again, start again, see what you come up with."

While Fran reassessed her badly hacked fish in a low, crotchety mumble, behind Chloe's station, Paul continued their earlier argument in a low, crotchety mumble.

"What do you have against Jeff Goldblum?"

Chloe continued to break down her fish carcass according to Big Sky guidelines. Calling back over her shoulder between hacks, she said,

"It's a both/and problem, Paul. Can Mr. Goldblum assist us against a swarm of eels? Maybe, he's a talented man. If something is going to flash before my eyes before I die, though, I'm just sayin', I would rather my handsome stranger be wearing a subtle pinstripe than Jeff, still sexy at seventy. But that's me. You do you. And now, I'm gonna go wrap a dinosaur in wheat and goat cheese, because apparently, somebody thinks that's a good idea."

"It isn't," Paul said with an unnecessary chop that took off a fin.

"Is this your Waterloo, Paul? The challenge you go full rebel, put up a pan-fried, largemouth bass, and tell Chef Cooper to eff off?"

"Maybe," he said, clipping another fin. "Except Oliver is right, as always, it ought to be perch."

Chloe put down her cleaver for a moment to better face down this crisis.

"Have you ever had sturgeon *en croûte*?"

"No. No one should."

"*Hrmmm*. Well...why don't you see this as a teaching moment? For them. Show them that even Paul can't make a bottom-dweller do the right thing, not with this recipe, and help guide them into finding better ways to use up this much product. Today is the "before", the Jake Sexy. The Reinvention Challenge will be the "after", the right way, the Paul Standard. If you don't give them your best "before", how will they learn? Maybe in their heart of hearts they think if they just tried a little harder, they can make this dish work."

"They can't. It shouldn't be done."

"You're right, of course you're right, but the only way to snap them out of it is for you to make one. Just one. Just this one time. If they don't change their ways after eating your Reinvention dish...well, you'll know you've done everything you could. It's an invasive species that grows to the size of an alligator, they must be getting desperate out there in the back beyond Yellowstone. Show them a better way forward, Paul."

Paul stopped chipping away at the edges of his sturgeon trying to make it symmetrical since he couldn't make it disappear.

"Alright. Just this once. But I am putting my side of the story into my interview segment, so the audience at home understands why I am doing this."

"Great idea. Educate the masses on what to order at a fishing lodge. That's advocacy, that's what that is."

"Do you need more parchment?" she asked, holding out her industrial sized roll.

He checked the stock on his bench.

"No, I am good, thanks."

"Go team!"

Chloe returned to her dish. Hearing an authoritative thwunk! shortly thereafter and turning to see Felix absentmindedly wipe a trace of sturgeon splatter off the back of his neck before settling into his crimping technique, she knew the crisis had passed.

After repeated assurances from Rachel the PA that they were trout fishing not killer eel hunting for the Group Challenge, the contestants who survived the dinosaurs started to look forward to their next off-site adventure. They weren't near any body of water large enough to involve charter boats, or weather, so they imagined a placid day spent at an alpine lake, floating around on various skiffs, channeling their inner *On Golden Pond*. Maybe they'd learn to toast fish on sticks over a campfire. When the vans left the house at dawn and traveled higher and higher into the mountains, too high for a simple day trip, their Henry Fonda fantasy just expanded to include a few days in a lodge by the lake. Those in the second van spent many miles wondering if this lodge had a hot spring.

Where they were taken was up into the heart of Rocky Mountain National Park to Fern Lake. Well, near Fern Lake. Access to the actual water required a hike of 3.6 miles, uphill, according to the brown Park Service arrows. Walking the trail, Fran suggested the rangers made a rounding error and it was actually 9.2 miles. In Vivian's opinion, it just felt good to have a proper workout, prompting her Echo to lie and compare the climb to an easy 5k run. Yet still Janiva didn't trip her for it, even when she had the chance at around mile marker 2.4. As a reward for her restraint, her team gave her the last energy bar when they stopped at the lookout rest area near the summit.

The hike reminded Chloe of Seoul with more greenery and less chance of backtracking or getting turned around. To be absolutely certain she only took on the Department of Interior's recommended daily allowance of hill, she toiled her way up behind Travis, watching his feet as he picked out the easier path, and set a slow and steady pace. She became very familiar with the scuffed tree logo on his worn hiking boots, and somewhere between mile 37 and 48 – Chloe thought it best not to be too informed during the "not there yet" phase of the adventure – realized he had a deep scratch on the inner side of his right heel. She also tried to take in the vast cathedral of trees, the scent of warm pine, and be a team player and keep an eye out for bears, but mostly she followed Travis' boots up and up and up.

Adding to Chloe's lassitude, after the mining catastrophe her team picked her last for the upcoming challenge. Whenever cooking in the warehouse littered with kitchen stools and lounge chairs, she maintained the general, early impression of her as a steady performer without the expertise of a Fran or Travis, or Vivian's gamesmanship or, of course, Paul's soul for food. Off-site, though, not so much. Everyone noticed that in the field she lacked "focus" and the 125% effort needed from a teammate, and viewed her as the nicer, unluckier version of desultory Jake. It appeared no one on set yet realized that Jake was making a choice, while she was making the best of a bad decision.

She had thought completing each challenge would help her, bit by bit, gain strength. She thought wrong. Every week she felt physically weaker and more tired. Exacerbating the situation, apparently nowhere in Colorado was on the level. When the excursion train suddenly plunged into darkness, for a moment, a tiny moment, the shock added to the heat and overexertion caused her heart to give out. It came back on, but it took a moment, and as usually happened during an "episode", her fingers temporarily lost their grip. In such a small space, rocketing down an incline, dropping a spice jar had an out-sized impact on her dish and standing in the competition.

Even with this unexpected window of quiet time, though, she still couldn't think of any better strategy or adaptation other than pushing through on sheer willpower. With a sigh, Chloe fixed her eyes back on the boots made for walking and trudged on.

Unbeknownst to Chloe, the incident that startled her startled Travis more. The lights came up in time for him to see her change color from red to white to blue. In a flash, he understood the discordance between her serious mind and her bright, silly misdirections. This was how she dealt with living under the shadow of death, and the word salad and non sequiturs was her way of whistling in the dark.

He retreated out onto the coupling to de-anise because it was the pragmatic, right decision, but also to prevent Chloe from teetering out there herself and falling off the train. Coming back into the galley, he continued to block the exit until she forgot about her own personal hygiene and returned her focus to her dish. Silently, he helped assess and mitigate the damage from a small cloud of errant spice, while he tracked her pallor and steadiness, and evaluated what it meant. Her dish was the least thing affected. What with the rocking of the train, her honed ability to control her body even through a syncope, and his own broad shoulders protecting the plates, the accident hadn't done much damage.

His sudden, radical departure from the ancestral wisdom teachings of America's number one jack o' lantern producer, though...Yeah, that had an impact. Perhaps weeks of exposure to the shenanigans of his roommate, Jake, finally rubbed off in his sleep. One second he was holding the near-empty spice jar and watching the servers' unsteady progress down the corridor to collect their plates, and the next, almost on autopilot, he dumped a new layer of fennel on Chloe's chicken. If Owen the Roadie hadn't collided with the narrow galley door frame as the train rounded a bend during his handoff, Chloe would have gone home. Even competing against two missing pork chops and one-third of Owen's intended serving of grilled artichokes, the judges' decision could have gone either way. Moving forward, no one expected her to long survive Chef Parker's ire after the food he normally found reliable as a favorite sweatshirt lulled him into a fatal complacency at Judges Table, an added reason they picked her last for the team challenge.

Silently hiking the long road to Fern Lake, Travis still wasn't sure he regretted his knee-jerk foray into sabotage. Except that it hadn't worked. Also, that savvier competitors knew it required his own action or inaction for such a glaring error to make it to the pass, and so would his grandfather. Chloe herself refused to believe it. Would that change once seconded by a patriarch during a "friends and family" interview segment? Should he tell her first? Would she give him his name back if he did? Travis didn't know what consequences might yet lay ahead regarding his past act, but listening to her stumbling and lagging footsteps following his, mile after mile up the mountain, he was already wracking his brains for what he could try next.

the landslide

The contestants spent several hours toiling through a dense forest of tall, spindly aspen, ponderosa pine and Engelmann spruce. The trail finally reached a large, greenish blue alpine lake framed by three summits of the mountain range, with each of their tree lines giving way to grey, rocky crags. In twos and threes, the teams debouched onto a pebbly beach and looked around for their skiffs. The PA's, still wearing their black clothes now augmented with lug-soled motorcycle boots, directed them instead to a pile of waders and to the stream that fed the lake. They instructed the contestants they weren't just fishing, but fly fishing to source their protein.

Chloe found she didn't care for the sport. It required standing in glacial mountain waters and involved a lot more arm waving than regular fishing. Nor was she very good at it, even after a whole afternoon learning how eddies worked, and how to flick a very long stick at them.

"That's not a pool, it's a rock," Oliver counseled, pausing by her section of riverbank. "You'll have more luck finding something moving by aiming your line at something moving."

Oliver spent most of the assignment shuttling between clusters of flailing amateurs, teaching them how to get their fly on and get busy. He didn't land everyone's fish, but was usually nearby when it happened. Sharing his expertise and personal fish magnetism with the contestants was especially kind because he did it before the producers demanded he do so as payback for overlooking his "vegetables under the sea" debacle, and without his assistance, no one else would have caught anything. Even Travis, and Travis never out and out failed any task. Oliver still caught the most fish, despite having his line in the water a fraction of the time everyone else did, but it could have been an embarrassing blowout victory.

After achieving the objective to source their protein for the challenge, the contestants were ready for the hot springs. Once again, their hopes were dashed. Having survived the day imagining some rustic cabins located further along the trail, they were directed towards the nearby camping area. The team who caught the most fish, or as the rules adjusted to ground conditions, caught anything the soonest, that team won the glamping version. The losers were shoved into the adventure-hiker setups. Chloe would have preferred a tent with headroom, and a cot, but it was exactly the level of camping she did at home, except with a much nicer sleeping bag. There was the added consolation of fireflies in the meadow, and the night sky visible through the roof vent was awe-inspiring. If only it wasn't all so incredibly labor intensive, the whole preindustrial, living on the side of a mountain thing, the Gone Fishin'! field trip might have been fun.

As they gathered around the campfire that night, the day's star and superhero was given the spotlight. He told them stories of harrowing nights at sea out catching "real fish" and shared his food dream – to open a kitchen side to his family's fish empire. His niche idea was to prep and serve whatever the tourists brought back from their charter fishing trips. The contestants thought it was a great add-on service, having just come off a hard day's work themselves, and turned their campfire chat into an impromptu focus group.

Some debated rustic candlelight dinners versus a more pirate-y campfire meal. Others suggested he should offer his guests a fancy dinner to refresh their weary souls.

"No, he shouldn't," said Travis, who had seen years of city folk exhausted by picking out a pumpkin. "Do you want to worry over two forks and three knives tonight, or do you just want to be fed?"

"*Touché*, big guy," said Paul.

Vivian and Ashley agreed that for their money they would expect him to use his considerable talent to transform any sad flounders or undersized blues into lobster, which sounded wasteful to Oliver and a lot like cheating.

"You don't fish for lobsters," he corrected them in a tone that echoed the crackling and popping of the campfire. "You buy them at our lobster shack. And pay for them."

The liveliest discussion centered around how much they would pay him to oversee all things fish moving forward in the competition. Those still gainfully employed and on leave from their jobs, like Fran and Paul, started the bid with cash.

"Five grand, easy money," offered Paul.

"Twenty-five percent of the take," countered Felix, who gambled it all to quit his job.

Jake, still employed, but not by someone who offered weeks and weeks of paid leave to persons planning to immediately quit on return, staked twenty percent of the finale pot.

"But I'll actually pay out," he said, "unlike the unemployed kid."

Neither the show lore or annals or video evidence ever did reveal whether any negotiation started under cover of darkness continued off-mountain, but the eventual winner of Season 14 didn't know nothing about fish, nor care, and they did survive the Week 8 fish fry, so...

That night, however, Oliver's buddies became increasingly unhappy to see him gaslighted about what he would get out of doubling his workload, and elbowed Ajiz to break up the bidding war by reminding the contestants what really mattered up there on the mountain. Whether James Taylor's claim, *"there was a young cowboy, who lived on the plains..."* was true, and whether they could believe it, if it helped them to sleep. That led, naturally, into selections from John Denver, David Wilcox, and other obligatory musical numbers to be sung when in the Rocky Mountains at night. Oliver also contributed a sea shanty, which while it didn't go with the mountains, he insisted went with the stars.

Tired of talking fish so far from proper water, he asked Chloe about her own food dream. She gave the group an outline of her condiment line, but unlike his plans, and many others shared as they went around the fire, hers felt vague and unformed. The work would be done sitting down, and was therefore an equally reasonable dream as Fran's café which wouldn't even be serving greens cooked in bacon fat, but given her performance thus far, she remained doubtful whether her food was worthy enough to have its own labels. She always fulfilled the brief, unlike Paul, but never made a winning dish like Vivian, Fran and Travis now battling it out for first place or know exactly why she survived every recent catastrophe. Perhaps, God forbid, her hope of a food empire was based on Juan's temporary favoritism, rather than the moderate talent needed to produce a solid dish.

Chloe tried cheering herself up by being grateful she lasted long enough in the competition to experience the joy and wonder of Paul's campfire chili – which was totally different than his cooktop chili – so, that there alone was a darn fine reason to climb a mountain and turn around. Wasn't it? Maybe. Of course, he would have made it for them out on the terrace back at the house, if they asked, but now they knew to ask.

She also knew who else to ask for help when down and troubled.

"Ajiz!" she called across the fire. "Can you sing *Landslide* for us?"

"*Ooohhh*, good mountain music," he said with enthusiasm.

"And a good fish song," agreed Oliver, who joined in for the watery parts.

"*...Can I sail thro-ooough the changin' ooo-cean tiiidddeees, can I...han-dle the seasons of my li-i-ffee...*," they crooned.

"*Mmhhh-hmmm, I don't knowwwww...*," Chloe sang back to them.

She, and really everyone, did feel a little better after such a discouraging day in the field and stream knowing that Stevie Nicks understood. And put it in a song that didn't require hauling a guitar to the top of mountain to sound pretty okay sung though the blowing smoke of an inexpert campfire. God bless that gypsy.

The next day, sixteen disheveled and slightly grubby contestants tumbled out of their various tents and lined up on the small beach to tackle the cooking portion of the Gone Fishin'! Group Challenge. The judges instructed them to produce glamping-worthy dishes made over portable, charcoal hibachis to be judged by the paying guests of the outfit supplying the tents. The latter were represented by two families of strangers, augmented with a few hardy friends of the judges staying at the lodge down near the trailhead, and who hiked up to Fern Lake for the day.

By the end of the cook, more contestants than just Chloe missed the lesser aerobic commitment needed to prepare food on a horizontal playing field. And running water. And product to cook with. Oliver led the Red Team to victory, of course, finishing the week with a trifecta of wins, but Ashley surprised everyone with her ability to work an open flame. Her bison chops were both perfectly cooked, and according to Chef Juan, had perfect grill marks. If she hadn't fallen into the producer's trap of resorting to a cooler full of supplemental protein, she might have been a contender. You know, if any of the judges ever tried her food.

As the teams congratulated Oliver, relieved and excited their survival cooking experience was ending and they could turn their charcoal-smeared faces towards home, Rachel the PA started clapping her hands to call them to attention. Instead of distributing advice and water bottles for the descent, she announced they were staying on to film Spice Mountain! Week. Ajiz launched into his Poppin' John happy dance to hear Week 6's theme, but the rest just stopped mentally reviewing all the corners and pockets of their tents where they might have shoved stuff, and started debating the merits of lake water versus mountain stream water in washing off excess carcinogens.

Under the guise of lessening the burden on their gravity showers, Chloe recommitted to skipping any off-hour group hikes and all other wandering about that wasn't directly related to the challenges, and tried to find the bright side. For the Spice Mountain! challenges she would only have to walk from her tent to the beach, and that was a shorter walk than from her workstation in the warehouse to the mini grocery store in the back corner. Maybe she could finally rest up? Sort of? And maybe, if she could get it together and really focus, at all times and under any conditions on the task at hand during this simpler, primitive existence, Week 6 would be her time to shine. Maybe.

CHAPTER TWENTY-NINE

too hot

Up on Spice Mountain!, Chloe found one positive aspect about cooking grubby was that no one noticed how pale or off-color she got. Fran did ask why her lips turned funny, but Chloe told her it was just charcoal and Fran believed her right off. Travis, lurking around their cook station, scowled at that answer. He was a much tidier person, though, and obviously still mad about the train thing.

She and the other contestants were delighted, however, when Rachel announced that for the Group Challenge, they would be cooking indoors again with clean faces, hands and aprons at the Greywater Canyon Lodge. The change of venue also greatly benefited the guest judge. He carried his spice rack up to Fern Lake, grumbling the whole way, to allow the contestants to properly make his Mughlai for the Imitation Challenge. The film crew was even more excited.

Normally when working on location, management and staff worked to stage a few "interactions" in corners and time gaps where they could fit both the film equipment and a contestant wielding sharp objects and getting mad about stuff, hoping the invented combo was interesting and related to the actual events of the episode. The latter part, the reality part, got pieced together by rumor and scrolling through footage for lucky glimpses on various nanny cams. The Greywater kitchen, however, was open and well-lit, and allowed the cameramen to set up the perfect stationary long shot to track any snafus and contretemps when and as they actually developed.

The crew was also pleased when an added twist, one both unexpected and readily understandable to the home viewer, developed within the first hour of taping. One of the Lodge's main, eight-burner cooktops, the one installed originally as a cost-saving factory second that never really worked properly and had been due for replacement six months ago, that one, it went kaput. It was the first time this problem happened during Season 14, and created a fresh, new opportunity for failed teamwork to impact service. It was going to be a great episode.

For most of the contestants, the timing of the new crisis was especially unfortunate. After several challenges using a campfire to sanitize raw protein, the knowledge they were cooking in a four-star lodge put maximum strain on available burners. Only a few lucky contestants were oddly prescient regarding the unexpected deficiencies of a luxury hotel kitchen. Vivian stood ready to adapt or reinvent her dish whether the primary heat source was broken, fixed or missing, almost as if she toured the exact property months ago for a completely unrelated purpose. Jake luckily snagged an early slot in the lineup to minimize the impact of any equipment crunch on him. Their Ashley barreled ahead with her own dish regardless, as usual, but it was a slightly more informed wrongheaded idea. All three then smirked their way through the menu planning process and encouraged their teammates to make as many unfortunate decisions as possible regarding other dishes.

The guest judge for Spice Mountain! Week was, of course, Madabhooshi Rajpayee, that well-known spice master and regular panelist on the network's professional cooking competition, *If You Can't Handle the Heat*. Many home viewers, and most contestants, were also familiar with his flagship restaurant that featured the flavor of the Indian highlands, called with more exactness than creativity, India. He was slumming it to fly in from Atlanta to judge a bunch of amateurs, but he liked hiking and owed Chef Juan a favor.

Vivian's lack of appreciation for spice, Indian food, or foreigners left her no one that week to impress, and with no suspense about the outcome, she used the Group Challenge to take a mini break. She offered to prepare a throwaway ceviche with a cliché spice blend to open the meal for the Blue Team. Even if the judges managed to remember it, or Chef Raj forgave it, the audience at home would never expect it to send her home. It would be both complete, and being a raw preparation, cooked properly, two feats likely impossible for the last few contestants in either lineup.

Ajiz took an entirely different approach. Excited to finally have a guest judge who understood his flavor profiles, and that this meal he could grind spices with a mortar and pestle and not a rock washed in lake water, he made a series of dipping sauces to accompany the Red Team's lamb kebab appetizer plated in individual pinch bowls. The sauces ranged from "mild", which was hot, "medium", which was uncomfortably hot, and "hot", which was unfortunate. The fourth sample his team rejected as "insane", and not to be placed near consumables in case of accident. The judging for this segment was to be conducted during a sit-down, family-style meal, and given the expected distraction of chatter across, down and around the long table, the risk of such a fatal inattention among the select guests was particularly high.

"Word," counseled Chloe, looking up from her yellow pad where she was jotting down the team's dish progressions. "Think of your long-term brand. "Fiery" and "stupid" speak to two very different diner demographics."

"I think Ajiz should do Ajiz," said Jake, offering his minority opinion with a stab at Fran-level conviction. "This is his chance."

Surprised – and suspicious – to hear Jake chime in to support another contestant's food, Travis dissented strongly. For Travis.

"That's bad advice, Ajiz. Don't do it."

Lawyer Paul nodded along with the majority consensus, relieved his teammates had not lost their minds up on the mountain along with his flip flops.

"You want people to eat your food, not dare other people to eat it," he warned.

Ajiz's prudence won out over self-expression, and the squeeze bottle of red insanity was put aside. Not destroyed, however. He sent his less-than dish out second, but still hoped for a surprise, guest judge walk-through where he could demonstrate his full embrace of Scoville.

For the remainder of contestants, their success was tied to actual burners now needing to be shared with the opposing team. When half the available equipment changed from problematic to nonexistent after Ajiz's dish safely made it to the pass, Travis drew up a hasty schedule to go sharesies, and tacitly made the enforcer of it. During any competition squabble, they all had learned to trust Travis to stand there, tall and square, sensible and silent, until the drama brought by the other party burned itself out. Only once had they seen him "get excited" in the kitchen. Back in Week 3, Jake was telling Paul a story Paul wasn't even listening to, and gesticulating with his knife, he nearly stabbed Chloe passing behind him with a tray of durian custard cups. It surprised everyone to see Travis glower and threaten even more than Troy, but it was the exception that proved the rule. His proven, phlegmatic reliability led the long line of waiting contestants to spend their *mise en place* refining rather than readjusting their dishes.

Despite Travis' experience, temperament, and best effort to mitigate the pitfalls, twists and lack of fire and to shepherd his Red Team to victory, however, in that Greywater kitchen, Jake would once again be his undoing.

hot damn

Instead of bringing the heat, Jake brought the sexy to the Spice Mountain! Group Challenge. He prepared a flashy but relatively simple shrimp scampi with an extra two dollops of red pepper flake afterthought. Two weeks in a row Jake's plates received the classic warning trope, "if it's this simple, it better be perfect", but he refused to allow threats or direct comparison with much better chefs to impact his cooking style this far from the semifinals. He met the moment instead by grilling an excessive contingency of backup shrimp while Sheriff Travis was busy out front serving his own dish, and frittered away unchecked as the burner schedule accordioned with every not quite quite crustacean.

Third to last in the lineup, and thanks to Jake, now with sixteen fewer minutes to complete her own dish, Chloe found herself in the weeds and longing for her inexpertly stoked brazier at Fern Lake. After receiving key pointers from Oliver on how to crisp trout skin during the Gone Fishin'! Group Challenge, she had hoped the cutthroats would work for her this time. The Lodge cooler held a generous haul, versus making do with what she (and Oliver) could pull from the river, allowing ample product for error and experimentation to get the cast iron skillet heated to Oliver's expert specification.

The challenge and the guest judge also offered a great opportunity for feedback on the "Marsden Sweet & Sassy" condiment line. Chef Raj owned a line of branded grocery products, and today's plates showcased three of her recipes for his expert assessment. Her *juje* and concept might also redeem her reputation with the cool kids. She completed the bulk of components during *mise en place* without issue in the flat, lit and tricked out kitchen, and they now sat lined up on the small section of counter she commandeered for her prep. The dish only needed the trout to crisp up and come off the grill to be assembled into greatness.

After Jake hogged the burners for all of eternity, however, it would be a near thing if the trout alone, now needing to be made last-minute and in smaller batches, made it to the plate, and without another five minutes on the competition clock, the dish would only be a trout, alone, on a bed of wild rice. Even Jake couldn't sell that to the judges as "minimalist", and "a pure expression of the ecosystem from which the protein came". Although he would probably try. More than once Chef Juan sighed, off-camera, at Chloe's lack of Jake-level verve when presenting dishes the audience at home couldn't actually taste. Standing over the grill station, wishing she risked pan-seared sea scallops, Chloe knew the plates about to go out, combined with an honest, lackluster defense, would both infuriate her teammates and almost certainly send her home.

Unexpectedly, Fran offered to help on the assembly line. That was a competition twist. If Chloe unknowingly caught fire, she liked to believe that Fran might alert her, maybe, but Fran ignored any lesser troubles impacting other people's food production. Fran's dish was last on the menu and also waiting on the burners, though, so perhaps the faster Chloe got out of the way the better. Grateful, whatever the reason, Chloe shoved a sauce boat into one of her hands and a squeeze bottle into the other, pointed to the mock-up dish for reference, and recommitted herself to frying twelve perfect trout.

Holding the two condiments and waiting for Chloe's cutthroats to arrive, her weird flash of generosity baffled Fran, too. The other three-quarters of her mind occupied itself with determining the exact level of char she desired on her game hens. It blocked out altogether Vivian poking around the kitchen with Ashley, making disparaging remarks about other people's food, until she heard her name spoken.

"Hey Fran, can I see that for a moment?" asked Vivian, interrupting Fran's mental rehearsal of when to flip her birds.

"Huh? Oh sure," she replied vaguely and handed over the squeeze bottle pointed at by Vivian. Taking advantage of her momentarily free hand, Fran then turned and added more cream to her mashed potatoes.

"Stop adding fat!" Chloe called out from her cook station.

"I'm trying to make it like Paul's."

"That's a white whale, Fran. And Paul's food doesn't openly try to kill people. Balance!"

"Fat adds flavor. I'm serving it with a lean protein, and it's practically next to three green beans."

"You're a menace with the sides, Fran."

Fran made a face, but put down the wooden spoon, turned around and retrieved Chloe's red sauce.

Handing it over, Vivian asked,

"Are you sure you know where everything goes?"

"Are you kidding? There's the test dish," Fran answered defensively, uncertain why Vivian would care.

"Pour the chutney," she said, holding up the sauce boat, then waving the bottle added, "squeeze the spicy goodness, and Chloe comes behind with the *piece de resistance*, the artichoke relish."

"Well, don't forget to tell the judges you helped her," counseled Vivian, "they should know whom to credit if one of her dishes actually succeeds."

"Nonsense. She made it, I'm just squeezing it."

"If you say so," Vivian said and moved away, opining before she got quite out of earshot, "well, I know I wouldn't pair up those three condiments. We'll see what the judges think."

"She should at least learn how to pan-fry before she tries to get "creative" with her plates," agreed her Echo, making the appropriate air quotes as the two walked off.

"Meow meow meow, King Friday," Fran scoffed at the pair's relentless, on-brand commentary, and went back to rehearsing her hens.

Jake, too, had gotten bored waiting in the Lodge's employee break room with the finished contestants. Possibly, he didn't like all their dirty looks. Like Vivian, he amused himself by poking, spying and prowling about the kitchen without any intention of being useful. Finding a convenient section of counter to lean against, he watched Chloe's trout come off the grill, the rapid and efficient team assembly, and the excited and grateful arm clutch Chloe gave Fran as the servers collected her plates. When Chloe followed her dishes out into the restaurant, he drifted back to the lounge.

"THIS IS MY SWEET & Sassy cutthroats with wild rice," Chloe announced with confidence, standing at the head of the long table and introducing her dish to the judges and guests.

Chef Matteo briefly thanked her and dismissed her to clean up her work area. After waiting for the swing doors to close behind her, the diners began a short discussion about her presentation. Then Chef Juan ate one forkful of her dish. And started coughing. He then took the remarkable and drastic step of spitting out her food into his napkin.

"Oh my God, what did she put in this?" he managed to choke out. "Don't eat it!"

By then it was too late for Chef Raj, but he gave an alternative response.

"Oh! That sauce over the protein has a nice heat. Doesn't go with trout, but I like the boldness."

The other judges and guests took the middle way between the two experts and the three additional zippy eaters now coughing and crying along with Chef Juan. They picked at the edges and safe places away from the liberal squirt of red insanity and went back to gossiping about whether Charlie Adams should have opened that third restaurant, and how soon it would fail, and who they hoped would replace him at the Aspen Food & Wine Festival that year, if it did.

Chloe was still wiping down her station with unnecessary meticulousness, waiting about in case Fran needed her to return the favor of a last-minute assistant, when her trout plates came back. Largely full.

"What happened?" she asked the nearest server. He only shrugged, as if he hadn't just eavesdropped his way around the table and knew all.

Grabbing a plate off the tray as it went by, Chloe examined her dish closely. Dipping her pinky into the red sauce, she tasted it, and immediately yowled and wheezed her regret.

"Since when do you hate your own food?" asked Fran, achieving her second empathy milestone of the season by noticing another human choking to death two feet away.

"It's not my food," Chloe gasped, "it's Ajiz's."

"Oh," said Fran, no longer interested, and continued making twelve perfect gravy schmears.

Chloe, still gasping and tearing up, walked into lounge area to find Ajiz, and find out how the...*Ahem.* How might that sauce have ended up on her plate. When she ran him down, suddenly a more immediate concern surfaced.

"Hey, Ajiz! Don't you know how to make a lassi? Isn't it a required safety skill for you heat people?"

"Sure, it's easy."

"Help me, quick, I just need a small one," she said.

She grabbed his arm and pulled him toward the kitchen. At doorway of the lounge, she turned back again and pausing to brush her still watering eyes with her palm, asked,

"Hey, Linus! Can I use your leftovers? Please."

"Sure, what...?"

"Tell you in ten minutes."

Returning to the kitchen, she and Ajiz found an empty corner, and a blender, and quickly concocted the cooling beverage with the remains of Travis' spicy Greek octopus dish. After taking a large gulp herself, she poured the lassi into small glasses, added a sprig of mint as garnish, put them on a tray and took it over to the servers now waiting to bring in Fran's hens.

"Hey, could one of you please slip in and give these to the judges?' she asked. "Please. My dish was unexpectedly spicy and may have burned their palates."

The servers looked at one another noncommittally.

"Wow, team players. You must all be here auditioning for *Backstage Front of House*. I'll be sure to put in a good word."

Carrying the tray herself, Chloe headed for the swing doors, hoping to get her drink delivered and consumed ahead of Fran's judging. She slipped in quietly and circled around the table behind the diners, placing a lassi next to each water glass. She nearly made it back to the exit before she was spotted.

"Chloe!" said Chef Juan.

She wheeled around, holding the empty tray against her chest.

"What is this?" he asked.

"Just a lassi. For anyone who tasted my dish. It should help neutralize the heat and restore your palate."

"You should have served it with your plates. It won't be judged now."

"I know," she said, and turned to leave.

Chef Juan decided to use this opportunity to educate Chef Raj and the other guests on a potentially unfamiliar nuance when judging amateurs.

"Our contestants' spice levels are often wildly inappropriate," he explained, "especially those from cultural traditions that don't use them."

"Unlike your generations of expertise," he added in tribute to Raj's well-known pedigree.

What Chloe heard was condescension and an unfounded accusation that she thought scotch bonnet was a food. Words she hadn't intended to say, not there, not with Fran's plates arriving any minute, flashed out.

"That wasn't my sauce!"

"Which sauce?" Chef Juan asked.

Gritting her teeth with a quick mental reminder that a tray should not be used as a projectile, not without her Troy's supervision, Chloe made an effort to speak more calmly.

"The hot sauce on my plate, that was Ajiz's."

"It wasn't. We tried his already."

"We told him not to use that one. His was a series of Mexican hot sauces, mine was a mild *gochujang*. They were similar colors in similar squeeze bottles, that's why I didn't notice the switch at my station, or the pass..."

As she talked, Chloe replayed the scene in her mind's eye – her last-minute grilling, the other people milling about the busy kitchen, who was holding the wrong bottle.

"Wow, Fran," was all that Chloe said out loud, but Joey on Camera 2 expertly captured her shoulder sag and the resigned sigh.

"Why, what did Fran do to your dish?" Chef Parker responded, just as Fran entered through the doors at the head of her phalanx of servers.

"Which one is she?" Chef Raj whispered, curious to learn who among the contestants could make a decent condiment.

Fran took her mark at the head of the table and hearing her name invoked asked to camera,

"What did I do?"

"I think we should save this discussion for Judge's Table," answered Chef Matteo, always mindful to have each conflict during its proper segment. With a reassuring shake of her head, Chloe mouthed "it wasn't you" before scuttling off to the kitchen.

After Fran presented, and before trying her dish, Juan stared at Chloe's lassi, picked it up, smelt it, and then took a small taste.

"Oh, that helps," he said, and finished the glassful. "That's much better. I was afraid I wouldn't be able to taste food again before Christmas."

"Are you sure it isn't poison?" asked Chef Parker, who had seen Chloe's nostrils flare during Juan's earlier "exposition".

Chef Juan shrugged.

"Chloe isn't a star, but she's a pretty decent home cook. She wouldn't screw up yogurt."

"You said that when she ruined fennel for me, and I still say, then maybe you should take her home to cook there."

"I don't agree," interjected Chef Lucy Sharpton. Because she could. As only a special guest at the table, Chef Lucy had the freedom to say what she wanted, even if it was the truth and inconvenient with the contestant's elimination schedule. "The microscopic bite I sampled had balance, and the plating was quite rustic professional."

"I don't think it was that red-headed woman's fault, either. She blames that Fran person," mumbled another guest seated across the table from Lucy, trying – and failing – to get some screen time.

"Whatever happened, it was Chloe's own fault," insisted Chef Parker, staring down the row, "it always is."

Chef Raj, a veteran regarding contestant shenanigans, offered a wider and more nuanced perspective.

"Chloe's dish wasn't spiked, that was a proper red sauce. Why would Fran make a Trojan *Roja*? This is a French dish."

"I still say," Chef Lucy insisted, "if it wasn't doused with fire, hers wouldn't have been my bottom dish of the day."

The other guests looked around the table, counting the double negatives and trying to work out if that was a good final review, or bad. Chef Matteo simply gave Chef Juan the look that eliminated Chef Lucy from the shortlist of next year's guest judges for being both vague in her pronouncements and relentlessly not a team player. He then picked up his fork, and redirected everyone's attention, finally, to Fran's dish.

CHAPTER THIRTY-ONE

showdown at the oh no corral

After Chloe's late-breaking, fire-breathing, cutthroat drama, which is how it was later described in the show's commercials, Spice Mountain! Judge's Table really brought the heat (ditto). Gathered together in Greywater Lodge's smaller dining room, the panel sat at a long table against one wall, the contestants clustered against the bar on the opposite wall, and the alleged perpetrator of the Spice Bomb stood alone in the center of the dance floor waiting for her chance to explain herself.

The panel focused their critique on getting Chloe to admit her crime, while blaming someone else, hopefully with recriminations and tears escalating into a fight with somebody. Anybody would do. To elicit the desired outcome, they launched a series of penetrating, rapid-fire exchanges.

"Ajiz, do you know how your sauce ended up on Chloe's dish?"

"No, but she and I used the same bottles. We even made a joke earlier about mixing them up."

"Chloe, you should have used a different bottle."

"I needed a squeeze bottle."

"Then you should have handed Fran the right bottle to begin with."

"I thought I had."

Nothing seemed to spark the hysteria or blame-fueled implosion the judges wanted.

Their emphasis on her mysterious use of industry-standard supplies provided by the show, and their reliance on the contestants' recollections of what other people might be doing while they themselves scrambled to get their food to the pass suggested, perhaps, a lack of interest in the event beyond fully exploiting its dramatic potential. Otherwise, they could just ask the cameramen, who filmed the entire crime, to play it for everyone. Chloe had full faith that if Al didn't catch it, his number two, Joey, had. The crew filmed Vivian making a *ceviche*, they were that all-in for the Greywater kitchen.

Whether or not anyone cared about the truth, everyone expected Chloe to be eliminated over the mix-up. Also, that the editing department would cut and paste clips of her Fennel Incident together with today's debacle to send her home with the permanent moniker "Idiot Spice Girl". Chef Parker set the narrative by offering his long-familiar, sneering homily on cooks who didn't taste their dishes before service, and his level of snark clearly indicated Chloe's time on *Yes, Chef!* had come to an end.

Listening to her weeks of effort reduced to a mistake and a badly paired sauce, neither of which she made, Chloe's hands slowly contracted into fists. Forcing them back open, she pressed them against her legs as she fought to keep at least one audition promise and face the whole of the competition with open hands. Chef Matteo noticed her struggle, and elbowed Chef Juan. The two shared a silent, knowing laugh as they watched her fingers clench and unclench.

She also resisted funneling her righteous indignation into a rambling, disjointed defense with a shrewd certainty that kept her mouth clamped tight. Any allegation she made was unlikely to stick to Vivian and might instead risk framing Fran as a saboteur. Ajiz, too, might get roped in as the silent avenger for his rejected sauce, now being praised by the guest judge. Without access to the raw video footage, oh that Vivian, she got them good.

Standing on her mark, stiff and straight and trying not to cry, Chloe's sole consolation was that people this happy to see her bomb would have torpedoed her career eventually over something. Anything. It didn't make her feel better, but it did help keep her peace.

"And stop expecting your team to defend you when you aren't defending herself," she reminded herself again and again, hoping the silent crowd at her back also might bother her less in time.

"So, who do you blame for catastrophe?" Chef Matteo finally asked Chloe, as if her view on the events mattered. "It could have caused real harm to our guest judges."

"Space aliens?" she suggested.

Al quickly spun his camera around to capture the looming meltdown, or possible seizure. Not that he wished either eventuality on Chloe, but it was Season 14, and an Emmy was an Emmy.

While the contestants behind her tittered nervously, Chloe gave Chef Matteo a long, considering look. Then she took a deep breath and accepted full responsibility for her part in the disaster.

"I lacked the ability to get my dish to the pass under today's burner constraints without assistance," she admitted. "Chef Parker is correct. I could have tasted my dish one last time."

"Was it Fran who helped you? Isn't she partly to blame? Fran, please step forward."

Chloe gave Chef Matteo another long stare as Fran moved into position.

"I told Fran to pour and squeeze, and she did. The dishes looked exactly like the mock-up."

"I thought you achieved a good spice level," said Chef Raj. "*Roja* just doesn't pair well with trout."

Chloe had just enough emotional bandwidth to turn and seek out Ajiz, saying with almost – almost – a laugh,

"Look! You were right, Mr. Heat Miser!"

Turning back to Chef Raj, she pointed out the true creator of the sauce.

"That's Ajiz, our spice guy. He said people who like spice would get this one, we voted no, and he was right. Well, kinda, but allow me to make amends for my uninformed veto by facilitating this coming together of like-palate'd people. *Forged in Fire*. No wait, there's already a show named that. No anvils were involved in this sauce-making."

Ajiz waved his hand to Chef Raj, and in return for Chloe's non-combative, rambling re-introduction to his favorite network judge, tried harder to stop shifting his weight back and forth on his heels in time to his silent rendition of "*...you dropped the bomb on me, ba-by...*".

Janiva noticed he stopped moving and whispered her support of his restraint.

"This is not a day for disco."

Chef Juan had a different response to the unexpected injection of *kumbaya*.

"Well, I'm glad some people benefited from my loss of taste," he said with uncharacteristic sharpness. "Do you have anything to add, Fran?"

Scouring the surrounding faces, Fran saw, or thought she saw, the assumption that she either accidentally or on purpose sabotaged Chloe's dish. No one yet knew Chloe handed her the wrong bottle. Over and over, she chastised herself for violating her own rule to mind her own business during the cook. Before launching a full-throated defense, she looked once more over at Chloe, willing her to say something, anything, to alleviate the need to throw her under the bus with her own two hands.

Chloe continued to stare straight ahead, hands pressed to her side, waiting. Her only movement was a tiny shift in her shoulders, as she squared them to better take the blow.

"I just did what I was asked to do...I don't know how this happened...I...I..." began Fran.

Standing alone on one island, Fran continued to look across to Chloe standing alone on another, her disappointed and undermined friend, talking up Ajiz's treacherous spice mixes while no one was interested in her own condiment line. Her reaction baffled Fran but was consistent with the Chloe they all knew. Chloe shifting the blame, even by silence, though, was weird. Did she think the mixup was Fran's fault? Was refusing to openly accuse her as far as Chloe would go for friendship? Except, Fran knew she had only stood there, holding...

"Sssssssss."

As Fran faltered in the midst of her opening argument, the room heard Chloe quietly exhale. It kinda sounded like the hissing of snake, if one wasn't trying to be that accurate about it, but it might have been her best imitation of a balloon deflating. Either was appropriate under the circumstances.

Fran heard "snake".

"Oh," she said suddenly.

Chloe finally turned towards her. That one sliver of understanding temporarily overwhelmed her dead calm. Disappointment pricked at her eyes.

"I'm sorry, Chloe," responded Fran.

Chloe jerked one shoulder in her direction and tried to offer an understanding smile.

"It wasn't your fault," she said with a bit of a wobble. Quashing it, she turned back to the judges.

"That's right," Fran realized. Chloe publicly vindicated her from the beginning.

It was later agreed among the crew that Joey's solid camerawork best caught that enigmatic exchange between two former partners in crime, now partners in a crime. Really, he was on fire that day. Al, though, redeemed himself by his better knowledge of human nature. He turned his camera on Fran, focused in for a closeup, and waited for her next move.

Fran dimly guessed that somewhere in Chloe's silence was a warning to be careful...about something. If neither of them started a red herring blood feud by blaming each other, though, maybe if the judges got a hold of a new, dramatic twist – like the truth – both she and Chloe would be vindicated. Maybe? She turned back to the panel.

"I have something more to say. Chloe passed me the bottle when the fish were going down, and other than Vivian holding it while I stirred my potatoes, it never left my hand. Before that, though, the bottle sat on the counter for a long while, and her station was miles away from Ajiz's graveyard of bad ideas."

The judges hadn't bothered to interview the crew, or review the tapes, and were not going to. Their sole focus was to make an obvious and dramatic mistake into good television. Whose mistake was much less relevant. But Chef Matteo was listening. Once Fran mentioned Vivian's presence on scene, he understood Chloe's earlier, mocking look. Like her, without knowing exactly what happened, he knew exactly what happened. He decided it best to end the segment there, and closed the critique with a brief,

"Thank you, Chloe. Thank you, Fran, Ajiz."

He then dismissed group at large.

"The judges and I will deliberate, and let you know who won and who will be going home. Thank you."

The abrupt conclusion surprised the contestants, but they obediently shuffled and jostled their way back to the break room to await their fate, sneaking shifty looks at Chloe, Fran and Ajiz, and then each other. Unlike Aaron's odd blueberry barbecue departure Week 2, this appeared to be a real thing about a real thing that really happened. It was just as unclear, though, what exactly did happen and who was to blame.

After the contestants filed out of the judging area and the PA closed the doors, Chef Matteo turned to the other chefs to ask,

"Fran won, right?"

"Right?" he said again, looking around for confirmation. "Juan? Raj?"

"Okay," Juan agreed, and Raj made an assenting gesture.

"Isn't she on the wrong team?" asked Parker, stretching his hands over his head with a yawn. "Send Chloe home and pick somebody else to win. It just can't be Vivian, putting up that empty plate of nothing. Make it quick though, I'm tired. I don't want to bother."

"You must. Chloe's dish was sabotaged, and Vivian is the saboteur."

"*Ughhhh...*not today," protested Parker. "How?"

"Why?" he asked after a short consideration.

Matteo shrugged.

"I'm sure it's on tape. Fran and Chloe must have missed the switch, but they're not accusing each other. That's information."

"That's weird," responded Raj. "Don't they know this is a competition?"

"Raj, Season 14 is all weird. Juan insists on putting though people who lack the gameplay to win at tic tac toe."

"Nobody wins at tic tac toe," said Juan defensively.

Parker returned to practical matters.

"So, now what? Will Fran watch Chloe get eliminated without making a stink about it for the fans at home? Not for Vivian she won't."

"Are you sure it's on film?" asked Raj.

Matteo sighed.

"The crew won't shut up about their "all access" kitchen today. Also Raj, for most people, putting nuclear hot sauce in one's mouth, that shows up on camera. It had to have been a last second switch."

"Well, don't look at me, I never have these problems on my show. My contestants are professionals who know what it takes to win. Step one – don't get caught."

"I still say Chloe never tasted her dish and is entirely to blame. Again," insisted Parker, "but if we give the challenge to the Red Team and Fran wins, then from the Blue Team...Reid? How about we send Reid home?"

Raj nodded.

"The curry? Yes. Him. Definitely."

"How does that happen, Raj?" Parker asked. "I could see the spices in it, you can actually see them, yet I couldn't taste anything except salt and cream."

"I don't know, man's a magician. Or a vampire. All those spices, poof, gone. He should go to."

Chef Matteo assented to the change.

"Fine. We'll say Chloe's team saved her and send her home next week. Whether we let Vivian get caught later or never, let the editors see how it fits. For now, I just want to get off this mountain before dawn. Can you believe the Lodge wants us to pay for that cooktop?"

"Scam artists, the lot of them," responded Juan. "Who broke it? Please tell me Chloe did."

Matteo rolled his eyes with disapproval at another example of ineffectual gameplay.

"What? She won't have dinner with you, so your new plan is to downgrade her from intern to indentured servant? It was probably Vivian. On purpose."

"Make her father pay for it, then," said Parker. "Why can't she just leave her winning to us? I don't want to see that woman for at least another twenty-four hours."

"Well, you're in luck. Tomorrow is their day off and except for Raj, we don't have to see any of them until the start of the Pastrry Week," said Matteo.

"Who's coming for that?" Raj asked, moderately interested in a potential new professional contestant for his *India Bakes Against...* series.

"Some Korean hotshot, we'll vet him for you. He once worked on the Rue de Rivoli. Not Angelina's, but the hotel down the street."

"*Oooh la la,*" responded Chef Juan. "Do we have to speak French?"

"No," answered Matteo.

"Do we have to speak Korean?"

"No.

"Yay. What's he bringing?"

"The dish is called "The Wood Planers" or "Sunflowers" or something," answered Matteo.

"What are you talking about?" interjected Parker. "You booked someone who named a dessert "Wood Planers"? And you expect me to eat fourteen of them?"

"Only thirteen after tonight, and maybe the title got translated wrong. All I know is that he was late with it, and the PAs are fuming. He'll be lucky if he doesn't find bootmarks on it during his reveal. He's won several awards, though. You like food that wins things."

"He sounds like a nightmare."

"That's Monday's problem. Tonight, let's just get the elimination in the can, and go back to our mountain where people know how to install stoves. Rachel! Call the contestants back, please, so we can go home. Thanks."

The contestants straggled back into the judging area. Lining up again on their marks, they learned the surprising end to their time in the wilderness was that Fran won the day, Ajiz got special mention from Chef Raj and as a result (obviously) of Chef Juan's continued advocacy, Chloe squeaked by again. Ajiz then went from elated to crushed as his dance acolyte, Reid, got sent home for his tasteless curry, just nudging out the fatal spice bomb. Vivian's name wasn't mentioned at Judge's Table at all. She, at least, enjoyed a restful week on Spice Mountain! and was now more than ready to Gimme Some Sugar!

CHAPTER THIRTY-TWO

after we bomb

Following the elimination segment, the contestants removed their dirty aprons, collected their belongings, and made their way out to the waiting vans for the long drive back from Rocky Mountain State Park. Amid the bustle, Chloe quietly separated herself from Fran and climbed into the second van. Nature abhorring a vacuum, and often preferring to give misfortune a wide berth, that may be why the seat next to her normally reserved for Fran ended up occupied by Jake. A few elbows and nods among the other occupants casually noted that unusual seating mix-up, but by then the gossip had already moved on to Reid's curry, and Ajiz's heartbreak over Reid's curry. That, too, petered out once they started driving in the dark. It wasn't worth the energy to talk, never mind re-canvass what was so last hour. They'd care again tomorrow after a proper shower and coffee made with the proper whirring noise, not stewed over a burning log.

Sitting in the second row behind the driver, looking out the window at the night forest rushing past, Chloe was grateful for the silence, and the long, empty road down the mountain to try and forgive her friend. Fran had been tricked. True. Holding a grudge about it was the second half of the trap laid by Vivian. Very true. Fran already apologized. Publicly true. And yet...boy, did Fran let her down. Handing anything to Vivian was madness. It was Week 6, everybody knew that. How could it have taken Fran forever and a good ten minutes to discover who really started the fire? A lot happened that day that made Chloe mad, but she was most mad about Fran becoming Vivian's useful idiot to torpedo the Marsden Sweet & Sassy empire on day one of its launch.

One fact Chloe seized onto as it floated by and away downriver in her mind was that if Fran hadn't helped her at all, Chloe wouldn't have had a dish at all. That was most true of everything. The judges may not have tasted the condiments she took such care to make...

Chloe bit her lip as a wave of disappointment washed over her.

...still, Fran replicated the plates perfectly. That took careful thought, and time out of the competition clock, and effort. Focusing and refocusing her mind from that perspective, Chloe began to chip around the edges of the lump of ice in her chest.

Her eyes continued to well up, though, over yet another cinematic team challenge failure. Maybe she, Aaron, Troy, Butterfinger Bobby, and the eliminated contestants from that awful Sushi week could rehabilitate their reputations through a podcast, or at least start a Zoom support group.

The immediate threat, though, was to the magic and harmony of the cool kids club. Chloe could no longer be friends with Fran if she secretly blamed her for this debacle, making the contest unbearable on top of it being unwinnable. And who would get Paul in the divorce? To avert a further, future disaster, Chloe knew she must leave it all here on the mountain. The miles and the forest and the darkness whooshed by as she did the hard work of trying to accept a situation before it had yet to be made right. It would be. It didn't feel like it ever would be, or ever could be, but someday, it would be.

"Do not worry," she reminded herself, *"be not afraid."*

Faintly silhouetted by the starlight and moonlight outside the van window, it was easy for her seatmate to watch her contend with sadness and disappointment. Jake saw the tears glint and fall silently, and her shoulders collapse inward as she grieved her loss in the kitchen. As he monitored her, he also calculated how long before some bright spark mentioned he witnessed the event, and weighed the benefits of a preemptive confession.

Rejecting the latter, he stuck to his brand. He patted his shoulder and offered it to her as a head rest.

"If you want to take a nap, feel free to use me."

"Thanks," she replied, "but I'm good."

His quick ear caught the quiet sniffle, and also her effort to put a friendly smile into those words that softened her "no". As did several other listening ears. Suddenly, they both felt a sharp jolt in their backs, and heard a low mumble behind them.

"Sorry, I was just moving my legs."

"*Our Linus, so reliable,*" Chloe thought, taking the hint and gaining a comfort.

"It is dark in here," she agreed, calling over the high seatback. "Hey, thanks for doing the schedule today. Without you, fearless leader, I wouldn't have gotten a single trout to the pass."

"Yes, you would," was the slightly less mumbled response.

Chloe gave a low snort of amusement as she readjusted her wedge against the window, her elbow resting on the tiny ledge and her head in her hand. Their Linus always rejected her highly positivity-forward way of stating opinions. His Eeyore-esque gloominess cloaked a solid, non-combative dependability, kinda like the burnt parchment covering Oliver's excellent halibut *en papillote*. Many contestants were lovely people, despite being fierce competitors. Paul, making his magic even over a hunk of charcoal on the side of a hill, steady, drama-free Janiva keeping it real while she smoked everyone but Travis when cooking a steak, Ajiz who brought the soundtrack to their lives, and their superman of the sea, Oliver. His generous advice led to her trout from today that nobody much tried turning out far more successful than last week's trout everybody tried, and this from the man who chastised her Week 1 not to tell anybody anything that might improve their skill set. Chloe even could also now acknowledge – inside, where it counts – it wasn't Jake's fault he was so handsome and charming, and that she was two sizes larger than she wanted to be. She felt kinda bad she held it against him.

Why that man was spending valuable nap time flirting with her as they drove down the mountain, though, she had no idea. Perhaps he found it a challenge that her interest in his beach bum style only extended to whether it indicated a working knowledge of sharks. Whenever he fished shirtless up at the lake, his waders bunched around his hips to give Al his best Brad Pitt, *A River Runs Through It* realness, she clucked at him asking if he needed help sorting out the buckles to get dressed properly, and volunteering Paul's services if he did.

"That water is frigid, Jake," she would warn him in her mom voice, "and unskilled people are waving sticks with hooks on the ends of them. It isn't safe."

Chloe was correct that Jake found her a very weird woman. During their turn to collect kindling, instead of flirting him into carrying a double load of heavy objects up and over obstacles on an incline, she used the opportunity to distract herself from being tasked to carry heavy objects up and over obstacles on an incline, and listened to his confession that he liked the celebrity part of celebrity chef. She saw how he would be good at that, in a detached, twenty-thousand-foot perspective way that lacked any reference his hair, chin or abs. You know, that kinda way.

"You have a lot of charm," she assessed dispassionately, sitting down for a few minutes on a log on the pretense that her bundle of sticks needed reorganization. "If you learn to turn the sexy off, in that not every situation needs "more", it might really need less, the network would probably love to create a Jake brand. The camera loves effortlessness, even when the result is less than Paul in a bad mood and not feeling it."

It was sound advice from someone who didn't even think to sit on his lap to "avoid spiders".

Sitting next to him in the tight confines of a dark van, Chloe had become so inured her to Jake wandering around in the background with an overexposed six-pack and no boundaries, she even forgoed the opportunity to guess the brand of cologne he wore, a competition she, Fran and Janiva had been having since Week 2. In fact, she ignored him altogether while she made a fresh effort to stop rehashing the last fatal four hours.

Maybe she was tired, she decided, maybe she let things get too big. Twenty-three people would crash and burn with her, and poor Aaron got tripped out with a pretty good barbecue. Plus, it was Season 14. Twenty-four times fourteen seasons was...was...

"Linus," she asked though the gap between the seatback and the window, "how much is twenty-four times fourteen? I suck at night math."

"Three hundred thirty-six."

"Our Linus. Thank you!"

That's a lot, Chloe told herself, and almost all of them left without the consolation of tasting Paul's (mother's) short ribs. Poor things. Everything would be alright in the end. Maybe when she got home, she would try running away to Paris. Doc would never think of looking for her there, not after faking him out with Asia, and there were human limits to how unhappy one can be at the D'Orsay.

"See, look, come down a couple of hundred feet in elevation and there's a Plan. Oxygen, that's what I was missing on the mountain."

Now, she just had to live through the next few days of televised sucky, suckyland. The only real decision left was whether hiding under a bunk bed was still her most viable intermediate Plan B. All this unpleasantness would be over even faster if she refused to come out and film stuff.

"Are you sure you wouldn't feel more comfortable leaning the other direction?" offered Jake a second time, mistaking her sighs and head shakes and nods as a protest against the discomfort of the tiny window ledge.

Chloe tilted her head to look at him sideways, her head still in her hand. He was more of a shape than a person in the dim light, but still a charming and handsome one. And dangerous. After such a lousy day, what a pleasant, temporary consolation it would be to lean on his shoulder, as invited. He probably knew a dozen surreptitious ways to hold a woman's hand for the first time at if it meant something, and was just bored enough to try to kiss her, if they weren't in a van with Linus sitting behind them. He might, possibly, also, in his Jake way, be making an effort to comfort her after her loss.

And yet, she reminded herself. Firmly. Who encouraged Ajiz to embrace his hot sauce soul earlier? No one imagined that would end so well for their Mr. Married Spice. Jake also hadn't yet tried the consolation of apologizing for hogging the burners and being the reason Chloe needed Fran's help in the first place. Plus, he had an open relationship with the woman who just destroyed her career prospects in North America, you know, that.

"Let's not end our day leaning against the enemy, please," she admonished herself. *"Sexy Jake is Jake Sexy, fool."*

"No, thank you," she demurred out loud, trying to sound friendly and normal, like when Oliver offered her a bite of his lobster. "I'm just trying to think through today, and how I can do better. I appreciate your kindness, though."

"Then why don't you let me be kind to you?"

Chloe gave a short, silent snort that Jake was this bored and this awake this late at night. She turned back to the window, instinctively moving forward a tick to lessen the impact of any second kick from the back row. Her new posture, or perhaps her lack of response, seemed to forestall the latter. With sudden clarity, Chloe realized if Linus and Jake switched seats, her day might have ended even worse. Linus would be a lot harder to resist, and just as bad a decision.

"Geez Louise and a bucket of snakes, don't tell me Fran was right. Is today also the day to give Travis his name back?"

To her added dismay and annoyance, Jake still had not yet decided to stop Jakin'.

"What about it?" he asked again, reaching out and running his hand up and down her arm.

"Wow, are you believable when you do that," she thought, before adding with a skosh too much snap,

"Being nice to the chubby girl just because you had an extra espresso in the lounge, that's not really your style, Jake."

A sharp intake echoed through the silent van. It wasn't certain who gasped, but quashing her temper, Chloe quickly responded before anyone else did.

"I'm sorry, Jake. I'm the one who always wants you to put your clothes on, remember, so you don't get cold, or splattered, or damaged."

Too late, it occurred to her that kind of advocacy would get back to Paul, if it hadn't already. Now, she'd never get him in the divorce.

"Today sucked," she continued. "Can we just agree that today totally sucked? I miss my man. He might even be able to cheer me up here, in a dark van, with the rest of you."

"I didn't send Troy home," Jake insisted, finally giving himself away in his quick, wildly off-topic attempt to defend himself.

"Oh, really? Then you know who did. And my man is a completely different person. For starters, my man likes women, let's begin there."

"Such a nice man," she added, comparing the memory of one chef's warm, spontaneous clasp to Jake's practiced caress. "He apologizes when he does something wrong."

"I think you're making one up," countered Jake.

"Well, you would."

Trying again to sound normal, and change the subject away from the quagmire of fake boyfriends, Chloe added,

"Hey, since you're obviously still jacked up after your "perfect" shrimp today, any more ideas for your show?"

"I still don't believe you," repeated Jake, refusing the offramp.

"Doesn't make it not true."

In the echoing silence of the van after that witty riposte, Chloe heard the captive audience of avid gossipmongers and one seat-kicker waiting for Jake to call her the b-word or the l-word for the crime of repeatedly and publicly rebuffing his advances. They were probably already voting via hand signals whether and how Troy would get involved at the Reunion Special. In tired desperation, Chloe took the Ajiz way out and resorted to the Carly Simon songbook to end the conversation.

"In the weeee small hours of the mor-ning, when the whole wide world is fast asleep...," she began.

Pleased to hear her voice sounded in tune, especially so late in the day and at such a low volume, Chloe finished two whole verses as a lullaby to the van, an homage to her lost *entremets*, and an apology for being so disruptive. After her solo, she settled into a new, more comfortable wedge against the window, shut her eyes, and tried to ignore the crack and pop and smell of char as she burnt her bridges with both Jake and Travis over her memory of a ghost.

"Today effin' sucked," she accidentally mumbled out loud, forgetting it was nighttime and Sunday and dead quiet in the van, shocking everybody. She would regret it later, after the guys quoted it so often that fans of the show turned it into a meme, but it came from her soul.

CHAPTER THIRTY-THREE

the cool kids come back

A few hours before the winning team was to head out for their rodeo Group Reward with Chef Raj, Fran noticed her roommate was missing. Going to search for her, she came up empty in all Chloe's usual morning haunts. She wasn't on the wicker loveseat out on the terrace, she wasn't stretched out on the green and red plaid couch in the living room, she wasn't even sitting around the table amid the clutter of coffee cups and notebooks and contestants getting butter on the pages of the reference library cookbooks. Fran finally discovered her sitting on the top bunk of her bed, working on dish ideas in her food journal, and finishing her late breakfast of two granola bars and a glass of tap water.

"How's it going?" Fran asked, seating herself on the lower berth of the opposite bed and glancing uneasily up at her. After Tammy left, they both regularly used their top bunks to get away from it all, but Chloe taking the high road without her morning caffeine or berry-stained fingers looked ominous.

"I've got an idea for how to plate tortellini that I wanted to get down on the page," Chloe answered, continuing to work on her sketch. "What's up?"

"I'm sorry I let Vivian ruin your food," blurted out Fran, "and your chance with Chef Raj. I know we joke all the time about her taking us out with the van, but...I really didn't expect her to...I just thought if I had a free hand, I could stir my potatoes."

"She must have been watching for just the right moment," Chloe responded, popping the last hunk of granola in her mouth. "She made a *ceviche*. That left a lot of time on her hands."

"Well, thanks for not blaming me at Judge's Table. The saboteur label would have stuck to me all the way to the end."

Chloe began erasing her sketch of tomato wedges and started again with tomato slices.

"It wasn't your fault."

"Still, in the heat of the moment, them going all out to blame you for doing something you didn't do, you must have been wild," countered Fran, who was right. "And it was my fault."

Also, true.

Chloe lowered her pencil. Taking quiet breath, she looked directly at Fran for the second time since Judge's Table.

"I forgive you, Fran. You didn't do it on purpose. You also did a great job replicating my plating, and I don't want Vivian's nastiness to overshadow our dream team fabu teamwork. It must really suck to live in a world where nobody likes you, and everything you have was paid for by selling your soul. Her man hit on me in the van, by the way."

"Like you needed that."

Chloe gave a short laugh in agreement.

"And Travis kicked the seatback – he was behind us – at key moments. We really don't progress much farther than eighth grade as humans, do we?"

"You're calling him Travis now?"

"Yeah, I'm giving him his name back," she answered, meticulously brushing away eraser dust.

"Does he know this?"

"He will. Did you also hear I ended my fabulous day by becoming officially entangled in the myth of the fake boyfriend? It didn't even work. After the thirty-seventh rejection, Jake very nearly called me a lesbian. I thought I was going to have to channel my inner transgender woman in the wrong bar on a Saturday night about to have to explain modern living and ready for things to pop off. That can get a little intense in a closed compartment."

Fran didn't respond, except to make a mental note to get the full story from Oliver. A silence fell on the room, broken only by the scrape and rasp of Chloe's pencil.

"I wish there was something I could do to make you feel better, Chloe, because I know you don't."

The pencil stopped for a moment, before Chloe shrugged again and continued giving a lemon wedge unnecessary 3D shading.

"It's just a bummer knowing there isn't any point to being here. Instead of demonstrating steady improvement, gaining fan support for my food line, and leaving because it was "my time", I've become a laughingstock who can't rise above the flavor profile of rice pudding."

"It isn't over," Fran insisted, "anything can happen."

"True, but anything good? Not if the judges have their way. Don't worry, I'll get over it. Look," Chloe said, waving her pencil, "I'm working on a new dish. Isn't this a can-do attitude?"

Fran continued to watch Chloe's bent head with doubt.

"Well, for today, try to just enjoy having a roof over our head and running water again," she counseled. "At least you still have Travis to kick people when you're down."

Chloe nodded.

"I know, that's why I'm extra staying away from him today."

"Why don't you just go for it?"

"Because he's not my guy. He means well, and even when he's wrong it's for the right reasons. That's awesome. If he could kick my seatback, though, couldn't my captain, o' captain stand up for me at Judge's Table?"

"Maybe he thought you screwed up the bottles."

"Absolutely. Which is fine. I just think my guy would know that I would be the first to realize and admit it. The admitting part, on camera, is of course an untested theory. I may be delusional about my skills and abilities in a moral crisis, but he could at least bring some Percy Sledge to the action."

"Maybe Travis didn't think he had the right, or think you wanted him to."

"Totally maybe. He might even be 1,000% right. He's a farmer, the man knows things. I'm sure I am being unreasonable. Warning me first about Juan and kicking me later over Jake is a lot, so it's super unfair to want him to...I don't even know what. There are a lot of men running around interfering with our lives here, it's just a shame none of them are our hero."

"*Where have all the good men gone?*" sang Fran.

"*And where are all the gods?*" Chloe sang back, "*Where's the street-wise Herrrrrr-cu-les to fiiiiight the rising odds?*"

Chloe pushed away her notebook, and the two began to dance it out – Chloe from her bed and Fran taking the floor – through two verses and one chorus of some Bonnie Tyler classic. Trailing off once they reached the instrumental break, Fran leaned against the ladder of her bunk bed, while Chloe flopped back on her mattress to catch her breath.

"I feel so much better now, Fran," Chloe said, looking up at the ceiling.

"Really?"

"Bonnie Tyler, she tells it like it is. He's gotta be sure, and he's gotta be soon and he's gotta be larger than life, Fran. Do we know anybody like that, Fran?"

"No."

"No, we do not. But we have asked for one, and that is the first step. I really do feel better now."

"The *Yes, Chef!* Dance Party, it does a body good. I'm going to get some water from the kitchen, do you need anything, Chloe?"

"Nope."

"Pie?"

"Nope."

"Sure?"

"Yup."

"Then I'll be back."

Instead of heading for the kitchen, Fran went down the hall and climbed the stairs into the loft looking for Oliver and Paul. Not finding them, she tried the living room where she discovered most of the guys watching soccer, plus Ashley strenuously leveraging her time on her high school JV team to be a part of.

"Who's winning?" Fran asked, coming in to lean on the back of the buffa-lo-check couch. With a series of head jerks and shoulder taps she managed to corral Oliver, Paul, Felix and Ajiz away from their game and out onto the terrace.

"Strategy meeting," Ajiz said to the others as he got up. "A Pastry Week has to descend on us sometime, and we're claiming Felix and all that lies beneath ahead of time."

"Within," corrected Paul.

"Beneath," insisted Felix. "I'm the sugar assassin. You wait, I'm gonna make something that isn't a pie and take you all out."

"Yeah, we know," said Paul, "it'll be a cake."

Gathering everyone in the seating area out on the terrace, Fran waited patiently for the chairs to stop creaking and scraping as they all sat down. Noticing how the sound echoed and carried, she looked back towards the door and up to the windows overhead, then shook her head.

"Nope, we gotta go further. Follow me."

"Where are we going, now?" Ajiz protested. Having successfully maneuvered for the best chair, the one that got the most sun, he had the more reliably dry cushions.

"*Shhhhh*," she replied, "it's important. Follow me."

Fran led them over to the stairs and down off the terrace, and they regrouped below in the lower garden. Glancing around again for any face peering over the parapet and keeping one ear cocked for the sound of the slider door opening, she briefly explained how the spice bomb really went down. Or off.

"Oh my God!" exclaimed Ajiz. "Is that what happened? I thought she accidentally picked up the wrong bottle after our sauce tasting."

"Wow, that sucks," said Oliver.

"The worst part," continued Fran, "is the one time she used her Sweet & Sassy condiments, nobody tasted her food. Or cared. Meanwhile, in the middle of total disaster, in the middle of being thought a compete idiot, she took time to help you out, Ajiz. Would you have?"

"She did," he agreed. "I thought she was just trying to laugh off her own mistake. I thought distracting her from that was being nice."

"I was already in the lounge when the incident happened," explained Paul. "I assumed the prep chaos must have been high for you to volunteer, and that you switched the bottle by accident, Fran. I didn't know if saying something would make the situation worse."

"I get it. Probably some people think I did it on purpose."

"Can't we just say who did it?" asked Ajiz. "Do you know? What if they think I did it? Will anyone think I did?"

Fran shook her head.

"If the judges wanted to know, they would just look at the tape. It happened in the middle of the kitchen. It must have been filmed."

Felix, the former engineer, was confused.

"Why wouldn't they want to know?"

Lawyer Paul was not.

"I think the reason doesn't bode well for any of us."

"Bingo," agreed Fran, "and we don't know who else Vivian did this to. I don't think anyone who went home so far could have won, still, it's got to hurt going out by someone cheating. Look at Aaron's meltdown. Chloe's really upset, and she's still here. Even if she doesn't blame me, which I don't believe, none of us backed her up. That's a fact that can't be changed."

After an awkward pause while they considered Fran's words, Ajiz with his mouth open in shock, Felix asked for more information.

"What are you going to do?"

"I don't know."

Paul looked for solutions.

"What are we going to do?"

"I don't know. I just thought you guys should know what really happened."

Oliver reached down, picked a strawberry, and ate it thoughtfully. He knew Vivian was trouble from the word "horseradish".

"Don't eat those without washing them," said Paul, taking the half-eaten berry out of his hand and tossing it off the terrace, "and we better think of something quick. Today we have to go to the rodeo with Chef Raj. That's going to get awkward."

"Actually, she isn't going," said Ajiz, "I thought I told you."

"What happened?", "Why?", "Oh, what now?" the rest wanted to know.

"She said she couldn't watch bull riding with someone who thought of her as Idiot Spice Girl and asked me to represent for both of us."

"Wow, we really suck," said Fran.

"Why?" asked Ajiz. "Do you mean me, or do you really mean us?"

"It's our fault. If we backed her up, today might be a second chance to promote her condiment line. Instead, she's letting Ajiz here suck up to his new best friend after his loco *Roja* ruined her dish."

"I didn't know it was partly my fault, I really didn't," said Ajiz, kicking at the nearest clump of kale.

"It wasn't anybody's fault, so stop taking it out on Travis' greens," said Paul.

"Do none of you know how to interact with produce outside of Whole Foods? Anyway. It was Vivian, and she's made everybody feel bad about her own crime. That she got away with."

"Well, what are we going to do?" asked Ajiz once more. "Let's ask Travis. Well, first tell him I harvested that clump wrong, and then ask him. He'll know. Won't he?"

Tired of shaking her head, Fran just stared at him.

"He won't?" said Ajiz with surprise. "Yes, he will."

"Why not?" asked Paul, believing Fran the first time.

"Because he might know."

"What does that mean?"

"Work it out, Paul."

"Then what are we going to do?" Ajiz lamented.

Fran suddenly held up her hand. In the silence they heard the creak and swoosh of the slider door opening.

"Let's get through the bull riding and rodeo clowns, first," she whispered, "think on it, and regroup tomorrow night over, I don't know, the magic healing power of short ribs. I just didn't want you guys to keep..."

"Putting our foot in our mouths?" said Paul in an equally low tone. "Wise precaution and appreciated. Let me look at what we have in the freezer, and meanwhile, we should all keep our eyes open. Who knows when Vivian will strike next?"

Nodding to each other in silent agreement, the cool kids climbed the stairs back up to the terrace.

rocky road

As had already been tattled to Chef Matteo by the prodution assistants, while the contestants struggled through the challenges up on Spice Mountain!, back in Denver, Chef Ji Kyung-ho's looming television debut as a *Yes, Chef! America* guest judge loomed large to end in disaster.

His sole responsibility, prior to his opening segment, was to provide an appealing signature dessert that popped on TV for his Imitation Challenge. Ideally, its mere appearance would terrify the average home cook, including the contestants he would set to replicate it, while inspiring mass viewer pilgrimage to his new store in New York to taste the real thing. If it looked extra terrifying, maybe the viewers would get on a plane to Korea.

He arrived in Denver with three viable options, preselected by his sous chefs. They planned for to him to make a final decision after a half-day spent in his test kitchen adjusting to the unfamiliar altitude, and an afternoon culinary tour of local pastry shops to research what ingredients commercial suppliers would haul up to the top of a mountain. The remaining contingency window before the shoot he planned to spend in his hotel suite, complaining to Wallace about what he wasn't accomplishing back in his home kitchen, and wondering if the Hu's liked their wedding cake and whether it brought Little Paris any new referrals.

It was a good plan.

Instead, Kyung-ho spent his first days in Denver re-testing decades-old recipes. Today he was remaking Option 3, Little Paris' version of *riz à l'impératrice* with black sesame. It was not going well.

9,941 kilometers away, his staff produced two hundred servings of the same dish that same day with their usual calm precision. Alone on this side of the planet, in the gleaming, cavernous and rarely used commercial kitchen borrowed from the convention center and loaned out to this season's guest judges, Kyung-ho attempted to make three. As he pulled out another tray of shapeless and smoking improperly incorporated sugar butter lumps wishing they could be a biscuit base, he acknowledged he still had yet to make one.

Everything in this new, much better-appointed environment – the stove, the equipment, the ingredients – was conspiring against him, the foreigner, to ensure he fail. Even the bulk flour seemed to harbor ill will. What big mouth let it be known that despite Kyung-ho's very expensive classical training he still loved rice more that wheat he couldn't say, but looking down at the smoking lumps it was clear somebody must'a.

It was also possible, maybe, that stress, lingering jet lag, the extra 5,198 feet above sea level and some bad math in switching between metric and imperial measurements helped produce the array of test pastries lined up for review. All were slightly underdone or under-risen, burnt, bland, or just ugly looking. Whichever the root cause, and surely it was 6/8^{ths} the flour having a chip on its shoulder, you couldn't tell Kyung-ho otherwise, none of the final products remotely fulfilled the producer's brief.

Trying to find a proactive, 11th hour solution, Kyung-ho Googled the exact distance between this kitchen and his own stand mixer to double check it really was not within walking distance.

Night came on, and with it the deadline for submitting both his final recipe and sample products to the production assistants responsible for sourcing the food stuffs needed for the show. Kyung-ho knew it was the last day, the absolute last day before they loathed him en masse for making them shop last-minute. And really, that day was yesterday. Tonight was a rush to prevent them deliberately tripping him as he walked out onto the sound stage as just desserts for his inability to meet even the contingency window of his basic contract obligations.

Despite the time pressure, and notwithstanding his proven skill and experience with gluten across three continents, Kyung-ho continued to stare at the last round of failed components, bewildered, and reflecting on life and where it had all gone wrong for him. Or at least why something he could make blindfolded in Korea, Paris and New York could not be replicated in this one foreign kitchen on top of a mountain. Perhaps he needed wheat that arrived by sea. Kyung-ho Google'd that in case it was a thing.

His sudden inability to apply basic laws of chemistry to any recipe, that might be science. He was cooking in a cloud bank. His uncharacteristic inability to commit to any one recipe was weird. Again, he oscillated between perfectly fine option a.) which he didn't feel like baking, and perfectly appropriate option b.) which he knew wasn't going to fly, and today's option c.) which he was never going to make for the show anyway.

Absentmindedly taking a bite of a test pastry, and then spitting it out, Kyung-ho suddenly, and finally, took a different path.

With one outward sweep of his arm, he shoved the rejects into the large, nearby trash bin and committed to what he intended to make all along. His signature, not made for TV, most popular *entremets*. The one he knew best, therefore, the one most favorable to the intuitive adjustments needed in this freaky, traitorous kitchen. It was also the one most certain to suit a Western palate, which is perhaps, maybe, why he named it for one – Chloe's Starry Night.

So what if a marketing decision impacting Little Paris' entire American launch was a wee influenced by the possibility that having made it to the West, she who never returned to the East might see it on TV. That didn't make the decision wrong, just layered. It was absurd to think she would remember him, one shop, one encounter on a multi-country tour of Asia. Still, she did find him his target audience and saved his fledgling business. It was therefore only right, he reasoned, if one happened to wander within a likely 2,500 kilometers of her own domain, and be given the opportunity, to give credit to the woman who made his success possible. On national TV. Where she might see it, although, it would be silly to think she would remember him.

Post dithering (about food), Kyung-ho settled into the task with an unexpected enthusiasm, enjoying the chance long-denied him back home as executive chef and owner. He made the dish start to finish without any interfering tastes or unwanted contributions of a large kitchen staff divvying up production of the components. As he worked, he jotted down the recipe, a slightly looser version than the precise and regimented one scaled up in sets of fifty servings in the binder on the shelf above his desk. It being already the next morning in Korea, he did momentarily consider the expediency of calling whoever was on *mise en place* to just read it to him. Between the possibility of being tripped on national television for his wayward tardiness by one set of antagonists, and the certainty of being kicked for his last-minute re-vision of his international launch by another, he chose to go it alone. Maybe by the time the show aired, his own staff far, far away would forget not only how Starry Night was not selected as an option, but that it was specifically and roundly voted "no" by the committee.

Kyung-ho's new commitment and focus, or perhaps finally doing the right thing, suddenly overcame his long war with American source materials. He quickly manifested, step by step, an especially good solo version of the dish. The lemon mousse was luscious and cloud-like, the gelee flavorful and piquant, and flakiness, sandiness, and buttery goodness appeared in due season as required and expected from *un maitre patissier*. Halfway through the bake, he even found himself singing, a rare occurrence indicating a happy, relaxed mind with some free time on its hands.

Alone in the echoing kitchen, it didn't matter which song he chose to sing, so he didn't bother to examine why Bob Dylan became his warm-up for relying heavily on English in the week ahead. If *To Make You Feel My Love* stuck in his head for another reason, or whether it influenced him to place the gold-leaf moon that could go anywhere on the marbled, glazed surface with such precision, well, who had time to cook, sing, and also ponder such mysteries. He hadn't burnt anything in three hours, that was all he needed to know.

Stepping back to assess the completed dish, alongside the two required backups in case anything got dropped, smacked against, or preemptively eaten during taping, he wondered what the producers would say. Would it pop on camera? He didn't know. Would the show's junior staff forgive him? He wasn't sure. Would it make his girl happy? Yes. As in most crossroads in his career over the last year and a half, he let Chloe have the final say.

CHAPTER THIRTY-FIVE

what's an entremets?

Nothing announced the start of Gimme Some Sugar! Week more than Felix exiting the warehouse locker area with his apron tied with extra neatness and wearing his best kitchen tee shirt.

"You are a vision in unstained white cotton, Felix!" Chloe called out from her yellow club chair. "It's Week 7, sweet thing, show us how it's done!"

"It's also Chloe's week to get eliminated," predicted Vivian to Ashley, seated together on the farther couch.

"I suppose both can be true," Chloe agreed, overhearing the aside above sound of eleven other contestants milling about between the coffee machine and the lounge area waiting for the start of morning taping to be announced.

Fran brought over her mug of coffee to perch on the arm of Chloe's chair.

"Don't listen to her, Chloe. New week, fresh start. Look, we're cooking indoors on a flat surface with plumbing again, let's get excited."

"I thought she was trying to motivate me. Sad, how unhelpful some people are every...time. Anyway, oh, I wish we had an amazing blueberry thingy to get our head in the game for this nightmare week."

"Is that a flavor of Glenn's donuts?" Fran asked. "Are you going off about donuts again? During donut time of the day?"

"*Shhhhh*, Chef Parker might hear you. How, how can I bribe a man without my phone? Anyway, would a Cider Hill moment make this moment better? Yes.

Today, though, I need me those blueberries I eat with a fork, so, extra *shhhhh*, 'cause I ain't sharing that with him, either."

"She certainly doesn't need more donuts," commented the irrepressible Ms. Slim Shady.

"What protein goes with that?" interjected Travis, looming nearby and doing his part to talk over Vivian. "And since when does Italian food have blueberries in it?"

Chloe shook her head at such collective ignorance.

"The amazing blueberry thingy I am referring to is a plated dessert made by this handsome like the sun Korean chef who owns a teeny, tiny pastry shop in an alley somewhere near Seoul. Naturally. As if I could be speaking of anything else. Also, secret fact, man's a genius and a marshmallow. He can look all Mr. Grim, but oh no, don't be fooled."

"How is the sun handsome?" asked Fran. "And isn't he not single? Why are you wasting my time?"

"Wow, haven't you've had a big breakfast and can move up on your Maslow's hierarchy. Yes, last I saw he was dating a Bond Villain. Or maybe she worked at the World Bank. Or both. You know her, we all know that woman. She was even wearing Bond Villain shoes, which is beyond provocative in a town that is all mountain."

"Nobody dating a Bond Villain is in an LTR. It won't last," pronounced Fran.

"Ever the optimist, Fran. But aren't we underestimating, to our peril, the tenacity of your average Bond Villain? Look how tenacious I am after one dish and a four-minute interaction, and I can't even get my ruthless on for national TV."

"It isn't your mindset," continued Vivian, "you just can't cook."

"Thank you, Vivian. There would be something extra depressing about getting sent home simply for not trying."

Travis again interrupted the escalating tension.

"What's provocative about shoes?" he asked. Because he didn't know, and apparently Felix, now sitting straight and still in the chair opposite Chloe so as not to crease his apron, wasn't going to help run interference today and ask himself.

Chloe explained.

"It takes a special fitness about one's hamstrings, Travis, for a woman to walk up hills in heels. Me, ain't got it no more. And I may have given her the stink eye simply because she does. Perhaps I did. I can't remember."

"Oh," he replied.

Just "oh". The ordinary, one-word response Travis often made when receiving new information in the warehouse kitchen. One almost might not know, unless, say, one had shared the stress and pressure of a national cooking competition with him for the last six weeks, that the ground under him shifted ever so slightly as Chloe gave him his name back.

"You're calling him that now?" Fran asked, casual-like, because somebody had to and God forbid Vivian got there first.

Chloe answered with an equally casual reply, almost as if they were having a real conversation.

"Yeah. He's probably going to win, so I am practicing being his sworn enemy. It'll take effort, that, so best start now. So, I'm giving him his name back."

Is what she said. As if that made any sense.

Nearby, Oliver and Paul leaned against the back of Vivian's couch, drinking their first on-set cappuccinos and talking liability laws in international waters. They really didn't want to be sucked into other people's conversations, but even Oliver's stirring and tragic recounting of his uncle's wife's brother's boat meeting a rogue rock in the North Atlantic faltered as they assessed the immediate crisis.

"Paul?" asked Oliver under his breath. "She's really gonna call him that?"

"Let's not talk about it," he whispered back, his courtroom experience allowing him to do so without moving his lips.

"That's what I thought. Do you think she found out?"

Paul turned his back on the group to better gossip freely.

"If she doesn't know, she don't wanna know. Like he'd miss that amount of fennel on a piece of white meat. I think it was him being captain of the bomb squad, though, that tipped her over the edge. Let's not talk about it! Not here."

"Well, can't say she didn't call it. Spice Mountain! effin' sucked. You definitely have to make your (mother's) short ribs again tonight, for everybody's sake."

"We don't have any! How are we doing on favors with Rachel? We couldn't keep up her supply of chocolate chip cookies last week while we only had hibachi's."

"Then grab that young PA," said Oliver. "We can use his phone to order in more of Glenn's donuts."

"Please stop forgetting Troy's not here anymore to take it away from him. And you want to risk Chloe finding out Glenn has been hooking us up? You think today is the day to confess?"

"Ugh! I can't handle the intrigue. I can't handle it!"

On the other side of the seating area, Fran's interrogation on the topics that mattered most to herself continued.

"Be honest, is that chef truly as handsome as all that?"

"You really don't care about sweets, do you? For you, I shall stop thinking about what I need and give you what you need. If one of Michelangelo's angels, you know, the statue," Chloe explained, pointing down.

"Not the painting," she continued, pointing up.

"Anyway, if that guy got bored after centuries of just being aesthetic perfection and decided to try his hand at making aesthetic perfection, you know, *juje* his life, that would be him. And why wouldn't that man date a Bond Villain?"

Fran's moderately blank expression suggested she either did not share or couldn't follow what Chloe thought were widely held assumptions regarding the career and dating aspirations of Renaissance art. Chloe tried again in the vernacular.

"His desserts rock the house, that's all I'm saying, and I happen to find him attractive even when he doesn't shave and his hair's a mess. I would prefer both the art and the artist to come cheer me up, but I am settling for the one that can be frozen and overnighted to me in a small cardboard box."

"Why were you in Korea?" asked Travis. "You're an Italian cook."

Since Paul couldn't put both hands over his ears to block out the sound of Travis asking a question that he knew Travis didn't want answered, not until he found a place to put down his coffee cup, he resorted to just closing his eyes, but behind his mug Oliver insisted,

"It was a good try to be normal. Come on, it was a good try!"

From across the seating area, Chloe saw Paul's head flop forward. Taking it as some hint...about something, she answered Travis with added caution.

"Oh, you know, I ran away from home. When you're committed to the process, you have to go somewhere nobody will look."

"Ran away from home?" sneered Vivian, "What are you, twelve?"

"When I was twelve, I didn't have credit cards."

"Like I was saying, Travis," Chloe continued, "I did a tour of Asia, and our ship stopped for the day at Incheon. They will make ninety stops in Japan, but Korea is an in-and-out thing. Why, I ask you? Have you seen a Japanese man in a suit? How is that culturally superior?"

Felix, suddenly finding his voice, interrupted her sartorial harangue to get to the sugar.

"You were about to find a skilled pastry chef. We want to know about that part."

"Oh, right. As I strolled along, snow coming down, damp, unhappy, as one who has run away from home is wont to be, suddenly the wind blew me around and into his shop, which by a miracle was a patisserie not a chicken gizzard barbecue. It was like being half-shipwrecked, half-Dorothied on the isle of blueberry lemon happiness."

"What dish is that?" asked Travis again, quickly seconded by Felix.

"Right, get to the food."

"And when do we get to the handsome part?" interjected Fran.

"And did you go back a lot while you were there?" Felix added. "Did you try anything else? Get to the food."

"And when do we get to the handsome part?"

"No, Felix. My ship left on the next tide, and I gave his business card to someone in country."

"They have invented Google," sneered Vivian's Echo, finally getting in the game.

"Can you Google in the Korean alphabet? I don't even know the name of his shop, never mind how to type pictographs into my computer."

"Get to the food!" Felix insisted.

"It's an *entremets*, alright already? Lemon mousse with a blueberry glaze and lots more secret bits. You should see his chocolate work. I can't order a two-tiered cake that doesn't come with a 3-D chocolate butterfly anymore. Well, you get it."

Felix nodded, all in now that he had the full picture. Fran still didn't get it.

"How is this a story about a handsome man?"

"Places, places everybody," interrupted Rachel, walking through the room clapping her hands to get their attention.

Everyone lined up in their rows, and to the great relief of Paul and Oliver, the conversation turned to general speculation on the new guest judge.

"Who do you think they got?" Janiva asked, turning around from her spot in the front row. "Felix, who's hot in desserts these days?"

"Do we think French?" Paul wondered from the back row.

Fran remained gloomily certain that whoever showed up would not be a friend.

"Maybe they got that Australian," she speculated. "He made a whole generation of savory home cooks afraid of a *croquembouche.*"

Chloe grimaced back at her with unexpected solidarity.

"So not a fan of hard caramel with my eclairs. At least we're in the second row, and nobody will see my disapproval. Safety first."

"Nobody better see that face," Fran answered with a warning elbow, "you and Felix are our two dessert-loving ambassadors."

"I promise to duck behind Janiva – hey girl, hey! – during the reveal if anyone shows up trying to ruin *pate du choux* with a marble veneer."

While Chloe put her hands on Janiva's shoulders and practiced different ways of hiding behind a woman two inches shorter than herself, Felix wished again that someone, anyone, would show up with a cake.

"Yes, we know," said Paul.

"I'd settle for cooked flour coming out square," Fran whispered to Chloe.

"Let's at least not go splat on the pavement," Chloe whispered back. "No smoke, no fire, no mixing up sugar with salt."

Hearing the low bar the women set for themselves, Felix reached over and patted Chloe's shoulder, wondering if the judges would notice him making double-sized components and being inexact about which side of their shared bench he left them. He still owed her an amends for initially coming down on the wrong side of the spice bomb.

"Thank you, Felix," she responded to his silent encouragement. "Good luck to you, too! Channel your inner Saturday night Paul. Feel it, baby."

Fran elbowed her again.

"Stop encouraging him, the food gods are probably already letting him eat cake. We're here to destroy the competition!"

"The world can't afford to lose a pastry chef, they're essential workers."

"She's right, mean Fran. I'm essential, and I have the tidiest apron here. You shouldn't alienate the only person showing the new judge respect."

The entrance of the main judges limited further trash talk between Felix, Chloe, and Fran to an exchange of raised eyebrows and belligerent chin gestures until Felix's attention was wholly claimed by Chef Juan officially opening the week with his introduction of the guest judge.

THE SAID GUEST JUDGE STOOD backstage with his business partner, insulated by two, thick double doors from the talk regarding what would happen to him if he showed up with French wedding pastry, and waited for his cue to Enter with Cloche.

"Do I look alright?" he asked anxiously.

Wallace gave him the side eye at this unusual, third-party appeal from a man notoriously "flexible" in his presentation. He suspected he was not being asked for his opinion on fashion and the modern chef uniform.

"Of what are you inquiring?"

"Do I have flour anywhere? Is my jacket buttoned crooked? It's wise to double-check before I go out there."

"Yeah, sure that's what you meant. This is not an idol competition. Worry about your food."

"Our business model depends on my making an all-round good impression, so I was just asking."

"True," Wallace conceded, crossing his arms over his chest.

"So does your raise."

"Point taken. I still don't believe you that's what you meant, but point taken."

He looked Kyung-ho over objectively, as requested.

"Your chef coat is clean and properly fastened, you've shaved your entire chin this morning, and none of the backstage grime is streaked across your forehead," he affirmed, holding up his own palm marked from moving the cart a foot closer to the brick wall. "Whether these people will appreciate any of that over your food, couldn't say. You know you need to keep them talking for at least fifteen minutes, right?"

"About what? Why can't we do *Oui, Chef! Francais* instead?"

"Are we discussing this now? Here? You chose the dessert with all your fancy chocolate work, right? *Oohing* and *ahhing* will eat up a lot of time. Who doesn't love a 3-D chocolate butterfly?"

He reached for the cloche. Kyung-ho swotted his arm out of reach.

"Never mind that now, don't make it slide around on the plate and start a whole bunch of other problems."

"You'll be fine," Wallace said soothingly, "look how handsome you are in your new chef coat. You like the new logo."

"They're going to get my name wrong when they introduce me."

"Yes, they will, that's why it's embroidered on your clothes. Just remember BTS has gone before you, so the whole world is K-pop nation."

"It's not actually comforting to be sent out to deliver dessert to people who would rather eat steak and watch a boy band."

"Thirty seconds," warned the headsetted person on Kyung-ho's right.

"Opening the door, chef," warned the headsetted person on his left.

"You'll be great," Wallace replied. "If you screw up your words, just remember they think it's cute when rockstars do it. In your country, you are a rockstar."

Carefully lifting his cloche off the cart, Kyung-ho negotiated it past randomly moving people and equipment, hyper-alert for potential tripping hazards, both sentient and inanimate. He assiduously mended fences with the show's lower echelon staff over the last few days, including bribing them with a fourth sample dessert made, he was careful to stress, "just for them". On set, however, he remained deeply wary of any sudden movements in case he missed anybody.

An absurd amount depended on him successfully carrying a metal container out a crowded door opening, past a few rows of amateur cooks, and placing it on the cloth-covered table near the front of the room. His expansion into a major US market, his ability to meet payroll for forty-seven employees next month, the reputation of Korea. It was almost equally absurd that his primary concern, other than remaining upright and dignified and his sudden fear he didn't actually know fifteen minutes worth of English words, was whether if by chance, his long-lost happenstance angel watched the Food Network. He was at least not so absurd as to tell Wallace that last part, and keeping his peace, peeked one more time under the lid of the cloche.

"You all set?" asked the headsetted person holding the door handle. Giving her a brief nod of professional assurance, the door yanked open, and after taking one more looksee around for protruding limbs casually blocking his way, Seoul's current Top Pastry Chef, Korea's Top Ten Most Handsome CEOs, the Hallyu social media darling and now *Yes, Chef!* Guest Judge for Gimme Some Sugar! Week strode through the opening and onto his American television debut.

CHAPTER THIRTY-SIX

the trumpets shall sound

Beyond the doors of Kyung-ho's isolation booth, the contestants stood in their three shifty rows, listening to Chef Juan enumerate his impressive achievements. Chef Jimmy Bob from Week 1 only need a few words of introduction, Chef Bowen came to them out of an advertising cartoon from the last millennia, but this new guy had a much longer resume full of benchmarks they envied and understood. Glancing up and down their ranks, they shared looks of respect, and fear. No one, however, could match the resume with a name. Even the exhortation from Chef Juan for everyone to "Please welcome... from Seoul, South Korea...*Cheeeeffff* Ji Kyung-ho!" enlightened no one.

Their complete ignorance regarding his contribution to the field of pastry, however, did not diminish the enthusiasm of their standard welcome given to all guest judges. Clapping madly for him, whoever he was, the contestants turned around as soon as they heard the door in the rear of the hall rattling open, and jostled and peered around each other to watch him walk down the room past their cooking stations, along the far side of their ranks, and around to the judge's area, tracking every moment of his ceremonial entry like a field of sunflowers following the sun.

Chloe looked over and around and stood on tip toes like the rest with only moderate results. The kaleidoscope impression from glimpses of half a profile or the top third of his head provided only enough information to confirm he was a man with pale skin, a good haircut and a confident, upright bearing carrying a shiny, domed metal object. She failed entirely to connect this potentially handsome and most definitely lauded professional with a not-yet-successful, small business owner she met on the far side of the planet, and who by rights, ought still to be there.

Once Kyung-ho safely deposited his cloche and turned to face the contestants, however, she suddenly blinked a few times at the resemblance. She shook her head and tried blinking harder, but the vision did not dissolve no matter how the view was blocked by half of Vivian's shoulder or all of Janiva's head. Unbelievably, unexpectedly, it was he.

"Snow blindness," she said, and clutched Fran's arm tight.

"Huh? Why are you cold?" Fran whispered, trying to balance Chloe's sudden drag on her right side with her own efforts to get a better look at the cloche from the gap to the left of Jake, as if that would tell her anything.

"No way," Chloe repeated, over and over, vigorously shaking Fran back and forth. Fran lurched against Ajiz on her other side and started a jostling, domino effect down the line.

"Stop doing that! What's wrong with you?" Fran said.

"What did I do?" complained Ajiz. He hadn't even started singing yet. They did blame him for the spice bomb, he knew it.

"He did it," he heard Chloe say, confirming his suspicion.

Making a heroic effort to stop banging Fran into other people, Chloe further tightened her grip instead.

"Oh, I'm so proud of him," she breathed. Ajiz didn't hear that part.

While Chloe dislocated Fran's dominant arm and used her *in toto* to pinball and bruise the rest of her competitors, and make Ajiz feel persecuted, the regular judges exchanged greetings with their guest. It surprised and gratified Kyung-ho to receive such a warm welcome from both the amateurs and professionals, all of whom he was certain had never heard his name or eaten his food.

Except one, he reconsidered. Within the shifting crowd, one red-headed woman shoved the contestant next to her in a manner that suggested a fan's enthusiasm. Somebody's fan.

"Wallace, if I'm being confused with Su-ga, you're so fired."

Kyung-ho turned back to Chef Juan. A well-practiced description of his new shop used up thirty seconds of all the English words he knew, but he gained confidence from Chef Juan's responses that he answered questions actually asked.

Looking out at the wider audience to gauge their reception, the shifting bodies parted again. The movement suddenly brought Kyung-ho face to face with that fan. Her expression startled him. It wasn't giddy excitement, or disappointment that he, in fact, was not her favorite Korean rapper on a side-gig. She looked...as if reuniting unexpectedly with an old, good friend. Kyung-ho felt support and encouragement shining out from her, along with a sense of homecoming. It was a powerful, oddly familiar, but momentary impression. She immediately bowed, leaving only the top of her head visible. Kyung-ho politely and reflexively responded, and as his own head came back up, his attention was reclaimed by his fellow judges with questions about his work in Paris. Another thirty seconds, and he still had English words left in the tank. Wallace must be proud.

"Why are you bending me over?" remonstrated Fran in whisper. "Stop moving me around so I can hear what they're saying. It might be useful for the cook."

"We're being polite," Chloe hissed back, "play along!"

Dragging Fran back upright again, Chloe became more forthcoming as a team player with inside information.

"Behold!" she said gesturing with her chin toward the newcomer. "Trust and believe! I knew he worked in Paris."

"Everybody who hands back their empty plastic cups before the plane lands at Charles De Gaulle says they "worked in Paris". Plus, Chef Juan told us that already."

"*Pffttt.* Amateurs. My man is *properly* French-trained, and – and! – the man brought me sumpin' to eat. If that isn't the man. Reliable. Handsome like the sun, dead reliable."

"Staring into the sun makes you go blind."

"Exactly. I told you I never got over it."

"W...w...wait...this is your guy? Your chef guy?" sputtered Fran, so struck by the coincidence, she even kept Chloe rooted in place for a moment. "No way. Is it? What's he doing here?"

"Way. The OG himself. The OG delivers. Told you so."

"Oh m'God...Oh my God!" Fran said excitedly, trying to take in the news and pass it on down the line at the same time. "That's the chef Chloe was JUST talking about."

A wave of surprise, doubt and speculation quickly spread outward from Fran. Vivian, as expected, came down authoritatively as the leader of the skeptic faction.

"Chloe knew he'd be here," she scoffed, with a nasally Echo adding,

"Or she overhead the PAs talking at craft services."

"Nope," the accused replied. "I wish for him all the time, no reason to think today he would come true."

"Why didn't you tell me?" complained Felix. "Reading off his resume took an hour and a half. There was time."

"I'm sorry, Felix, I guess I stopped listening to a word Juan says. Look, I snapped Fran's arm like a chicken from the shock, and I still can't let go of it."

"Please try," Fran requested.

"What do you think he brought?" Chloe asked instead, giving Fran another shake of excitement.

Fran took the small win that Chloe was getting her head back in the game.

"Finally! That's what I have been trying to find out."

"Too small for a *croquembouche*," pronounced Felix.

They all craned their necks with increased efforts to see the full cloche, as if a better look at a standardized metal kitchen object would provide the edge and definitive answer regarding what was under it.

Meanwhile, the judges were laughing in sympathy over the supply house sending the wrong spatulas to Kyung-ho's new shop.

"We finally used up twelve cases of gold leaf after a junior staff member checked the wrong box on the form," he complained, "and now this."

Chef Juan began interrogating him as to how one got customers to consume that much precious metal, while Chef Matteo's experienced eyes noted the wave of excitement among the contestants, and that Chloe appeared to be staring at Kyung-ho while the other contestants stared at her. He nudged Chef Juan to bring the larger group into the conversation.

"Are you familiar with our guest judge's café, Chloe?" Chef Juan asked, taking the hint. "You seem...overwhelmed."

Kyung-ho froze.

"What a coincidence," he told himself. *"It must be a common name."*

His head slowly and calmly swiveled toward the person so addressed, checking slightly as the red hair reentered his peripheral vision. It couldn't be her, he reminded himself, so no need to...to...

But it was. Flaming hair and shining eyes, they really belonged to only one person, even this far from home. His shock was superseded only by the unexpected gratification to relearn, unequivocally, that a happy American is an unmistakable thing.

"She remembers me. Isn't that nice."

His public-facing austerity thawed in a rush of a sudden joy. All his waiting for returns and reunions, he finally admitted, was complete balderdash. He hadn't expected to find her again, he expected to find her dead. And here she was, here, now, now well enough to be...

No. No, he didn't think she was.

While Kyung-ho grappled with such wildly varying revelations without the resources of a Fran to lean on, Chloe managed to answer Chef Juan's question with only an occasional need to re-injure her much needed prop.

"Annyeonghaseyo, Chef," she said, tipping Fran over with another bow before turning to Chef Juan. "I had the...*shake, shake*...honor of trying Chef's food when I was in Korea. He was always a genius...*shove, lurch*...so I am not surprised to hear all his recent accolades, but it is SO wonderful...*shake, SHAKE*...to find out his talent, courage and tenacity were finally rewarded."

"You so need to stop that," said Fran, trying again to dislodge her arm.

Kyung-ho bowed in acknowledgment of Chloe's words.

"And," Chloe added, returning his bow before scrunching up her shoulders with happiness, taking Fran along in both directions, "he brought his food with him. Reliable, the man is reliable. I have missed you, Chef."

"What do you think is under the cloche?" Chef Juan asked Chloe.

"Heaven."

Fran rolled her eyes at Chloe's continued inability to be useful over such a significant question.

"She wants this blueberry lemon thing he makes."

"True, but he wouldn't know that," Chloe said repressively in an undertone, "and this show is all about expanding our horizons, so let's practice gratitude for what he did bring. It, too, will be amazing."

"She wants this blueberry thing."

"I am very partial to Chef's *entremets*," Chloe conceded to Chef Juan. "Alas, I lost his business card, so I couldn't have it again. Or find it again. Or find it to have it, you know, mountains. Whatever."

Fran again explained.

"She means he doesn't have a franchise in her time zone."

Kyung-ho reached in his pocket and pulled out a small, white rectangle stained with a blueberry thumbprint. Silently, he held it up and waved it, before tucking it away again.

Chloe recognized it instantly.

"It went home!"

"*De.*"

"He put it on the tour?"

"*De.*"

With her free hand Chloe gave a high fist pump of satisfaction.

"Yes! That's so...!"

She suddenly trailed off. The card was in his pocket? It was theoretically possible it would still be somewhere, maybe, but in his pocket? And why did he know it was there? That was confusing. The continued discussion between Fran and the judges about their past connection swirled around Chloe unheeded. Keeping her head cocked and eyes fixed on his pocket, she waited for the card to explain itself. It didn't seem to have anything it wanted to share.

"Maybe it's his lucky card. That makes sense. Lucky card," she decided after a long minute, and let it go at that.

Fran took advantage of Chloe's silence, and her staying static for ten seconds, to offer the judges the "real" story, which they hoped included a lot of spice, drama and bad feelings. Juicy intel prior to Chloe's elimination tomorrow would heighten the suspense and audience investment over who went home.

"...she went to Korea before her operation...she always craves it when she isn't happy, or not feeling well..."

"You're unhappy today?" asked Chef Parker, always researching seeds of discord.

"Why aren't you feeling well?" Kyung-ho mused silently.

Chef Parker's question recalled Chloe's mind to the present.

"Huh? Obviously last week was unfortunate, and I doubt today, being pastry and not pasta, will be my finest hour, so yes, I am having a feeling."

"Ugh! And now I am going to bomb in front of my hero," she added to her near neighbors in line, dropping her forehead on Fran's shoulder with a groan.

"Luckily, he will jack you up on sugar, first," consoled Fran, "and didn't you bribe Felix for just such a moment?"

"Not enough to wrangle with this Iron Dome of doom," she replied, and banged her forehead a few more times against Fran's shoulder. "I just never plan ahead."

With a sigh, Chloe straightened back up and turned to face the music.

CHAPTER THIRTY-SEVEN

the miracle
and the madness

"You were sick," Kyung-ho said unexpectedly, and unexpectedly harshly. "Why are you here?"

His sudden animosity startled the judges who were listening, and even the contestants who were not. The cooks and crew members shuffled around to face the right direction to watch...whatever this was, and Chef Parker discretely gestured to the other two chefs that they should let this play out, whatever...this was or was going. Chloe just turned to glare sideways at Fran, again, and shake her head to prevent further revelations, but she lacked Oliver's authority.

"What?" said Fran in response to her look. "It was in your intro package, remember?"

"He doesn't need to know," Chloe whispered under her breath.

"How sad," interjected Vivian to camera, jumping in to offer the audience at home color commentary on today's unfolding drama in the kitchen. "Obviously, Chef isn't as big of a fan of her, as she is of him."

"Maybe he's just afraid it's contagious," echoed Ashley. "Is it?"

Exasperated by big mouth Satan and friends, and also trying to course correct after hanging back on Spice Mountain!, Fran jumped to Chloe's defense.

"She was dying and now she's not, so the what and whatever is nobody's business."

Boldly glaring directly at today's guest judge about to critique a dish she could not make, she added,

"You should be nicer to your fans."

Chef Parker disagreed strongly with both Vivian and Fran. It wasn't sad at all, it was his business, and guest judges didn't need to be nice to nobody. A spice bomb having a conflict with the visiting chef, what great timing to counter any mid-season rating slump. He stood ready to make the most of it, and silently prayed for a sex scandal reveal. He then looked over at the cloche to calculate whether Chloe could be maneuvered into knocking it onto the floor, until receiving a sharp elbow from Chef Juan.

"Too much?" Chef Parker whispered.

"*Tch, tch, tch*, nobody make up stories," Chloe countered in a vain attempt to diffuse the sudden tension. "That isn't his mad face. Wouldn't I know? Wouldn't I be upset? Trust and believe, I would. The man likes his customers, and he likes them to be alive. Let the man have his PTSD."

"Meanwhile, let's blame Fran," she said turning to her. "Look what you did. It's his debut and you made him grumpy with news of my demise."

"You broke my arm."

"You put out the sun."

"Wait, you said you went to Korea to run away from home," said Travis, unexpectedly breaking into the conversation with an uncharacteristic, Fran-like thirst for information.

"Well, technically I ran away from my doctor. My home is very nice. Running toward Chef's desserts, though, is always the wise decision. If only his *tart tartin* could transit through Customs."

"Why come back before you'd eaten everything?" asked Felix.

"You can't die in someone else's shop. That's rude," Chloe answered, writhing once more over her nervous habit of running her mouth instead of shutting it. "What I mean is, Chef's desserts make life worth living, but some things do actually require medical intervention."

"But, of course, you are better now," Kyung-ho replied. English was his third language, though, so he might not have got the sentence structure right. What he meant was, "what the hell are you doing, missy?"

Chloe responded with a bright smile. In American that meant "yes". He immediately and correctly interpreted it as a "no", made without having to lie about it. His frown deepened. She stuck out her tongue as a rebuke, but only for a second, and Al missed that part, so it was like it didn't happen. But he got it.

"Meet our star pastry contestant," she continued on, reaching over to clutch Felix's shoulder. "Please give him all the guidance you can."

Kyung-ho bowed at her request and, equally important, acquiesced to her tart and panicked appeal to remember why they were all there. He turned to ask Felix where he studied, and his area of expertise.

Felix just managed to stutter that he hadn't been to culinary school, yet, but that he really like cake-making. Chloe shook his shoulder in a manner intended to express encouragement, or perhaps a subconscious attempt to dislocate another competitor's arm before the start of the challenge.

"There's no need to be nervous, F, Chef really is a marshmallow. Trust me. Right now, he's just...It doesn't matter," she said pulling herself up short. "He'll help you out all he can. Really. You're our Felix and he's a genius, it'll be great."

"It'll be great," she said to Kyung-ho with another bright smile.

ALL FOUR JUDGES RECOGNIZED THE opening segment of Sugar! Week had gone off the rails. Three of the four loved it. One rubbed the bridge of his nose and waited for his business partner to burst through the doors, interrupt the taping and smack him upside the head. Americans might not notice, but if the episode ever aired in Korea, they might wonder why he was yelling at a stranger, and demanding a public accounting of what that Fran person correctly asserted was not his concern.

Even in the grip of strong, wholly unexpected and unhelpful emotions, though, Kyung-ho marveled at how Chloe continually and relentlessly marketed his brand, or tried to, under such shifting conditions. To demonstrate he could be team player, and because what he was about to say was true, he made an unexpected contribution.

"I brought you something," he told her.

Chloe looked at him, then the cloche, then back at him with a wide smile of anticipation and gratitude that he was ready to put aside the drama and get down to the sugar.

"Do you want to see what is under the cloche?" asked Chef Parker, his tone openly inviting her to bring the snark against this unexpected enemy, if she wasn't.

"Well, yes. And no. Mostly extra yes. But no."

"What do you mean no, you weirdo?" said Fran. "Even if it's a *croquembouche*, you are going to eat it and like it."

"*Croquembouche* don't fit under a cloche," Felix corrected her. "You don't even know what one is, do you?

Chloe just yanked Fran upward with another righteous shrug.

"*Tch*. I'm so misunderstood. I'm not being pessimistic and distrustful," she declared, even though she kinda was.

"Please, show us what brought, Chef," requested Chef Matteo, moving the show forward to the next segment.

Kyung-ho reached for the cover to his dish.

"I call it...*Chloe's*...*Chloe's*..."

Kyung-ho choked momentarily on giving the dish its proper attribution. What seemed necessary information to an audience of four million felt shameless to an audience of one. After a short pause, he recommitted to using the full, actual title of his signature dish.

"*Ahem*. This is...Chloe's...Starry...Night," he said and lifted the metal lid with a flourish. Glancing casually around to assess the contestants' response, he allowed a good minute to elapse, or at least a good four and a half seconds, before he looked to Chloe for her reaction. Which he considered a very long time and a valiant effort.

She didn't hear a word he said.

Despite the joy, anger and writhing embarrassment of the last ten minutes, Chloe never lost sight of what this debut on *Yes, Chef!* meant to Kyung-ho's business. As excited as she was to see him, she was more excited for him. During the reveal, she watched his face not his hands, and listened only for how his moment of theater was received by the crowd. The gasps of approval and groaning acknowledgment of the dish's skill were enough. When he finally glanced in her direction...something in the way he raised his eyebrows at her... only then did she actually take in the murmured speculation from her fellow contestants regarding why this dessert had her name on it.

Chloe's eyes dropped down to the plate.

"No way," she breathed, and with one last squeeze and death rattle to Fran's arm, burst into tears.

On the exposed metal disk centered on the white, cloth-covered table, its careful plating undamaged by all its travels, there it sat, yet another twinkling, shiny, visceral reminder that with this man, managing one's expectations was entirely unnecessary. The thing she loved and could not find, from across thousands of miles and the whole of the deep blue sea, it found her.

"*Tch*," she managed to get out, gesturing with her chin her appreciation for the new marbled glaze, the golden moon, and the tiny stars.

Fran hadn't listened to Kyung-ho's reveal either, little interested in what a man she already didn't like had to say about food groups she didn't eat. The outburst of emotion so close to her ear, however, recalled her attention. Turning towards Chloe, and discerning the hiccupping sound was from happiness, not anger or disappointment, she took another look at the blue dessert.

"Wait? No way. No SUPER way," Fran exclaimed, pulling on Chloe's arm in turn. "Is that? Chloe, is that? Wow, he did deliver."

Grateful for the distraction of having her own arm painfully yanked about, Chloe smiled and nodded and patted away her tears with her free hand.

"Told you so," she choked out.

A possible culinary danger suddenly struck her.

"It's not the last one, right Chef? Chefs?"

Kyung-ho's stomach dropped.

"Wait, should I have brought something new? Tae-Ho warned me this dish would be a disaster."

Confused and startled, for once, by his expression, Chloe quickly tried to assess whether her question had been culturally rude, or an English word that phonetically sounded rude, or what just happened.

"If there are twelve more backstage," she rapidly clarified, pointing to the plate, "I won't have to go *Squid Game* over this one. But if cooking in a borrowed kitchen made you never want to make this dish again, it will be boots on, knives out."

Kyung-ho silently balanced relief with trying to understand what American ritual involved footgear and sharp objects, with wondering how she heard about his trials with unsea'd gluten.

Watching his face, Chloe let out a sigh of relief.

"Phew, glad that's resolved. And that there's more."

"He hasn't said anything yet," Travis pointed out.

"Yes, he did. The rest of him is taking in the idiom. Attacking a judge happens all the time on Japanese reality TV, and he hasn't been in the country long enough to know that we have liability laws. Although, some things are worth getting sued over."

The contestants turned back to Chef Kyung-ho for confirmation.

What they saw was not the face of a chef who felt understood and respected, standing in front of a very happy superfan. Chef Parker's eyebrows went up and Chef Juan pursed his lips as they telegraphed to each other that boy, was this man mad. They thought he was mad earlier, but they were wrong. Had Chloe worked as a food critic in Asia?

Ajiz leaned around Fran to nudge Chloe and call her attention to the looming crisis.

"Hey, Chloe, uh, we think you're funny, but I don't think he gets you."

Paul agreed.

"I don't think he can follow your English."

Vivian, ever the peacemaker, added to camera,

"Leave it to Chloe to insult a foreigner and a guest judge."

The man himself, or rather the two thousand years of hitherto unknown patriarchy lurking in his modern, egalitarian, you-do-you soul, was indeed having a feeling. Acutely aware from the opening of his segment that Chloe's death grip on Fran was not excitement, it was how she was holding herself upright, he felt like he was watching a tired free climber refusing to be sensible and come down to earth. Each time Chloe readjusted her grip, she struggled to get her stasis back. Now, after the excitement of the reveal, and the small alarm over something about knives, sheer willpower alone prevented her from falling down in front of an audience and a camera. Instinctively, Kyung-ho checked his watch and calculated how long he need linger outside his own country, culture and empire where this absurd test of stamina, right in front of him, too, like she was trying to piss him off, such things would not be allowed.

"You shouldn't be here," he said aloud with Fran-like conviction, looking up from his Seiko.

Once again, Vivian was right there to support him.

"That's what I have always said."

In a flash of temper, to either or maybe both of them, Chloe answered by pointing to his dish.

"Apparently, God doesn't agree with you."

"Then why do you always lose?" asked Vivian.

"I won." Chloe clapped back. Tamping down her ire, she continued in a lighter tone. "What's a quarter of a million dollars? Anybody can have one of those. Everything I loved and lost in a back alley on the other side of the planet has found me, and this isn't even my mountain. And I keep telling all of you, I am one of his favorite customers."

"You know I'm right, don't you?" she asked him directly, encouraging him again to remember they were at work.

"I am more right," was his swift reply.

The camera swung around for a closeup, hoping now was the start of that second reveal, and Kyung-ho felt a sharp twinge of contrition. His outbursts danced very close to outing Chloe as a medical liability, and made her look disliked. It was absurd their interaction could be so misconstrued, but people who believed she could stand for more than four minutes at a time would believe anything.

"*Mianhada*," he said to her with a half-smile of apology.

Chloe nodded and lowered her gaze. As his plate came back into view, her eyes welled up again. It was all very confusing and emotional, but he had brought her what she wanted to eat, and she knew how short-tempered he got when stressed.

Chef Parker, disappointed and confused that the mad guy just apologized, moved the segment forward, hoping the storm would kick up again if Chloe tried Kyung-ho's dessert and hated it.

"It's time for tasting," he said, and the contestants surged forward, glad to be released from the odd, crackling tension.

a moment of forever

Felix eagerly grabbed at a spoon and lunged for the shiny edible object on the white tablecloth.

"Not before Chloe, idiot," said Fran, holding him off with her arm, and batting away the other contestants clustered around the judging table ready to taste test the new Imitation Challenge. "It wasn't made for you."

Chloe leaned in, but her spoon only hovered over the dish, dithering whether to start by trying a star without moon, or ruin the picture by going all moon, or begin with just marbling, because gold...he used it, it must be edible, but...wasn't it a mining product?

Her view of the dish was suddenly blocked by an impatient, outstretched hand. Kyung-ho snapped his fingers twice and held his hand back out. She turned the spoon over to him with a docile,

"*Yeeesss*, Chef."

"Watch the moon," he instructed.

After a sharp tap, the metal utensil cracked the golden sphere to release a tiny wisp of smoke, and with it the scent of a lemon tree. He then ruthlessly but efficiently carved out a balanced bite and offered the spoon back to her.

"Oh, wow," said Felix in wonder.

Chloe just re-clutched at Fran's arm and teared up again. After another short pause, instead of trying to negotiate the transfer of cutlery that he once more gestured toward her, she reached for his hand and guided the spoon up to her mouth to take the bite.

"Is it good?" asked Felix, "is it how you remembered?"

"Wow, you don't say," he continued, as the group watched her whole being light up and relax at the same time.

Monitoring her response, Kyung-ho noticed something else. Other than how pleased he was with himself. His brain rapidly reviewed the ingredients in the dish and their medicinal qualities. Antioxidants. Vitamins. Sugar? What combination would have that result the instant they hit her blood stream?

"Anthocyanins," he concluded. *"That's what she needs. Anthocyanins."*

Then he simply took a moment to enjoy Chloe holding his hand and looking at him as if a working knowledge of molecular chemistry and how to cook with fruit made him the most amazing person in the world. It was just as fun, and exactly how it felt the first time. Consistency, it's so important in French cuisine.

"It is good? Is it how you remembered it?" echoed Chef Juan, who hadn't been listening. He and the rest of the panel used the distraction of the reveal to turn away from the cameras and quietly confer. All three restaurateurs understood the politics of dish naming, and it didn't usually end in a fist fight with the customer.

"Sex scandal," Parker whispered confidently to the others, "gone wrong."

They smugly turned back to the contestants, better sure of their footing for the day's taping ahead.

"Try it," Chloe replied to the group at large, dropping Kyung-ho's hand and stepping back. "Take in the magic."

A cluster of unhesitant spoons dived in, and the contestants began the process of devouring the dish as step one in replicating it.

"Fran?" Chloe asked.

"Ooohhhh..."

"You're welcome. And see, I'm always right."

"I can't make this thing," pronounced Ajiz, sparking a wave of sad nods and elbows.

"Yes, okay, maybe pairing citrus with dairy without curdling anything is going to suck for most of us," she agreed, "but at least he fed us first. How the Bond Villain did it, I will never know."

"I mean, *ahem*, World Bank chick. How's our girl?" Chloe asked with another bright smile.

Chef Parker laughed out loud.

"Who did what? Story?" asked Fran.

"No story, just tiny, the woman was tiny. His shop is on a hill, so there's that, but how can one not be a 9,000-pound shut-in if this is what you eat every day? She was full Bond Villain."

"Maybe...?"

Chloe giggled inappropriately at Fran's innuendo and smacked her silent at the same time. Fran subdued her own laugh to a smirk.

"Let's not break our hearts thinking about it, Fran," Chloe mumbled. "Hills. Hills, metabolism and magic. What do we know from Bond Villains, and I'd hate to be wrong. Or right."

"Who's the World Bank chick?" Chef Juan asked on behalf of management.

"He's dating somebody from the World Bank," offered Fran with a snarky eyeroll, still not on Team Kyung-ho.

"Actually, I said a Bond Villain," Chloe corrected her, perhaps under the influence of a sugar rush. "Same thing, but I am on record for voting no. That should be understood."

"Please tell me not out loud," Paul interjected.

"Oh, I disapproved, and I expressed myself. What can't I say to a complete stranger? I would like to think I provided clarity. I'll tell you about it later."

Paul shook her head in resignation, while Fran eagerly awaited the inside story.

Belatedly, Chloe re-remembered that Al was her documentarian, not her friend, not with his arms full of heavy equipment, and neither country needed to know what she really thought about whom a visiting guest judge slept with.

"Anyway, moving on," she said. "This recipe better be accurate or I'm going to be mad at you, Chef. You know we can't get the balance right on the first try, you getting all getting funky with your individual components. *Tch tch tch*...Mean. Except good, of course. Super extra beyond good. Good now, mean later."

It was Kyung-ho's turn to shrug.

"See look," Chloe pointed out to the group. "I told you he was funny."

Nobody got that.

"It's not really fair," Vivian complained, "us having to make a dish you have had before and thought about. You have an advantage."

Everybody got that.

"If I made that, it would be completely not this," Chloe protested. "I had the prototype. Can no one follow our conversations? I thought we covered this."

"No, you're still holding out on me," said Felix, angling for more data. "All you've done is glare at each other."

"I said, *tch tch tch* and wept. For goodness sake, the stars are new, the moon, the glaze, I still have no idea what the crunchy stuff is. I don't know what more I need to do to express all that in a positive and supportive way. He got it," she said gesturing again with her chin to Kyung-ho. "You got it right?"

Kyung-ho's eyes narrowed again, which again looked like annoyance, but this time it was Chloe that laughed out loud.

Fran looked at her with deep concern.

"What? He thought that was funny," said Chloe. "He knows full well I can use words when I want to. And you should be glad he is laughing now, as it lessens the risk of him shooting the messenger at Judge's Table. And by that, I mean you."

"What did I do?"

"It's what you said, Fran. You shouldn't have distracted him on his big day with my little problems."

"He was being mean to you."

"He is constitutionally incapable of that."

"You're a nutball. Babble and obfuscate all you want, but everyone can see this reunion is not going well. Everyone."

"I insulted his girlfriend. People like their life choices to be approved of. Even when they're wrong."

To Chef Parker's disappointment, Kyung-ho's only response to such bald provocation was to rub the bridge of his nose and laugh a little under his breath. Trusting in the vast opportunities later in the day to reignite the war, Parker closed out the segment and Kyung-ho stepped back into line with the other judges.

Standing like a soldier, hands behind his back, Kyung-ho looked straight ahead at nothing in particular, while they all pretended to listen to Chef Juan enumerate the rules for the Imitation Challenge. He kept Chloe well within his peripheral vision, however, and continued to track the lasting impact his food had on her pallor and energy level. She oughtn't to be here, and as soon as he was no longer under contract to be here either, things would be going back to how things ought to be run. For the next few days, though, she would at least be where he could feed her properly. He risked a momentary direct look at her face. Success, fame, paying the rent on time, these were wonderful things, he liked them, but once more he was forcibly reminded how taking care of Chloe felt even better, and the one area he felt uniquely skilled.

"I should do that forever," he decided.

CHAPTER THIRTY-NINE

chatter boxing

When Chef Matteo dismissed the contestants back to their benches, Kyung-ho watched for the moment Chloe let go of her prop and was left to her own devices. He then shook his head disapprovingly at her departing form.

"She's usually so kind to everybody, I hope you aren't offended," lied Chef Juan, responding to his sigh.

In that quick defense, Kyung-ho instantly recognized a rival, and in the condescending and careless manner, not a very good one. He asked,

"Have you gotten to know her well?"

Chef Juan answered with a swagger.

"Of course. She's going to intern at my restaurant."

"Oh no, sir, she is not, Mr. Fancy Pants."

Kyung-ho forced a tight, polite smile.

"Is she? Doing what?"

"Haven't decided. Maybe start her on the grill station at my casual dining place?"

Kyung-ho resisted the urge to punch him in the nose for trying to kill his wife.

"Are judges allowed to hire contestants?" he asked instead.

"Sure. Job offers promote the pool of applicants for next season."

"Well, good luck with your hiring process, Casanova" interjected Chef Matteo, then turned to Kyung-ho. "We're so glad you are here, Chef. Chloe is getting cut this week. Your surprise connection will enhance her exit drama. Did she cause trouble in your café? She does that periodically."

Kyung-ho countered Chef Matteo's request for information with one of his own.

"Did something happen during the last elimination? I thought I heard the contestants mention explosives."

"A spice bomb," Chef Matteo reassured him, conceding that resolving fears over a potential on-set terrorist threat momentarily trumped scandalmongering. "That's an American culinary phrase. She put the wrong sauce on her dish. You're Korean, so I don't know if you would have noticed, but one of the expert panel...it was ugly."

"She didn't do it," added Chef Juan with a pastiche of loyalty, "but it was her dish. And my palate."

Chef Matteo corrected himself.

"Right. It was an "accident" with her dish, so it counts against her. Vivian has the subtlety of a rhinoceros sometimes."

"I think we'll miss that rivalry. It's heated up lately," said Chef Juan, still playing for time to keep Chloe in the competition.

"Jake is at it again," reported Chef Parker. "Vivian took notice."

"Which one is Jake?" Kyung-ho asked.

Chef Matteo discretely pointed him out.

"The handsome blond kid over there in the plaid shirt."

"He lacks my mature charm," said Chef Juan.

"You keep telling yourself that."

"He seems to be missing a few too many buttons to be working around food," remarked Kyung-ho, "and is Vivian that dark-haired woman? She's very pretty."

Chef Juan concurred with both statements.

"Don't expect him to find them, and expect her to vamp you all week until you tell her so."

Kyung-ho responded with a quick dissent.

"She's not my type."

"Who isn't? Chloe?"

"Vivian. And Chloe just likes me for my food. The pastry business is like that."

"Did she work for you?" asked Chef Parker, seconding Chef Matteo's attempt to dig up the secret discord between them.

"She connected us with a culinary tour offered through Holland America. My first shop is in one of those "authentic" neighborhoods near the marina."

"That won't upset the elimination schedule at Judge's Table, will it?" Chef Parker asked, still not seeing where it all went wrong.

Kyung-ho shook his head and cleared his throat.

"I don't have a problem with her leaving, and she expects it based on her skill set. What if she performs well?"

"She won't. Whatever you do, don't turn out the lights or she'll ruin a whole flavor profile for you."

Chef Matteo interrupted before Chef Parker could enlighten him further about that startling pronouncement.

"Before we start the next segment, Chef, I wanted to give you the heads up to use your own style to critique the contestants, but there's no need to be too honest when it comes to Vivian."

"What does the show not want the audience at home finding out?"

"She's smart enough to play the game for the cameras, we've just identified her as the season winner. Will your girlfriend mind the beautiful American vamping you on TV?"

Kyung-ho gave a short laugh that turned into a cough.

"She will mind, but she's not liable to get confused about Vivian. I hope she keeps her distance. Love triangles aren't good for my brand. One public scandal can tank a Korean company."

"An angry Vivian isn't good for your business, either," Chef Matteo replied, balancing the equities. "Her father ships food stuff. Do we ship wheat to Korea or do you get it from Ukraine? Anyway, best of luck to you and your supply chain, you've been warned."

"Well guys," he said looking at his watch, "I guess we can start walk-throughs. We don't have to stop at every station, Kyung-ho, just if you see something interesting. Watch your back, though. Literally. These kids will knock into you with a pot of boiling water, or a knife, or open an oven door against your calves without a second of thought."

Kyung-ho coughed again.

"Yes, Chef."

"Are you getting a cold, Kyung-ho?" asked Chef Juan. "Maybe someone should check with a PA and see if we have any lozenges on site, or at least flag Rachel down to bring you some water. You've got a lot of talking and eating to do in the next few days."

"Thank you, I will. I didn't feel anything earlier, but something seems to be coming on now."

"It's probably just the pollen from the garden, and the dust in here," suggested Chef Parker. "The PA's have been measuring out all the contestants' flour as we have been talking."

"That's probably all it is," Kyung-ho said, clearing his throat again as they walked towards the front row of workstations.

In TV land, the contestants were dismissed from the tasting segment back to their stations to jump into the cook, but in real life there was a short break for the camera crews to reset and the PAs to stock the workstations with any perishable items. As the contestants refueled, rested up and waited for their next call, Fran pulled Chloe aside to do her own hard-hitting interview on all that tension with a guest judge.

"What did he say to you?" Fran asked.

"When? You were there."

"He was talking Korean, start with that part."

"Oh. He said he's sorry for being grumpy."

"And what did you say?"

"I thanked him for bringing me m'stuff. And now we're friends. Except, one cannot be friends with a judge. We'll be friends later."

"That totally didn't happen."

"Did, too. He's launching an empire, by the way, so whatever you think of him, don't let it affect what you say about his food on camera. I told you he was handsome, that should be enough for you. Deal?"

"No deal. He's only moderately good-looking, and boy, is he a whole lotta mean."

"Not to us."

"No, to you. It sounds like you actually like him, your mean, horrible chef."

"You knew that before he showed up this morning."

"Well, he doesn't like you back."

"Can't think of why he would. All I've really done is trash talk his girlfriend and told a stranger about the best thing I ever ate. How is that sexy? Trust me, though, he owes me one, so if there's any more sabotage, he isn't going to look the other way."

"*We've got a gold-en tick-et,*" Fran started to sing. She meant it ironically, but the power of Charley Bucket quickly triumphed over sarcasm, as it always does.

Chloe started them back off from the top.

"*I never thought my life could BE, anything but ca-tas-tro-PHE…*"

"*…Sud-den-ly I begin to seeeeeeee a bit of good luck for MEEEEEEE,*" added Felix, joining them after collecting a fresh cup of competition jet fuel.

"*For we've got a GOLDEN tick-et,*" they sang, and the day's *Yes, Chef! America* espresso-fueled glee and get down dance party kicked off in the corner by the entrance door, as it was wont to do when their breaks went long. Or when anyone among the cool kids was having a feeling and wanted to sing about it. Oliver and Paul, back over in the lounge trying to finish their earlier conversation, shook their groove thing in solidarity, and Travis, as always, stood listening for their next call. Somebody had to, Chloe always maintained.

"One day you're going to crack and join the fun train," she said to him as Ajiz transitioned them into *"I Want Candy"* and before Oliver brought some 50 Cent into the action. "It's just a matter of time, and the right song choice."

"No, I won't."

"Yes, you will. Choo choo!"

Kyung-ho, witnessing the phenomenon for the first time from across the room, interrupted the judges' discussion about SEO metrics and new franchise name recognition to look at his companions with a raised eyebrow.

"They dance at the beginning and end of things," explained Chef Matteo with a shrug. "It's what they do."

CHAPTER FORTY

sweet tea and no sympathy

Before the dance party drowned out the other noises in the warehouse, Chloe thought she heard Kyung-ho cough. It might have been anyone doing anything, there were a lot of noisy people between the mini grocery store and the door to the restaurant all the way across the room, but she thought not. When she happened to be looking in the direction of the judges, he coughed again and confirmed it. It was also coming on not passing off, because once the challenge started, she could track the judges' movements by the ever more frequent hacking that carried above the clatter and bangs and whirs from the intervening cook stations.

While she whisked her mousse, the panel passed by two rows ahead of her. She watched Kyung-ho stop to turn his head until a paroxysm passed. That didn't look good. She wondered if he would recognize or use American medicine, and looked around to see if a PA was nearby that could find him cough drops. There must be a stock somewhere, although she wouldn't be surprised if Chef Parker used a more old-fashioned show business nostrum, like gin.

Her eyes fell on Felix's bench and the day's ingredients lined up and organized. Seen as a tidy group, she recognized the ginger, lemongrass, lemon balm and honey made a tea that calmed the symptoms heard from across the room. Possibly. Unless she remembered wrong. It was an Asian flavor profile, though. Perhaps what it lacked in efficacy, it might supplement in comfort.

She finished her mousse, congratulating herself that it set well, while boiling a pan of water. She then prepared a quick tisane before moving on to the next component. As it steeped, she glanced back and forth between the simmering pot, and the one melting sugar for the glaze, and over to where Kyung-ho stood across the room, debating whether to keep the drink hot until the judges got to her station, or risk a burnt caramel by walking it over to him immediately. Fortunately, Rachel the PA passed her station and broke the tie. Flagging her down, Chloe poured the beverage off into a mug, stirred in a good dollop of the honey and asked her to please deliver it to Kyung-ho.

"It's for his cough," she explained. "They drink this in Korea when they're sick. Possibly I mean China, but I think it's Korea."

"That's nice of you," said Rachel.

"It was so nothing. Just hospitality for the stranger in a strange land with a cold coming on. If you or anyone else needs any, I've got at least another mugful. They're welcome to grab it off my station."

"Do you want me to...?"

"Just shove it into his hand and go back to being slammed with your real work. He'll know what it is, and whether he needs it."

Rachel picked up the mug and threaded her way over to the judges. Kyung-ho felt her light touch on his shoulder, heard a low "Chef?", and saw a disembodied arm reach through the knot of people and cameramen to press a large, warm mug into his hands.

"Thank you," he said as the arm disappeared. Sniffing what it handed him, he took a tentative sip.

From her vantage point across the room, Chloe saw he did not burn his tongue or abandon the mug on the nearest countertop, and was satisfied. She returned to her work. It further gratified her that soon she could no longer locate him by ear alone, and noted he still carried the mug with him twenty-five minutes later when the group passed by her station with a simple, "Everything going alright, Chloe?" from Chef Matteo.

She thought no more about it. Until it came time to make the crumb component with what was left of her knob of ginger root. With an exasperated sigh, she realized she failed to check the quantity needed for the actual recipe before macerating an overly generous portion for the tea, and now had to choose whether to tweak the recipe to fit the remaining finely grated paste or make a full-sized component with a weak ginger vibe. Deciding to stretch a smaller, properly made quantity, after a brief struggle with math changing the ratios, she moved on.

Another hour elapsed, and Chef Matteo called the end of the cook.

"...Three, two, one, hands up! Please step away from your bench," he shouted to the contestants.

Chloe looked down at her version of (her) Starry Night. The internal layers weren't quite level, giving it a bit of a tilt, but a Van Gogh was not a Mondrian, so, you know, and she did remember the exact placement of the decorations. With a nod of moderate satisfaction, she joined the general post-cook ritual, craning her neck to look around at what everyone else had put up. She caught Fran's confident eye and Oliver's assured head shake, and Felix gave her two thumbs up from the adjoining bench. She also noted Vivian gilded her *entremets* like the dome of a smaller Buddhist temple, Ajiz's turned pink, there was no getting away from that, and Paul's stacked up two fingers too high, he must have added an extra layer somewhere. Still, not hearing anyone wailing, the cook seemed to have gone well all-round.

Twenty minutes later, upon receiving the signal from the judges and consulting her checklist, Rachel announced,

"Chloe, you're up!"

Chloe waved her hand to acknowledge the summons and climbed down off her high stool where she had been resting, chin in hand. Reaching for her dish, suddenly she felt her head spin and her muscles get wobbly. She paused a brief second to let it pass off, picked up the plate and carried it across the room and through the glass door Rachel held open for her.

"Hello, Chefs," she said pleasantly, entering the formal judging area.

The four men sat behind a string of four-tops pushed end to end in a room otherwise set up as a small restaurant. Placing her dish in front of Chef Matteo, Chloe stepped back to the mark on the floor, careful to disregard all other persons in the room wearing black and milling around off-camera. Ignoring the working people still felt rude, but she learned to save her belated, unprofessional waves and nods for whenever the cameras, and the judges, turned away.

The four men stared at her offering, then Chef Juan started off the critique.

"How did it go today, Chloe? Is this dessert as good as Chef Kyung-ho's?"

Chloe smiled slightly. She considered the six ways Vivian, ahead of her in the queue, might have used his rhetorical question to flirt with the guest judge.

She was just his type, very Bond Villain their Vivian. With a wry grimace, Chloe refocused on her own business.

"I appreciated the clear and easy to follow instructions, thank you, Chef. My dish isn't perfect, but I'm happy with what I put up."

Kyung-ho returned her thanks with a slight bow, looked over at her plate and then back at Chloe. A simple glance showed she achieved a perfectly acceptable bake, and that it was slightly more visually accurate than the contestants before her. Kyung-ho's experienced eye also recognized enough imperfections to legitimately second whichever flaw the others chose to highlight.

He was far more concerned, and more acutely aware, that he was tired, and already tired of talking so much, and getting a cold, although thanks to the mug of tea Juan sent in earlier, that was better. Some people, he knew, were at an increased risk of being unreasonable when they were sick and tired. Watching Chloe swaying slightly in her effort to keep on her mark, he suspected – without being convinced – that yelling at her to go lay down and leave dessert-making to him might be an overly strong, potentially confusing, possibly fever-induced outburst that lacked the pastiche of judicial impartiality.

Still, he refused to remain completely silent in the face of overwhelming provocation. Looking down the row at the others, he asked,

"Are they all going to stand? Maybe because I have a cold, but it makes me dizzy watching them shifting around waiting for bad news. Can they sit on something?"

"Oh, they can sit," responded Chef Matteo. "Chloe, do you want to sit down? Take a chair from…"

"I see it," Kyung-ho announced before she could turn her head in the right direction. Pushing back his own, he stalked over to collect the one he chose two contestants ago. She stepped out of the way, and he plunked it down on the contestant's mark with a firmness that both relieved his feelings and communicated them. He then returned to his seat.

Chloe immediately flopped down with gratitude.

"Thank you, Chef. It has been a day."

Taking action made Kyung-ho feel better immediately. Chloe wouldn't fall down in front of him, and that was a gain. His complaisance as a successful problem-solver, however, was fleeting.

"Now, we will try your dish," Chef Matteo announced. Reaching for her plate, he sliced the dessert down the middle to expose its internal layers, and then divided it into four portions, plating one for each judge.

"*Hmm-mhh,*" responded Chloe with indifference. No longer needing to make an effort to remain upright, she slumped in her chair and let the tiredness wash over her. As her head lolled around, her eyes came to rest on Kyung-ho. Watching him at work was still like a glass of cold, clear water after a hard workout. Sugar! Week was going to be full of lingering wonder. Well, until her elimination. And as long as he didn't fall for Vivian right in front of her.

Kyung-ho's plate was handed down the line, and as he received it, he looked over again at Chloe. It took a moment to summon an admonishing response to her sleepy, candid look, but he did. He then waited until with reluctant acquiescence, she slowly sat up properly and adopted a more alert pose, before he hurriedly caught up with the other judges putting their silverware down with small clinks.

Despite her newly focused stance, and full expectation of terminal criticism, the ensuing attack caught Chloe wholly unprepared.

"This isn't good," pronounced Chef Matteo, poking at his remaining portion of her dish. "Where's the ginger?"

Chloe blinked a little and raised her eyebrows slightly at this strong response to what was a blueberry and lemon dessert, but otherwise did not respond.

"The blueberries could use salt," said Chef Juan, "and without the ginger, it's just too sweet."

Chef Parker simply remained on brand.

"This is not an award-winning dish. The mousse, it's kind of claggy. More ginger crumb would have given the dessert texture."

Politely swiveling her head back and forth to look at each judge as he spoke, Chloe's only other reaction was to raise her eyebrows a skosh higher after each comment. All this relentless negative Nelly, and right in front of Kyung-ho. How very unexpected.

His critique came last.

Chloe watched him drag his fork through the crumb. The gesture appeared more fraught than necessary. Her eyebrows at the ready, she awaited his thoughts on her artistically tilted, gently spiced version of her own damn dish.

"There is almost no ginger in here," he echoed, and then relapsed again into silence.

Kyung-ho raised his eyes too late to notice the tiny, frozen pause before she refocused her attention on the bits and remains left on her original plate. If he had to guess her reaction to his critique, and it would only be a guess because obviously he missed it, but if somebody made him guess, her following head tilt and two quick bites to her lower lip might suggest *et tu Brute*. Seen only in profile, however, it could also indicate a long-standing feud with the boom mike operator, whose equipment nearly buzzed her head just out of frame.

Maybe. It could.

Not content with giving just their top-line impressions on how much she sucked at incorporating sugar with Asian tubers, three out of the four judges again canvassed the lack of ginger. Chloe waited silently. Despite the crisis, she found it slightly – slightly – amusing they chose to highlight the flaw with a redeeming story behind it. Also, that Kyung-ho kept poking the crumb looking for the ginger stewing in the mug next to it. Still, it wasn't that funny.

"The judges are never near this mean on Yes, Chef! Australia," she silently complained. She considered interrupting their good time to solve the great ginger mystery for them, but it felt cheap to leverage unrequested medicine as a mitigating factor in an unsuccessful dish. It might even dock her more points.

Instead, Chloe pressed her open hands against her legs, and since nobody was talking to her anyway, continued to list objective truths, hoping to calm her growing ire with facts. The judge's underlying assumption that she couldn't measure ingredients properly, well, the spice bomb wasn't her fault, and the dried fennel, sure, that happened, that was on tape, but it was a mining accident, not a rounding error. She refused to get excited about (allegedly) bad crumb and the catastrophic omission of an eighth of a teaspoon of sea salt. Her first skirmish with molecular gastronomy produced fog, that was something to be proud of.

Having debriefed her bake with still some lingering agita, Chloe moved on to counting the tables in the restaurant. There were seven. She checked back in with the judge's discussion.

"Would you serve this in your restaurant, Chef Kyung-ho?" asked Chef Matteo, looking down the row at him.

"No."

Another simple statement, and true, and correct. Chloe did not possess one tenth the skills to apprentice in his kitchen. Neither did they. Again, Chloe felt pique growing into anger. She looked up and counted the can lights overhead, stopping at ten, a nice round number, because staring at lights was unproductive.

It was an education to witness the art and alchemy of the judges condensing her overall show performance into the archetype she would be assigned in the editing room and grafting it onto the dish that showed up at their table. "Ghost ginger" wasn't the ideal mistake from someone who would mix up her own gochujang with someone else's dragon boat of hellfire, but wow, look at them making it work. A deep suspicion grew in her mind whether Butterfinger Bobby dropped all those ramekins in Season 11, or whether he dropped the first one and afterward a PA got assigned to creep up and say *"boo!"* whenever he went to collect his serving dishes.

Kyung-ho echoing the chosen strategy, though, clarified the real source of her anger. All four professionals lived and died by online reviews yet had no regard for the power of their randomly assigned, big, fat lies on anyone else in the room. None of the viewers at home would purchase her grocery store products now. If Juan expected her to work for such careless man, or thought any of this was sexy, well, then, he was capable of anything, but watching Kyung-ho come into her kitchen and silently pick and poke her dessert while she was slandered and ganged up on...

Betrayal. Chloe's head snapped up as the right word echoed in her mind like a gong. Biting her lip again to disrupt the pricking behind her eyes, she lowered her gaze back to her plate. This was not the time to evaluate three-syllable words about trite and mostly accurate comments. This was their exit process, and she would have to live through it. Disciplining her expression into a mild, listening face, she fixed her gaze on Chef Matteo and waited for her dismissal.

CHAPTER FORTY-ONE

chloe needs another hero

Kyung-ho sat hunched over his cold mug at the four-top closest to craft services, watching and waiting through Chefs Parker, Juan and Matteo's interminable discussion on missing ginger root, like it was a thing. He was trying to stay out of what only needed to be a three-to-one decision, while having a wee bit of a panic attack. He only contributed five, perfectly neutral, possibly mistranslated words to the critique of Chloe's dish, and brought her the chair she was sitting in when she heard them, and yet somehow it got him tossed into the outer darkness with the Juan's of the world. Those people expected people to stand while listening to yammering nonsense. It was an uncomfortable and disorientating fall.

Turning suddenly to the Juan sitting next to him, he asked in a low voice,

"Is today an elimination?"

Chef Juan shook his head and whispered back,

"We thought about it, but this dish isn't bad enough to bother throwing off the numbers for the team challenge."

With a flash of thankfulness, Kyung-ho rubbed the bridge of his nose and wished this critique segment would hastily finish so he could...do...something, anything, to get off the Juan bus to nowhere good.

After one more round to briefly cover how unsalted blueberries ruin everything, Chef Matteo decided they filmed enough tape of the judges' critique and moved on to get the necessary contestant engagement.

"So, Chloe, do you have anything to say about your dish?"

Calmly shaking her head "no", she attempted a wide-eye, ready-to-go, smile, and leaned forward a little in preparation to standing up. Not eliciting the response he needed for the segment, Chef Matteo nudged Chef Parker to try a different tack.

"I'm afraid Chef Kyung-ho doesn't find your unskilled attempt to replicate his signature dessert successful. How does that feel?" he asked. Kyung-ho glared down the row at him for the untimely shout-out, and blame.

"A first attempt could never equal the work of a Cordon Bleu graduate, and shouldn't be sold next to it," Chloe replied with outward calm and indifference. After another pause, she leaned forward a little more to better indicate that today she played for Team Parker and would not hold them up any further with meaningless twitter.

Matteo tried his other elbow.

"This is the fourth challenge in a row you haven't performed well," Chef Juan pointed out with a heavy slather of Juan-esque sympathy. "It's a shame you couldn't deliver for the guest judge you have a history with."

Chloe's eyes flashed briefly in his direction. Realizing, however, that leaning and staring and silence would not end her segment, she resettled herself in the chair, replaced her hands flat on her thighs, and went back to counting can lights. Desperate times.

"Don't you have anything to say about your performance?" asked Chef Parker. "Where's the chatty Chloe we've gotten to know?"

"You are providing me input regarding my deficiencies, and I am evaluating and incorporating that input," she replied, looking vaguely in his direction. The temporary black spots in her eyes from staring at light fixtures prevented her from seeing him properly, but his red coat made it easier to pick him out of the lineup.

"I agree with Chef Parker," said Chef Juan. "Wow, twice in one show! Did something happen in the past with Chef Kyung-ho? Is it his fault?"

Chloe found Chef Juan even easier to re-locate, the loud plaid covering his shins jumping out from under the table to even a visually impaired person. She turned her blinking stare in that direction, and decided a row of lying liar spice freaks didn't need to know.

"Nope," she replied briefly.

It was Season 14, however. Everybody knows the Friendly Judge never takes no for an answer.

"We haven't asked you yet how your name got on an *entremets*," he continued with hearty enthusiasm. "Chef Kyung-ho said his business benefited from your past random act of kindness. Tell us about it."

"Did it? Huh. It might have been kind, but I wouldn't call it random," she countered. "I do not go around willy-nilly suggesting people engage in ill-advised ventures with unknown schmucks. That would damage my brand. And his."

"You have a brand?" asked Chef Parker.

Chloe reminded herself, firmly, it wasn't her job to teach Chef Parker that being mean was easy, and anyone could do it. Starting with the person who led him astray with the shade of his signature jacket color. That wasn't a friend.

"You seem to be nodding your head," she heard Chef Juan say.

"Am I? Sorry, Chef. I started singing to myself there for a second."

"Singing what?"

"*Lady in Red, say Lady in Red,*" he willed silently, hoping to finally mark that one on his *Yes, Chef!* bingo card.

Chloe let him down.

"Bonnie Tyler."

"Oh," he responded, disappointed, "you mean *Total Eclipse of the Heart?*"

"Doesn't have a drum line. *I Need a Hero* is the latest cool kid anthem."

"*Where have all the good...,*" he serenaded her in a spontaneous and mistaken belief that he, too, was a cool kid. He regretted it instantly.

Chloe directed a clear-eyed look at him that Chef Matteo recognized from the previous week.

"Dooooo doo. Doo dooooo," she said, speaking the backup singer part back to him almost the way she did when Ajiz started off a song. Almost. With that, because it didn't matter anyways and it relieved her feelings, Chloe went back to staring at the can lights and singing to herself, adding what for the cool kids was some very minor silent chair dancing.

"*Where's the streetwise Heerrrcules to fight the riiiising oddddds...?*" she asked herself, inside, where it counts, with subtle head bob, while playing the drum line quietly against the side of her chair and the top of her leg with her thumbs. Later, the audience at home could tell by her two, small, sharper head tilts when she got to the "*wahhhhhhh, wahhhhhh*" part, but she doubted anybody in the room did.

"What just happened?" asked Chef Matteo staring first at Chloe ignoring them, and then at Chef Parker. "Did…? What?"

Chef Parker just shrugged in Chloe's direction.

"How would I know?"

Chloe made an effort to stop expressing how she really felt and turned another blinking stare straight ahead at the shape of Chef Matteo.

"I can bring some Bonnie and listen at the same time," she replied. "Someone was telling me I don't have a brand out in the real world?"

"Oh. Well, like we were saying," said Chef Matteo, trying a third time to get the interactive footage needed for the segment so they could bring in Travis. "For such a competent person that you say you are in business, it's a shame you keep making extreme rookie mistakes, like too much fennel, too much spice, and now no ginger."

"Yes, I do say," she responded in a bland tone that made one judge lean back and try to hide behind Juan. If she couldn't see him, she might think he left after getting her a chair.

Up on Spice Mountain!, Chloe's focus on shielding Fran and squashing her own hurt feelings allowed Vivian to slink away unchallenged. It was too late now to change her trajectory on *Yes, Chef!*, but since they kept asking for some self-assessment to close out the segment, she decided to give it in the area she felt most qualified and expert.

"You're so right about me making dumb mistakes," she continued affably.

Kyung-ho leaned a skosh further back to better limbo under the sword he heard whistling toward their row of necks.

"Fran and I have been on the show long enough to expect Vivian to switch any sauce handed to her. It is Week 7. I guess we both just lack imagination when it comes to cheating. I wonder if she has done this before. She seemed so good at it."

"Why would you say that?" Chef Parker sputtered. "Do you have proof?"

"Me? Well, I do have a better knowledge of Fran's character and my kitchen habits than you do. Then there's science, but we could just ask Al, who filmed the whole thing. I don't see why in his quest for an Emmy, he should be denied his Pulitzer. Right Al?" she said, turning to the cameraman.

For a moment, Al stopped spinning around capturing reaction shots and his eyes peered around his equipment to look at Chloe the person, and not Contestant X on a monitor.

"I'm here for you, Al," she said, and turned back to the panel. "As I said last week, if I sauced my own plates instead of delegating, the dishes wouldn't have gone out. A *Roja* is slightly the wrong color, and ask Chef Juan whether sentient humans could miss the taste of Ajiz going all-in."

"Well...Well...," Chef Juan began, quickly trying to invent an on-brand interaction the editors could choose from other than a cheating allegation against the season winner, "...at least you are still here in the competition to have the dessert Chef Kyung-ho made for you."

"He didn't make it for me," Chloe said, returning to her former calm, businesslike manner, "he made it for you. I just happened to be there."

"*Ohhhh*, snap!" said Felix. That is, months later when the episode aired. Kyung-ho responded by looking down at his chest, checking for holes and whether he was bleeding out. Given the differences between the two men's vernacular, however, it worked out to the same thing.

Chef Matteo offered another, more neutral, transition option.

"Well, we'll consider what you've brought to our attention. We've seen a whole different side of you today."

Once again Chloe leaned forward silently as if to stand up and stared him down. This time, he wisely dismissed her.

"Well, thank you Chloe, that will be all."

CHAPTER FORTY-TWO

winners and losers

After Chloe left the warehouse restaurant, and while Kyung-ho acclimated to his new life cast into outer darkness, now with grievous bodily harm, his companion in exile turned in his seat and addressed him with approval.

"You're going to make an unbiased judge after all, Kyung-ho. It's a shame about her bringing up the Vivian stuff, but we're glad you let her get that mad without jumping in to mitigate it. I know she's still a customer."

Kyung-ho tapped his fingers on the wooden tabletop with apprehension, hoping against hope Juan was mistaken. He was wrong about the internship, it was possible.

"Are you sure about her being angry?" he asked. "She didn't expect a good critique."

"Very. At the audition we called her hands girl. She has this philosophy about open hands make an open mind or something. Anyway, when she presses them against her leg, the process isn't going well. If she was a lemon, she would be squeezed dry today. It was probably your fault."

Taking his next to last sip of tea, Kyung-ho decided to change the subject to one where his life was heading in the right direction.

"Thanks for having the tea made up, Juan. It really worked."

"Have what made up?"

"The tea. It really helped my cough. I could use another cup."

"I didn't have anything made up. What are you talking about?"

"You didn't? Where did it come from?"

Kyung-ho took another experimental sniff of the dregs. After a rapid review of the ingredients, he sighed and mentally kicked himself. Then kicked himself harder and banged the mug down on the table.

"What's the matter? What's in it?" asked Chef Matteo. He stretched his arm in front of Juan to pick it up and take a whiff. "Oh."

"Oh, what? Do you smell bitter almonds?" asked Juan. "Is Vivian now trying to take out a judge?"

"No. Ginger, lemongrass, melissa and honey," listed Matteo, leaning back in his chair, "and there's only one person who ever makes extra beverages this season."

"At least we know now where the missing half pound of ginger went," said Parker leaning over Matteo's arm. "*Hmmm*, smells good. I wonder if we can get her to make us some. Is that Thai lemongrass, Kyung-ho?"

Kyung-ho sighed again and started hitting his forehead with his fist.

"Don't worry" responded Chef Matteo, handing him back his mug. "Even though it's your cold, it's still not your fault she screwed up her dish. She does weird things all the time."

"But how do I get more tea? Now?" asked Kyung-ho in despair.

"Just ask craft services," said Parker. He then added with renewed optimism, "Hey, maybe Chloe is secretly planning to poison Vivian and steal the crown, and all these extra beverages are red herrings. I hope she does it on camera."

"I hope she doesn't," countered Juan. "She can't intern at my restaurant from jail."

Kyung-ho decided, once again, that discussing topics that made his fist all twitchy and gave him a headache was not a productive use of his time. This time he tried refocusing on mitigation strategies and damage control.

"That second person we judged...Fran? Is that her name? If you're getting rid of Chloe, have you thought about keeping Fran around long-term? I may be biased in favor of anyone who can make a decent mousse, but from the little I saw earlier they seem like "winning it for the both of them" contestants. If Vivian is as volatile as you say, and she does anything you can't cover up, it might be best to have Fran as substitute for the finale. You'd get good dramatic tension, either way."

"What a great idea. Thanks Kyung-ho," responded Juan. "So great to get a fresh opinion. You can map these things out from the start, but you have to adapt to what actually happens. Especially when not everybody flames out just because it's their turn, and Vivian did cheat on camera."

"Glad to help," he said.

Chef Matteo looked at his watch. "That's plenty of deliberation time. Rachel, can you please send in the next person? Thanks."

It took two hours and nineteen minutes for the entire cast to move from their workstations into the judging area and then out to the lounge. That still wasn't enough time for Fran to elicit why Chloe entered the restaurant with casual nonchalance and left in a blazing fireball. Unlike Ashley, or Ajiz or even Paul, the judges never sandbagged Chloe with new flaws and failures she didn't already know. It was weird. Now with all thirteen contestants gathered again in one space and called to line up on their marks in front of the cook stations for the results, Fran hoped she could get the full story.

The winners were announced first, and today it was Chef Parker's turn to do the honors.

"Will the following please step forward," he said. "Felix..."

"Yay!!! Our Felix!!!" was heard from Chloe and Fran.

"Janiva..."

"Yay!!! Hey girl, hey!!!!"

"...and...*pause*...Fran, please come forward."

Chloe had to push Fran out of line amid more clapping, cheers and several whispers of surprise before she walked in a daze to join the other two. Once Felix's dish was given its accolades, followed by a supportive "told you so" from the contestant side of the room, and after Fran – still dazed – and Janiva, steady and confident as usual, were given special mention, the Top Three were dismissed back into line.

Chef Parker moved on.

"Now, for those of you in the bottom. Will the following three step forward. Ashley. Ajiz. And...*long pause*...Chloe. Please step forward."

The three took their positions against another background of rustling confusion from those who expected to hear Jake's name called last for serving a blue moon dish without any moon. Chloe and Ajiz linked hands to await the judge's stock ire together, while Ashley just looked surprised.

"Ashley, what was that?" Chef Parker began. Then spent the obligatory five minutes reviewing why she didn't read the instructions, and cooked how she, who was not a pastry chef, felt dessert got made. He then turned to the next problem dish of the day.

"Chloe, where was the flavor? It was like you didn't use half the ingredients. Or any salt."

Letting go of Ajiz, Chloe shoved both hands into the side pockets of her khakis, causing her stained apron to scrunch and flare around her arms, and now without a plate to stare at, directed her eyes to somewhere around knee level of the judges. After a blank pause of nobody saying nothing, she gave Parker's slight about a ginger-scented blueberry lemon dessert that triumphed over molecular gastronomy, unlike some people's, the shrug she thought it deserved.

Chef Parker rephrase his question.

"Did you use all your ginger root?"

"Yes. I macerated a portion before I realized it had to be finely grated."

"And which part did you waste making a tea for the guest judge?"

Out of the corner of her eye, Chloe saw Kyung-ho hold up his mug and waggle it a few times to get her attention. He failed. So did Chef Parker. Chef Parker, though, continued trying.

"Why didn't you tell us earlier what you did?"

"We never mention small mishaps that occur during a cook."

"But it impacted your dish. A lot."

"So can using the wrong spoon."

During this exchange, Ashley turned to look at Vivian, Ajiz looked down at Chloe's profile, Al moved his camera into position and quite a few in the crowd looked to Fran to interpret what was happening. Obviously, Chloe had done something wrong, again, although what tea had to do the dish, and how Chloe turned into Travis after ten minutes behind a closed door, not even those closest nudging and elbowing Fran for more information could solve.

"Did somebody start talking about Troy in there?" Oliver whispered to Paul.

Chloe turned her head slightly to better hear the low chatter behind her.

"Tell me you didn't poison one of them, Chloe," Fran hissed, "did you?"

She smiled at Fran over her shoulder and shook her head.

That brief interaction, and her small, quiet snort over how little Fran understood the toxicity levels of dessert ingredients, restored some of Chloe's equilibrium. As a prophylactic measure against losing it again, she began to count how many rows of bricks were visible on the wall behind the judges, starting from over their heads to as high up as she could look without putting her head back or making funny eye movements she wouldn't want Al to record for posterity. Without squinting, she thought there were nine.

"Is she ignoring us again?" asked Chef Matteo.

"Please tell us why you made Chef Kyung-ho a tea, instead of making Chef Kyung-ho's dessert?" he finally asked her directly, "and why we shouldn't send you home for it."

The murmurs turned to gasps at the threat of an unexpected elimination. Chloe remained nonplussed.

"I heard Chef cough," she explained to the third brick over Chef Matteo's head. "Finding substitutes for even common medicine is difficult when far from home. It was a simple courtesy to a fellow traveler."

"It's a wonder you got any dish up at all," sneered Chef Parker, "spending all that time playing apothecary."

"It took a nanosecond of thought, and about five minutes to make. Ajiz told Paul his cream was boiling over, and I always leave my flour bin out for Felix to use after he's dropped his, it's how the cool kids roll. The tea had almost no impact and nothing to do with you not liking my dish."

"It was excellent tea," Kyung-ho said in a burst of instinctual unwisdom, trying again to separate himself from the other judges and the elimination process. "I could use another cup."

Chloe turned her head to look vaguely in the direction of Kyung-ho's shins, without making any effort to find the right shins.

"There is one mug's worth in the fridge, third unit from the back. It hasn't been sweetened. The honey is on the far wall with the spices."

Kyung-ho received the information in blinking silence. Obviously, she would not deny a person access to lifesaving medical treatment, but otherwise he was on his own and waving empty cups around making demands wasn't helping.

"We should all try it, then," said Chef Juan injecting some welcome friendly banter. "Chloe, would you make the rest of the judges a glass, too?"

Felix's earlier, mumbled, "why do I feel all oogie?" received several nods of agreement, but the momentary silence following Chef Juan's request startled even Vivian. Chloe did not, could not have sworn at a judge. She hadn't said anything. Had she? Oliver's head movement said it all. He had been in the van down from Fern Lake, so he knew. Before Kyung-ho's hand could reach the bridge of his nose, however, Chloe spoke the calm and correct response.

"Yes, Chef."

Felix quietly elbowed Fran.

"Drink it at your peril," he said.

She nodded.

"More fool, them."

Chloe wheeled sharply around and the ranks of contestants quickly stepped out of her way. She returned to her station to make the additional beverages. Chef Parker then called the group back to attention. Turning now to Ajiz's dish, he noted Ajiz's failure regarding a basic mirror glaze, and asked how a blue dessert somehow became pink.

"I was thinking of the wrong painting," Ajiz explained, now a veteran talker in a Bottom Three crisis situation. "This is more of a...a...of a Monet...?"

The idea visibly struck Kyung-ho, especially now that Little Paris had no more gold surplus, and he unexpectedly supported Ajiz's monumental error.

"It could be done in strawberry," he agreed, and began counting on his fingers like a fortune-teller, a clear indication he had withdrawn from participation in the remainder of Ajiz's critique, and instead was contemplating various flavor profile combinations for the crumb and glaze components.

Chloe returned a few minutes later with three small glasses and an espresso cup on a tray. The glasses she handed to the regular judges, and the cup she exchanged for the mug in Kyung-ho's hand.

"Why is his different?" asked Chef Matteo.

"His is medicine, the other three are just iced tea," she answered and stepped back into line.

The judges each took a sip.

"Oh, this is well-balanced," said Chef Matteo, "I like this."

"This is the second time in a row the beverage is better than your dish," commented Chef Parker.

"You should run a tea house, Chloe," said Vivian from the crowd behind her, adding one decibel lower, "and leave the cooking to rest of us."

Chloe gave the judges' praise the same indifferent silence as Vivian's censure.

"You won't regret wasting your time and ingredients on this add-on? Even if we send you home today?" asked Chef Parker.

"We are the choices we make. I already made it." she said calmly, sparking another wave of discomfort among those who heard the silent "you – insert swear word of choice – idiot" part, like the "w" in "sword", drowning out even Parker's threat.

"Of course she should go home," said Vivian, finding a camera near her and again trying to be the voice of America. "Why all the drama? She could never replicate a dish this perfect. She lacks my skill with sugar work."

"It wasn't perfect," Chloe snapped with quick derision. "That was the challenge."

The shuffling, agitated audience froze.

"Do you mean Chef's desserts aren't refined?" asked Vivian. "Or you just hated this one?"

As the silent the room waited for her response, Chef Parker imperfectly restrained a gleeful smile, Paul grasped Oliver's arm in genuine alarm over whether Chloe understood defamation law, and a cold finger of fear went down Kyung-ho's back regarding his launch.

Chloe stared again at the row of shins in front of her biting her lip. She decided that payback is a bitch, and after a short internal tussle, that unlike some people, she wasn't.

"A foreigner working on the Rue du Rivoli better be embracing their *plus royaliste que le roi* over how pastry is made, if he doesn't want to get assassinated," she replied. Taking a moment to congratulate herself on remembering the phrase, and on her accent, she continued.

"Chef's shop offers all the classics, like *tart tartin*, madeleines, napoleons," she listed off from the image in her mind, "but for specialty items, perfection is too static, too cold, possibly not how Koreans do things."

"He adds a little *chkt*," she said, making gesture like she was turning a dial. "A little dissonance. It's riskier than perfection, and braver, it ain't French, and the component with the dissonance will always taste wrong on its own. That's why I said it would be hard to replicate the dish on the first try. The man's a genius. Nobody ever listens to me."

Glancing back towards Vivian, Chloe nostrils flared with contempt at her disappointment.

"Duh-uh," she concluded.

"Is she right?" Matteo asked Kyung-ho.

"She is always right," he responded with a wondering, rueful awareness of how well this stranger intuited his cooking philosophy after eating two versions of one dessert, while being visibly and extremely upset about her own problems, both times.

"Then why is she angry that you brought her her signature dessert?" asked Chef Parker, this time because he genuinely didn't get it.

"Please make it stop," Oliver said to Paul, before turning around altogether.

"As I said before," Chloe answered Chef Parker, "he didn't make it for me, he made for you. I just happened to be there."

"Oh, snap!" said Ajiz, which is probably where Felix got it from. Even Paul, largely bored by the bad cross-examination over a petty misdemeanor in a room that earlier witnessed at least two murders and a travesty, turned around with Oliver, and started randomly pointing at equipment and workstations as if that somehow...something.

It was Week 7, however, and the contestants had learned a little bit about how show business worked. Chloe decided it was past time to launch into the guaranteed segment-ender – talk amongst yourselves.

"I thought the pink was pretty," she commented to Ajiz.

"Chef's going to use it in a new, strawberry version. I gave him the idea," he responded with pride. "That happened while you were gone."

"*Pret-ty in, pretty innnnnnn pinnnnnk,*" Chloe sang back with what only insiders would recognize as a nod the Psychedelic Furs. Thankfully, Ajiz was an insider, and could hum and head bob along with her as they turned back to face the judges.

Chef Matteo, instantly paralyzed by listening to amateurs having thoughts on how to tweak a real chef's high-end food, with song, closed out the segment in an almost knee-jerk haste.

"Well, you three will have to raise your game tomorrow to avoid elimination. I hope all of you have chosen the components from today that you want to reuse tomorrow for the Reinvention Test, and I hope you chose wisely. For now, go home, get some rest, and we will see you right back here tomorrow."

CHAPTER FORTY-THREE

Released for the day, the rows of contestants broke into chattering groups and headed off toward their lockers and the doors to the drive, while the judges turned and moved together back into the "restaurant" and through the farther doorway to their private lounge.

"I don't think she will be making you any more tea," said Chef Juan in a low voice to Kyung-ho as they walked.

Chef Matteo was more sanguine.

"She did offer."

"No, we drank that part already."

"Really? I think I got lost in the bizarre gameplay. Who makes a companion beverage and doesn't serve it with their dish? That's twice she did that."

"Well, I still don't know why she is mad to be in the bottom three over it," Juan said, "but you better stick with CVS, Chef."

"Say-vee? I don't know that word," replied Kyung-ho, hoping it was American for "time machine". Alas, Wallace had not booked him for a *Dr. Who* reboot.

"C-V-S. It's a drug store. I'll have the driver stop by on the way back and come in with you."

In the car with Juan on the final leg to their hotel, clutching his bag of cherry-flavored cough drops and some orange liquid Juan swore was more effective than Chloe's tea – so obviously, that wasn't true – Kyung-ho did clear up one pressing issue on his conscience.

"She isn't really getting sent home over two ounces of grated ginger, is she? It was a blueberry dish."

"Why? Do you feel bad?"

"Even if it was missing all four ounces, there were several dishes far less successful, plus that tea was excellent."

"True. She would do better as a sommelier. If only she drank."

"She doesn't drink?

"No, isn't that annoying? I had a bottle of good wine and several reasons we should share it all ready, too. What do you use to invite women over in Korea?"

"Ramen."

"No booze?"

"The soju is implied."

"Well, tomorrow is a whole other dish, and if she beats out Ashley, which she did by a country mile today, she'll hang on through the Group Challenge. She should have waited to make the tea then. No planning, that woman. She knows Parker has it in for her."

"Well, she knows enough about pastry to promote that Felix kid," countered Kyung-ho. "He did a great job without any formal training. What are the show's plans for him? Can a pastry chef win?"

"We already did that two season ago. Why, do you want him for Little Paris?"

"It might make a good crossover promotion between the show and our opening, if he went out on a high note. Otherwise, he's of no use."

Juan gave that some thought.

"We could have him sacrifice himself for the savory chefs in the last team challenge before the semifinals. Customers love that."

"Well, once you cut him Little Paris will have a better idea how to use him," lied Kyung-ho. "Hey, how will today impact your own recruitment of Chloe?"

"She'll get over it. She's the forgiving type."

"I hope so," Kyung-ho said fervently, also hoping to someday get credit for his relentless backstage Friends & Family reward campaign. He fully intended to tell Chloe all about it at a later date. After somebody calmed down enough to distinguish between one man finding her a chair and the other offering her a stupid internship.

THE DISMISSED CONTESTANTS LEFT THE taping area in the opposite direction from the judges.

As soon as Chloe came within explaining distance, Fran asked,

"You did poison Chef's tea, didn't you? Is that why you've been weird for the last three hours?"

"That is more of a C-drama than a K-drama. I whipped up a tisane for his cough, and silly me, used up too much ginger. All that *contretemps* got invented because it's my week to get eliminated. Let's talk about what really matters, your big win! That is amazing!!! Top Three. Congratulations."

"Thanks! How crazy was that?"

"And you promised to fail right alongside me. Where did it all go wrong?"

"The instructions. It was so weird, I just understood them, and since he was supposed to be your friend, I followed them. Turns out, I can follow directions. Who knew?"

"Trust. It changes everything," said Chloe as they reached the locker area.

"Hey," began Fran, then paused, as usual, to remember her combination.

"32-8-17," Chloe prompted her.

"Thanks. So, can we talk about that super extra grand gesture gone sideways today?"

"I don't know what you mean."

"How did he go from hero to zero in one Judge's Table? And don't say "what?" because I know a splat when I see one, whatever this tea business was about."

"He was mean to me," Chloe mumbled through the fabric of her apron as she pulled in off over her head.

"I told you so," said Fran, grabbing both their aprons and tossing them into the group laundry basket.

"Oh, I got so mad. Oh, Fran. Oh. They went off on the lack of ginger, as if I replaced it with salt. Or red onion."

"Did they say anything good about your dish? Did he?"

"Not one thing. You would think I was on *Worst Cooks*. Then the judges decided that my helping his business was the random act of an airhead, because, you know, they were there so they must know. The weenies. That may have contributed to my emotional inner life temperature heat-ness."

Fran slammed her locker shut.

"I think you mean being so spitting mad you swore at a judge. Don't think we didn't hear you. Well, if Chef can't run his shop by helping the people that help him, then I say, he can hawk his empire somewhere else. Come on, let's go find out what Paul is making for dinner."

"Wait, Fran, first I have to tell you," Chloe added in a low voice as Fran shepherded her toward the outer doors, "...I...This time I told them we knew about Vivian switching the bottles. On camera."

"Look out! How did they respond?"

"They said nothing. Literally nothing. Matteo just went straight to the "okay, thanks, bye" part. There was certainly no, "gasp! We had NO idea! Oh. We have wronged you." Vivian sure got me good."

"She won't get away with it," Fran responded confidently over her shoulder as she yanked open the heavy entrance door and held it open for Chloe. "They're probably holding it over her."

The vans having not yet arrived, Chloe moved over to the brick wall of the building and leaned against it.

"Hey, how did I win?" asked Fran suddenly changing the subject. "It meant kicking Vivian to number four. If they want you gone over the spice bomb, they probably don't want me hanging around as a witness."

"No idea. It couldn't have been a three-against-one vote, Chef can't possibly be that stupid, so it had to have been at least a three-to-one for."

"Wait, what? You know you suck at math. Did you count right?"

"If anyone voted against you, it was only one person, and that person wasn't him."

"Not yet getting your math, but I'm still going to punch him in the nose the next time I see him."

"Do you think he had his reasons?" asked Chloe. "I helped him in Korea because I like to interfere with stranger's lives, it's what I do, but who knows how many times I am wrong about these things. Maybe..."

She trailed off with a shrug of acceptance.

"Oh, he had a reason," said Fran. "This isn't a logic problem, it's a character flaw. He thinks one or two grand gestures give him license, or runway, to be utterly self-centered the rest of the time, he's that guy. Why is not our concern, nor does it matter. Mixing it up like that probably goes down great with Bond Villains, where he can step off to."

"Maybe you should choose Travis," she suggested, again. "He at least knows how to respond appropriately when Jake tries to stab you."

"I have already not chosen him, Fran. Let's do this. We'll pretend Chef made a mistake, and I'll ignore him for the rest of Sugar! Week in case he makes more. A non-native speaker jettisoned into all that politics and excitement and cameras, it can happen. It did happen. Oh Fran, it was bad in there."

"I know, it sucks. We knew the judges were out for you this week, but it still sucks to live through it."

"He did get me a chair, though. I forgot that part."

"What chair? Who, Al?"

"No, Kyung-ho asked the judges if the contestants could sit down, and then actually went and found me a chair."

Fran grudging accepted this new information.

"Okay, he occasionally doesn't suck, but he could glare less and make a wee effort to support your own food journey."

Chloe nodded.

"Just for accuracy's sake, you know, just to be strictly fair and impartial, he wasn't being mean before the cook, just not helpful which might be the same thing for different reasons. He's remarkably observant. He saw things even I didn't know about."

"What didn't you know?" asked Fran, turning to her with a new, sharp suspicion. "Chloe?"

Chloe fiddled with her purse strap for a moment, and then decided to finally come clean.

"I haven't recovered enough to be in this competition. I guessed I was, but I guessed wrong, that's why I keep having weird screw ups. He's just more mad about it than I am. It's probably the jet lag."

"Like it's any of his business. What does it mean going forward, though? How bad is it?"

"They're kicking me out, so that solves that. What to do with my life is the problem," Chloe said, looking up at the big, puffy, white clouds with a loud exhale and watching one of them reform into a bunny rabbit. "All I've proved by coming on *Yes, Chef!* is that I lack the strength to get through one service without getting wobbly bobbly and causing a culinary disaster, which I guess is information. If I can't pull a miracle reversal, though, and I've tried that three weeks running, the show is going to trash-talk my one, tiny, sit-down business idea out of existence. For Vivian."

"Come work for me, I don't cook with spices."

Chloe shook her head.

"A bijou enterprise requires staff to work super extra hard, which we have established, no can do. But I shall always be your *pro bono* advisor. You can pay me in grilled cheese."

"You're too independent, Chloe. You're always helping other people, but never let anyone help you."

"Really? I don't see that."

"Yeah. I know. You're as bad as Travis."

"Huh. Maybe that's why I like him so much. As a guy," she added, "over there. Whom I am not sleeping with."

"Those shoulders, though?" Fran said as they both looked appreciatively at Travis chatting with Ajiz on the lawn side of the sweep. "They're very square. Think it through."

"All yours, Fran. The gift of a grateful nation. I don't think you get how good your onion rings are."

the end of the affair

Returning to the hotel, Kyung-ho ditched Juan, took his medicine and went to find Wallace to have dinner. And probably get yelled at.

Wallace had waited backstage just long enough to see Kyung-ho receive his warm welcome from the judges and contestants. The rest of his day he spent working out of the hotel suite on the New York launch. Looking up from his laptop as Kyung-ho came lagging and drooping into their shared lounge area, he asked,

"How did it go?"

"Fine."

Kyung-ho plunked himself down onto the camel-colored, tufted leather club chair. Digging behind his back to remove the collection of bright, chenille throw pillows piled there, he tossed them onto the matching leather couch where Wallace was working, sunk back against the remaining teal bolster, and stared up at the plaster ceiling.

"Did I really see a fan among the contestants?" Wallace asked absent-mindedly, pushing away the electric green pillow that landed against his thigh and continuing to click away on his keyboard. "How do you manage it?"

"Because I'm a handsome genius," he answered, leaning forward to see what Wallace was working, then put his feet up on the shorter of the two round, nesting coffee tables. "What do you want for dinner?"

Wallace stopped typing to consider the options.

"Do you mind if we order in?"

"A meal with zero chance of running into the other judges sounds like heaven. Where is the...thing?"

"It's over there on the desk."

Kyung-ho retrieved the red leatherette room service menu and brought it back to his seat. Flipping through to the dinner section, he asked,

"Do you want the burger again?"

"*Mmmhhm.*"

"What do I want after my day? Fish?"

"We're on top of a mountain. In America," Wallace reminded him.

"Right. Steak."

"Actually...*uhhh*..," Kyung-ho continued, looking up from choosing his sides, "that was Chloe."

"Yeah, I noticed you went your own way with your signature dessert. I won't be the one telling Tae Ho, that is all on you."

"No, what I meant was, that was Chloe. The fan. That was Chloe."

"Shakespeare chick!" Wallace said with surprise looking up from his work. "Person, woman, I mean. What's she doing here?"

"Isn't it crazy? My day was crazy," Kyung-ho said, tossing the menu onto the coffee table.

"That's...wow. Was she glad to see her dessert again?" asked Wallace, his interest and attention waning as he clicked through his emails one last time for the night.

"I think now she hates me," Kyung-ho answered, skipping to the end. "Or she always hated me, and I didn't pick up on it. She completely understands my food and despises me as a person. Why couldn't we go to Qatar? What do you have against sand?"

Wallace looked over at Kyung-ho, hit 'save' on his computer and closed the lid.

"What did you do?" he asked, leaning back as well, and folding his arms.

"I think I should order."

Kyung-ho went back over to the desk to call room service. When he returned to his seat, Wallace hadn't moved.

"They said it would be forty-five minutes," he reported.

"Uh-huh. What did you do? And please tell me it wasn't on national television or impacts our launch. Does she not like the new dessert? Did she tell people that, on TV?"

"I don't know what I did. You know my English isn't 100%. Whatever happened during the critique, though, was not my fault. They pre-decided it's her week to be eliminated. How is that my fault?"

Wallace waited for the punchline.

"While you provided the moral outrage in support of the one person in America we are certain likes your food?" he asked.

Kyung-ho shrugged and squirmed in his chair, making the leather crunch. With an extra loud crunch, he stood up and moved back over to the window.

"No?" he replied, looking out at the office building across the street.

"You helped eliminate a woman and expected it to end well? Go away and let me work," said Wallace, reaching for his computer.

Returning to his seat, Kyung-ho sat back down with another crunch. With his elbows on his knees and chin in his hand, he looked ruefully at his business partner.

"This is about work. It was only Day 1 of Sugar! Week."

Wallace sighed, crossed his arms and leaned back again.

"Start from the beginning."

"I didn't ask her to make me tea, but she made me tea."

"Beginning. You showed up with her dessert. Happy happy, yay yay, that was just before I left."

"Her sidekick mentioned during the reveal that she was terminally ill. I did not handle that information well."

"You couldn't have known," Wallace protested. "Anyway, now she's cured."

"I did know, and no, she isn't. She almost fell down right in front of me before the challenge even started. I can't believe the show is letting her compete. By Judge's Table I had had it. So, I got her a chair. That helped everybody. I should get credit for the chair."

"Am I going to have to wait for the show to air?" Wallace asked. "You run into your long-lost muse unexpectedly, and she is dying, and you got her a chair. When does the yelling start?"

"She didn't yell. She just got really mad. I had a cough, and she used up all her ginger root to concoct the kind of tea you always have to get around Chinese New Year. We didn't know during the critique I was drinking what I was supposed to be eating."

"That's kinda funny. Who cares if that dessert has any ginger in it? Why she hates you has not yet been revealed in this narrative. How did you compliment her dish? Did you get the yeses and nos in the right place?"

"*Uhhhh...*"

"Did you mention her business acumen in setting us up with Bangtan Tours?"

"Yes. And the judges agreed, on camera, it was a great random act of kindness for the business."

"Dude. She didn't step up to run the cash register on a busy Tuesday. Instead of gratitude, and returning the ginormous favor, you patted her on the head and jumped on the missing ginger bus, which was irrelevant and your fault? On television? Where she's trying to launch her own food career?"

"Oh. *Ohhhhh*," Kyung-ho said with sudden realization. "I'm in trouble. I told you not to make me do the show."

Wallace snorted.

"Well, you should have at least familiarized yourself with the premise. Good luck coming back from this one, dude."

"Maybe she was just being professional? She got very professional during the critique."

"I think the word you are looking for is "had it with that fool". Let's not confuse ourselves with euphemisms. She didn't – and this is important, so do try to remember – didn't get back at you by trashing our own brand? Did she?"

"Oh, she thought about it, but she changed her mind."

"Wow, I like this woman. And you kinda suck."

"It's a rigged show," said Kyung-ho, sitting up straight again and reasserting his natural confidence, "and I already decided she's going to come work for me. I just couldn't see beyond how...that needed to start immediately..."

He trailed off as Wallace shook his head at him.

"Says who?" Wallace countered. "And not now she ain't. Do you really think it only matters that you respect her talents, without actually telling her, or anyone else? Dude. You better stay away from sharp knives around women."

"She shouldn't be competing."

"That is not for you to decide. It's none of your business."

"It will be."

"It ain't."

"But one of the judges wants her to intern as a line cook. She'll drop dead in a month."

"Maybe. Still none of your business. It's possible she doesn't see what you see, or just not want anyone else to know, or you're flat out wrong, but she must want to get something out of being on the show to make the effort."

"Well, she has to stop. She can't put up a plated dessert for four without almost fainting."

"The dish you couldn't find one nice thing to say about? That's a lot of undermining and letting down, and she couldn't stand up before you did this."

"Oh." Kyung-ho blinked and stared at Wallace for a moment. "This is bad."

"Yeah."

"It just snowballed. To know she was working herself to death for a rigged show...things snowballed."

"Did she get eliminated?"

"Tomorrow. That part doesn't have anything to do with me, she knows that. And I got her a chair, that should count."

"It's probably why she let you live."

"And I brought her her dessert. It made her very happy."

"Until..."

"Oh God, what did I do?" Kyung-ho said, clutching his head again with both hands.

"I leave you alone for eight hours, how could you have done this much of an Icarus? Hey, didn't you two meet because you were screaming at Soon-yi and didn't think anyone was in the shop?"

"Yeah, that was her."

"She probably thinks you have anger management issues. I'd let it go."

"No," Kyung-ho replied looking up at him from between his hands.

Wallace recognized that tone. Kyung-ho used the same one when he refused to switch from Belgium to Thai chocolate, despite the import tax hike.

"Well, if you don't like her food, at least tell the world about her business sense," Wallace suggested, as he returned to his typing, "and how much Ji Foods owes her. Forget about love and start with justice. And just know she isn't going to go anywhere with you because of your big feelings. Love is an action. Naming that dessert means she inspired you, not that you care about her, and if this is the level of support you can offer her here, and while she is literally about to drop dead, why would she follow you halfway around the world? So, she can be let down in another language, in a foreign country, where she has no friends? When is the taping over?"

"Monday."

"And when do you fly back?"

"Tuesday."

"Well, good luck. You have less than a week get your act together, do a 180, and add a marketing genius to the payroll who understands our brand and the American and Korean market."

"You'll be glad if I can pull it off, just so you know. She gets my food. At a core, deep level, she totally gets my food. I told you she understood the blueberry."

"Well, here's hoping it turns out better than if we risked getting shot during a layover in a Middle East country having a civil war. I think that's room service at the door," Wallace said as the tinny buzzer echoed through the room. "You get it."

"*Ugh*," he mumbled at Kyung-ho's retreating back, "he's gonna get so weird again..."

CHAPTER FORTY-FIVE

decisions,
decisions

The next morning, Wallace and Kyung-ho breakfasted in the hotel restaurant. After a long silence punctuated only by the low hum of other guests heading to the waffle buffet, and the occasional "more coffee, hon'?", Wallace looked over the corner of his newspaper and announced,

"I think I'll visit the set with you today."

Kyung-ho glanced up from pushing his Denver omelet around on his plate, wishing it would turn into one of his shop's croissants.

"What? Why? Don't you have the final media packet to work on?"

"No rush, Chloe will do that next week for me. Right? I just thought I would stick my head in, do my part to ensure you don't blow my chance of having a decent PR director to finish said media packets."

Kyung-ho picked up his coffee cup, put it down on the saucer again, then picked it back up and took a sip, all without answering.

"Breakfast abroad is torture for you, isn't it?" Wallace asked sympathetically.

"I like other people's food," Kyung-ho insisted. "I eat it."

"Not when you're stressed."

"*Humph.* Do you really want to come to the set?"

"Who else is going to kick you if you do something dumb? Again. You do know what this gesture means?"

/ 287 \

Wallace drew his thumb across his neck in a slicing motion.

"Yes."

"Great, as long we're clear. I think those are all the signals we need."

Wallace disappeared behind his *New York Times*, and Kyung-ho went back to sighing over eggs that weren't French pastry.

An hour later, the contestants arrived at the warehouse to find Chef Kyung-ho prepping a small basket of Asian pears at Vivian's assigned front-row workstation, supervised by a new, unknown, dark-haired stranger.

"There are more of him," Fran whispered to Chloe as they moved through the competition hall towards the locker room, "are they both on Team Vivian?"

Around them, the contestants began the morning ritual of putting away their outdoor things, grabbing their knives, and donning their aprons in readiness for the Reinvention Challenge.

"It's the wonder of K-dramas," Chloe whispered back. "Well, that man looks Chinese, but it's the same principle. Just when you think, surely, that tiny country has shown us all their handsome, talented men, they make more."

"Although, I'm pretty sure that guy is from China," she added as she shut and relocked her own unit, "which makes it less remarkable that out of a half-billion to choose from, they sent us someone so adorable."

"Who is he, though?" Fran asked.

"No idea. One of his sous chefs? Maybe Chef brought staff with him."

"He's probably mean, too," Fran sighed with regret.

"Quick, who's who?" Wallace asked Kyung-ho in Korean, as the contestants started exiting the locker area and heading for the lounge and the coffee station.

"Chloe, red hair. Her sidekick and attack dog, the one with light brown hair with, you know," answered Kyung-ho, waggling his finger around.

Wallace supplied the missing word.

"Curls."

"Yeah, and here comes our winner."

That was the last of the cheat sheet Kyung-ho could safely transmit before a contingent led by Vivian approached his (her) workstation.

"Ah," said Wallace appreciatively. "Well, if you're going to get vamped..."

Kyung-ho elbowed him.

"Be useful."

Wallace addressed the group in English.

"Good morning, ladies. And gent."

"I don't believe we've had the pleasure," slinked Vivian. "Are you Chef's personal assistant?"

Wallace and Kyung-ho exchanged glances in mutual understanding, and shared opinion, of the implied elevation of Kyung-ho's status and denigration of Wallace's.

"For today, I am," Wallace answered.

Kyung-ho elbowed him again.

"No fair," Wallace complained, "I can't hit you back when you're packin'."

Kyung-ho immediately put down his razor-sharp *nakiri* and Wallace took up a fighting stance. The two squared off for a moment before Wallace pushed Kyung-ho's shoulder good-naturedly and leaned back against the counter. Kyung-ho resumed his rapid slicing, focusing most of the group's attention on his hands as they memorized the needed sequence of cuts to turn an irregular polyhedron into little, seedless squares.

Wallace went back to complaining.

"We both know you can't block my saber strike, but I don't want my new assistant to be mad at me. She doesn't even like to beat you up herself. How can we fix that?"

"Do you mean me?" Vivian asked, naturally assuming that Kyung-ho's randomly selected workstation must be a personal compliment. "It would be a terrible shame if our superstar judge was injured, even accidentally. Can I help, Chef? My *mirepoix* always gets special mention. What fruit is that?"

Another looked passed between the two men. This woman's relentlessness was impressive, but her situational awareness, not so much.

"Asian pears," answered Kyung-ho.

"You know, these mean "get lost" in China," Wallace mentioned conversationally, as he handed the next one to Kyung-ho, "or do I mean goodbye?"

Satisfied that he almost made Kyung-ho laugh, Wallace again made the conversation general.

"I'm here to help with recruitment for Ji Foods," he explained. "Chef is a genius in the kitchen, but not always the best with staff retention."

Felix's eyes became round with excitement hearing this announcement, but Vivian continued to disregard all the hints and information she didn't understand, or care about, and the low-status messenger delivering it.

"Do you run a strict kitchen, Chef? I can tell you have high standards."

"I have a temper," he answered. Glancing again at Wallace, he added, "My girlfriend and I met, actually, because she disapproved of how I spoke to our counter help. Wallace still hasn't forgotten it."

"A woman interfered with how you run your business?" responded Vivian. Her faux shock and horror, however, received only tepid answering shrugs from the group around his bench. They were far more interested in Kyung-ho's expert treatment of pears, and growing impatient with her tangents continually interrupting his knifework.

Kyung-ho was also on Team Shut Up Vivian.

"She interferes whenever she gets the chance," he answered tersely, scraping the bench with the back of his knife to move bits of core and seeds out of his way. "I find it best to listen to her about everything."

"Wow, that's really sexy in a man," she answered, adroitly changing tactics.

"Vivian, let the man chop," said Janiva.

Looking at his phone to hide his own response, Wallace was reminded that time was ticking down before the start of the show. The target and sidekick had chosen to gather in the lounge area, covertly tracking the activity at Kyung-ho's bench instead of joining it. Direct interference was required.

"Is that the woman you designed the dessert for?" he asked, pointing across the room.

Kyung-ho glanced over at Chloe while he picked up another pear.

"Yes," he answered, rolling the fruit in his hand before setting it down in position.

"They had quite altercation, yesterday," Vivian explained to Wallace. "She ruined Chef's dessert by leaving out the ginger. Last week she put ghost peppers in a red sauce. She's that contestant. Poor thing only gets attention when she screws up."

"*Hmmm*," he responded, "that sounds more like sabotage."

"You know, my oven..." Janiva started to say, before Vivian cut her off.

"She's ranked at the bottom, why bother to sabotage her?"

Kyung-ho stopped chopping again to everyone (else's) disappointment and looked Vivian full in the face.

"What stupid person...," he began, before Wallace reached over, took the pear out of his hand and started eating it. The two men squared off once more, but this time Kyung-ho resorted to the cannister holding utensils. Selecting a large wooden spoon, he turned back to Wallace defiantly.

"I think we both see why Qatar was out," Wallace responded between bites of pear. "If you think you're Jackie Chan in this kitchen, God help us if I let you transit through a war zone."

Across the room, as suspected by Wallace, Fran and Chloe closely surveilled the group around Kyung-ho. That is, Fran provided a running commentary. Chloe pretended to be engrossed in last-minute prep work for the elimination round about to start. When Kyung-ho stopped chopping the first time, Fran wondered aloud,

"Are they going to fight?"

Chloe risked a direct look over now that violence might be involved.

"I doubt it...except maybe," she responded, reading the two men's body language.

"He knows martial arts," said Fran.

"Who, Chef?" Chloe asked, studiously peering into the half-opened door of the mini grocery store, trying to determine whether all the ingredients she needed for her Reinvention dish were available.

"Nope, the other one. See, you can tell by how he stands."

"Huh. Well, good luck with that," answered Chloe, refusing to turn back around before she spotted the current stock of lemons. "Clearly, he's your department. I have enough trouble ignoring the guy with knife skills."

Fran continued to monitor the situation.

"Wait, now what's going on?" she asked a few moments later. A new, unexpected sharpness in her tone made Chloe look over again.

"What the hell?" she, too, responded.

Fran glanced around the room confused. She noticed something vague and weird happening over at Chef's workstation, but not that weird.

"Goodness me, what is goin' on?" Chloe continued. With one hand she covered her eyes and the other grabbed at Fran's sleeve. "Look. I can't look. Don't make me look, but you look."

"What? What don't I see?"

Fran canvassed the room again. Was Ajiz teaching someone else to Pop? That would make for a long day. Surely Janiva would not let herself get sucked in…

"That!" Chloe insisted, letting go of Fran's arm long enough to gesture more accurately, if blindly, towards Kyung-ho's onlookers. She then opened the smallest crack between her fingers, and with the added protection of hiding behind Fran's shoulder, watched Vivian lean her elbow on Kyung-ho's countertop and draw a seductive finger through the pear detritus, seemingly oblivious he was holding a wooden spoon without any discernible culinary objective.

Fran just saw Vivian doing Vivian.

"That girl is out of her mind," Chloe pronounced. "For your edification, now that is his mad face."

"Why? Doesn't he look the same? How do you know? And why do we care?"

Chloe dropped both her hands. Even from a silent distance, it was obvious this conflict was real and not deescalating.

"How does this man stay out of trouble when I am not around?" she asked, hauling herself off the couch. "Pardon me for a moment, there's a homicide in progress."

Fran grabbed at the side of Chloe's apron to hold her back.

"I thought we talked about this?"

"No worries. I just gotta go smack him upside his head to snap him out of it. You'll like that part, take all of a second. We really don't want to find out what he can do with a prison canteen. It would be interesting, but not that interesting."

Pulling away from Fran, Chloe strode with determination across the room.

The cluster of contestants in the lounge started following Fran's dispatches once the action got to the martial arts stage. Watching Chloe leave in a huff, they gripped their coffee mugs and leather knife rolls tighter, and settled in to watch a new drama unfold they did not understand, but still gleefully anticipated.

The group around Kyung-ho's workbench were equally surprised, and a few just as gleeful, to hear Chloe's voice moments later calling, "Kyung-ho-*shi!* Kyung-ho, darling" from half-way across the room. The Asian delegation was the most startled. Vivian remained focused on employing her best flirtatious culinary move. She gave Chloe one warning snarl over her shoulder before turning back to Kyung-ho with a much softer, more intimate look that invited him to share her opinion of Chloe as the unwanted intruder with very bad timing.

Kyung-ho responded to Vivian's appeal by directing a forbidding stare at the woman bearing down on him, causing one or two of the contestants to step back themselves. Chloe continued to move forward into the oncoming fire.

"*Annyeonghaseyo,*" she said politely to Wallace with a friendly bow as she approached the bench, adding a "*nǐ hǎo*" for good measure. She then reached out and laid her hand over Kyung-ho's fist, the one still holding the spoon in a sea of chopped pear preparation.

"*Annyeonghaseyo,* sweetheart, dear...," she began, turning to address Kyung-ho and searching for the right word.

"...*Oppa,*" she landed on confidently.

Wallace put his hand over his mouth to smother a laugh, while Kyung-ho shook his head a little, unsure he heard correctly. The contestants just thought she switched from Korean to Southern to Greek.

Looking down at his hand to gauge whether her word choice startled him enough, it pleased Chloe to see his knuckles no longer white.

"*Merci,*" she said, giving his hand another pat. "*Oppa,* I'm beginning to not trust you with the implements of your office. How about we express ourselves without cutlery. First. See how that works. Just say it in Korean, you'll feel better."

Whether from the unexpected endearment, or unexpected touch, or his complete surprise at this new development in what should have been a routine *mise en place,* Kyung-ho's grasp loosened enough to lay the spoon on the bench.

"Thank you," she said. "I only know so many foreign words, so you get what you get to get this to happen, but I will withdraw the first one and the inappropriate manhandling as rude, if you promise to keep your word. So *gamsa-hamida,* and don't make me come back here."

Chloe removed her hand, gave Wallace another friendly nod, and turned back towards the lounge.

"So weird," Vivian said pettishly, "and interrupting just to be weird, as usual."

Kyung-ho's hand closed once more over the spoon. Catching his small movement before she quite turned around, Chloe put one hand back over her eyes and reached the other behind her to pat his fist again.

"*Oppa*! Now, now. I'm not saying you are wrong. I'm just saying didn't we just agree? That's all I'm saying. If it feels French, go French."

This time Kyung-ho ignored both the overture and request. He didn't feel like it. Perhaps due to his anger tinged with relief that her blind groping hadn't landed on his *nakiri*. You know, maybe.

"*Tch*," Chloe said feeling his resolve through his hand. She opened her fingers covering her eyes and looked at him through the small gap with a twinkle of blue tinged with both humor and firmness.

"Okay," she conceded, "I won't do it again, but two wrongs don't make a right. This is my country and I'm the one with the familiarity of the criminal code."

"Chloe, maybe you shouldn't get involved," spoke up Fran, hesitantly, from across the room, "in whatever you're getting involved in over there."

"Too late! Not his mad face, Fran."

Kyung-ho and Chloe stared at each other for a moment of strange alchemy. The colder he tried to look, the warmer she felt. This time he spoke first.

"*Ajumoni*!" he declared. That, of course, was cheating, but did break the impasse.

Chloe gasped, dropped the one hand, took back the other and stepped away from the counter.

"Well, I never! Fine. You young people have your zombie apocalypse, see if I care."

With a final *tch*, she turned and stalked back across the room to rejoin Fran in the lounge.

CHAPTER FORTY-SIX

across a
crowded room

Chloe returned to the lounge and sat back down next to Fran on the yellow couch with a loud crunch.

"What did you do that for?" Fran whispered. "Didn't we agree we were going to ignore him? And what did he say?"

"He said "stop interfering, you old nanny", is what he said."

"He didn't! Wait, he couldn't have. He didn't use enough words."

"It's what he meant, and not an *au pair*, either. It's not my fault. I didn't know we would need a contingency plan for him getting all up in his feelings while holding a deadly weapon. I'm trying to use my brain in a pro-ginger direction today, not solving his stupid problems."

"It was a spoon."

"In the hands of a professional. A grown man with a quality wooden utensil, that'll leave a mark."

"I just wanted to break his train of thought," she added with a touch of genuine seriousness. "You're right, of course, it was none of my business. I won't be sorry for being kind, but you're right. Yesterday he showed me he is an ungrateful jerk, and I should believe him and keep my distance."

"Right. We agreed."

Chloe looked down at her hand, deeply regretting having touched him. Her fingers seemed to be on fire.

"Yup," she said resignedly, "that'll leave a mark. The sacrifices I make for other people. I really need to stop doing that."

ACROSS THE ROOM WALLACE ECHOED Fran.

"*Ahem*," he said to Kyung-ho, "I thought we agreed on today's agenda?"

Kyung-ho looked over at his friend's laughing face and made a sudden feint to again whack him with the spoon.

"You're lucky I came with you today," Wallace said in Korean, dodging the blow. "Somebody needs to remind you that I need a new director, and that you are an ass."

Kyung-ho lowered his weapon and leaned against the counter, waiting for him to continue.

"I do see why she throws you off your game, is that an American thing? But you need to stop letting the other team win. And fix things."

"I'll talk to her during break, I promise, when things quiet down," Kyung-ho replied, straightening up and preparing to return to his work. "I'll explain..."

"Dude, you can explain if you want, and she may find that moderately interesting, but what you need to do is stop. If you can't take her side, you can at least stop pretending you're on her side."

"I am on her side."

"Well, then you suck at it. She just saved you, again, and she was right, again. You shouldn't lose your temper like that in the kitchen. What did you do about her being insulted? Nothin'. Worse than nothing, letting yourself get vamped right in front of her, and then calling her an old lady in front of the vamp. If Chloe doesn't care, her sidekick does, and she is not on Team Kyung-ho."

The group around the bench listened closely to the two men's unintelligible conversation. Then watched both stop talking and look across the room at Chloe, now ignoring them with a greater commitment, and at Fran, who very much was not. They nodded knowingly at each other. It didn't take a crash course in Babel to realize yesterday's mysterious conflict was apparently going to be a thing.

"Except, why is the new guy mad?" asked Felix in an aside.

"And where does Fran come into all this," wondered Janiva.

Jake just hoped the men's conversation switched back to French, so he could eavesdrop properly.

Ignoring the murmurs and sly elbows, Wallace continued his reality check.

"I know there are too many people around, and too many cameras, and it's making you turtle. It's hard to communicate with your head stuck in a carapace, it is. But she's here to get work done. If a random, silent, grumpy lump caused you one tenth this much bother in your shop, in the middle of a weekend rush, heads would roll."

"Alright, alright," Kyung-ho conceded, "I just thought waiting for the right moment, in private..."

"You thought wrong. Every minute you're becoming less of a man in her eyes. Tick tock boom."

Hearing Wallace's last words, the contestants looked at each other with excited anticipation. "Boom" meant boom in any language, they silently telegraphed each other. Didn't it?

Kyung-ho blenched. He placed the wooden spoon he somehow still held back on his bench with a firm, sharp clap that made Janiva jump and Felix sigh over yet another interruption. Wiping his fingers on the dish cloth tucked into his apron string, he turned and crossed the room over to Chloe.

The two groups again fell silent. Wallace crossed his arms, readjusted his own lean against the workbench, and hoped for the best. Chloe just hauled herself out her seat again and braced for another round of unpleasantness coming her way.

Reaching the group in the lounge, Kyung-ho first bowed politely to Fran.

"Annyeonghaseyo."

She gave him just enough leeway to not suspect he was swearing at her, but no more.

Kyung-ho then turned to address the woman standing quietly in front of him, staring straight ahead at his embroidered name and top two toggles of his chef coat, waiting for him to do something even more annoying. He sighed. Fifteen hours was more than enough time being a Juan in the world. Besides, he thought, as his face softened, she needed him in his rightful place in the universe.

"I'm sorry," he said, breaking the silence.

"For what?" answered Fran. "Being mean all the time? Because nobody cares if you flirt with Vivian, that's your business."

He turned toward her with an unexpected smile.

"You're a good friend. I'm relying on you when I am not around."

"Told you so," mumbled Chloe automatically.

Kyung-ho turned his eyes back to Chloe's downcast face and continued his public apology.

"I shouldn't have lost my temper yesterday. Or undermined your own marketing campaign. That part was by accident. English is my third language, and I lost focus on the bigger picture trying to follow the immediate conversations."

After a short pause, he continued on with a stern firmness that suggested he still hadn't quite found his *sang froid*.

"You know that in my empire many things are not allowed."

Chloe gave the slightest eyebrow twitch to indicate she understood what he meant regarding Vivian and the judges. Not enough to indicate she absolved him from making all that additional trouble, but enough to acknowledge his awareness that she was competing in a snake pit. That amount of twitch. Then, as the silence lengthened, she realized he also was still complaining about her presence on set. After another minute of nobody saying anything, she responded to the latter with a shrug.

"Maybe you're wrong."

"I am not wrong."

"Well, it's not your place to point it out to other people that don't need to know."

"You're right. I'm sorry. I was just surprised to see you here. But I am not wrong to be mad. You're mad, too."

Chloe made another twitch of acknowledgment that his bossy unprofessionalism was at least grounded in fact. She considered whether a vague, cheap shot at the judges would terminate the conversation in friendly unanimity. It was an unworthy solution, but better than crying.

"They don't like my food. I like my food. Eh, peasants. I appreciate your apology, though, and I did like your food. Always glad to see that coming."

"Ha!" is what she said on the inside. *"Beat that for insouciance. Go Fran Plan, go!"*

"They expect you to work in the industry," Kyung-ho responded, almost as if that mattered, and he couldn't read the clear, unspoken subtext in her furrowed brow and pursed lip. "The harder you fail on the show, the more likely you will welcome gainful employment."

She relented enough to roll her eyes at his jacket embroidery in a shared moment of disbelief that such tactics could work.

"Of course, none of this is the point," he said.

Chloe scrunched up her forehead, wondering if she had lost track of the point. Arguing in public, in code, to a non-native speaker, it was so easy to go astray.

Kyung-ho decided it was time to fight dirty. He reached out and put his hands on her shoulders. Desperate times. After all, only Wallace knew how very rude it was for him to do so. She could only guess it was rude. And she started it, touching his arm while they were both inside of Korea and complete strangers, then grabbing his hand earlier and giving Wallace a heart attack. Whatever, he was doing it.

"Wallace wants me to bring you back to work for Ji Foods," he said.

To the avid eavesdroppers, that sounded like an apology with a consolation job offer. None of them, of course, had the sightlines to see his thumbs caress the edge of her clavicle.

"I don't work for Villains," she responded swiftly, trying to stay strong.

"Neither do I," he replied to the question directed at his top toggle. "Five minutes after you left, I already started inventing the blue moon component of your dish. Gastro molecular fog takes doing, you know, you gotta want it. You should also know, my staff wanted me to bring you a mooncake with lotus root and a fried egg in the middle, but I vetoed it. When will you give me credit for all the things I do that don't make you mad?"

He felt her shoulders twitch with a silent laugh as she took in the update on his life back in Korea, and the near-miss culinary disappointment, but the others only heard her terse, prim,

"Thank you. It's a beautiful moon."

"*Toi aussi.*"

"With a little help from Wallace," he continued, "I did hear you say goodbye. Coming back to develop a strawberry moon would benefit everybody. And by everybody, I mean you."

"Inventing misty-moisty lemon is not the same as being helpful," she replied, making another valiant effort to not choose someone who brought her occasional and rare joy, but did not make her world a better place. Not right in front of Travis.

To soften her calcified disappointment with reasonableness and professional support, she added,

"Thank you for the apology, though. I do appreciate how stressed you are with the launch. You and The Westin, I love that partnership."

Kyung-ho ignored her proposed offramp.

"I should also get points for the chair," he continued. "I planned ahead for that."

He felt her shoulders relent with another silent laugh.

"Let's not move into crazy talk about fictional, oblivious people. You always got points for the chair. Ask Fran," she said, pointing over at her. "It came up. She knows."

A room full of silent heads swiveled in Fran's direction, only to see her shrug and mouth back at them,

"No, I don't know. I can't help you."

No one believed her, but their heads swiveled back to the action.

"Well, one of us is crazy," Kyung-ho said.

Chloe's eyebrow twitched again.

"I will take that under advisement. For now, let's focus on boosting the brand. Both, if it can be resuscitated, mean man. Less drama and more usefulness is even better than fog and apologies."

"Don't think I am going to help," he unwisely retorted, his uncontrolled fear and anger letting him down again, "because I'm not. I said no and I mean it."

Since it was hard to shrug "alright, already" with so much weight on her shoulders, Chloe made a concessional head tilt, and with a sound very similar to the one Al made picking back up his heavy camera after a long break, she stepped back slightly to dislodge his hands. Kyung-ho's hands involuntarily clamped down on her shoulders, and he felt her sag under the added weight.

"I do appreciate the apology. Really," she said. "And after I am done with my work here, vent then, there might not be much to vent about."

The tension in the room ebbed greatly at this calm resolution, but the stabbing alarm Kyung-ho felt the day before returned two-fold. He spotted a nearby empty chair, and gently pushed her to sit down. Dropping to his knee next to her, they could now converse almost eye to eye. Except, Chloe lost interest in his chef coat and focused on having a silent opinion on the dark-washed denim covering his knee while she waited for him to go away. Baking people, they naturally possessed more innate patience than someone who pan-fried things, but he would go away eventually. He had chopping to do. With Vivian, and the popular kids.

As a polite, civilized person, however, she did respond to his gesture to again actively find the chair.

"*Gamsahamida*. Verticality is a challenge."

He stared at her bent head for a few moments. Suddenly, he stood up with a jerk.

"Stay here," he replied with heat and frustration. "I'll be right back."

The "woman!" part was silent, but she heard it. She wondered who else did too.

"You're yelling again," she said to his retreating back.

"Yes, I know."

CHAPTER FORTY-SEVEN

kyung-ho gets game and matches

After clambering to his feet, Kyung-ho quickly headed back across the warehouse kitchen to where Wallace still waited, leaning against his workstation. Behind him he heard Ajiz's loud, carrying, "what was that all about?" and Fran's speculative, "I think they're having a wrongful termination dispute?".

"It's nothing," Chloe responded quietly. "He just wanted to apologize for being grumpy yesterday and get my opinion on his new menu. He has a cold, and with the launch, him being here is very stressful."

"Don't worry, that's not his mad face," she lied, "we're good."

Kyung-ho held his tongue and kept moving forward. From the sound of her voice, she was leaning back in her chair and not getting out of it, avoiding at least one power struggle. He gave himself a three-minute grace period until she changed her mind.

Wallace watched him approach with disapproval.

"How's our staffing issues?" he asked in a low voice as Kyung-ho reached the bench.

Kyung-ho leaned on the butcher block countertop with both hands and dropped his head between them for a moment before replying.

"Help," he said in Mandarin.

"What did you do? And Korean is safer," Wallace advised, switching over. "Smaller country, better odds people only know how to order barbecue."

"She told me to go away and let her finish the competition," said Kyung-ho. "Do you know they sent them out hiking the mountains the other day? Mountains! No wonder she's so exhausted. I can't let her do this."

"There's nothing much you can do. It's her decision. And you're a judge. Maybe you just need to relax, let her compete and rig the outcome?"

With an expletive the surrounding contestants could feel, if not follow, Kyung-ho pushed off from the counter. Wallace was wrong. There were a zillion things he could do and it was past time he started doing them. He returned to the lounge and knelt down next to Chloe again.

"I've changed my mind," he announced, and watched her last, lingering doubt that he was anything other than a burden in the competition kitchen harden into acceptance.

"You still think I'm an idiot because I didn't know how to market my first shop, don't you?" he responded with exasperation. "There were a lot of moving parts. I had the inventory solved, didn't I? Didn't I? And did I bring you a mooncake and expect you to be happy about it?"

"Heh," she conceded. "You're right. And you're right. Okay, this is me trying not to be intractable and prejudicial. You had something further you wanted to say?"

Kyung-ho put his hand on her knee to get her attention, an intimacy that made Wallace gasp from across the room. The others just waited for him to get injured, wondering if Troy taught her any special self-defense techniques or if she would go old-school American with a *Dallas*-esque face slap. Chloe only stared at his hand. She knew he meant it. She just didn't believe it.

"Your decision is not wise, and you know it," he said. "I will support you, though. So, good news, you no longer have to wait until the contract runs out to discover all the other things I'm good at. In return, you must promise me nothing worse will happen on the job, and when I get mad, acknowledge I am right. I will make an effort, and you will make an effort. That's fair."

Her downcast face suggested she either did not understand, did not care, or was not yet a believer.

"If you spent more time sitting down and eating properly," he protested, "you wouldn't need me to point out that bringing a blue moon not a moon cake was a fully informed decision. It proves I can be just as right as you with just as little information. You can apologize for that confusion later. For now, I just need you to know that I did what I did only to make you stop. Everyone in Korea knows how brilliant you are, I forgot you hadn't heard."

He paused for a moment to let that new information sink in.

"Moving forward," he continued, "just know that what I will do to not be mad at you will put you so far on the deficit side of our ledger your head will explode. And I plan to get happy, that I can promise. I went to school in Paris."

"I don't even know what you are talking about," she said with a laugh. Because it was true. She couldn't even pretend to guess what the maker of her Starry Night could or would put his mind to next, now that he had seen the error of his ways.

"Oh, it's on," he said.

"You be an intern," he concluded with disdain, just to relieve his feelings, "who ever heard of such a thing? Ji Foods always had right of first refusal."

"Are you offering her a job to make up for being a jerk?" asked Fran directly. Everyone else was darn glad she did. Whatever his amends, it still sounded like it had a fight attached to it, and now they were all confused. Either way, though, they were pretty sure Chloe was not having it.

"I think she's going to say no," predicted Oliver to Paul as they again watched the action from behind the far-side couch. "I think she's just being nice about it."

Paul agreed.

"He is a judge. Let's hope today she'll stop swearing at them."

Several others nodded in Oliver's direction, especially when Chloe answered,

"I don't know what I am going to do next. This is not really working out."

"That's a no," whispered Paul.

Kyung-ho responded to Chloe's scrunched forehead by answering Fran's question.

"Yes, I am offering her a job. As my *anae*. Wallace, of course, has some other paperwork he wants to review with her, but it isn't his empire, it's mine. She has no reason to sign on to the project, it's only just after breakfast, but by tomorrow lunch, she'll see that I am right."

Chloe's turned her head away again to think with fewer distractions, but he saw her cheek twitch and heard another small snort of laughter as she worked out which TV characters used that title, and therefore, what it meant.

"You can't possibly know that," she protested.

Kyung-ho responded with a self-deprecating shrug and a few condescending pats to her knee. He wasn't stupid enough to think she trusted him about the Man part being real and permanent, that would have to wait for at least halfway through today's shoot, but he had a long enough list of things he thought needed doing on set immediately that would reset her expectations about what one looked like in action.

"What's an *anae*?" Fran asked.

Chloe gave another short laugh.

"I think it's in the marketing department. He would never let me work on the line."

"Absolutely not."

"*De, Oppa*," she replied.

With those two words Kyung-ho got to his feet and gave both arms a nice stretch, letting one chunk of his recent tension drain out of him while trying to hide his face for a moment. Competitions, launches, visas, death, citizenships, these were all just details. After a year and a half, plus a very bad night, everything was finally understood between them. Or enough for him to risk a relieved and smug satisfaction to be back in the corner of the world he belonged. Juan only wished he knew about this place or had his staff recruitment skills. Like any woman wants to be an intern, child please.

"Wait, did he just win the argument?" whispered Felix.

Ajiz, who should have recognized a married people fight that he had four times with his wife before entering the competition, asked,

"I wonder what it was about?"

"Respect on the victory," said Oliver, accompanied by his best "mad skills" head shake.

Chloe craned her neck to look up at Kyung-ho.

"What's the Korean word for no?"

"I'm not telling you. Let's go meet Wallace."

"Fran," she said, accepting the temporary defeat that came from being in a Google-free universe, "let's go meet Wallace."

"Who's this Wallace?" Fran asked.

"Business partner."

The trio walked back across the room. Holding Chloe by the elbow, Kyung-ho formally introduced them to each other.

"May I present Wallace Yan, the CFO of Ji Foods. He came out West to deliver me at gunpoint to a show only he wanted me to do and stayed over to see American mountains and hopefully a real cowboy. Today he was having trust issues. Wallace, please meet the woman who saved the empire."

"So, you're the one," Wallace said.

"And you're the only," she replied.

Wallace laughed appreciably and capitulated to the boss's point of view.

"Meet Fran," Chloe said, her quick eyes noticing he wanted to do just that, further cementing such an important relationship. "She was very interested in whether you have martial arts training. Hint, false advertising is not a good look, but elementary school counts. You know, you learned the basics and since then it's been independent study. I'm sure Kyung-ho-*shi* needs you more than Studio Dragon or the Triads, so what can you do?"

Fran turned away, flustered by Chloe's raillery, and missed Wallace's speaking look of thanks to his new best friend to whom, he belatedly acknowledged, he also owed his job. He stepped around the bench and began to ask Fran polite, rudimentary questions about the competition.

"What are you doing?" Kyung-ho asked, watching his employee go over to the enemy.

"Bribing your staff. Duh-uh. Obviously with a few spies and allies, we wouldn't have these problems."

Chloe saw him laugh, but everyone else just watched the grumpy one in the relationship move around the bench to take up a deadly weapon again.

"They can't get along for two seconds," said Paul to the group in the lounge. "Did she cause an international incident in Korea?"

"Well, she would, so it's possible," agreed Ajiz. "She doesn't seem to be all that bothered about it, though."

"He said Chloe had gotten on his wrong side of...a ledger, something?" Oliver added. "Then he stormed off. Or back? I don't know. Was there money involved?"

"Should we get money involved?" asked Ajiz. "I bet ten dollars..."

And so, the legend of some deep, mysterious wrong between Kyung-ho and Chloe that neither party could be induced to mention but sometimes could rise above officially became a thing, and with it a ninety-dollar prize to whomever guessed right who started it. It was, perhaps, a sign of the intensity of the production schedule, and the contestant's need to conserve every ounce of creativity towards their own standing in the competition that not one posited what became patently obvious once the editors cut and pasted clips from Sugar! Week into three, cogent episodes. How Kyung-ho wanted to ditch the competition two minutes and thirty-seven seconds after he put down his cloche, go home to his own shop and take Chloe with him. And was spitting mad because she wouldn't go. And that it was his own damn fault. After Sugar! Week aired, however, and Fran scooped the first pool, a second, more informed debate began about whether if Chloe stopped her flip-flopping and made a decision earlier, would he have just left the country, contract and schedules be dammed. And would, maybe, things have turned out differently.

Fran, though, never wavered that it was always going to end the way that it did, and they could at least all agree that Fran should know.

sweet caroline, that's a good smoothie

Chloe discovered in just fifty-two minutes that life with Kyung-ho doing what he felt like doing in a competitive food environment was a lot like Paul in the home kitchen – a bunch of alright.

First, she learned he made a darn good smoothie. As the Reinvention Challenge got underway, and before the judges started their walk-through, Kyung-ho commandeered a tiny section of craft services and whipped up a drink for Chloe with blueberries and ginger and secret kale. It was practically near savory-adjacent and still a quality beverage. Mad skills that man.

Second, unlike Chloe, he did not use the PA delivery service. Slipping around behind Felix, he brought it to her station himself. Chloe was not aware of his presence until she saw his arm come past her from one side and felt his other hand steady her hip. The latter was a wise precaution – and in the kitchen, safety first – as his sudden appearance caused her to jump back in surprise. She might otherwise have smashed the dozen eggs on Janiva's station behind her. *Quelle horreur.*

Safety can be too much of a good thing, however, for a person with seven components to deliver in two hours. Startled back against his chest and into a brief, partial embrace, Chloe inexplicably froze in that position for several minutes afterward, almost long enough for him to slip back to his proper place over by the judging table. While staring at condensation forming on a smoothie glass might look like a moment of menu planning, it was not.

A loud bang and louder swearing from Janiva as she dropped a tray of scones broke Chloe out of her trance. Reaching forward she picked up the smoothie glass and took a sip. Giving it a head shake that fans of Oliver would know connoted the wondering satisfaction of a surprise job well done, Chloe returned to peeling ginger with a spoon, refreshed and ready for greatness.

Sometime later, in the relative mental quiet of pasta making, Chloe's wonder at both the smoothie and its appearance resurfaced, and with it, a growing need to have a feeling about it. Cranking the handle of her Marcato, an automatic process that required limited vigilance, she began to monitor Ajiz's station two rows ahead. During the switch from the roller attachment to the cutter, she finally saw a good moment in Ajiz's cook to call out to him.

"Ajiz, dear!"

"Yes, Chloe?" he answered back over his shoulder.

"Please sing *Sweet Caroline*."

"Right on!" he said, always the team player.

"Was it the spring...?" he began, bringing his spoon up to use as a microphone, *"...and spring became the summer, who'da believe you'd come a longggg..."*

By the time he reached the fourth line, the universal and infectious spirit that is Neil Diamond took hold of their section of the kitchen. All the other cooks – the ones with a soul – joined in at *"...warrrrrmmmm, touchin' warrrrrmmmm, reachin' out...touching me, touch-ing youuuuuuuuu..."*

Across the room, Chef Juan caught one of the PA's as she flew by him.

"Rachel?" he asked.

"Yeah?"

"What are they doing?"

She looked over to where he was pointing and saw amid the general bustle mid-cook, Ajiz singing into his spoon, Chloe and Fran waving theirs over their heads, and Felix on the drums, banging away at his pot. Paul and Janiva, checking their bakes behind them, opened and shut their oven doors on the down note.

"Uhhh...Chloe asked Ajiz to sing *Sweet Caroline*," Rachel said, nonplussed. "Anything else? Because I just found out our melon supplier..."

"No. Just checking."

Never ones to get too distracted from the job at hand, this being *Yes, Chef! America* not *American Idol*, everyone knew that, the contestants immediately resumed their work after one verse and one chorus, all the better for a moment of Neil.

Twenty-seven minutes later, Ajiz called back across the benches.

"Chloe!"

"Yes, Ajiz."

"Now I have that song in my head."

"It's Sugar! Week, Ajiz. Feel it. I feel it."

"I'm naming my dish after it," said Felix. "It's called "Sweet Carolina". I'm doing a hummingbird cake, only different."

Travis scanned the ingredients on Felix's bench.

"You're not using banana. Or pineapple."

"I told you, it's the same, just different. Chef is from Korea. He won't know either way."

"Hear that, Ajiz?" said Fran. "You've inspired the sugar baby to new heights in imaginary food. That's a win-win for all of us."

"Chloe survived without ginger," Felix countered.

"No, she got in trouble," corrected Fran, disappearing as she leaned down to check her oven and then reappearing again. "Big trouble. And her dish came with a restorative beverage."

"Well, it's going to work for me, I'm feeling it."

"Do you need another verse, Felix? To make the leavening disappear, as well?" asked Paul, who had switched out the mandatory ingredient, Asian pear, for rice flour and the ginger for cinnamon because that was what his dessert required. Janiva, finally back on track with her scones, already could tell by the smell his dish was going to be amazing.

He continued his jibes at the naive and uninformed substitution decisions of the younger generation.

"Maybe you should conjure up some non-dairy, frozen, dessert-like ice cream. That would take your dish to a new level."

Felix staunchly defended his vision.

"No, Paul. I don't need another verse. I can't percuss anymore, now, my cake is in the oven. But an *a cappella* hum during judging would not go amiss. And you can try to send me home with a Season 2 Cool Whip fiasco, but I ain't dumb, and I ain't leaving."

"Word," said Chloe. "Hummingbirds, they're the invisible avian, I think you're on to something new and mystical in a baked good. Your cake smells almost as good as Paul's."

The judges stopped by Chloe's station shortly after. Kyung-ho tried to hide his pleasure with her earlier song choice, the empty glass, and the impact his sharp eyes saw the beverage had on her physically by being extra polite to Juan when they knocked into each other while arranging themselves in the crowded space. Poor thing, Juan, believing women wanted to be interns. No wonder he was still single.

Chloe had reached the hot and bothered portion of her cook with three burners and four components going at once. She clocked Kyung-ho's extra-squared shoulders with a smile, but only partially listened to the judges' greeting while she stirred a pot, opened the oven and scanned her bench for a missing ingredient, all at the same time.

Looking around her workstation, Kyung-ho noticed the pepper mill sitting on their side of her flour bin and moved it out into view. Chloe blinked a few times at its sudden reappearance before her hand shot out and picked it up.

"Thank you, Chef," she said.

"How's it going, Chloe? What's the dish?" asked Chef Juan, as they watched her grind pepper across two of the three pots on the stove.

"I don't know, exactly. Since I have abandoned sugar – sorry, Chef – I am embracing pepper," she said waving the mill before putting it into Kyung-ho's outstretched hand. He replaced it back on her side of the flour bin.

"Pepper wasn't in yesterday's Imitation dish," Chef Matteo reminded her.

"I know, but ginger was. I am going ginger, ginger, pepper, pepper. With lemon."

Chef Parker said,

"I don't get it."

"It doesn't have a story yet," she agreed. "I haven't found the right inspiration to organize my thoughts. The spiciness of ginger is just speaking to me today. I'm getting my Ajiz-lite on."

"We're halfway through the cook," remonstrated Chef Juan, "when is this story showing up?"

"*Ugh*, that darn timer. You know, if you guys weren't so obsessed with clocks, you too would know the genius, joy and wonder of Paul on a Tuesday. These things come with their own punishments. Sad, so sad."

Kyung-ho continued looking in Chloe's pots and around the bench as the other judges talked. With a small cough that might have been a laugh, he interjected,

"Summer on the farm. Saturday lunch."

Chloe stopped to blink a few more times at Kyung-ho. She scanned her bench again.

"Song?"

"*Jump in the Line?*"

Chloe laughed.

"That was me being greedy, you had me with summer farm. Thanks for playing along, though. Thank you all. And now go away. Please."

"Hey, Free Bird!" she called over to Felix, hoping to assist the judges' getting gone process. "Are you ready for genius?"

Felix made a panic scan of his own bench.

"No? Maybe?"

"He's making you a cake," Chloe said to Kyung-ho, pausing in her internal "*shake, shake, shake, Senora*" as she made another pass over her dishes with the pepper mill. "If you have any mid-sponge tips..."

Seeing the wry glance of the other judges, she finished with,

"...because making him cry at Judge's Table is not a good look, if it could have been avoided."

"The point of the show is that we know how to cook, and you don't," said Chef Parker, "and why do you insist on helping your competitors?"

"He's just a kid."

"I'm not a kid!" Felix yelled over, "I'm 27!"

"Why is he now called Free Bird?" Chef Juan asked, in search of updated background.

"Oh, you shouldn't hear that from me. Enjoy your day!" she said and shooed them to move along, "Go, go, I need to feel my souffle."

"What souffle?"

"The man said Saturday. I mean...honestly. If he said it in French, maybe we would be confused, but he did say it in English."

With that Chloe got out another pot and ignored the judges altogether as the camera crew backed up and the entourage slowly made their way over to Felix's workstation.

When the judges passed by to talk to the next row of contestants, once again Chloe felt a hand on her waist and saw its counterpart move towards her bench, this time to pick up a spoon and sample her souffle mixture. Confident and fearless that unexpected ghost hands weren't Juan being an extra ass, she felt almost accustomed to that kind of interruption. Instead of jumping back in alarm, she only leaned back a little, and that mostly to better hear the pronouncement being whispered in her ear above the general clatter of the busy kitchen. Mostly. Sure.

"A little more zest," Kyung-ho advised.

"Yes, Chef!" she said, with a slight, extra, unnecessary lean so she could crook her head to say it to his chin. That felt important, you know, getting the angle right. But then, immediately and heroically, she moved forward and away to take up the microplane and return to her cook. Safety first.

AFTER JUDGE'S TABLE, WHERE THE curdled ginger cheesecake sent...*sniff*... their CPA back to his day job before the contestants...*sniff*...fully grasped how 1099's work, Chloe put her knife set away in her locker for what might be her own last time in the *Yes, Chef!* kitchen. Tomorrow they would be off-site for the Group Challenge, and she doubted she would return from whatever warzone hellscape the producers had up their sleeves this week.

Today's Reinvention Challenge, however, had been a redemptive success. She finished just out of the top three with her "Mill on the Floss" dish – lemon, pepper and Asian pear chicken on angel hair pasta with a ginger and pear slaw, black pepper biscuits and a lemon ginger souffle – a personal best and a fabu plate. It was so good, Chef Parker said so before he remembered he was supposed to find it flawed and less-than. She was doubly pleased Kyung-ho tasted her food in its proper form and context. The show editors could still cut and paste today's win into a loss, but now they would have to work for it.

The dish might have placed even higher if she hadn't gone savory for Sugar! Week, but given the prevailing head winds, a solid fourth place with integrity was as good as a confetti cannon to Chloe. It might even be possible, maybe, a little, and she wondered if she was jinxing herself even thinking it, but maybe today's plate secured her more time in the competition? Could she next crack the team challenges? Word on the street – that would be Fran – the next cook had something to do with melons. Most likely she would join her poor Troy in being taken out by a gourd, but if she didn't...if she could...

She slowly closed her locker and walked towards the lounge area where her teammates awaited the arrival of their transportation back to the house.

"Chloe!" Ajiz called out as she came into view, "how does paella sound for dinner?"

"Paul can't make paella."

"I'm teaching him to make paella," said Oliver. "It's a nine-seafood recipe. It's going to be epic!"

"Wow. Sugar! Week must be getting you extra down."

"Sugar and fish, there's just no place those two things intersect."

"I hope you like paella," said Fran. "Once they got onto the exact crunch needed on the rice, it was like a runaway train. There's no stopping them now."

"Is there bacon in paella?" Chloe asked Fran in a low voice.

"No."

"Huh. Yet they're getting excited. A nine-fisher sounds very non-Paul, and something they won't finish before midnight. How about we have some of my leftover lasagna and pretend to be either "full" or "asleep" when dinner is ready?"

To Oliver and the group at large, however, she replied,

"Well, isn't that a plan. I am cheering on your collaboration in salt and look forward to seeing where you land on crunchy rice. Before our ride shows up, though, I'll be in the garden trying to think up dishes for tomorrow. Do you need me to grab anything?"

"I'm good," Oliver answered, waving a fistful of herbs he already gleaned. "We're ready."

"Go team," she said and moved toward the front door.

"Don't think too long," warned Fran as she passed, "the cars will be here in fifteen."

Chloe gave her a thumbs-up over her shoulder and continued out the main entrance. Perhaps a moment's quiet and a few deep breaths of lavender would calm her mind after such a big day and recharge her spirit ahead of the next impossible – possible? – mountain to be climbed.

CHAPTER FORTY-NINE

birds, bees and the westering sun

Chloe crunched down the gravel path, turned the corner of the warehouse, and cannoned into Kyung-ho. As she bounced off his chest, his arm shot out and pulled her up against the sheltering wall. She found herself sandwiched between brick warmed by the afternoon sun and a vista of unfamiliar linen. She almost didn't recognize him, or rather his chest, without the cotton and toggles of his chef coat.

"Are you alright?" he asked.

She nodded.

"Chef, where did you come from?"

"I'm a judge, we have more doors than you."

For a long minute they stood against the wall, connected only through that strong clasp.

"Is Sugar! Week over yet?" he asked.

She shook her head.

"Two more days of filming. And Al has eyes everywhere, it's his profession."

Kyung-ho sighed.

"Thanks for the tip. Two days sound like forever right now."

He released her with a gentle push that pressed her back against the warm brick, and stepping away, moved over to the nearby garden bench. As he took his seat, he glanced towards the corner, inviting her to join him.

Bereft of his support, Chloe slid down the wall like an untethered pea vine. She landed in a heap on the grass, one white calf escaping beneath a canopy of dirndl skirt. He half-rose to go help her up, but she forestalled his assistance.

"No, I'm good. I'm going to pause over here. Safety first."

Closing her eyes, she tilted her face to the setting sun. Together they sat a while listening to the evening birdsong, breathing in the heavy scent of *herbs de Provence* from the surrounding garden beds.

After several long, slow minutes, her low voice broke their silent rapport.

"Earlier it seemed you had something to report?"

Kyung-ho stared blankly at a clump of rosemary. His mind reluctantly dragged his thoughts away from the present moment and back to the loud bother during the judge's lunch break. It led to the reemergence of his actual "mad face" with regular frequency during the afternoon taping.

"The producer showed up with the dailies from last week. Remind me to have you show me how to get fish skin that crispy."

Chloe nodded silently. After another quiet pause, she spoke again.

"Did she get caught?"

"Busted. She knew about the camera in front of her, but not the one behind her. The editors strongly protest wasting such dramatic action shots, so they sent it up the chain of command. Why didn't you say anything that night?"

"I was busy trying not to cry on cue. It seemed like a good idea at the time. Looking back, I don't think I was the target. I think it just amused Vivian to take out Fran by starting a cat fight between us."

"So, now what?" she asked. "The producers will hate to waste my nickname as much as that footage. That one will outlast the franchise."

"It hasn't been decided. They are still in the "yelling at the judges for allowing it to happen" phase."

"At least now the storyboards won't write themselves. Do keep me posted. Hey, more importantly, didn't I knock it out of the park today with pepper, pepper, pepper, ginger, ginger? Didn't I? You know I did."

"*De, de,*" he conceded.

"If I keep putting up plates like that, somebody might think a white hat/ black hat matchup makes good TV, change the plot line and keep me until the end. Well, if I can crack the nightmare that is the off-site challenges. Those require MacGyver'ing a meal using, like, two sticks, a blowtorch and half a cow, while standing at a forty-five-degree angle. In the warehouse kitchen our stations are at least plumb and equipped with stools, like civilized people."

Again, Kyung-ho's mad face made its appearance.

"You're not strong enough to finish the competition! I saw your sassy plates. The only thing you need to try harder at is to avoid being sabotaged, and I don't want you to die trying. It's not worth it!"

Chloe opened one eye to consider him appraisingly, and then shut it again. Dropping her light, bantering tone, she addressed his actual concern with quiet earnestness.

"I can't quit the show. You're not wrong and thank you for being angry about the situation, and for your strong support of my food, but I don't know what else to do. You're an international superstar and for now I'm the Idiot Spice Girl. The press will tattoo that label on my forehead for as long as we are friends. It will be a disaster for both of us."

"Or worse, you're so much more established in your career, what if I am tempted to hide in your shadow and hope nobody ever notices me? If the show kicks me out, I'll go, but you can't ask me to slink away like what they've said is true. I've hung on for one more challenge, I must fight on. I don't know how else to get my name back."

Kyung-ho struggled for a moment between the justice of her words, the injustice of the situation, and his impotence so far to champion her. He ran his own empire. It was absurd that here he had no power at all.

"Let's not believe they're going to win, not yet," she said, hearing his snort of impatience. "Vengeance is mine saith the Lord, and we should believe Him when He says stuff. He's already come through with a vengeance, maybe He has a way to ditch the moniker."

"What revenge? Where? You haven't heard the editor's list of cut and paste options."

"Ah. Well, fun times ahead! You can now see, though, how getting within cloche distance for the super extra secret bonus prize of Starry Night took divine intervention. My plan for that day was to hide under my bunk bed until discovered by housekeeping. So, I already won against Vivian herself, and that was before I knew you owned a collarless linen shirt. You're the gift that keeps on giving, by the way."

Kyung-ho put his arm up along the back of the bench, leaned his chin on it and gazed at her, a tangle of blue skirt and white limbs, and the evening sun burnishing her hair. He breathed in the scent of the garden and with it the certainty that her enemies' power was temporary and insignificant, and that hers was permanent.

"When we get home..." he began. Then stopped abruptly.

"When do you go?" she asked.

"Tuesday."

Chloe gave a small sigh.

"When will you come back?"

"I won't. Wallace can handle it."

"*Hrmm*. Do you have a garden?"

"No, should I get you one?"

"Will there be bees?"

"There will probably be bees."

Chloe opened one eye again briefly and shut it with another sigh.

"You are impossibly handsome today, if you don't mind me repeating myself. I hope I don't turn into a helpless ingénue once you're gone. You know I rely on you for everything."

"I can't say that I know what you are talking about. You haven't relied on me yet for anything."

"Chloe!" they heard Fran suddenly call out as she came around the corner, interrupting them before Chloe decided how to respond to his actual question.

"Chef, where's Chloe?" Fran asked.

Kyung-ho pointed a lazy hand towards the wall.

"Chloe, why are you sitting there?"

"Seemed like a good idea at the time. Are the vans here?"

"Just pulled up. Need help?" Fran asked, standing over her.

Kyung-ho had already slipped around the bench, and silently anticipated Fran's offer.

"Yes, very much so," Chloe replied, taking his outstretched hand and letting him hoist her to her feet.

"He is much stronger," she explained. "You're...a delicate flower."

"Yes, I am," Fran agreed. "Stop spacing out, we gotta go."

Chloe continued staring down at the grass, softly clicking her teeth in thought.

"Am I? How 'bout that."

She chose not to break the peace of the garden by arguing that Fran was completely mistaken. But Fran was completely mistaken. She was not spaced out. She was fully present and actively waiting for Kyung-ho to let go of her hand. He didn't, he hadn't, and snatching it back felt so unfriendly, that couldn't be right, not standing in a garden under the westering sun.

While waiting, and having nothing better to do, it seemed like a good time to respond to his latest complaint.

"Chef, will you make us something for breakfast?" she asked.

"Chloe!" Fran remonstrated.

"What? He's far from home and his people, and has nobody to cook for. It's important he feels appreciated to keep his spirits up. We need to eat."

Fran glanced nervously at Kyung-ho's impassive countenance.

"Not his mad face, Fran."

"What would you like?" Kyung-ho asked in a tone that to Fran sounded curt. Chloe felt his thumb run along the inside of her forefinger, and naturally, had a different perspective.

"*Ummmm*...Something sweet that pairs with strawberries? We have a strawberry patch, so that part is covered. I'm still crying over my moon that became fog, though, so just make something you like making."

"I'll see what I can do."

"Not if you're too tired, though," Chloe added, relenting to conscience, "or too busy. Or have to stay up late. Or get up early."

"I'll see what I can do."

A car honked impatiently in the distance.

"Our chariot awaits," she said. Reluctantly taking the initiative before it left without them, she let go of Kyung-ho's hand. "Home, Fran."

Moving towards the drive, she turned back one last time.

"Have a good night, Chef. Thanks for finding my pepper mill. And for the promise of bees. And for wearing linen, such a good look."

With a twinge of embarrassment and impatience, Fran pulled her quickly around the building and out of sight.

IT PARTIALLY MOLLIFIED THE LAST carload of contestants to see Fran and Chloe hustling as they crossed the sweep towards the van.

"Sorry to keep you guys waiting," Chloe apologized, wheezing slightly as they piled into the waiting vehicle.

"Did you find your inspiration?" asked Travis.

"No."

"Nothing?"

"Doomed-a-rama. But," she announced to the van at large, "I hope I made my delaying the paella party worth it. I was organizing a breakfast treat for you."

They all looked at Fran, as usual, for an explanation.

"This woman actually had the nerve to...you will...She asked the guest judge to bake something for us."

"She what? You WHAT?" exclaimed her fellow travelers with one minority, "I love this woman" from Felix.

"Forget that," said Ajiz, "how did you dare? After he yelled at you all day?"

"Did not."

"Did too."

"Did not."

"Why don't you tell us what happened," interrupted Travis, aware as they all were that Ajiz could go on like that for hours and still expect to win something.

"Well, as thinking people with souls are aware, in just days Chef's gonna be on the other side of the planet. We need to eat his food while we can. It's good for him, too. It builds character and helps him understand his customer base."

"He's opening a café two hours from your apartment, dummy," said Fran. "You can just eat there. Without being either weird or a Vivian."

"But I want the unadulterated, made-by-the-man, version. Trust and believe, it's not the same thing."

"Is too," said Ajiz.

"Is not."

This time Fran interrupted them, both with words and the threat of a sharp elbow.

"Is this what happens to brains fried by sugar?" she asked Chloe.

"Hey, at least I'm using my crazy for the good of humanity, Ajiz is just being contrary. You'll all thank me later."

"I'm thanking you now," said Felix.

Travis, talking over the subsequent knuckle bump between those two that almost took out his nose, tried getting the actual story out of Fran.

"Did she really do this?"

"Right to his face. Ya' know his death stare?"

"*Tch*," Chloe responded. "The man's a giant marshmallow, don't you guys get that yet? If, you know, Michelangelo worked in marshmallow."

"That makes him a Peep. Are you calling him a Peep?"

"Peeps don't have cheekbones."

"We have forms in the HR department for people like you," said Fran with exasperation.

"Yes, they're called citations. For my ability to source award-winning pastry. You're just prejudiced because you don't yet know where he stands on onion rings."

"Isn't he still mad at you?" repeated Ajiz. "We all thought he was going to take a whack at you with that spoon. Are you sure "cook" isn't another word for "poison"? English is not his first language."

"I don't care, I'm still eating it," said Felix.

Chloe reached over the seatback for another knuckle bump before correcting Ajiz.

"It's Vivian who almost got the spoon. All that slinking, pretending he has some mad crush on her. I think she's trying to get him fired."

"Fired for what?" Travis asked.

"Consorting."

"Takes one to know one," said Fran.

"What? Huh? What. I was sitting on the ground, ten feet away from him. I don't think that's the right verb. Anyway, today ended twelve times better than expected, and with any luck, tomorrow Felix and I will both fall in love with a Little Paris food item that can be shipped via FedEx. Starry Night kinda loses something once you turn it upside down and toss it fifteen feet every time you switch conveyances."

A startled Travis tried one last time to get the real story.

"Chloe, why were you on the ground?"

"I was doing my garden gnome imitation."

"In front of Chef?"

"No, behind his back. The bench faces the other way."

Adding this new revelation to the previous mish mash, he, too, was forced to concur with Fran.

"You have officially lost your mind."

Perfectly content to learn that a simple insanity defense could obfuscate a blatant pastoral interlude, with a man, in public, near cameras and feet from a score of nosy gossips, one of whom was even a farmer who should clock a PI when he saw one, Chloe closed her eyes with a smile and dozed for the rest of the ride home.

pain is sometimes a bread product

Dawn found Kyung-ho alone his test kitchen making his *pain au chocolate*. When he unlocked the side door to the convention center, he experienced a momentary qualm over whether the old flour war would mysteriously reignite, but the process was smooth and quiet, and only required turning on the bank of lights over one section of prep stations. While the pastries were still warm, he loaded them onto a platter and into his car, and drove them out to the contestant's lodging.

As his footsteps quietly creaked up the wooden stairs of the cabin's long porch, he set a fixed intention to hand over the plate and leave. That was for the best, and all that was required. Then Rachel answered the door. With her cell phone glued to her ear, she silently waved him in, and looking down at what he carried, pointed toward the kitchen before disappearing into the butler's pantry she was using as an office. Being a team player, he abandoned his own plan and followed the orders of upper middle management.

He set out his platter on the granite-topped island, making a quick, professional assessment whether that particular swirl of grey-brown was a help or hindrance when rolling out pastry. He then looked around the empty kitchen. After approving the brand of stove and disapproving the refrigerator placement, his mission at the house appeared complete. He only needed to go find Rachel to tell her the croissants were for the contestants, and he was now leaving.

Perhaps, yes, she was already aware of both pieces of information, but it was the polite thing to do.

Wandering through the now-empty butler's pantry, he exited its other door and found himself in the also empty hallway. Wandering further, he found the empty common room. Leaning his hands on the back of a sofa, he looked out the picture window to search the empty terrace in case she stepped outside. She appeared to be the only one up yet in the silent house, and somehow to have disappeared.

Nervously tapping his hands on the seatback, Kyung-ho began to decide to really leave. Turning toward the hall, however, he discovered the woman he was actually looking for lying below him on the other side of the sofa, asleep. Already disturbed by the doorbell earlier, and further wakened by his banging on the furniture, she opened her eyes to see his face leaning over a wall of red and green plaid.

"Good morning," Chloe said drowsily and without surprise, "you came."

He reached down to brush her hair off her forehead.

"Why are you sleeping out here?" he asked.

She shook her head.

"Didn't. Unwise. Came out early to wait for you. Are you very tired?"

"What kind of coffee do you want?" he asked.

She started to rise, as if his question required her participation, but was immediately checked by the pressure of his hand on her shoulder. She relaxed back into the cushions.

"A sweet cappuccino, please."

Across the room, the slider door creaked open, and Travis reentered the house carrying the morning strawberry harvest. Finding Chef in their living room, he came up short. Chef's softened expression startled him more. He craned his neck to see over the moose-patterned club chair between them to ascertain whether he was alone, vaguely but half-unbelievingly expecting to see Vivian. Instead, he glimpsed an unmistakable shock of red hair. With a sharp sense of loss, he realized he wasn't getting his nickname back.

Spotting Travis by the door, Kyung-ho nodded a greeting and returned to the kitchen. Travis followed him out of the room.

"Chef, what are you doing here?" he asked.

"I made *pain au chocolate* for all you contestants."

"Thank you."

Turning on the sink faucet, Travis began rinsing the berries.

"I can take it from here, Chef," he said. "I'm sure you have lots to do."

Kyung-ho looked steadily at the quiet, well-liked giant. Unlike Fran and Chloe, he was certain whose cuisine reigned supreme with Travis, and unlike Juan, here was a rival not to be despised. Kyung-ho was clearly the shorter, slighter man, who sometimes communicated by intuition rather than a full grasp of the English language. Travis also had been supplying Chloe with strawberries for weeks and judging by the movement of his hands under the tap, knew how to wash them properly. Still, Kyung-ho reminded himself, today was a breakfast challenge and one of them had run a five-star Parisian hotel kitchen. And had already made the croissants.

"Are those for everyone?" he asked, indicating the basin of fruit.

Travis nodded.

"We get them out of our garden."

"Great, thanks. I'll just chop Chloe's, then, and leave the rest of the grunt work to you. Help yourself to some *pain au chocolate*, they should still be warm."

The men worked without further chatter to organize their own breakfasts. That is, Travis watched Kyung-ho expertly chop and steam and plate, while making a decent pretense of waiting for his turn at the coffee machine. Kyung-ho finished his design on Chloe's cappuccino foam with an unnecessary flourish, then finally broke the silence.

"Have you mastered latte art yet, Travis?"

"What? No."

"*Hmmph.*"

Picking up the five-star coffee and breakfast plate ensemble, Kyung-ho moved into the dining area. The light clink of servingware placed on the table broke through Chloe's doze.

"Come and eat," Kyung-ho said, reappearing by the side of her couch.

Catching at his arm, she used it to pull herself upright. Still holding it, she stumbled after him to the table where he had set out a cappuccino with a swan design, sliced berries, and his renowned-on-multiple-continents *pain au chocolate*.

"Aren't you eating?" she asked.

He shook his head.

"I think it's better that I go."

"You're assuming I intend to let go of your arm."

"Sit, eat your breakfast."

"Alright, but I am only choosing the food option, this one time, because it's perishable and I asked you to make it."

Releasing him, Chloe slid into the chair. Kyung-ho clasped his hands behind his back and waited for her verdict.

A sudden clatter of footsteps on the stairs announced the arrival of a wave of other contestants coming down for breakfast. Like Travis, Paul stopped abruptly to see Kyung-ho standing in the dining room, causing a minor, temporary pile-up.

"Behind, chef, behind," a voice could be heard grumbling from above.

"Good morning, People," Chloe sang out. "Check out the kitchen for what Chef brought us. And, uh, told you so."

She waved a croissant at Paul and the series of heads that appeared over his shoulder. Turning back to Kyung-ho, she took a small bite.

"It's hard to compliment you while mentally preparing myself for being left on the wrong side of the world," she responded. "No good, no good at all is what is coming to mind. If one has two more, will that make this experience even worse?"

"I don't know," he replied, "that's not very French."

Chloe laughed softly and took another small bite.

"I hope you appreciate, then, the sacrifice I'm making. Market research, I'm just trying to be thorough. Needing to force myself hereafter to eat something that will be wrong and not remotely what I want, however, will be unpleasant."

"It's not like you to talk down my shop."

"I won't complain in public, but you've already ruined *entremets* for me, and this here is a staple pantry item."

Vivian entered the dining area carrying two croissants and a glass of cranberry juice. Catching most of their conversation, she turned to her those following her and remarked in a loud whisper,

"Oh my God, Chloe just told him his food and his shop both suck. Can you believe her?"

Chloe took another small sip of coffee, careful not to slosh the pattern, and stood up.

"I'll walk you out, Chef."

Silently, she accompanied him to the hall. Silently, he passed through the door she held open for him, and once more his footsteps clattered across the porch and down the steps.

Returning to the table, she found everyone chattering excitedly about the unexpected meal. They momentarily fell silent as she entered.

"Did you really tell Chef these pastries are sub-par?" asked Fran. "And are they? Because, what do I know."

"I am disturbed and concerned for you all, accusing me of things that are not humanly possible," she answered.

Returning to her place at the table, she gestured to her cup.

"Look, he made a recognizable swan in cappuccino foam. The man's a genius."

"You don't seem glad he did what you asked, though," said Travis the Observant, noticing her lack of cheerfulness with a last flicker of hope.

Chloe looked again at the perfect balance of butter, sugar and bitterness.

"You're right, Travis. When somebody gives you heaven on a plate, one should at least live there for a while."

"What did you really say to him?" inquired Fran.

Seven avid faces, three disgruntled ones, and one still wishing people would talk secrets in French turned towards Chloe.

"I merely objected that without proper supervision his baristas will make a leaf pattern on my coffee foam, if not a spludge of white nothing. I'll drink it, but I don't see why I have to pretend it's the same thing."

"And what did he say?" asked Fran.

"That the cost of an international plane ticket will triumph over my standing coffee order. Our Travis is right, though, what is far more important is the here and now. So, ha ha ha, oh look, I was right."

Kyung-ho sat in his car without turning on the engine, which was as far as his resolve to leave had taken him before petering out as a thing unhelpful. She didn't thank him, or properly compliment him, or even say goodbye. As he passed through the doorway, she simply touched his back as he walked by. He still felt the brief, light pressure landing on his right scapula. It momentarily checked his progress, like the moon pulling on a satellite before it spins past out of orbit. Taking his finger off the starter button, he jettisoned his plan to review a very pressing occupancy permit issue, surrendered to gravity, and gave his full attention to inventing a legitimate reason to return to the house and sit down at her table.

CHAPTER FIFTY-ONE

the food fight

Again, the doorbell rang at the contestants' house, and again Rachel answered it, phone still in her ear. Again, she found Kyung-ho standing on the coconut fiber welcome mat demanding entry.

He bowed to her, and mouthed,

"I left something in the kitchen."

She nodded, stepped back and again vanished.

Kyung-ho crossed the entryway and turned into the dining area, which was not the kitchen. The chattering room again fell silent.

"Thank you, Chef," Chloe spoke into the void with quiet surprise. "*Ahem.* We were all agreeing about how amazing these croissants are. Weren't we team?"

A chorus of yeses went around the table, with one or two dissenting "well, she wasn't".

"Please join us," Chloe continued, sparking a slightly less enthusiastic chorus of assent, and whispered confusion over the reason for his reappearance.

Kyung-ho bowed slightly and took the only open chair, the one next to Vivian.

An awkward silence settled over the group. Conversations were half started and then abandoned as everyone monitored Kyung-ho, Vivian, and Chloe to see whether a war might break out somewhere, and whether they could follow the why, or know who to root for. Finally, Paul – trying as usual to be the grown up in the room – asked the obvious question.

"So, Chef...how long have you and Chloe known each other?"

Kyung-ho looked down the table to see how she would field that.

"We met for ten minutes about a year and a half ago," said Chloe.

"Forty-seven minutes and nineteen seconds," he corrected. "She advised me on a startup venture. She is extremely knowledgeable about niche markets."

Chloe demurred.

"You've all eaten his food, he's an easy sell. Where's Wallace today?"

"Back at the hotel."

The conversation petered out again.

Kyung-ho chastised himself for succumbing to his impulse to behave like a middle-schooler. Placing his hands firmly on the table, he prepared to return the world of adult responsibilities.

"Actually, I thought I left my phone in the kitchen," he began.

Before he could take further action, though, or the lump in his breast pocket started beeping, he felt Vivian's restraining hand on his arm. Having done all she could earlier to educate Kyung-ho that Chloe liked his food only in front of a camera, and willing to let that stew a while until he was ready to see the truth, she moved on to other topics guaranteed to drive a wedge between them.

"I hope," she began, "and I don't want to embarrass you Chef..."

Kyung-ho glanced at her with alarm and leaned back to put some distance between her and wherever this was headed. The others watched with varying levels of expectancy that the curtain was finally going up. Chloe tried not to hiss.

Vivian continued.

"...but I hope you being here this morning doesn't get Chloe in trouble with Juan. We all think there's a little something something there."

"Chef Juan's an equal opportunity guy," interrupted Fran in a quick defense of Chloe's reputation with the company at large. "He hits on everybody."

"Is that a hint she is already with Travis?" asked Vivian, doubling down.

Chloe picked up her croissant and took a tiny bite in a dual effort to keep her mouth shut and make the pastry last as long as possible.

"Only she calls him Linus," Vivian explained to Kyung-ho, continuing to offer herself as a helpful navigator regarding insider show gossip. "She says she's living for his pumpkin patch. Isn't that cute?"

"Everybody with a soul loves a giant pumpkin and Travis' steak *au poivre*," Chloe responded tartly. "Stop making the boy feel oogie and weird over his muesli."

In the new awkward silence, punctuated only by a few clinks and tinks of spoons and saucers, Chloe stared at the large, nature conservancy wall clock over Kyung-ho's head looking for something to count. She settled on watching the seconds hand tick past a cardinal, blue jay, and a robin before opening her mouth, and then only to take another tiny bite of pastry. Refreshed by time and sugar butter, she looked down the table and tried to change the subject.

"Hey, any chance of dessert with lunch?"

Kyung-ho's free hand suddenly thumped down on the table making all the contestants, and their servingware, jump and clatter. Pushing back his chair, he stood up and stalked into the kitchen, grumbling in Korean all the way.

They all looked at Chloe for a translation, or explanation, but she had none.

"I only know how to say "hello" and "yes", that kinda stuff. If a pastry chef didn't want people asking for more pastry, though, he should be a broccoli farmer. He wouldn't get mad about that."

Had Wallace been there to translate, he could have informed them that Kyung-ho, now loudly opening and closing cabinets to find another plate, was just complaining about watching someone pick at his food.

"This woman, I am going to lose my mind before this stupid week is up," he griped and grumbled, until relinquishing his attempt to find the right cabinet, he banged the last door shut, walked over to the island and picked up the whole tray of the remaining croissants. Turning back, he strode the length of the dining area to thwunk down his burden in front of Chloe.

"Eat," he said, "and stop worrying about lunch before you've had breakfast."

"That's more than two."

Putting one hand on the back of her chair and one on the table, he loomed over her.

Chloe lost the ensuing staring contest. Possibly because she knew he was right, or perhaps because his fighting stance allowed him to rub her back with his thumb, a tactic several orders of magnitude more effective than rubbing her clavicle. She reached out and put another pastry on her plate.

"Mean, that's what you are," she complained.

"Uh-huh."

Looking up at the avid, startled faces around the table, Kyung-ho offered his own version of events.

"When she's stressed, she doesn't eat. If Wallace doesn't get his new PR director, he might just fire me."

Responding to her side glance with raised eyebrow, he added,

"What? You nibbled at my *pain au chocolate* while sitting across from me. Is that how we are going to play this? Really?"

"Go away," she replied. To the surprise of everybody, he did.

"Wait," asked Ajiz, "do you know Chef, or the other guy?"

"Wallace is her biggest fan," Kyung-ho answered retaking his seat, content to see Chloe eating normal bites of her breakfast, and that before she distributed the extra pastries among her side of the table, she put another one on her plate. "She helped create his Blue Suede Shoes dessert at the same time as Starry Night. He is very fond of that one."

"Oh, what's in that?" asked Felix eagerly, co-opting Kyung-ho's attention to talk sugar. Long before he discovered all he wanted to know about toasting bananas, conversation restarted again around the table to where Kyung-ho was just one of many voices.

Too soon, however, Vivian took the opportunity to unexpectedly, if predictably, try again to ruin it for everybody.

"Chef, would you mind driving me to the set?" she interrupted with a tug on his sleeve. "I could use some quiet time before today's challenge."

Eleven out of twelve heads swiveled in Kyung-ho's direction to watch him politely, but firmly refuse.

"I'm sorry, but I don't feel comfortable driving someone who isn't my girlfriend. I can ask Rachel if..."

"Is she that jealous? How insecure," Vivian responded, goaded into unwise speech by his choosing public rejection instead of public coercion.

Kyung-ho's look of such concentrated dislike penetrated, if only momentarily, her obliviousness. His answer, however, was more quiet.

"One never knows when the paparazzi is around, and I don't like her bothered by the unnecessary. If a picture is going to get into the tabloids, it should at least be true."

"Who is your girlfriend, anyway?" Fran asked bluntly.

Kyung-ho didn't answer.

"Chloe," Travis said.

"Yes, Travis?"

"Do you know who it is?"

"The Bond Villain?" whispered Fran eagerly before Chloe could reply.

It immediately revived and delighted Vivian to be reminded she was just his type.

"Did you really date a Bond Villain?" she asked. "If she doesn't like you driving rivals, how does she feel about you cooking for Chloe?"

"She hasn't really said." Kyung-ho replied. Or complained.

"Huh," said Chloe through a mouthful of pastry. "Bet you she has. Bet you you weren't listening."

a road trip changes everything

The interrogation of Kyung-ho regarding his current relationship status was (mercifully) interrupted by Rachel entering the room to announce the vans had arrived. Spotting him seated at the contestant's breakfast table, she said,

"Chef, glad you're still here. You've got your SUV, right?"

He nodded.

"Can you take a load of the contestants to the site? Actually, I'll trade you for the van. We need backup melons for the shoot, and I can take the rental to go pick them up."

An uncomfortable silence descended among the contestants, but Kyung-ho assented readily enough.

"I've got enough room in mine," he told Rachel, after a quick, mental head count. "You keep the van. It's easier to load, and you might need the extra storage."

"Dibs for the Blue Team!" Chloe said, causing this week's Blues to look at her with consternation, regretting they chose her over Ashley.

"Trust me," she responded to the subtle wave of dissent, "it'll make a nice change. Honestly, I feel so completely unknown here."

The contestants scattered to collect jackets and purses and water bottles. Chloe retrieved hers from her bunk bed and followed everyone outside to find the rest of her team standing around Kyung-ho's car. Crossing the sweep, she heard a familiar step behind her and the car beep as Kyung-ho remotely unlocked the doors. The team continued to exchange looks without getting in the car, however, unsure of where to sit given Kyung-ho's rebuff of Vivian.

"Shotgun!" Chloe called out, approaching the passenger side. Seeing her team's response, she added, "If it makes you feel better, I'll ask. Chef, may I have shotgun?"

Kyung-ho nodded and moved around to the driver's side.

"Marshmallow," she whispered as Kyung-ho got in and shut his own car door. "I keep telling you that, and you should believe me. Who got you *pain au chocolate*? He likes *us*, he just can-*not* stand Vivian. What did you want him to say? Please evil one, let's spend some quiet time together? Keep up!"

Chloe opened her door, and the rest piled into the back two rows.

The sound of seat belts clicking into place and seven people settling themselves echoed through the silent car. Once they pulled out of the driveway following the other van, Chloe swiveled around, stuck her head in the gap between the front seats, and announced into the void,

"Now, for Part B of my genius plan."

"Chef?" she asked turning to him. "What don't we know about running a group kitchen thing? Tell us everything."

Kyung-ho glanced at her sideways before returning his attention to the road. Giving his forearm leaning on the armrest between them a reassuring pat, she turned back to others.

"This is our seventh team challenge, guys. What don't we know? Think! We have an expert," she said with an added squeeze to the expert's arm, "our secret weapon *du jour*. And now we've got about twenty minutes to let it change everything for us."

After another long pause full of stares, eyerolls and elbows, Ajiz broke the silence.

"Well...how do you choose the right items for a group menu, Chef? I still don't get it."

"A buffet or a progression?"

"What's the difference?"

"A lot. We don't supply the dinner part of the meal, but I can tell you how we plan the dessert menu for one, versus a dessert buffet, and you can see if you can adapt it."

He then gave them a caterer's cliff notes on how to balance variety with production constraints. His brief but helpful suggestions started a lively discussion. He had tips on judicious *mise en place* and fancy edible garnishes, when to avoid recipes where everything must go right, and how to build in flexibility in case things went wrong. He told pithy anecdotes about assigning tasks according to politics over talent and wasting specialty items on a bad client. His best advice was a warning not to catastrophize failures and mistakes during the cook, especially when said disasters were entirely their own fault, an issue that particularly derailed Fran and Oliver. Their only job was to succeed under any and all new constraints.

"No one here expects you to deliver what they ordered, even on your best day. Not making any food at all is the real danger. Success is first and foremost about mental discipline."

Out of view from the others, Chloe spoke little, except when she popped her head between the seats for a comment or vote, using the hand she left on his arm (to save time and effort) as leverage to pull herself forward as needed. The bulk of the drive she sat sideways in her seat, watching his profile and enjoying his native reticence relax into confident authority, measured enthusiasm and bursts of humor.

During an interval where her team conversed among themselves how best to incorporate his latest suggestion. Kyung-ho looked over and asked in a low voice,

"Are you still mad?"

"No...Am I? Maybe," she said, trying to forget the image of Vivian confidently and openly touching his person. "I think I'm more tired and scared about causing the wrong publicity and/or having a disaster day. She got me good with the spice bomb. If she gets angry with you, or you get angry..."

"I can handle Vivian and will try to control my temper. You just focus on today's cook. Are you going to make spicy food for your customers?"

"No."

"Then what happened in the prior episodes are mistakes, not a disaster. Everybody goes home, which means everybody makes them, and I trust you to talk your customers out of any box Juan or the editors try to put you in."

Chloe closed her eyes and smiled as she absorbed his much-needed support.

"*Sa-rang-haeng,*" he added under his breath, mistakenly thinking she couldn't understand him.

"*Mon amour,*" she replied softly, because she did. Before any eavesdropper did too, she quickly asked how Wallace was responding to the new staff change.

"He's getting insufferable about being the one to talk me into doing *Yes, Chef!,*" Kyung-ho replied. "He's going to want a company car at this rate."

"That's why I love him so much already," answered Chloe. "He's so right. He deserves wheels for that."

"Oh, does he?"

"Hey, if you help him get a girlfriend," she suggested, "won't he be no longer terribly interested in what you're doing?"

"Help me to help you," she said with a subtle head tilt in Fran's direction.

"You think?" he replied. "Well, if you are wrong and he implodes during the launch, I'm banning you from the New York shop."

"Heh," she laughed. "I love how bad you are at threatening me."

CHAPTER FIFTY-THREE

blue melon
kisses

When the Blue Team tumbled out the SUV onto the sidewalk in front of the Mile High Diner, Fran's pronouncement that Chef was surprisingly human and unexpectedly helpful represented the consensus opinion. All but one of the team also shared her desire to canvass a whole new info dump regarding the Kyung-ho/Chloe drama.

"She likes his business partner? Isn't that what she just said?" asked Oliver.

Paul agreed.

"I heard her trying to get Kyung-ho to set them up."

"But Chef cooked for her," said Fran, equally confused and secretly disappointed, despite being far better informed.

"Love triangle?" posited Oliver.

Paul nodded back at him.

"Have you noticed they never fight when they talk business?"

"Business love triangle?"

Chloe pretended she wasn't listening.

THE BRIEF FOR THE SUGAR! Week Group Challenge was a dinner menu pairing watermelon with protein, as the closest to sweet things two out of the three regular judges would accept after a week of sampling amateur desserts. The teams then gathered in their designated corner of the diner's seating area for the allotted fifteen-minute, pre-shopping strategy meeting. Instead of getting down a plan, however, the Blue Team stared at each other in dismay.

"Do you...? Watermelon...?"

"I don't."

"Travis, you have a farm...?" began Fran. Everyone turned to look brightly and expectantly at Travis, Farmer, and Their Savior.

"We grow pumpkins. Different gourd."

Instantly and unanimously, they demoted Travis to Farmer that Grows Nothing Useful. Except Chloe, who loyally added the caveat,

"Still, love me a giant pumpkin."

"The last preparation for watermelon I saw," she reported, causing suddenly renewed, brightly expectant faces to turn in her direction, "was sliced down the middle and being eaten raw on a Korean television show. Or was it Taiwanese?"

Oliver shook his head.

"That is not helpful."

"I used to eat watermelon Now-N-Laters as a child?" said Paul.

"Again, not helpful."

"Well, we don't have Glenn, and we don't have donuts, so listening to Chef must be the solution," announced Chloe, taking charge of the collective panic attack threatening to derail both their meeting, and any chance they had in the competition. "This is going to work for us. Let's start with what we know. None of us eat watermelon, Travis refuses to even grow them, so...so...odds are few guests will have eaten many for dinner, either. Where does that get us?"

"If we see the problem as a parameter, like Chef said," offered Paul, "then... what if cook what we want, and pretend that that is what watermelon is used in? Who'll know different?"

"Great thinking," said Chloe. "It's tart, right, and things called water are probably mostly water. Wait, it's not like Greenland, is it? Watermelon has water, right?"

They looked to Travis for confirmation. He nodded.

"See, farmers know some things," she said. "What if we view it like a damp lime or a lemon? And put it near crispy things without getting them soggy?"

"My signature onion rings," piped in Fran, "always a crowd pleaser."

"Yum-o-la," agreed Ajiz, "but haven't you already made them. Twice?"

"Not the Cajun-spiced ones."

Paul enthusiastically jotted that dish down on the menu plan.

"What else?" he asked the group.

"Fish, watermelon needs a fish."

"When you are right, you're on fire, Oliver."

Panic turned to enthusiasm and even a cohesive, watermelon-forward menu as Kyung-ho's advice and strategy took hold. At every hard choice or knotty compromise, "Kyung-ho says what?" became their guiding principle. It even inspired them to an unusual height of prudence. For once, they thought beyond the wished-for final product, and discussed equipment needs and divided up responsibilities and how to best stagger the day's pressure points to achieve a final product.

Their new mantra also proved effective in the field. When the team regrouped in the check-out line, Ajiz reported that when faced with the potentially disastrous news that the Whole Foods stock of tuna steaks let them down, one timely, "now, what did he say, Oliver?" led to a resigned acceptance of snapper, rather than a knee-jerk panic request for lamb shanks. The team recognized this as a personal best for Oliver in a fish counter substitution crisis with a round of high-fives.

Driving back to the diner, another "Kyung-ho says...!" – quickly gaining recognition as salient and useful in any emergency – was silently telegraphed to each other when Ajiz realized he left an essential ingredient behind in the shopping cart. The team virtuously refrained from acknowledging, out loud, that what really happened was the item was so obvious he forgot to write it down on the shopping list, and that is how it got overlooked. Again. They knew it, but they didn't say it, and instead, spent a productive following ten minutes adapting to the omission that was too late to fix regardless.

By the time the team returned with their bulging shopping bags to face the day's real test, using an unfamiliar product while discovering and navigating the quirks of someone else's old, tiny, and creatively equipped kitchen, the rallying cry had been shortened by time constraints to "KHS!". When Paul's burners were turned up instead of being shut off, a timely KHS! (which cool kids pronounce "k'yes") turned his frown upside down. Instead of tossing out thirty-eight minutes of prep and all their stock of Swiss chard in a pique of despair, he abandoned the side dish nobody thought worked anyway and added a charred element to Chloe's salad.

"Depth," pronounced Ajiz tasting the new collaboration, "the char adds depth. Balances the sweetness. KHS!, baby. Groovy."

With an exasperated KHS!, and – possibly – a muttered expletive, Fran announced the fryer was hopeless and unreliable. However colorfully expressed, they marveled how a KHS! led her away from a meltdown, as her one chance to shine, ever, in the food world was sabotaged by the equipment decisions made in the last century, and redireced her towards an oven-baked version the Blue Team marketed as "calorie-conscious".

"I'm not saying it's better," said Oliver with a full mouth, as he sampled the newer version, "but it is darn good, and now I feel justified having four, not one."

"That's good customer relations," Chloe said, grabbing a second handful, "we should get extra points for that. And now you can make your signature dish again with proper equipment, because it's a duo. That's a totally different dish."

"The Mile High-Low Plate, what a great idea," Fran said.

"You're welcome. KHS! forever," she said, grabbing her third, and last, handful. Definitely last. Sure.

By a series of such miracles, and the time saved not arguing whether any one happenstance or idiocy was really a secret attempt to ruin each other's lives on national television, the Blue Team dishes came out surprising well. The contestants themselves fared slightly worse. At the end of *mise en place*, Travis chose to "just move on" in his search for the lid to the blender, the one sitting on the bench in front of him, right where he put it. Each person's exact placement in the kitchen when he hit the frappe button could be mapped by lining up the splash of watermelon puree across aprons, backs, and at least one forehead.

"I think the owners are going to be finding surprise traces of your watermelon sauce for decades," said Paul in the dramatic pause after Travis turned off the blender.

"Or ants."

"If we give them a watermelon-free menu, and call it an intentional decision, would that be read as avant-garde?" asked Oliver while they waited for Travis to guesstimate whether enough product was left to avoid another major menu alteration. "Blue Team – The Rebel Kitchen."

"Maybe?" said Ajiz, ready for any excuse to switch back to his regular flavor profiles for red sauces. "We can leave empty spaces on the plates to imagine their own version of watermelon."

"Does anyone really want the real thing? Even Travis won't grow one," declared Fran.

"We grow pumpkins!" said Travis. "We're a pumpkin farm! And I'm going with what's left of the real thing, and making it work. There should be just enough."

"You KHS! those two tablespoons," said Chloe. "Even if whirly tools are a culinary bridge too far for you, I still believe you can triumph over a watery red melon.

"Hey, Paul doesn't know how to work a two-top," said Travis wiping down his arms and apron, and getting back into action. "When I burn food at least it still has a purpose."

While most of his team stared open-mouthed at Travis making a joke, Paul recalled them to the business at hand.

"Whatever, tick tock, people! Debating over sticky fruit wall art is so last hour, I'm KHS!-ing back to what really matters in life — making the perfect *au jus.*"

A KHS! sustained their team spirit even while wearing a schmear of fruit stickiness and fully aware that Paul never looked a clock when making a gravy. When time was called, they chose unity and the person easiest to clean. Instead of sending out Oliver to leverage Travis' mistake as a scapegoat for everyone else's menu deficiencies, they gave Travis' forearms a quick extra scrub down, KHS!'ed and said goodbye, and shoved him through the door.

The judges might have accepted Oliver's *deshabille*, but Travis' flat, bland explanation for the splatter pattern on his apron was too intriguing to accept. The whole group was called out front and reluctantly lined up like a subdivided Jackson Pollack. The crowd laughed, but the Blue Team's unflagging commitment to the man, the mission, KHS! preserved their cheerful sense of accomplishment, and camaraderie. To the end of the jeers, they presented a picture of hard-working amateurs who had faced some challenges while leaving their mark in the Mile High Diner, rather than a ragtag group of resentful, failed rookies in need of a clean-up on aisle 5.

CHAPTER FIFTY-FOUR

the last
judgment

Two very different teams stood in front of the judges back at the warehouse kitchen. The Red Team – professional, united, and confident they delivered a solid performance, and the Blue Team – an equally united, kindergarten cooking class gone right, undaunted by others taking the cleaner, sterile road to supplying ninety-five covers of a watermelon-themed menu.

"Blue Team, you look like you had a busy day in the kitchen," observed Chef Juan.

Chef Parker seconded him.

"It looks like you're wearing it."

"That's my fault," admitted Travis.

"Lids," said Oliver, "they can be anywhere."

"Or, right where you put them," agreed Fran.

"Otherwise, the cook went well," Travis continued, speaking over their words and stray jabs.

"The Blue Team got professional help during their drive to site. That isn't fair," Vivian tattled, as expected.

"Oh, yeah," Travis confessed. "Chef told us deep, professional secrets like focus no matter what on the challenge in front of us. My grandfather says the same thing every time he teaches someone to drive the combine. If that counts as a watermelon preparation, it went right over our heads."

"Plus, by the end," added Fran, "we were on our third..."

"Eighth?" Ajiz corrected.

"Split the difference, eleventh recipe, so if he had given us a menu plan, we would have blown through it in the first hour."

"Do you even cook with watermelon, Chef Kyung-ho?" Chloe asked.

"No."

"Well, there you go. Our Travis can work two tablespoons of puree like they were a gallon," said Chloe, "but he won't grow them."

"We grow pumpkins, we're a pumpkin farm!"

"It's been eight hours, and he still won't admit it. I think the watermelon lobby got to him."

Chef Juan abandoned any attempt to disentangle such an unproductive backstory and turned to the Red Team.

They chose a more traditional Judge's Table strategy. Upon being informed the guests particularly liked Janiva's Watermelon Sweet and Sour Chicken, a dish everyone had touched at some point, they all tried to take credit for it. Vivian's "involvement" in what Janiva invented, insisted on making and cooked was to shove the plates out of her way when she needed more room before her own service. Naturally, she was the loudest to insist her participation made all the difference. To be fair, it probably had. Janiva was certain the Red Team would have received even more votes if each dish was complete.

Just as strategically, and unanimously, no one on the Red Team could quite remember how the flavorful mushfest that left their kitchen a watermelon-glazed steak made it to the pass. Jake made noise that it might be a Blue Team dish? Somehow? Who could remember something so long ago?

Chef Juan might swallow such balderdash, but Ajiz wasn't having it. He immediately began the Blue Team prebuttal to Jake's gaslighting with the low hum of Barbra Streisand. Fran elbowed him at his opening "...*Memmmmmmmories... light the cor-ner of my minddddddd...*", and Chloe put her hand over her eyes, but when Paul and Oliver joined in, it became a thing.

A little Barbra did jog the Red Team's recollection. Just when Ajiz told Oliver, with feeling, "...*Whattt's toooo painfullll to reeeemember...we simply chooosee TOOOOO forrrr-get...*" the entire Red Team capitulated to Jake's open disavowal of what he himself insisted during their menu planning would revolutionize steakhouses everywhere.

The judges again stared at Jake for a long moment, then turned with anticipation to discuss Ashley's dish. Her watermelon mousse schlumped into a puddle even as the servers carried it out. Oh, the unfortunate lesson in centrifusion to cooks and wait staff alike when the trays were brought down off the first two servers' shoulders. Epic. Truly, epic.

"...*fooorrr it's the laugggghhhhtteeerrr...,*" the Blue boys sang in an almost reverential hush as their team learned of the incident for the first time.

Ashley making it rain demoted Chloe's spice bomb to a minor error almost not worth airing, and it not being the panel's necks that got watermelon'd down on, delighted all the regular judges. It scarred Kyung-ho for life. Having watched the event in horror with his hand clapped over his mouth, he swore to evermore include this footage as part of his staff training regarding the dangers of self-delusion and uncertainty when working with all things gelatin. The other three panelists just looked forward to using the anecdote to scare the Season 15 contestants.

Turning now to the Blue Team's critique, Chef Matteo's impeccable segue timing was a skosh off. Their melody suffered a little during the Ashley recap, but they had not lost track of their place in the song. Three sour and annoyed judges and one rubbing the bridge of his nose could not make them stop five words before Ajiz and Oliver's hushed denouement, "*of...sniff...the wayyyyy weeeee werrreeee*".

As they fell on each other's....*sniff*...shoulders with emotion, Chef Parker struck a blow from the bench over the musical delay. He launched into the dreaded, team-spirit-destroyer question – who should go home and who should stay. Alas for the cool kids' dinner plans, it was Paul that struggled most in the Mile High kitchen. The glee club immediately straightened up and got serious.

Even that on-the-spot character test of how well a randomly selected group negotiated exhaustion, fear, blame, credit, risk and regret, however, became a remarkably friendly debate about who deserved the KHS! MVP. Determining who, sadly, came last to the KHS! lifestyle felt much closer to waving someone off by bus than driving over them with it.

Fran began.

"No one person dragged us down, but if I have to pick a name, Paul took a minute to get his go go go KHS! on without a red meat protein. We love you, Paul, we know how awesome your food was, but that's all I'm saying."

"I'm the one he looks to to prepare a meal's piscine element, as he should," explained Oliver.

Chloe seconded them, but instead of twisting the knife like a normal person, refocused the discussion on the day's successes.

"He did use his body as a human shield to protect our *mise en place* from the red rain of death. It totally saved my dish, so that has to count as credit towards Best in Show."

"So, who should go home?" asked Chef Parker, again trying to pin them down and break them up with a classic threat. "Chloe? Who should go home instead of you?"

Chloe shrugged, instead of giving him the shiver of fear he expected.

"Since the worst dish never made it out of the kitchen, and it was only an extra side, it didn't really matter..."

"...Actually, it was burnt out from under me."

"...there was that, but besides sacrificing his body, and Paul likes to be tidy even more than Travis, like Oliver said, he doesn't cook fish or watermelon so his (mother's) zero to hero pickled rinds deserves special mention. What was the question again? We should just be given the win," she concluded, "we KHS!'ed it out."

Chef Juan took over from an exasperated Chef Parker and tried to at least discover what the Blue Team was yammering about now.

"Should we even ask what K.H.S. means?"

Spokesman Travis again answered for the group.

"If you'll forgive the informality, Chef, it means "Kyung-ho says what?". It's pronounced "k'yes"."

"It's not just a lifestyle, it's an adventure," added Chloe.

"Chef Kyung-ho, your name seems to be invoked. Could you fill us in?" asked Chef Juan.

Kyung-ho shook his head no. It lacked Oliver's authority, though. Possibly because it looked to the American audience like a "yes" and left the other three judges suspicious he was finally choosing partisanship with his demographic over an honest critique. His further explanation didn't help.

"I gave them a brief outline about catering a dessert course. It wasn't anything specific to fruit preparations, and I don't know exactly what they think I said."

Ajiz offered more clarity, in case it impacted their score.

"KHS! means get it done. Keep on keeping on. I know that sounds obvious to you professionals, but we've been getting hung up thinking how one french fry crisps..."

Fran waved a correcting finger at him.

"Onion ring," she said.

"You're right, onion ring. How this one battered vegetable..."

"Fruit."

Paul interrupted another Fran/Ajiz death spiral to sum up the new Blue kitchen strategy more cogently.

"If every fry of every fried side is determinative of one's success in life, it's impossible to get ninety servings to the pass in thirty minutes. During each catastrophe invoking "KHS" helped us focus and solve the immediate problem."

"Whatever strategy remains valid before and after the Great Blender Incident is a bedrock truth," added Fran.

"Wisdom for the ages," Chloe agreed.

Chef Matteo cut off further exposition with a defeated wave of his hand.

"Then who deserves to win from your team? We'll start with Chloe again."

"*Oooooh*, tough one. Fran's onion rings were my favorite thing I ate today, but if we are going with watermelon, Oliver's snapper."

"Fran?"

"Chloe. She led us through meltdown panic to success. Kyung-ho said it, but she understood how to apply it, and hammer it home. Plus, her salad was awesome."

"Ajiz?"

"I'm with Fran – Chloe."

"Travis?"

"Fran's onion rings."

"You didn't like my snapper," said Oliver. "Then I'm voting against you. I say Chloe."

"How do you feel about them singling you out, Chloe?" asked Chef Juan with surprise. "You've really turned it around this week. Do you think you can be this Season's *Yes, Chef!* Master?

"Yes, Chef!" she replied with Fran-level conviction. All three main judges took a beat in response to this new and unexpected confidence. Kyung-ho just smirked.

"Chef Kyung-ho's advice actually changed how you worked in the kitchen?" Chef Juan asked.

"KHS! baby," said Ajiz.

"Should we shorten it again to a hand sign?" he suggested, turning to the others and making a sign language "k" out of his thumb and first two fingers.

"What the heck is that?" asked Travis.

"It is a K. K for Kyung-ho."

"Looks like a claw."

"It's a K."

"I think it looks like you are trying to put somebody's eye out," warned Paul, "and you can't hear a hand sign in the kitchen."

"We can use it if we have to cook for SWAT out in the field," he countered. "Hey, if you open and shut your fingers it's an R-O-K. See?"

"Now it looks like a duck."

"But it's our duck."

Despite three of the panel thoroughly losing patience with the Blue Team's singing, meanderings and flashing gang signs, they still won the greater number of watermelon seed votes from the diner guests. Chef Parker lobbied hard backstage during deliberation for the Red Team win anyway to discourage future ridiculousness holding up his dinner plans, but Kyung-ho successfully intervened with more of his calm, rational and completely disingenuous competition wisdom.

"You can't ding them for that, it makes good TV."

Chef Juan also pointed out the Blue Team hadn't given the judges any material to justify eliminating Chloe. Grudgingly, Parker agreed to highlight Ashley's once in a TV generation failure instead.

The announcement that Chloe had received another week's reprieve and a wholly unexpected first win elicited another spirited round of "KHS!" from the Blue Team as they jumped up and down and high-fived, while Chloe shouted "we love you, Troy! This gourd's for you!" into the camera.

"Works every time," said Ajiz.

"Now, Blue Team, do you want to know what your reward is?" asked Chef Matteo with zero enthusiasm.

The winners clutched each other's sticky hands and shoulders, and waited breathlessly, while the losers scowled from the sidelines.

"Chef Kyung-ho, tell them what their prize is."

Kyung-ho waited out the dramatic pause, and then announced,

"Karaoke."

"Yes!" said Ajiz.

Fran agreed with him, for once.

"Oh, fun!"

Hearing a dissenting mumble beside her, she added,

"Have you ever been, Travis?"

"No."

"Do you sing?"

"No."

"*Tch*, Travis, as if we believe you," remonstrated Chloe. "You'll see. Everything's different when you are with your people. Sing us home, Ajiz!"

"*Celllll-e-brate good times, come ON*," he began, leading the Blue Team conga line toward the locker rooms without even waiting for Chef Parker to officially kick them out.

"Immediately upon his return to the hotel, Kyung-ho surprised Wallace with how easy it can be to join the group reward segment of a television show one was not signed onto, not even as a minor character.

"I need you to accompany us tomorrow night," he announced.

"What's that on your shirt?" Wallace asked.

Kyung-ho looked down at the remaining evidence of Ajiz's friendly jab to his left arm and Oliver's hearty clap on his shoulder.

"Probably watermelon. The Blue Team won, and I am taking them out to karaoke."

"Who's the Blue Team?"

"Chloe and Fran and..."

"In."

"Thank you. Oh, and Chloe wants to set you up with Fran."

"Wow, I think I would be in love with her, if I wasn't."

"There's trouble we don't need."

"Not a chance. I prefer someone more..."

"...into onion rings?"

"Are you telling me to work out again?" asked Wallace, looking away so he didn't have to see Kyung-ho's abs as he changed out of his stained clothes. "Hey, where did you go this morning?"

"To stop by the contestant's house," Kyung-ho answered, pulling a clean tee shirt over his head. "I brought them *pain au chocolate.*"

"And how did that go over?"

He joined Wallace on the couch with a smile.

"Have you met my wife?"

"Wow, don't you think you know. When is karaoke?"

"Tomorrow."

"Any chance of you doing something stupid between now and then?"

"None. That's the only segment on the taping schedule. Tomorrow is their day off."

"Should we try to do something stupid beforehand? We're risk takers, and we both fly out next week."

"No time, we're filming in the early afternoon. Actually, is there time? No. But I have a great idea for after karaoke. Chloe won today. She should get an extra reward."

"How does this involve me?"

"You're the one who is supposed to watch these shows. Don't winners always bring a friend to share the reward? Food is a team sport."

"That's just in Australia, but I love your creative mind. What are you thinking?"

Kyung-ho leaned back and put his feet up on the coffee table with a smirk.

"That your reward for providing cover for the need for a second, extra reward is going off wherever you want with your own date, and leave us alone to have a conversation longer than ten minutes."

"Wait, what about the cameras?"

"Crap! I guess...we'll ditch them? We are strangers in a strange land, it shouldn't be that hard to pretend we meant turn left when we said we were going right. If they can't take a hint, maybe they'll take a bribe."

"Shouldn't we save the ₩600,000 we have left in the expense account for after we get rid of them?"

"Water getting low?"

"Your willingness to sell that kidney we've been saving would not be taken amiss by the firm."

Kyung-ho sighed and stood up again.

"Let me make a cup of coffee, and then show me the numbers."

the blue team sings the reds and the pinks

Starlight Karaoke Lounge was thrilled – thrilled! – to have their establishment featured on an episode of *Yes, Chef! America*. Especially given the show scheduled the taping outside of regular business hours, and on a slow day when the best corporate suite was lying empty anyway.

Promptly near around 2 PM, the contestants, their camera crew plus Kyung-ho and Wallace gathered in the Grand Ole Opry Suite. A generously sized, country-themed room, it contained a u-shaped banquette covered in faux cowhide centered in front of a dinged and scruffy black stage that held a microphone stand, a giant screen for displaying lyrics and an olde-fashioned trunk full of props for the prop-minded. Various beverages and the promised dessert tasting menu items were heaped on a low central table in the well of the banquette. It being the Opry suite, the contestants found a comfortable gap between the seats and the table allowing them to stand up and move around without climbing over one another, if one was vigilant about limbs and where people put down their drinks.

After a brief introduction from Ajiz about how karaoke worked, everyone clustered in random groups and poured over the binders of song lists with chaos and enthusiasm. Groups shifted and reformed as they argued over song order, and organized duets and the must-have "all skate" numbers. The prop trunk they pushed aside for a day without cameras. As people always at risk of starting a grease fire, funny hats and lighted tambourines risked leaving a permanent and unserious impression on their fan bases.

Kyung-ho quietly communicated his Extra Reward plan to the contestants while the camera crew was busy working out their angles and doing a sound check. Filtered through the team in whispers, his attempt to hide its actual purpose raised the vague suspicion – among the uninvited – it had an important, secondary function. The impression quickly morphed, or rather solidified, into a conviction that by hook, crook, blackmail, or an old favor come due, the add-on event was invented to help Chloe get her big chance with Wallace. Fran was obviously taking one for the team and being brought along as the necessary fourth wheel.

Long before the quartet disappeared for Round Two, however, three out of the four odd-men-out anticipated a musical chairs evening of disaster, followed by an explosive next day on set and the end of a beautiful friendship, possibly a food empire. Travis provided the dissenting opinion, but the others ascribed his contrariness to him being both a farmer who hadn't seen much of the world, and a generally nice person who couldn't see perfidy and betrayal in other people, even when it happened right in front of him. From their arrival at the Starlight Lounge, everyone could see Fran monopolized "Chloe's man", and when Ajiz took the stage to start the festivities and up town funk them up, uptown funk them up, she moved over to the vacated seat next to Wallace with an alacrity that hurt some people to watch.

"Sing it like you want us to know something, Ajiz!" Chloe yelled, a sentiment equally hard to hear. It seemed almost as if she wanted to happen what always happens in a new relationship when Bruno Mars tells the people they're *"too hot, hot damn"*. The man has authority, even channeled by Ajiz. Everybody knows this.

Some would later argue, however, that so does Lady Gaga. Following Ajiz, Oliver gave it his all exhorting those that should know better that this was a *Bad Romance*, but before he even got to the bridge Chloe's bonus "reward" was doomed to go down in flames. Ajiz and Oliver hoped they were wrong, Paul wanted to believe Fran was just being welcoming to the stranger, Travis obviously wasn't paying attention, and Chloe seemed content to spend the group portion of her reward chatting with Kyung-ho while her best friend, only a kitty-corner of black and white leatherette away, undermined her one chance at happiness. Unsure what to do if Chloe herself refused to have a clue, the bulk of the Blue Team could only eavesdrop helplessly on the unsuspecting pair of villains and update each other on any missed developments whenever the performance schedule drew people and their attention away at key moments.

Chloe sang next and shocked everyone, not that they stopped chair dancing, not that kind of shock, but shocked everyone by finally admitting that *"all this time I was finding myself, and didn't know I was lost."*

"Wow, Chloe used the "l" word," said Fran, so surprised she interrupted her conversation with Wallace to address the group at large. "I feel we've made a breakthrough."

Paul agreed.

"It's the power of Avicii."

He then did his best, and Paul on his game was a formidable force of nature, to keep Fran and Wallace part of the general discussion by inviting everyone to clap along like a room without a roof. This was vetoed, however, as being too divisive under the circumstances. You know, if that was not what someone wanted to do. The group guided him towards bringing some LMFAO where everyone could have a good time, and also lose one's mind.

"It's the more inclusive option," said Ajiz. "This was a team challenge."

Alas, no matter how many times Paul sang the refrain, Fran remained unaware she chose the latter option. Gravitating toward any stranger who might know things, and peppering a newcomer with whispered questions about her best friend's love interest was her way to make a person feel welcome. Once she satisfied her public-minded and private curiosity, of course she intended to introduce Wallace to the gang. She was just working herself up to do it, nearly, sure, when Wallace opened his own line of questioning and derailed her plans. How was that her fault?

"Why are you looking at me like that?" is what Villain #1, that would be Wallace, asked over the rim of his glass as he took a sip of beer. Partly because he wanted to know, and partly because Paul once again failed to read the room, and in a pique for not being allowed to feel his Pharrell, busted out some Herb Alpert and the Tijuana Brass.

Wallace was all-in on the Alpert. A moderately fit, moderately tall man with a receding hairline and frequently in the presence of Kyung-ho, this much focus and attention from a woman was rare. It had been twenty-six minutes, and Fran had yet to be "nice" to him. When he told a joke, she laughed. Because apparently, she thought it was funny. She wasn't making allowances for his hair, and even seemed genuinely concerned this was his first afternoon off in a month and a half. For some strange, magical, wondrous reason – and was it Paul? We don't know – in a room full of deer trophies and cowboy hats, he, the Chinese national with an avowed affinity for K-pop and zero ability to follow his seatmate's deeply held opinions on Adam Levine winning *The Voice* with a country act, he achieved, without any discernible effort, the social pinnacle the Blue Team would readily designate as being "on fire".

Bobbing his head along with Paul's heartfelt, *"how cannnnn I SHOW you…I'mmmmm gladddddd I GOT to know ya"*, oblivious to the scrutiny of his three non well-wishers, Wallace researched this anomaly with an unusual, calm confidence. The afternoon was young, there was a million songs to sing to express himself, several entirely in Korean if he funked it, and never had he looked forward so much to signaling Kyung-ho to begin launching Extraction Plan A.

Humming right along with Wallace under the legitimate guise that everyone else was too, even the boom mike operator, Fran took another sip from her own glass and balked at any response to Wallace's question. It suggested she was behaving weird or wrong or otherwise needed to stop something. So, of course, she would. When she got a moment. Geez.

First, though, she needed to finish laughing at his impression of Kyung-ho which made her stomp her feet and cry. She was mostly done, but she might have to hit his arm a few more times just to be sure, and of course, he might do another one and restart the un-laughing process. Then there was the window of time needed to stare at his face, watching for his dimple to appear and disappear, and wonder if he knew he had one. That, though, at least looked like listening. If only Ajiz hadn't dumped half a Long Island Iced Tea on her, maybe she could have gotten it together.

What happened was, Ajiz stood up for his duet with Oliver, banged his shin against the table and hopping away on one foot, sloshed his drink on Fran's arm.

"That should have worked," he whispered, as he and Oliver tracked the aftermath of such a direct hit from stage. "I don't know what happened."

Fran didn't either. Ajiz's predictive model was flawless. The obvious next right action was to retreat to the ladies room to debooze in solitude, and hence be divided from Wallace forever. Instead of him waving goodbye to a star-crossed contestant and moving two seats over to talk to the woman he was being set up with, however, Wallace found Fran a napkin, and somebody's water glass, and – and! – wiped the drink residue off himself. That small initiative was so quietly manly Fran needed a moment. Sane persons do not encounter an albino leopard on safari and immediately ask what's next. They take a moment.

While Fran waited it out, a small, whispered altercation broke out among the co-conspirators.

"We have to stop this," said Ajiz, with his hand over the microphone. "Should I try a fuller glass?"

Oliver moved his own bottle out of arm's reach.

"We can't! Everybody's an adult here, let them work it out. Starting a flood is not how we solve problems on *Yes, Chef! America*. Not with the cameras here."

"On the day Chloe finally won something? We can't watch her best friend stealing her man when we ought to be celebrating. I have to do something."

"Don't do it."

"I'm doing it. Hey, Wallace!" Ajiz announced into the mike, "it's your turn to sing."

Wallace appreciated the assist. Hauling himself up off the low couch, he threaded his way past the intervening limbs and furniture to take the Starlight karaoke stage for the first time.

"Thank you all for letting me come out with you to celebrate the big Blue win," he said, as Ajiz handed off the microphone to him. "Chef is already working on a dessert to memorialize your success called Lucky Schmears or Victory in Blue Melon, something like that. I'm just going to sing about it."

"*Ahem*," he said, clearing his throat as the track started, "*...It's a little bit funnn-nnnyyyy, these feelings insi-i-ide...*"

"Well, he could have chosen worse," said Ajiz before joining in enthusiastically to support him in the chorus, it being karaoke law to do so.

"*...and you can tell evvvvrrryyyybody THIS is your sonnggg...*," they all echoed back to Wallace.

"*I hope you don't mind, I HOPE you don't mind*," added Oliver, getting all audience-bold going for the high note before he responded to Ajiz's second and far more effective ploy.

"Congratulations, bro, on splitting them up without creating a Starlite slip and slide. You did a noble deed for the team."

He then led them in the universal team (re)building that is AC/DC's *You Shook Me All Night*, before Ajiz grooved a celebratory *Watermelon Sugar High*.

"That's what the watermelon farmers need, a little Harry Styles action," said Chloe.

"Word," Fran seconded, as the power of music once again caused her to rejoin the collective. "That would get even Travis to grow them."

Filming the team response to the sample pastry platter, however, was what finally ostracized Wallace to reflect on his behavior. Nothing could tempt him to waste calories partaking a dessert not invented for himself. While the others leaned forward to bond and bicker over how many mini eclairs counted as "one", and whether "cake" and "cupcake" were the same food group, he leaned back against the banquette and made goofy smiles up at the ceiling.

Fran's own limited patience with sweet talk post the Sugar! Week elimination rounds lasted halfway through Kyung-ho's diatribe about how *petit fours* ought to taste. Banging her glass down on the table, she made her way to the empty stage. Oliver crossed his fingers and hoped for *These Boots Are Made for Walkin'*. The opening bars of a defiant and credible Etta James was a painful disappointment. Watching Chloe give a slow, overhead clap from the first "*attttttt laaaaaaassssssssttttt*" made him openly wince.

"I can't look," mumbled Ajiz, reaching for one more mini chocolate cupcake than he had intended to let himself eat.

"What's Kyung-ho doing?" Paul complained in a low voice, accidentally resorting to another *petit fours* and then needing a slug of beer to wash down his error in judgment. "One of us needs to have a man to man with him about his staff. I vote it be you, Oliver. Since Travis refuses to help, you're the tallest and work most with your hands."

Oliver nodded reluctantly and powered up for it with a raspberry mini cheesecake. Then a salted caramel mini cheesecake. His consideration of the added efficacy a plain mini cheesecake on his assigned task, though, got circumvented. Travis, their hitherto silent lump of a Travis, followed Fran and brought the house down with Lewis Capaldi's *Someone You Loved*. The shock and awe of his performance even caused Fran to make a hard right turn coming off stage and sit down on the other side of Chloe, garnering him three overhead thumbs-up from his team for finally showing up for them.

Wallace the outsider was unaware he was witnessing a musical miracle. He wasn't even polite enough to clap. Instead, he watched Kyung-ho twitch. Then twitch more as Travis approached the refrain, with feeling. Rudely taking out his phone, he suddenly discovered an incoming text that required his boss' immediate attention. In his haste to cross over to the other side of the couches, however, he "tripped" over Kyung-ho's leg and fell on him.

"Oh my God," said Oliver, "it's a fight! I know it's a fight."

"I told you Chloe deputized Kyung-ho," said Paul. "You know how she hates to kick anybody on camera herself."

In the distracted hoots and hollers for Travis, Kyung-ho disentangled himself. He and the farmer gave each other the side-eye as they passed on the stage stairs, and Kyung-ho cut in front of Paul's *Three Birds* to do a clap back. With feeling.

Annoyed but unintimidated, Kyung-ho debuted that night with *Make You Feel My Love*, which the karaoke machine had as the Adele version. If he couldn't get respect from the general public as to his crisis response when his uninvited subordinate ruined everybody's good time and own blind date, Kyung-ho at least got props that the boy could sing. In a formidable tenor he "*know'd it from the moment that wee-ee-e met...*" without his voice cracking, even a little.

The three amigos solaced themselves with "one" more mini eclair and the general opinion that a Korean ought to better at karaoke than they were. Also, at least Wallace was now sitting next to the right woman.

Stubbornly refusing to leave the stage until he had annihilated the opposition, Kyung-ho finished his set with *First Time Ever I Saw Your Face*.

"He even opened up the pipes this time," complained Ajiz, "is that even legal?"

"No," contributed Travis unexpectedly.

Oliver just shook his head and whispered through another mouthful of cheesecake,

"Poor Chloe, everybody's in love, but her."

Despite such drama, heartbreak and the impending train wreck, still, a very good time was had by all at the Karaoke Reward segment, and the pastry samples were judged perfectly decent except for the *petit fours*. Also, fortunately for the limited deviousness and shallow pockets of Kyung-ho and Wallace, and because it prevented Kyung-ho's finale from making the *Yes, Chef!* highlight reel, the camera crew went home once they captured a few performances and some shots of Kyung-ho presiding knowledgeably over the party platters for their B-roll.

Ajiz did make one last-ditch appeal to stop the train wreck from leaving the station.

"Chloe, wouldn't you rather stay?" he asked. "There's a half-dozen cupcakes left."

"KHS! forever Blue Team. I love you," she answered, "but I love me a

French plated dessert more than American buttercream. Plus, it's my only chance to make a sugar convert out of Fran. She didn't even try an eclair."

As if that made any sense. Thankfully, she was hustled out of the room before the sugar rush, and any residual Roberta, started her truth talking.

round two, take two

The quartet successfully exited the karaoke bar, alone and unfollowed, and paused on the sidewalk underneath Starlight's blinking neon sign.

"Where to next?" Wallace asked.

"There's an evening concert at the botanical gardens," replied Kyung-ho. "What are you going to do?"

"We can't come?"

"No."

"Did you actually want to come?" asked Chloe. "I mean music, flowers, he's wearing linen again, I'm all in, but is that your idea of a good time?"

"I love this woman," Wallace said to Fran.

"I get that."

"Do I at least get the car?" asked Wallace, just so he knew he had asked.

"No."

"We'll drop you off, though," said Chloe.

"No, we won't."

"He's still mad I tripped over him," Wallace told the two women. "For his own good! And the good of humanity."

Acutely aware it was more important to leave the karaoke entryway before a familiar grey van appeared than to gratify Fran's insatiable need to know and know now, Chloe quickly interrupted Wallace's recap.

"How about you go help Fran do some secret, *Yes, Chef!* research by eating and strolling your way through the 16th Street Mall?" she suggested. "There's a quarter of a million dollars on the line, and I think we all need to do our part."

"I'm in," agreed Wallace. "I don't know near enough about onion rings."

The trio trailed after Kyung-ho, who already walked off to get the car.

Ten minutes later Fran and Wallace were set down, or kicked out according to Wallace (and Kyung-ho), to explore the wonders of Denver's street food. Chloe and Kyung-ho drove off to go sit in a new and different garden with more people, a soundtrack and better seating than their old garden. Afterward they wended their way up to the Highlands to lounge on the sofa of a rooftop bar.

"Hey, did I tell you I actually have a shop in Gangham now?" asked Kyung-ho, sitting with his arm around her shoulders as they looked out over downtown Denver and picked a desultory path through the tapas menu.

"You haven't told me nuttin'. You've been too busy yelling at me to sit down. Now that I am, which looks remarkably like me finally listening to you, and honestly, haven't we all learned something about clearly presenting my choices...," Chloe trailed off as she looked up at him.

"This is me being grateful for tonight."

"I know. You're also tired, and afraid that if you don't stay keyed up, you'll collapse and end up lying on this couch for the next two weeks getting in the way of them running a bar. But I'm here now. If I have to carry you back, I'm more than okay with that."

"There are a lot of stairs."

"Then I guess I will only have the strength to carry you back to the hotel. Oh, well."

"You're safe now," he said, stroking her hair. "For tonight, you're safe now."

Chloe blinked a little and dropped her head onto his chest. He heard her give a small sniff, felt her body relax, and tightened his arm around her.

"Tell me about the empire," she said into his shirt after a minute or two. "What happened after I left?"

"Well, like I said, the first thing I did was break up with your Bond Villain."

He felt her shoulders shake as she laughed quietly. She turned her cheek to look back up at him, now with a few tears caught in her lashes.

"I apologize ahead of time if she burns down your shop over my trash-talking her on international reality TV. Did you really? That day? Really?"

He brought the thumb of his free hand up to wipe the moisture away from her cheek.

"I'm surprised she didn't pass you after she stormed out of the shop. She must've brought her car and parked it the other way."

Chloe leaned back against his chest with a contented sigh.

"Reliable. Good times. Now, tell me what happened with the tour group."

He reached forward, put a chicken wing on her plate, and handed it to her.

"Eat this, look at the city, and listen to my tale about how amazing you are and how much the neighbors love you. The morning after you left – we opened at 11 AM back then, it was so relaxing – anyway I was standing at the window of my shop..."

Eating sideways, tucked up under Kyung-ho's chin, Chloe listened carefully to his expansion journey, and shared with him highlights from the show, her surgery, and the outline of her food dream. Kyung chose not to mention he owned a commercial kitchen able to produce commercial-grade products within driving distance from a huge US military base. Time enough to talk about future plans after she left the competition, hopefully in one piece, if not holding a giant check.

"I can win this," she told his third button. "I think I've become that person. You know, the one who finally figures out how to succeed with the challenges halfway through the competition, and barrels past the front runners. I know how to use arugula in a sentence, Fran doesn't, and while Travis looks more reliable on camera standing next to an open fire, I talk better to it."

Chloe felt his Kyung-ho's chest move up and down under her cheek as he silently disagreed.

"I feel stronger, really," she insisted, "eating your food does wonders."

"I don't like leaving you behind when I go home. I don't trust you. I seem to be the only one who can say "no" and "stop" and "don't do that" with any effect. At least some of the time."

"Well, it helps to know how much you don't like to say no to me. That's information. I know I can be stupid, but know I am not doing it to be stupid. They told me I was going to die a long time ago, and by doing everything wrong I met you. Twice. It seems to be working for me."

Kyung-ho tried to take solace that in the immediate she couldn't stand up from the couch unless he let her. It wasn't much, but it was something.

Thirty minutes later, his phone dinged. He looked at the message with resignation.

"Wallace is reporting that your curfew at the house is in an hour."

"I hope he's saying that to be noble, and not because they are more than done with their own evening."

Kyung-ho laughed. Flagging down their server, he settled their bill, then reluctantly moving his other arm, helped Chloe to her feet. Hand in hand they slowly made their way down the stairs to the parking lot.

"Where are they waiting?" Chloe asked, turning on the car's GPS while Kyung-ho reversed out of the space.

"The corner of 16th and Curtis Street."

Chloe typed in the address and sat back as the familiar voice directed them to *"turn left, 15 feet..."*

Kyung-ho pulled out into traffic.

"Go straight, one mile..."

She shifted in her seat to face Kyung-ho, once again watching his profile as he drove, this time under a kaleidoscope of streetlamps and headlights.

"Thank you," she said.

He glanced at her briefly and smiled. Turning his eyes back to the road he reached out and took her hand.

"For dinner?"

"Yes. But also, for being what I call a fun person. I tell ya, a man who constantly surprises me by being helpful and reliable, it's a whole new world."

"That doesn't sound like a fun person."

"Oh, it's fun."

"Is Matteo actually right about you being weird?"

"No, I just talk weird. Listen, you'll see that I'm right. You know how when you're walking through the forest and see a bear..."

"We don't have a bear problem in Seoul."

"Just trying to be relevant in a landscape. Same difference with gangsters, which I know you have, 'cause I've seen them. As you know, because who hasn't this happened to, bumping into them is the start of a zillion different stories, and zero of them are fun stories if you are the only person who openly acknowl-edges bears eat people. Or that gangsters are human traffickers and thieves, if we're going urban jungle."

"Okay, already I don't get it. Remember English is my third language."

"That's my point. You're not an idiot. I love that about you."

Kyung-ho smiled slightly and wondered if this conversation would be easier to follow in Hangul, with at least all the yeses and nos in the right place.

"You do realize I don't know what to do around bears. Or gangsters. I'm not that guy."

"Neither do I. Together we'd probably get eaten or kidnapped, unless we had our Troy with us."

"Still not hearing the fun part."

"What I'm sayin' is, you are so much fun to be around during ordinary life problems, that I know if I end up getting eaten by a bear, you didn't do it on purpose. That's important to women. Men think they never get to make mistakes. Not true, we just don't like it when you do it on purpose."

"Maybe if you explain how I'm fun in ordinary fun...problems...?

"Oh, child please. I came in fourth today because you found my pepper mill, and do you realize that some PA has my phone, I don't know where I am, and the only reason I know what time it is, is because your car is telling me? Yet, I still have a better than reasonable expectation that I will arrive at my desti-nation safe and sound and before curfew. Reliable men rock. What am I going to do after Tuesday? Eighteen months and seventy-two hours in and I already rely on you for everything."

"Because I can find a kitchen gadget and take you to dinner? These are pretty small things, honey. Lots of guys would do lots of nice things for you, if you let them."

"You mean Travis," she acknowledged with a quiet exhale. "He *has* been a great guy throughout this competition. Right up until he sabotaged my dish. Other than that, he's been a rock."

"He what! When did that happen? And how did it get past you? This show really is a snake pit."

"I'll tell you the story another time. He meant well. And he doesn't know that I know, so don't tell him. I am not mad about it..."

"Yes, you are."

Chloe laughed softly.

"See how restful a person you are to be around? You do stuff *and* know stuff. What I am trying to say is that I know it takes effort and sacrifice to think about what I need and go get it. Even when it's just a pepper mill. It's what makes you all Man. It's like...you get to the future five seconds ahead of me, and by the time I show up, you've already made the world a better place. Oliver has a head shake for that, means mad skills, that's what it means."

"Maybe I just like how you look at me when you get there."

"Then it's a win-win. Seriously, what am I going to do with all this extra energy I no longer need?"

"Use it to live forever," he answered.

"*Humph*," She said with quiet snort, then added, "I still don't see what you get out of this. FYI."

"Men like being good at things, I guess. We think it's fun."

"Win-win?"

Kyung-ho brought her hand up to his mouth and kissed it.

"*...approaching destination on the right in fifty feet...*"

"Nice time?" Kyung-ho asked Wallace, as they drove along the dark, rural road after dropping Chloe and Fran off at the contestants' house.

"Yup. You?"

"*Hrmmh.*"

"That sounds like a half-yes with a complaint attached to it."

"I'm flying out Tuesday, right?" Kyung-ho asked.

"Yup."

"It has to be Tuesday, right?"

"Yup."

"It can't be a week from Tuesday?"

"Nope. Not to be crass and materialistic at this time of night, but it's a ₩2,000,000 ticket, and we are stuck with the commitments we made when you just wanted to get back to the shop as soon as possible. I built some contingency time into your schedule in case they shot an extra day or two, but you are needed back, and you were needed two weeks ago. What are you going to do?"

"I don't know. What are you going to do?"

"Oh, that's easy. Nothing. Let Fran get back to her competition, and I'll go back to New York to finish the launch and wait for her to win. We decided to reconnect afterward. I promised not to love her just for her quarter of a million in prize money, and she promised not to use me as someone who already has an established food business. She thinks I'm funny."

"You are funny."

"It's different that she thinks I'm funny. So, are you going to try a long-distance relationship?"

"Nope. I told you before already, Chloe's coming back with us."

Surprised, Wallace looked over at Kyung-ho, now visible under the streetlights as the car entered the city.

"When? Does she know this? What about her apartment? What about her stuff? What about her life?"

"Why do you think I'm resigned to leaving you on the wrong side of the planet? So that you can be useful. When Chloe's done here, she'll come out, get settled back home, and in a few months, we'll fly back to the US to deal with everything here. Or we'll make you do it. Don't worry, Fran's here to help. Give her a stipend, or barter with her for a dessert menu. The judges still want Vivian to win. Fran should be glad she has such friends to support her when she loses."

"Have you talked about any of this with Chloe?"

"No. She already knows."

"I don't think she does. Fran certainly didn't mention it."

Kyung-ho remembered how Chloe tucked herself into his chest and concluded he had the more up-to-date intel.

"It's not a one-step process, it's a two-step process. She already made the first decision, the second one we don't have to make for months. We could both be wrong. We aren't, but it's possible. I agree, moving to Korea with a month's notice might be incredibly stressful and challenging, maybe, but it will be a lot better than tomorrow."

He sighed.

"Tomorrow's going to suck."

"Why? What do they have you doing?"

"I don't know, cooking something. Meanwhile, the judges trash-talk her food, one of them thinks she's going to date him after sabotaging her for weeks, and you saw what is happening to me around spoons. She is the most beautiful woman in the world, and I am supposed to be looking at other people's awful versions of her dessert. It's a nightmare. Especially after tonight, when we got to just be us."

"How was us?"

"I like us. I really like her. Oh, I am so happy. I am so happy I'm going to give you a car. "

"Yay. Why?"

Kyung-ho laughed.

"Because she told me to. Hey, which one of these is the entrance to the parking garage, again?"

"It's that one with the green sign. Do you really still not know the English word for "enter"? In New York, the exit side has spikes to take out your wheels," Wallace warned, pointing to the left. "Are you sure you you're not reading the signs wrong with this woman, too? Might she be just trying to spend your money, while trying to bribe the money man to look the other way?"

"If you saw how she looked at me when I found her pepper mill," Kyung-ho countered as he reached out the car window to take the ticket from the machine, "you'd know I'm right."

"Should I know what that is?"

"It's a thing that grinds peppercorns," he answered, fussing with his visor before changing his mind and dropping the ticket in the cupholder. "Where we use half a kilo of capsicum, they like to sprinkle a little crushed peppercorn on top of things. It's kinda cute."

"Is this some expensive tool?"

"No, it's just a plastic thing this big," Kyung-ho said, taking one hand off the wheel to approximate the size. "Anyway, it was on her workstation, it's not like I invented it, I just moved it out where she could see it. She looked at me like I had given her diamonds."

"I don't get it. Oh! There's a spot. Over there," Wallace said, finding them an empty space. "Does she think you're a dowser, and will never lose her keys again? Are you sure that's the whole story? You're not very good at telling stories. Does she know that? Could be a deal-breaker."

"Oh, I don't get it, I was hoping you would." Kyung-ho said, backing into the space. "What level is this?"

"B2."

"B2, left of the elevator bank, remember that. You've got less on your mind."

"Well, if you would just date simple, straightforward women who like onion rings as much as I do, maybe you, too, could remember where you left your car."

"Chloe makes fresh pasta," Kyung-ho countered again, "and she asked me to give you the car, not her."

"You're right, diversity is a beautiful thing. B2, on it," replied Wallace, assuaging his concern with the knowledge that most transfers of cash required his signature, and the hope that if Kyung-ho was about to get duped, maybe he would at least stop being weird.

CHAPTER FIFTY-SEVEN

knives out, boots on

For the Masterclass, the crew reconfigured the main hall to turn the judging area into workstation for the guest chef. The contestants grouped their high metal stools in front of it, and sat, notebooks in hand, wracking their brains for an interesting question to ask that might garner them extra screen time.

Remembering the contestant's strawberry patch breakfast ritual, with perhaps a slice of malice, Kyung-ho chose to demonstrate various skills and applications of fruit and sugar through the components of his Strawberry Field Fantasia dessert. Felix was especially excited, and mimicked and memorized Kyung-ho's gestures throughout the lecture, particularly during his sugar work. Everyone else listened with moderate interest to learn how an ingredient that was largely water could be plated into shapes other than soup.

All were dying to discover, however, what happened the previous night, and what it meant for the competition. It split their attention between Chef the instructor, Kyung-ho the man, and staring at Fran and Chloe. The latter two seemed listless and sad rather than seething with jealousy, and Chloe and Kyung-ho were obviously ignoring each other. It was all very confusing. Oliver and Paul elbowed and dared each other to inquire after Kyung-ho's business partner, and whether he had a hangover, wondering if that would cause all kinds of sideways. That might be very illuminating.

In part to relieve the tension, and also because it felt so right, Ajiz reprised his *Watermelon Sugar High* performance as an obbligato during the pauses in instruction. Until they made him stop. Given his continued rhythmic head bob, though, they knew was just waiting for Kyung-ho to mention a melon, any melon, to bust out again. Eventually he stopped waiting. Kyung-ho looked up from demonstrating what Oliver designated his julienne 2.0 technique and saw half the group bobbing their heads along. The audience braced for the reemergence of his "mad face", but he added his tenor to the refrain, plus eight bars of K-pop shoulder rolls along with Ajiz just to show he could. Paul, speaking for them all really, did the "my head just exploded" gesture, with jazz hands.

Jake used the window of confusion to do his own reconnaissance. He heard a version of Chloe's heartbreak at breakfast, and always up for trouble-making, slinked over to Chloe's stool. Putting his arm around her shoulders, he whispered consolingly in her ear.

"I heard you had a tough time at karaoke. What an idiot that guy must be."

While Chloe considered how best to agree with him, Jake's shark-like approach, and the intimate gesture, had not gone unnoticed by others in the room. Kyung-ho exchanged speaking looks with her but chose to let her handle it. He resumed his knife cuts, intending to take his feelings out on the berries in front of him, like a civilized person.

And that's when sideways started to happen.

Paul elbowed Oliver to watch Round 764 of the Chloe/Kyung-ho war, which obviously had entered the Chloe using Jake to get back at somebody for something phase of guerrilla warfare, when they all heard Chloe yell.

"STOP!" she shouted.

The audience turned on their stools to see who finally got clunked on the head by the boom mike, while Kyung-ho paused at the top of his slice to look over heads and around bodies. It surprised them all to see Chloe scrambling away from Jake, pushing through the row of contestants between her stool and the front workstation. She made, and then kept direct eye contact with Kyung-ho, even while shoving and bumping everyone else aside.

"STOP!!!" she shouted again. "Put that knife down. This instant!"

Kyung-ho looked down at his bench to see a finger lying where a strawberry ought to be. He dropped his *nakiri* with a clatter. One of his hands had braced itself for the imminent leap over his workstation towards Jake's throat. The other had kept on being a chef. The sudden, divided purpose overrode decades of ingrained muscle memory and good habit.

Hearing the knife fall, Chloe paused her in forward momentum. Standing in a chaos of overturned stools and bodies, she continued to stare down what was now the top of his head.

"We cannot get you out of here fast enough, can we? Please don't leave anything behind when you go."

"Oliver!" she then barked. "Please bring your person, and your knives, forward."

"I don't have them," Oliver mumbled. "They're in my..."

Chloe turned her head, following the sound of his voice. As her eyes came to rest on the right person, he quailed under her uncompromising glare.

"Then...I'll get...I'll get them."

While Oliver scurried over to the lockers, Chloe began putting the front row to rights.

"Are you okay, Ajiz? So sorry about that," she said helping him up. Turning to Janiva, she rubbed her shoulder. "Totally didn't mean to shove you, Ms. J. Thank goodness Travis was there to keep you in your seat. Good catch, Travis."

"There was almost a culinary incident," she explained to the group, gesturing towards Kyung-ho. "Thank you front-row people for your sacrifice to save a Korean national treasure."

The row now righted and re-seated, Chloe moved forward and began bustling around Kyung-ho's station, filling a pot of water, putting it on the cooktop to boil and pulling over a nearby stool. By then Oliver had returned, obediently carrying his knife set.

"This is Oliver," she told Kyung-ho sweetly. "He has the best knife skills, so he's going to be your sous chef."

"Yay for Oliver!" she announced, starting a round of applause, and receiving a smattering echo of confused claps from the other contestants.

"I don't need..."

"Oh, don't even. Sit down!" she said to Kyung-ho, pointing to the stool. "You almost just lost your livelihood. You need a minute. If you take a minute, I promise we will let you get back to your regularly scheduled program."

"I promise," she reassured him. "Ten minutes...maybe twenty. Sit. We just suck at this, and we must accept it."

She turned a bright smile on Oliver.

"Please keep him away from sharp objects for twenty minutes, that's all.

He'll tell you what to do. Keep an eye on...," she waved her hand vaguely towards the cooktop, "...don't let nuttin' burn, and if anything sounds wrong, ask twice."

"I don't think he wants..."

"It's important Oliver," she said in her normal voice, giving her words much more emphasis than yelling. "You've seen this out with the fleet when someone almost gets knocked overboard by a runaway boom, or nearly loses a limb to the winches. It's like that. They just need a minute. I'll be back for the water. Turn it off once it boils, will you?"

She looked over at Kyung-ho, and making the universal hand gesture with head tilt for "duh, start already", turned and walked around the group towards the back entrance. With relief, she heard him instructing Oliver on the next round of cuts needed in the recipe.

As she passed along the outside line of stools, Fran whispered,

"Chloe, where are you going? And what did you do? And where are you going?"

"The garden," she whispered back. "I'll be back in like, two seconds."

Jake got up as if to follow but stopped as Chloe looked him up and down with cold appraisal.

"Oh. I really wouldn't," she said.

He slunk back down on his stool. Her withering tone also preempted the second cameraman, Joey, from following her to add a floor interview to the inexplicable but visually compelling footage of what was usually a dud assignment. A few seconds later, they all heard the large rear doors rattle open as she left the warehouse.

Crunching her way across the gravel, Chloe walked over to the herb garden. She took a moment to breathe in the scent of green things warmed by the morning light and listen to the buzz of a bee. After a few more deep breaths, she stooped down to gather some tea herbs into her apron and returned to the main hall. Walking softly, she crossed over to the equipment shelves, and then took up a workstation near the front of the room. Tipping out the herbs into a pile on the counter, she prepared the ingredients for a tisane, shaking her head at how often she felt compelled to make extra beverages lately. Then, waiting for a moment when the group's focus was away from Kyung-ho's cooktop area, slipped over and grabbed her boiling water.

After the tea had steeped and cooled slightly, Chloe quietly came up behind Kyung-ho.

"Drink this, so I forgive you," she said quietly in his ear.

He smelt the contents of the cup, his nose easily identifying chamomile and peppermint, and obediently took a sip.

Moving back to her borrowed workstation, Chloe continued to watch Kyung-ho's face. The worst of his shock seemed to have passed. When he stood up to show Oliver what he lacked the English words to describe, she responded to Oliver's nervous glance with both an okay sign and thumbs up. Kyung-ho sent his own wry glance back over the heads of the crowd, and his audience turned around in time to witness Chloe's characteristic "What? How is this my fault?" shrug, a clear tell she bore the brunt of responsibility for whatever had just happened. When the group turned back around, he resumed his solo instruction.

Her work complete, Chloe kissed her hand to Kyung-ho, retreated to the lounge area and laid down on the far couch to recuperate from her exertions.

CHAPTER FIFTY-EIGHT

the epic fail

After Kyung-ho's lecture ended, Fran immediately rushed over to the lounge where Chloe remained stretched out on the yellow couch. Hearing the approaching footsteps, she opened one eye to survey the landscape before shutting it again to enjoy her last second of rest.

"What the hell," Fran demanded, "was THAT?"

"Sorry about all the chaos," replied Chloe. Opening both her eyes and sitting up, she again apologized to Fran and the knot of injured folk trailing behind her snacking on strawberries and strawberry components. "Ajiz, are you really okay? Sorry Oliver, thanks for stepping up. You're a lifesaver."

"Forget that," insisted Fran, "what the hell were you doing?"

"Didn't you see? OMG, I'm going to have PTSD for a month and a half," Chloe said, stretching her arms above her head. "We almost had *Yes, Chef! Friday the 13th* edition. Oh...my...God."

"What are you talking about?" Fran asked, standing over her with both arms crossed.

"The knife. He almost chopped his finger off."

A series of "what!" and "when?" behind her echoed Fran's response. Even Felix paused eating the completed dessert he walked off with.

"Somehow his hand was in the wrong place, and a whisker away from kablewy. Like Oliver Day 1, only with better aim and more commitment."

"How did you notice?" asked Fran, while everyone else turned to look at Oliver. No one liked to talk about it, but that incident traumatized the witnesses and those who just saw the trail of red footprints afterward.

"Those of us actually trying to win this competition look at Chef's hands," Chloe said lightly.

"Bullying him like that, though, is that the way to handle things? While he was holding his *nakiri?*"

"I was in a hurry. Plus, Oliver got to learn super great new knife skill stuff, so, everybody wins."

Behind the throng, Kyung-ho hove into view.

"Excuse me, peeps," Chloe said rising from the couch with another stretch. "Gotta go get yelled at now."

With eyes lowered and hands behind her back in her best facsimile of the respectful, K-drama student, Chloe crossed the room to where Kyung-ho stood. As his feet entered her field of view, they turned and moved around the corner into the contestant's locker area. Chloe followed, smiling at today's lower look — high-water cuff, glimpse of ankle, rocking a no sock.

"Even his lower limbs are worth staring at. I was right to flip out over him near losing the extra good bits."

She checked her forward motion as the feet suddenly stopped and turned around, and waited for him to begin his diatribe. But he did not. After a minute, she dropped into a more natural pose and raised her head.

"I admitted to my own moment of Tammy-unaware during the Reinvention Challenge," she said as her eyes passed the hand that almost wasn't, closing them tight for a moment, "and now you almost turned into Captain Hook. Let's call it even, and both agree to focus more in the kitchen moving forward. Deal?"

Instead of agreeing to anything, his still whole and complete hand moved upwards and unexpectedly stroked her cheek before rotating to drag his knuckles along the underside of her chin. Chloe rocked back on her heels and blinked a few times at the intimacy of his touch. Making a heroic effort, she stepped away and not towards and cleared her throat.

"Well," she said, "I'm glad we could have this chat."

With another heroic effort, she got herself turned around and her own feet propelling her back towards the lounge. Her fellow contestants saw her scuttle back around the corner, seemingly almost immediately, her hands twisting in her apron.

"What happened?" asked Fran.

"I ran away. It seemed the right thing to do."

"Did he yell? We didn't hear anything."

"Koreans have lived, like, 2,000 years with paper thin walls. They don't need noise to communicate. It takes some getting used to on C-dramas, too, how much the Chinese whisper when they say something emotional. But you do. That's them, that's Asia."

Fran eyed Chloe suspiciously to hear her babbling. Paul asked for more salient information.

"How mad is he?"

"He's not mad."

"Then why do you look like that?"

"Well, okay, he was mad, but I was more mad, so I win. Then I said don't ever do that again, and he said he wouldn't, so we're good. Sort of. I think that's what happened, I could be wrong. But we're good."

"You don't look good," said Paul.

"Wait, he was the one mad, not you," insisted Travis.

"No, I was mad. Trust and believe."

"I'm confused," said Ajiz. "Were we there? She went crazy, knocked everyone over, he got mad, isn't that how I ended up on the floor? Why would he apologize for anything?"

"And why do you look like that, if you won?" asked Paul. "You like winning."

"When I saw his hand again, oh, I had a moment, but why cry in front of him, when I can cry in front of youse? So, I ran away. But I won't cry now, I'll cry later," Chloe said, retaking her seat on the couch.

"Yeah, whatever," said Oliver. "I think you leveraged a minor kitchen incident into a chance to goof off after staying out late last night."

"I wasn't goofing off. I know I don't understand the small fruit with smaller seeds family of products. Travis back me up, Travis knows I don't know. Chef was extra meticulous about how to use gelatin, thank you, Chef. And why are you stressing me out over a Masterclass that they don't care if we pay attention to or not? If I slacked off, it was off-camera, like a civilized person."

"I think Paul is right..." began Travis, "...you don't..."

"Van's here!" Oliver yelled out as a wall of grey flashed past the window. The contestants all began moving over to the outside door.

Fran directed a long, suspicious look towards Chloe while waiting for her to haul herself back off the couch.

"Now that I think about it," she said, "I don't think either of you were mad."

Chloe responded with a small laugh.

"Did I say mad? Maybe I meant crazy."

"I expect the real story later," said Fran, and turned towards to the door. Behind her, she heard the couch creak as Chloe stood up to follow. And then heard,

"Uh-oh."

She turned back around just in time to see Chloe crumple up and fall.

The earlier shock and fear, her mad dash to stop a horror franchise crossover, the competition, the yo-yo weeks, it was finally all too much for her long-overburdened heart. Realizing that this time she could not push through the familiar symptoms, Chloe felt a flicker of gratitude that at least the end had come saving his beautiful hands, and not fighting with the judges over anything Vivian-related. With her last moment of consciousness, she managed to aim her crash landing against the couch and not the sharp edges of the coffee table.

Fran's scream turned back the contestants still wandering around the set. They rushed to the lounge to see what happened. Once again, they were shoved and scattered out of the way, as Kyung-ho barreled through them from the back premises. Fran had moved forward to help Chloe, but she too found herself spinning backwards, followed by the coffee table, as he pulled both out of his way.

Dropping to his knees beside her, Kyung-ho gathered Chloe's limp form against his chest and with his free hand began lighting slapping her face.

"Chloe, wake up," he said in Korean, "wake up, Chloe."

The others stood around them, impotently asking each other what was going on, while Ajiz ran for the medical staff.

"I think she fainted," said Fran. "She was getting up and just went down. I think that's what happened."

As they watched and waited for help to arrive, Chloe opened her eyes for one more brief moment. Looking up at Kyung-ho, she managed a wan smile.

Only Kyung-ho and Travis, however, were close enough to hear her tired voice say, "good night, sweet prince..." before she relapsed into unconsciousness.

"...may flights of angels sing thee to thy rest," finished Travis mechanically.

"What's that? What did she say?" shrieked Fran.

"Hamlet," he answered. "She's dying now."

"Shut up!" snarled Kyung-ho.

Travis snarled right back.

"You knew this all along, didn't you? She never recovered. She was just pretending. Why didn't you do something? Why didn't you do your job?"

"I said shut up! Chloe would never let herself die in front of me. She knows I would go get her back if she even tried it."

"He's right," said Fran.

Heartened slightly by the ghost of Chloe's absurd and humorous logic, and Fran's confirmation of the words she was certain to say once she woke up, Kyung-ho gathered Chloe more firmly into his arms and willed his own strength into her.

"Just breathe," he said into her hair. "Let go of everything else, and just breathe."

CHAPTER FIFTY-NINE

heartburn

Documenting Contestant 16's exit from the show was a bit of tussle for the crew of *Yes, Chef! America*. Cameraman Joey heard the commotion and rushed in with his equipment only to be held off by Oliver and Paul from really good coverage of the staff medic providing CPR, defibrillation, and later the EMTs starting an IV line and intubation. The youngest PA also tried to supplement coverage with his cell phone. It was a short, hard-fought battle, but they lost.

Eleven minutes and thirty-six seconds later, an ambulance took Chloe and Kyung-ho away from the *Yes, Chef!* set forever. Forty-two hours and three minutes later, Korean Air took Kyung-ho even farther away back to his home country, and the next day after that Wallace left for New York. By then, the producers had given the contestants all the break they felt the production schedule allowed. They brought back Ashley to keep the numbers correct, and hopefully to top her watermelon mousse fiasco, and Fry Fry Away! Week lurched forward with the help of Abel Capshaw from Nashville's world-famous Fry Me a River restaurant and blues joint.

Among the general shock and on-air tributes of the remaining contestants, Fran stood out that week for crying her way to her high-low onion ring victory. Fans also noted taciturn Travis stopped talking altogether. Otherwise, the show rolled on, as the remainder continued their own death battle for the grand prize.

"I told you Chloe would make good TV," said Chef Juan, during an off-camera interval for "judge's deliberation" post Fry! Week's Reinvention Challenge.

"You were right," agreed Chef Parker coming back into the judge's lounge from his smoke break. "A medical emergency right before this week's theme – tacky, but timely. I hear it was a heart issue."

"How long do you think we should wait to announce today's results?" Chef Juan asked Chef Matteo.

"Let's give it ten minutes. Given the stress level this week, we should look like there was some debate before we send Ashley home again."

"I don't think that Vivian is gonna fly," Chef Abel interjected, as they began ranking the remaining contestants. "Who's dumb enough to get caught talking down, on camera, somebody going out a hero, savin' a man's hand. Cut your losses, that Vivian is no money."

Chef Matteo acquiesced with a sigh of regret.

"It's too bad her gameplay let her down, she's so skilled as a presenter. Do you think she should go out for her food, or disqualified for sabotage?"

"Sabotage," pronounced Chef Parker, with an eye to maximum drama.

"What if we brought her back?" suggested Juan following his own train of thought. "Might make even better TV?"

"How's that going to work?" asked Parker. "You and your one-track mind."

"Well, we can always ask."

"She won't do it."

"Still, we can ask, if we get a chance."

"These are darn good onion rings," said Abel, changing the subject again. "What's the name of that woman?"

"Fran."

"I vote Fran for winning the whole she-bang."

"You can't make a cookbook out of one item," Chef Matteo informed him.

"Sure you can. You were gonna ghostwrite the whole thing for that other one. Who's the expert here on fry baskets and boiling oil? That recipe comes from her soul. She at least has a soul."

"There is that," Juan conceded as the judges made their unhurried way out front to announce another preordained result.

THROUGH ALL THE VICISSITUDES AND departures of Fry! Week, across town, in a bed with an unseen view of the taller Denver office buildings, Chloe lay unconscious, like a fairy tale gone sideways.

On the first day, a small bouquet of garden herbs and flowers appeared by the bed. By the mid-afternoon delivery schedule, two professional arrangements, one large, one modest, also appeared. Every 2 AM thereafter, the telephone extension buzzed at the nurse's station. The person working the graveyard shift reported to the caller that there was no new update. Around 4:04 AM New York time, a panicked and heated argument over Zoom began and ended with Wallace's thin but true consolation that Fran was still there, and to wait and see. Only the wilting and failing greenery at Chloe's bedside marked the days. Until Saturday, when she opened her eyes again, on her own volition and without any help, to find everything all over and back to normal.

"It's about time," a voice to her right said.

"Yes, Chef," Chloe responded automatically, looking up at the unfamiliar ceiling, trying to guess where she was and what brought her there.

"*Mr. Grumpy, why are you here?*" she also wondered.

"What day is it?" she asked him.

"Saturday."

She nodded, taking in the information.

"Who won this week?"

"Fran."

"That's my girl," she said. She finally turned her head toward the speaker. "What can I do you for, Chef?"

"Are you kidding? I'm here for a visit! It's great to see you awake. We should celebrate."

"Uh-huh. You don't have the time. Are you checking in, or reporting up?"

"Hey now, aren't you glad to see me?"

Chloe turned away and noticed the large arrangement, the smaller arrangement, and the garden flowers on its last leg all crowded on the tray table next to the bed. She reached out and pulled the table across her bed and put the smallest bouquet directly in front of herself.

"That's getting pretty ratty," Chef said, "let me throw it away for you."

"The nurses were nice enough to keep changing its water, I'll enjoy it for a bit before it has to go. It's from our garden."

"Who told the contestants they could steal flowers out of the show's garden?"

"You have no soul, Chef. Thanks for coming by, though."

"You want me to go?"

"I just know you have many other places to be," she hinted, making a greater effort at diplomacy.

"Actually, I've been sent here. We want you to come back."

"Today?"

"No, of course not. Take a few weeks to rest up, and then you can take part in the semi-final. We give everyone sous chefs by then, so it'll be a light cooking schedule."

"Wow," Chloe replied. Chef Juan interpreted the small accompanying smile as gratified consideration of his proposal. He was mistaken, as usual. She was thinking about her Troy and wondering if his *Pu Bu* would also be making a reappearance.

"So, you'll think about it?" he asked.

"I'll talk to the doctors, and give it some serious, uh, thought."

"Great. Well, I better get back. Glad to see you're awake."

"Thanks for coming by, Chef," she said to his retreating back. "Oh wait, will you tell Fran right away that I woke up? Right away, right away, not later right away."

He turned around at the doorway.

"Sure. What about everyone else?"

Chloe gave a short laugh.

"Fran will take care of it. And tell her KHS. Will you remember that? Tell her not to worry, and KHS! forever."

"That stupid KHS! again. Does something from five episodes ago really have to be a thing this season? Whatever. Got it."

Chloe didn't think he had, but was confident Fran could win a game of telephone, even with Chef Juan. Even if he forgot half her message, and gave it to Ajiz, which was likely. The important thing was him leaving her hospital room, never to be seen again.

Chloe's next visitor was a middle-aged, authoritative cardiologist accompanied by a phalanx of white coats doing grand rounds.

"How are we feeling?" he asked. "Glad to see you finally decided to rejoin us."

"Hello," she said, and nodded to all the other faces. Turning back to their Chief, she asked,

"Do you know why I collapsed? I don't want to keep doing that anymore."

"Oh, we know what the problem is."

"You do?"

"I can't fix everything that's wrong, but the falling down part, there are three people in the country who know how to prevent that from happening, and I'm one of them."

"How handy. What are you doing on top of a mountain?"

"I ski?"

"Huh. Well then. Howdy."

Chloe's third visit was from the nurse to change her IV.

"We're glad to see you're back," said the nurse.

Chloe watched his practiced, jangling bustle as he turned off the IV drip, and switched the nearly empty hanging bag for a full one.

"Thanks," she said. "I haven't heard anyone beeping or yelling today, you all must be having a nice day."

The nurse laughed.

"It has been a slow one."

He checked the port on her hand, and Chloe held her breath hoping he didn't need to make a new hole. When he softly placed her arm back on the coverlet, she continued.

"Please tell whoever saved my flowers thank you. They're out of our garden."

"You're welcome. I know, I was here when the guy brought them in."

"Oh, has he been coming by?"

"No. He said he had to go home, but he asked us to try to make them last until you woke up."

"Of course he went home," Chloe told herself as her eyes welled up. *"You knew he would go home. You would have told him to go home."*

"He must be worried. I met him in Korea, and we ran into each other again when he was over here on business. I collapsed right in front of him, so embarrassing. I was really hoping to hold off on that until he got on the plane. How to let him know I woke up, though, is the problem. I still don't know how to spell his name in pictographs."

"He left his business card in the drawer for you," the nurse said, indicating the small table on the other side of the bed that held the landline phone and a small pitcher of water. He collected his tray of supplies and moved towards the door. "He also calls in every night. Do you want us to put him through?"

Chloe nodded with satisfaction.

"I tell ya, is there anything sexier than a reliable man? Please do. And if your shift stays boring, stop by and I'll tell you the story of how we met. We were a lovely story, right up until I dropped dead on him. So not sexy."

THAT NIGHT, CHLOE DOZED FITFULLY. Waiting. This time she heard the buzz of the extension out at the nurse's station sound through the quiet ward.

"Cardiology," said the night nurse, then after a short pause, "one moment please."

Chloe listened to soft footfalls approach her open door.

"Put him through, please," she called out in a low voice, "I'm awake."

Moments later the phone by her bed rang. Nervously clearing her throat, Chloe picked up the receiver.

"*Annyeonghaseyo?*" she said. "*Oppa?*"

There was no response on the other end.

"Everything's alright now," she continued. "Mostly. Mostly everything's alright, *Oppa.*"

A loud exhale told her they hadn't been disconnected. Chloe waited through another long pause, and then heard a somewhat unsteady,

"Thank God. I'm so angry with you, scaring me like that. Don't ever do that again."

"*Humph.* Did you get home okay?" she asked.

"*De.*"

"Did your empire survive without you?"

"*De.*"

"Are you in my favorite shop?"

"*De.*"

"How nice," she said with a smile. "Then part of me is, too."

"You know none of that matters right now, don't you? And don't think I missed that non-promise you just gave that this won't happen again. I'm sorry I had to come back."

"You had to. Empires need their fearless leader."

"Wallace had to drag me to the airport, personally. I wanted to be there when you woke up."

"Chef Juan took your place," she reported, settling herself back on her pillow. "It wasn't the same. Hey, guess what's nice about collapsing in Denver?"

"I can't imagine."

"The Denver Clinic has this guy who's an expert with my exact heart stuff."

"That's excellent. I should be there to see it for myself."

"We are poor people. We can't just do what we want. You couldn't stay here indefinitely, waiting to find out whether I would wake up or not. And you left Wallace behind."

Kyung-ho's heart turned over at the reminder of what almost happened.

"Wallace is in New York."

"See? He's practically up the street from where I really live. And Fran was still here in Colorado, that counts."

Sitting at his desk in his office, Kyung-ho stared at a picture from karaoke night he printed off his phone. Nothing counted other than her being alive, and to get her within arm's distance once again. He rubbed the bridge of his nose and decided that arguing about how she expected a man to act when his future wife nearly dropped dead in his arms could wait, and he plowed ahead acting like one until she got used to doing things his way. Too much time with the Juan's of the world, it showed.

"What did the doctors say? When do you go home?" he asked, his chair creaking in the background as he leaned back.

"They're only keeping me for observation a few more days. They don't need to make any more holes."

"What does that mean?"

"I don't need surgery."

"That's fantastic."

"The cardiologist says I need more antho...anthologies? That can't be right."

"Anthocyanins. I know."

"Yes, that. You sound so confident, I'm going with your answer."

There was a long pause as Kyung-ho considered what might have happened if he hadn't been on set augmenting her diet, followed by another fervent, slightly broken,

"Thank you, God. What's your cell number?"

Chloe gave it to him.

"What time is it there?" he asked.

"It's...," Chloe looked around the room for a wall clock. "2:14 AM. Is the shop busy?"

"We aren't open yet. You need to sleep."

"I will," she said pulling the sheet and thin blanket up around her chin as if that was the same thing. "I got the flowers."

"Good. I picked them the day after you collapsed. You need to go to sleep."

"The nurses stretched them as long as they could. Hey, did I mention that the judge who did not find my pepper mill, and who is *soooooooooo* happy I lived, dropped by to ask me to please come back and finish the show? 'Cause that's a good idea."

Kyung-ho exhaled with exasperation and a mumbled Korean expletive.

"I really don't want to yell when I am 8,000 kilometers away."

"Yell? I thought you would send Wallace to beat him up. Or you can deputize Troy. You didn't get to meet him, but he's a trained professional and I love him very much. The way I love Paul, only different, except the same."

Waiting through another long pause, Chloe added,

"...I'm sorry I collapsed, *Oppa.*"

"At least I was there. What I was most afraid of was you collapsing somewhere by yourself."

"Me, too. It was like living at the top of a waterfall. The second once gets tired and stops fighting over the edge one goes, splat. Although, you know, I would never actually die in front of you, not never."

She heard him laugh unexpectedly, followed by a "*De, de,*" before becoming serious again.

"I'm so angry I wasn't able to stop it from happening," he said.

"You're what kept me alive when it was happening, *Oppa,* that has to count.

When I was dying before, I would imagine myself back in your shop and just rest there in my mind. Going to a happy place always gave me that one little extra *umph* to hold on. This time my happy place came to me, so I had to make even less effort. You know I'm a huge fan of your right shoulder."

"Are you?"

"It's very big and strong, and I would much rather stay there than go with the dead."

"Good to know," he said, trying to smooth out the picture he accidentally crumpled in his fist.

"Anyway," she said. "This is too expensive a call, so I should hang up. When I find my phone, I'll text you."

"It's Wallace's job to be the voice of fiscal responsibility, not yours. I'm only hanging up because I think you need to rest, which I already said four or five times, and for no other consideration. Understood?

"*De.*"

For several seconds she listened to the squeaking of his chair instead of a dial tone, then relaxed into her first sigh of contentment.

"You're such a fun person, *Oppa*. Okay, I'll hang up first. That's the way it should be."

"Yes, that is the way it is."

"But I don't want to."

"I know."

"Do I have to?"

"Yes. And tomorrow you can let me know when you are coming out, and that will solve that problem."

"Out? To Korea?"

"Yes, out to Korea. You have two choices, *Anae*. Come here or feel bad about your negative impact on our source of income by making me try to run Ji Foods from the wrong side of the world."

"Tomorrow? You mean today tomorrow? Or your tomorrow?"

"Some time in the next eighteen hours tomorrow."

"Okay, we'll talk about this tomorrow. Bye, *Oppa*," she said, and after one more long pause, "okay, I'm doing it!"

"One, two, three GO!" she said, and hung up.

"*Anae*," she repeated to herself, smiling as she settled back in bed after replacing the receiver. "Oh, that man, givin' me some sugar."

She lay in the semi-darkness and looked up at the ceiling tiles, waiting for sleepiness to overtake her again, and occasionally chuckling over his joke that she come out to Korea immediately. She wondered when they would find the money or a window to see each other again. Maybe if his NYC shop had a special event or milestone that required the owner's presence.

"*Wow*," she acknowledged, "*him gone sucks just as much as I thought it would, and I've only known about it for a few hours.*"

Turning on her side, careful not to pull at the IV, she amended her assessment.

"*Actually, it sucks worse. Well...well...,*" she thought furiously, casting about for a bright side to forestall the sudden rush of tears. It took some doing. "*This time I have Wallace, and access to my dessert. Except that includes people to gossip with when my boy has moved on...Too much, too much, we'll think about that later.*"

Chloe abandoned her efforts to accept their inevitable future, and instead cast her mind back to the previous week sitting on the roof deck and looking out over Denver. Back to that brief interlude when she burrowed her head in his chest while his strong arm kept the world and its problems at bay. She decided, for now, it was still not unwise to go live there in the hollow of his arm. Pretending the rasp of the hospital pillowcase was the linen of his shirt, she fell asleep.

plan b: to sleep below a different sky

On Monday, the producers allowed a small contingent of the remaining contestants to make an unscripted and untelevised visit to see Chloe in the hospital while the winning team went whitewater rafting with Abel Capshaw. Travis picked her some strawberries (that Felix made into chocolate-covered strawberries), Fran snuck in some onion rings, the low-cal version, and Ajiz downloaded a get-well, recovery playlist to her phone which Rachel tracked down and sent over with them. Camped out on her bed and various chairs, they brought Chloe up to date on the show gossip and progression, snacked on their contraband fair food, and occasionally four out of five of them chair danced when one of Ajiz's musical selections brought out their groove thing.

Finally, Ajiz raised the essential question.

"What are you going to do now?"

"Go home, I suppose."

"What about your job with Kyung-ho?" Travis asked.

"You can't hire somebody that collapses all the time, it isn't legal."

"That's in the United States. I asked Paul," Ajiz reported. "Anyway, can't the doctors fix you?"

"*Welllll*, kinda. Look how far I came in the competition, though, with that nasty Damocles-y sword thing over my head. Wait and see what I can do with the ability to stand and no impending cutlery. You know, somewhere it's legal."

Ajiz looked surprised.

"You couldn't stand up all this time?"

"Didn't you notice her constantly leaning on Fran?" Travis answered for her.

"No?"

"No one was supposed to notice that," said Chloe. "What an amazing week you had, Fran, without a 140-pound drag your arm. Top three in Sugar, number one in Frying, go go go speed racer!"

"And, next week I won't be crying," replied Fran.

"Wow, anything could happen. Just remember I expect you all to team up and take down Vivian. If it wasn't for her, none of this would have happened."

"How is it her fault?" asked Travis.

"I don't know, but don't you think it ought to be? Let's blame her anyway."

After the cool kids left, taking the carnival evidence with them, Chloe turned on her phone. One of the last dings showed her Kyung-ho already texted so she would have his number. And a waiting text.

"*Reliable that man,*" she sighed happily, as she read his short message.

"*I miss you every minute, Anae. Come home soon. K.*"

Chloe read it another eight times before texting Kyung-ho back to announce the return of her personal telecommunication device. She hoped the proof-of-life documentation bought her some time before needing to respond to his actual question. Then abandoning her own life and problems, she watched an episode of *Goblin* on her phone and laughed hysterically, for the ninetieth time, at Lee Dong-wook's interpretation of a Grim Reaper on a date. Mentally refreshed, she turned to gazing out the window. The lights in the office buildings came on, and then went off again as the day waned, and other people went home.

What she herself should do next, however, remained uncertain. If she was never going to get well – and as pleased as her doctor had been with himself, and her progress, she was never going to get well, not really – her instinct was to avoid becoming a useless burden on someone else. Should she gamble on the finale? They would patch her up enough for that, surely, and maybe that would...? Something. A failed reality contestant with a dickey heart didn't seem like much of a life partner to a business mogul, but a comeback kid might, and it would test out the parameters of her new, new normal. Again. That would be... information, and good to know before traipsing off. Again.

Or, if she decided not to return for the finale, Rachel would book her flight home, and she could be back on her couch in just a few days to think through the problem in her proper thinking place. The PA's already packed up her stuff. Her suitcase arrived sometime while she was sleeping and was now shoved under her bed. A cat sitting on her chest, insisting that she remain still and let it nap was always a helpful outside perspective.

Chloe picked up her phone again, wondering how she made any decision about anything in the last month and a half without first referring to it. She clicked open her travel site app. She had never flown out of Denver before and didn't know where planes from there went. Like, whether the direct flights went to NYC, and if it made sense to avoid a layover in Atlanta by flying into LaGuardia, taking an expensive taxi ride into the city, hanging out with Wallace in an empty shop, and then walking down to Penn Station to catch the long train ride home. Not that that was a good idea, it wasn't even a plan, but she thought she would look it up anyway.

Chloe began to click through and click around just to see. Just to get more information.

Chloe's last visitor in the hospital was the most unexpected. Strolling through the doorway late in the afternoon, holding an inartistic fistful of garden greens, in came Wallace himself. How lucky, Chloe thought, not to be in New York City, banging on an empty shop door looking for him.

"Wallace! What are you doing here?" she exclaimed.

"The boss sent me. And also, these," he said handing her the "bouquet".

"Oh, you didn't have to go through the trouble."

"I assure you I did."

Wallace received his instructions from the head office Sunday, when Kyung-ho made his last dawn Zoom call to New York.

"She woke up, Wallace," Kyung-ho reported, wiping the emotion from his eyes. "The nurse put my call through to her room and she answered the phone."

"Oh, thank God...oh, thank God," Wallace responded with sleepy enthusiasm.

"Now, I need you to go back to Denver and get her to come home."

"Isn't that your job?"

"I am on the wrong side of the planet."

"They didn't cure her, Wallace," he added.

"Oh no. Are things going to be alright? What does that mean?"

"I don't know, but things need to not be alright somewhere I can keep an eye on her. She thinks a disabled person is a handicap for me, and the business. When I told her to come out, she thought I was kidding."

"How's that supposed to be a joke? Or funny? Never mind. What am I supposed to do? No, wait, why would she listen to me, if she won't listen to you? Please don't make me get involved," Wallace pleaded, shaking his head at Kyung-ho.

"You're just the messenger. I want you to go tell her that my life with her, even with her current health issues, is exponentially better than life without her. And you already know that. You just have to say it out loud and in person. Just a day trip, in and out."

"*Ohhhhhh*, dude."

"What? How else will you get a very powerful somebody on your side when it comes to Fran? When Chloe is happy, she wants everybody to be happy. Don't you want to be happy? Help me to help you."

"I don't know about this," Wallace continued to insist, but Kyung-ho could tell by his expression, even compressed into a tiny telephone screen, that he was wavering.

"It doesn't have to work," Kyung-ho reassured him. "I'll try to pick up some extra gigs and fly out in the next month or so. She almost died last week Wallace. She told me if I wasn't there, she might not have held on. She doesn't have to believe you, and she doesn't have to come, I just need to know I did everything I could this time."

The two old friends stared at each other though their small devices for a long minute.

"Well, then..." Wallace relented.

Kyung-ho pressed his advantage.

"Juan was there when she woke up, wanting her to come back and do the show. You know we need to shut that down."

"Wow," Wallace replied with a laugh. "Somebody needs to hit that guy."

"Spoiler alert, Chloe expects you to. She has some backup guy, too, but she volunteered you first."

"Again, how are these things my job?"

"Would you trust me to have an off button? With Juan? Whatever. The thing is, she doesn't yet understand Juan and I are making two different requests. To her they sound the same – speculation and chance now, with a slight possibility of some later benefit."

"Why does she have to decide now? She'll be home in a few days. I can meet her for coffee in another week or two."

"The show is flying her home. They'll send her to Korea, if she asks."

"No, they won't."

"Two weeks ago, you're right, but after collapsing on set? It's better to have her out of the country, busy with a new relationship, than hanging around, bored, thinking about suing them. We're doing them a solid. And isn't it better for Ji Foods to save the cost of a flight in case...someone else needs it?"

"*Wellllll...*"

"I know she won't do it. I just need you to ask."

"I'll go look up flights."

AFTER EXCHANGING SMALL TALK WITH Chloe about her stay in the hospital, and her visit from Fran, Wallace finally got down to what he was sent to do.

"I'm supposed to tell you to fly back to Seoul," he said, and found talking to Chloe in person much less awkward than thinking about it. She appeared very comfortable with people being weird. Maybe it was the being so near death thing.

"Don't worry, I'll tell him you were very eloquent," she replied, responding to Wallace's discomfort, rather than his mission.

"Are you going?"

"Of course not."

Wallace nodded, hearing what they all had expected her to say, and what he considered to be the wise decision. It was a long way to go and a long way from home to find out whether a relationship could work. Still, realizing that Kyung-ho would turn extra weird during this new phase of whatever those two were doing, he made one additional effort to fulfill his task.

"It's your fault about the window thing, isn't it?"

"What window?"

"He looks out windows ever since you left. He does it everywhere, but Thursdays are the worst. That's the day he works out of the old shop, and when he gets stuck on something, or is in a mood, or the sun goes down, he's always standing in that window."

"Isn't that the best table in the summer months?"

"You see my problem. I blame you. Not that I have ever understood your relationship. I count things, and date like a normal person, but you should know that he has been waiting for you since that day you left, and it's almost certain he will keep waiting for you until you come back.

Chloe remained unconvinced.

"His ex-girlfriend is a Bond Villain. I can't wear those shoes on your street, I can't compete with that. Not long-term."

"I hear you. Look at my hair, I get it. On paper, yes, he and Min-a were a perfect match. He already chose you over her, though, and hasn't once changed his mind since then. You understand his work and his food on a level she never did. And before you ask me embarrassing questions, if he thought of you as only his new favorite junior consultant, he would just follow you on Instagram and not send me halfway across the country to have awkward conversations with a near stranger."

Chloe considered this new tranche of information from someone who knew.

"I am not trying to argue with you, Wallace, I'm just trying to be practical. He's got a really busy life, being a rock star. I will just hold him back."

"Well, whose fault it that? What is also true is that he and I were banging our heads against the wall for months trying to get the first shop off the ground, and you solved the problem in one afternoon, with almost no information and a terminal illness. It's possible that the word "burden" means something different in English than in Mandarin, because otherwise, you're kinda not making sense."

Chloe pursed her lips and looked out the window for a minute, then decided to risk one more question.

"Wallace dear, we both understand marketing and obfuscation, and might have to know each other for the rest of our lives. You wouldn't start off our relationship by lying to me, would you?

"I don't think you understand men, Chloe. We like protecting women and providing. We invented superheroes, remember, so we can pretend putting on a polystyrene outfit will make us extra good at it."

After another long pause, she changed the subject.

"You're good people, Wallace. Anything I can help you with?"

"I can only afford grocery store roses," he blurted out, so relieved to talk about something else that he accidentally told her the truth.

Chloe considered his dilemma.

"Whole Foods will re-wrap them nicely, if you ask. Or you can have them wrapped with some bunches of spring onions with a funny note about your clandestine effort to smuggle in extra product. She already thinks you are a riot, that would be all winner for just an added $.65. One rose, a ham and American cheese on a white bulkie roll and some Ocean Spray is also complete thought."

"You have options," she assured him.

Wallace texted Kyung-ho on his way home from JFK.

"She looks good. Show already booked the flights, she goes home Wednesday, but I gave her a lot of new information to consider. Stupid show. Stood outside the warehouse a half-hour without seeing Fran. If she doesn't win..."

Wallace chose not to elaborate further on his discussion with Chloe. Kyung-ho would feel equally oogie hearing the details, as Wallace would relaying them. It was enough to inform him the task could be checked off the to-do list. He then spent the rest of his cab ride wondering if Fran received her contraband.

He almost missed his flight out of Denver waiting on the gravel sweep before a staff member was found with the authority to decide whether it was allowed, or not allowed, that a contestant receive a small bouquet from the assistant of a prior guest judge. Technically, receiving anything from the outside world during filming was considered an unfair advantage, but then, technically, Wallace was an inside man, who only days earlier could come and go freely on set as part of Kyung-ho's entourage. It presented a difficult legal morass.

Wallace finally broke through it using his boss's logic.

"Her best friend just collapsed on set. A handful of flowers will help the situation for everybody. Help me to help you."

Rachel's phone buzzed four times in her pocket while listening to his request and arguments, and finally she decided it was much more important to get back inside before she got fired, than to maintain the strict discipline of a normal *Yes, Chef!* season. She conceded to his request. With a twinge of less-than, Wallace handed his grocery store roses off to her, comforting himself that at least they weren't a bunch of weeds stolen out of somebody else's garden.

Fran received her contraband item between taping segments. She chose to put them in an empty pickle jar on the coffee table in the warehouse lounge area where all the cast and crew could enjoy them, subverting the letter of the law by not hiding them away in her now solo room at the house. Of course, Vivian's snarky comments about $9.99 bouquets cluttering up the set did give Wallace's tribute an outsized impact on the competition, validating Rachel's hesitation. Debating the power of pretty, red flowers in a pickle jar exacerbated the on-set tension about some people having friends in high places. The incessant reminders that she now had friends in high places, however, also fully restored Fran's Fran-like conviction just in time for the Thai Me a River! Week Reinvention Challenge Judge's Table. So, in the end, everybody was right, and thanks to Chloe's kind advocacy, once again Vivian got what she deserved.

CHAPTER SIXTY-ONE

home

again

Chloe flew out of Denver and back over the mountains on Wednesday, as planned. On the other end of the flight, she asked the cab to drop her off somewhat near home and walked the rest of the way, dragging her suitcase behind her. She still navigated intuitively when especially tired, landmark to landmark, and directions such as "four doors up from the house with the blue planter" or "left at the barbecue place, the good barbecue place, not the one nobody liked" lacked the precise GPS coordinates to be of any use to most cabbies. Taking advantage of living in a dense, urban environment, she aimed the taxi at a nearby popular and well-known destination rather than make any effort to explain where she really wanted to go.

Or, maybe, strolling along gave her one last window of time to debate whether to flag down the next yellow car and run away. Again. The heavy, red carryall she pulled behind her was the perfect go-bag. The show assigned a PA to do the contestant's laundry, so it was full of clean clothes, and they were much better packers than she. It would be an extra shame to waste it while wearing her favorite and most reliable walking shoe.

While Chloe meandered slowly along the sidewalk, hitching her way around cracks and over curbs, Kyung-ho looked out onto an alleyway bathed in bright sunshine. He had just unlocked the shop door and taken up his post in the window to wait for his first customers to arrive, his freshly stocked pastry case behind him full and fully expectant of the day's love. Well, his pastries waited for something to happen to them. He was just blocking the view from his best table and missing Chloe, and he planned to continue doing so until he could convince himself to go be less annoying and more efficient somewhere else. An influx of customers was likely to drive him into the back premises, though, so it was kinda the same thing.

Ding.

Hearing his phone go off, he pulled it out of his shirt pocket to look at the incoming text. Almost like magic, he saw a message from her.

"Where are you?" it read.

He texted back,

"At the old shop. Wish you were here. X."

He tucked the phone back into his pocket with a smile. Somehow, he felt that text exchange justified him standing in the window a few minutes longer, since that is what he said he was doing. Well, that is what he meant he was doing, and why stop now, he might look guilty of something. It was his shop. He could stand where he darn well wanted to.

Reading his text as she walked along, Chloe felt a rush of gratitude and instant gratification that she now had two reliable men in her life.

"Wow, Wallace, you're like a bonus Fran who understands subtraction and other life math. Don't you just know things."

Because of course it was Thursday morning where Kyung-ho was, and like Wallace said, that's where he still spent his Thursdays.

Ding.

Kyung-ho fished his phone out of his pocket again. He paused long enough to tell himself it was probably his supplier, and then looked down at a picture of the Incheon cruise ship terminal, one of the photos from her Asian adventure. It was sleeting by the time she arrived at his shop, and it comforted him to see that her day ashore hadn't started out that way. Maybe she would remember the city as less cold and dismal.

Ding.

The next text arrived before he put his phone away. Another picture from her trip, one of the Starbucks several blocks away from his shop, at the foot of the wharf.

"Stop promoting my competitors!" he texted back. *"Still wish you were here."*

Ding.

Savoring the feel of his hand buzzing with welcome news and information, Kyung-ho considered saving the message itself for later to make the sensation last longer. It might be important, though. It could be. And of course, it might well be his supplier. God forbid he lose track of their discussion about the bulk gold leaf needs of the modern pastry shop, what with the old order still on file with them. Clicking through his phone he found yet another picture in his inbox, this one of the sandwich board outside a popular seafood restaurant at the lower end of the food district. Cross-promoting within the neighborhood, that was more like it.

He guessed she also wanted to be informed, if he had a moment, what that place served, and why they were so busy, and how Little Paris could get them some of that. Their outdoor dining was very popular, maybe his shop should get a street permit for sidewalk seating. He zoomed in on the picture to read the signboard before clicking on the reply box to send back a translation and get her thoughts on benches versus tables.

"It says spicy summer special today on octopus skewers," he began, which sounded much better in Korean and kinda funny in English. He decided to play it safe and send her the French version.

"...spécial été...," he began typing, and then paused. *"That's summer, right? Why does that still look wrong..."*

"Oh my God," he said out loud, zooming back in on the picture.

"Is there a problem?" asked Assistant Manager Soon-yi, wiping down tables behind him.

Kyung-ho shook his head, which in American meant "yes".

"I'm sure it's nothing. I'm sure it's...the Internet."

Market research using screenshots off Google Earth was normal, everybody did it, especially someone who took such an interest in the business. He didn't believe for a second she could read the signboard. That proved he wasn't crazy. He went back to remembering the French word for "octopus".

Ding.

Another picture. This one of that nice hanging flower basket outside Yu's Be Well Pharmacy halfway down the block. He saw the owner watering it Monday. He wondered if it was a pharmacist thing to rinse off plastic flowers, and how long they had been hanging outside the drugstore without him noticing. Because people put up plastic flowers and left them up for years, that's what people did with plastic flowers. What a good neighbor, Mr. Yu, keeping them so tidy and hygienic.

Ding.

Kyung-ho stopped looking out his window many minutes ago in lieu of staring at his phone. How, then, was he still looking out the window? There in his hand was a picture of his shop bathed in the same bright sunshine, only the view was the wrong way round. Weird.

He heard the low rumble of a wheeled suitcase pass by while still looking at the blur that could be a man in a window looking at a phone. Of course, he chided himself, it could be anything, just like that sound could be a suitcase if you really wanted it to be, but it could be anything that rolled – shopping cart, wheelbarrow, runaway train, anything. Look at how wrong he was about plants. It was certainly highly unlikely such a common, urban sound could be a suitcase attached to anything or anyone important to him personally.

Ding-a-ling-clink.

While Kyung-ho zoomed in and out on the image, in case it mattered – it might – the bell on the shop door announced their first customer of the day. Soon-yi greeted the woman (person, Kyung-ho told himself, firmly) and he heard the woman's voice (lucky guess, it was a pastry shop) answer pleasantly back. That's when he looked up. Just to check out the window, though. Just to see if it was raining or snowing or there was an eclipse or anything other than the same bright sunshine he'd stared at all morning that somehow had gotten into his phone.

The woman stood in the doorway, studying the profile first seen another lifetime ago. How different it looked no longer angry. No longer broken-hearted and expecting the worst. No longer austere, and self-contained and professional. No longer waiting for her to come back. How different he looked when he arrived at this moment to find her already there.

Abandoning her suitcase as soon as it cleared the sweep of the door, Chloe walked slowly across the tiny gap between the entrance and his spot by the window. Slipping her arm into his, she leaned against his shoulder and gave a soft sigh of contentment. The sound he learned she made at the end of a long journey, and what had become one of his favorite sounds in the world. As his arm tightened involuntarily and his head bent to rest on top of hers, she sighed again.

"I agree with you completely," she said. "It's good to be home."

CHAPTER SIXTY-TWO

there are places i remember

5.4 million fans of *Yes, Chef! America* tuned in to watch the Live Reunion episode for Season 14, up 1.2 million from Season 13. Gathered once more in the beloved warehouse kitchen, all eighteen of the audience's favorite amateur cooks were back, plus a few faces the fans couldn't remember and one noticeable absence, ranged in tiers and sitting on their high kitchen stools.

"Hey everybody! Rhonda McAdams here," announced the emcee, opening the show with the same trademark bright, blonde enthusiasm she brought to *CBS Morning Poughkeepsie.*

"You loved them, you hated them, they set the world on fire and sometimes burned down the house, it's the live Reunion episode. Welcome everybody at home! We've got it all, the backstage drama, the battles, the chills and the thrills coming at you tonight. Let's get to it!"

The camera panned out to show Rhonda seated stage right of the contestants in one of the set's yellow club chairs, clutching an oversized microphone with both hands. Dressed in her signature electric blue jumpsuit, wearing far more makeup than anyone who worked near steam would dare, and layers of dangling necklaces just asking for trouble around pot handles, Rhonda looked more than ready to get to the bottom of all the show gossip swirling around social media. After all, she helped start most of it.

Turning away from the camera to face the contestants, Rhonda thrust her microphone towards the front row and this year's top-five finalists as if conducting a hard-hitting, guerrilla field interview, rather than asking questions from chatty people with their own mikes clipped to their shirts.

"First off, we have to start with our winner," she began, "how does it feel? Did you think you were going to win?"

"It feels amazing," Season 14's new champion responded, as expected. "I wasn't surprised. From day one, I knew I had everyone beat."

"Wow, I don't know if you can hear it at home," Rhonda said, turning back to the camera, "but those confident words set off some pretty loud groans from the other contestants. I'm guessing you don't believe her, Ajiz. What do you want to say to that?"

"She didn't do it alone," Ajiz countered from his seat in the second row. "I was there. I said it before and I will say it again tonight, it was my eggplant surprise that helped carry her to victory."

"I told you not to make it."

"You did."

"I TOLD you not to make it."

"You did. And I made it. You're welcome, Fran."

Fran turned back to face Rhonda with a shrug.

"I told him not to make it."

"What's the food dream, Fran?" asked Rhonda, as a voice in her ear barked a reminder that America never sided with Ajiz over Fran, and to move on. "What do you plan to do with your success?"

"Carnival truck," she announced. "When I started the competition, I wanted a small café where I had the power to kick people out to make them go away. Before our Chloe left us, though..."

She paused to choke down her emotion, then continued.

"...she suggested that if my café was on wheels, I could just drive away from them. Or, you know, over them. So, I'm going with a carnival truck. Fran's Carnival Onion Rings, you bring the big top, we'll bring the food."

"Oh, you mean a food truck," replied Rhonda in an unwise attempt to go toe-to-toe against Fran-level conviction.

"Carnival truck," Fran repeated with a withering glance at such an amateur combatant. "Food trucks don't have near enough windows. I need to see things."

"National treasure, our Fran's onion rings," Ajiz piped up, followed by a chorus of assent from among the ranks.

"Beloved institution, the world isn't ready."

"They need to get ready."

"Work out now America, you need to make some room in those eatin' pants."

"I don't get it," said Vivian. Still considering herself the voice of the popular kids, certainly the last one to be eliminated, she turned to look direct to camera for support from the viewers at home. The control room, however, took the reaction shot from Fran rolling her eyes at the audience, instead of sour grapes from the 5th runner up.

"Sounds like you already have your first regular customers, Fran, and a few people who are not yet believers. We wish you all the best! Let's turn now to our second-place contestant," Rhonda announced, moving down the front row, still vigorously pointing and waving her giant microphone at people as if it did something. "What a photo finish. Beets, it's the hill so many *Yes, Chef!* contestants have died on. How are you are feeling?"

"Fine."

"Any regrets?"

"No."

Thankfully, Al the cameraman, with help from the control room in his ear, was able to anticipate such a lively interview segment and augment it with more background whispers from the other contestants.

"Not one for words, our Travis."

"He just had to live up to that orange shirt, even after they only provided him with a butane stove."

"What's the plan, Travis?" broke in Rhonda over the murmurs, still confident she had the interview skills to weasel secrets and information out of a contestant notorious for letting his food speak for him. "Going back to the pumpkin farm?"

"*Uh*...carnival truck," he answered.

"Another carnival truck? We seem to be setting a new food trend here at *Yes, Chef! America.*"

"Should we tell her?" whispered Ajiz to Felix.

"She'll figure it out."

Oliver shook his head at them.

"I don't think she will."

"Even Fran knows she can't build an entire business with tempura as the only food group," interjected Janiva, the new proud owner of Okla-Somo Steakhouse and Sushi Bar. "Somebody has to at least offer her customers romaine wedges. "

"Let it go!" hissed Felix with some urgency. "If you guys start rumors on national TV, you know, two people, one truck and piss off Wallace before I start my new job, I will never forgive you."

"Tell her the name, Travis!" Oliver shouted down the row, knowing far better than Rhonda how to get their phlegmatic friend to finish his marketing pitch before the commercial break.

"The Farmer's Carnival," he replied, "our good time is good for you."

"America was behind you all the way, Travis, just as much as Jimmy Bob," said Rhonda, wrapping up the hostile witness interview with relief, and ready to move on to segments and topics more on brand for the shiny, happy, Upstate New York version of Chef Parker.

"America, Travis taken out by a root vegetable wasn't the only unexpected upset. Who can forget the tragic departure of fan favorite, Chloe? Fennel, fire, and then fainting, Fran, what would you like to say about your old roommate? Are you ready now to tell us about that sauce?"

"KHS! forever, baby. We did it!" Fran answered with another teary sniff, refusing the bait to vent about almost maybe losing out on her title, somehow, over a rogue red sauce, while behind her the former Blue Team members flashed their now-famous gang signs.

Fran's invocation of a mantra that inspired a nation required Rhonda to dig deep as a journalist and make the hard turn to cover the KHS! Experience among the top tier contestants. The one's with a soul, that is, and lucky enough to have survived past Week 6. Undaunted, she expertly guided the discussion to that week's karaoke reward and got the show back on track highlighting Season 14's second biggest scandal – how Ajiz sang Ed Sheeran's "Perfect" for his absent wife, which didn't make it into the show, and how Oliver sang some Flo Rida's "Wild One's" for Ajiz for his absent wife, which did. Rhonda tried to make it even more of a thing, but Oliver, living the KHS! life out loud, finally took the first step towards resolving the long war between their fan bases. Turning to Ajiz in a spirit of conciliation, he said,

"You singing, me singing, it's the same, right?"

"How is that the same?" Ajiz protested. Again.

"It was for the best?"

"How is that for the best?"

"*Shhhh,*" said Oliver, "they are replaying my big finish."

"Wow, I will never make you eggplant surprise again."

"Yay," said Oliver, as he finished mouthing the chorus, "and it could have been worse. Who would you rather your wife ask to sing at your 15th wedding anniversary, me or Kyung-ho reprising *First Time Ever I Saw Your Face*? I ask you, who?"

Ajiz paused.

"You and your music are always welcome in our home."

Disappointed again, Rhonda moved on to highlight other spectacular low points. Troy's soup had its moment of silence, while everyone on set and across America took a moment to ask themselves, "Gourds? What happened". If only, Rhonda lamented – inside, where it counts – Chloe was there to see his injured wrist in a sling and start threatening people on national television. That would make good TV.

Tammy Firestarter, the (former) ER nurse and first eliminated contestant was also given her own look-back segment covering all three competition kitchen fires, plus recent B-roll showing her newfound success as a critical care veterinarian assistant. Her crudité platters were a welcome addition at all staff picnics and pet adoption clinics in the Boise TriCounty area.

"Good fit," said Felix, while Paul tried not to feel bad his nickname had stuck.

Jake, taken out Week 10 for his hubris in trying to go head-to-head against the memory of Paul's meatloaf, reported that he was now Lead Instigator on *Love Trap*, the show where people tested their partner's faithfulness by secretly filming them getting hit on by far more attractive strangers, wondering what would happen. Jake played a variety of characters offering to cook the targets oysters and chocolate fondue. Not a show with a lot of suspense, it was no *Yes, Chef!*, but *Love Trap* successfully exploited how everybody loves a Jake Sexy from the safety of their living rooms, and was riding the schadenfreude train to syndication.

His on-and-off girlfriend, Vivian, had hung on almost a full week in the competition without him, and announced she was now the CEO of her father's food supply company, as expected, and had brought on Ashley as the Head Taster for their "re-purposed surplus" division.

"Who's Ashley?" asked Rhonda.

"She means Echo," explained Fran. Not that Ashley liked being called Echo, but it was better than being remembered for her peas.

Vivian frowned and looked around in surprise when Rhonda had no follow-up questions for her. Despite being such an early favorite, however, nobody at home much remembered her except as a vague, bad luck charm. Her only performance that made the show's highlight reel was her ability to make small orange squares out of carrots, and what was that compared to Paul's (mother's) short ribs and Fran's legendary onion rings in a rainbow of salt flavors? The clothing company that sponsored her outfits had tried to make a thing about dressing her like a Bond Villain, but even that didn't really catch on.

Echo, now that had caught on, and once reminded of Ashley's proper title, Rhonda began polling the contestants on their favorite snarky meme. It hadn't forwarded Ashley's career in food or media relations to be the face of ironic, "that'll never work" sentiment in America, or have her fifteen-second watermelon mousse fiasco video go viral on TikTok as a doomsday scenario, but still, it was better than being remembered for her peas.

"Why doesn't Aaron have a meme?" she complained.

Grateful for the assist, the cool kids abandoned the low hanging fruit of mocking Ashley and wrested the segment away from the voices in Rhonda's ear. As vowed back in Week 2, they insisted Aaron's new company be fully celebrated, despite its utter lack of dramatic appeal to hold the audience over through the next commercial break.

"What's the "Aaron Caters for You" house specialty?" Fran asked, because Rhonda wasn't going to.

Prompted by an encouraging clap on his shoulder from Troy, his designated bodyguard for the reunion, Aaron answered in a low mumble,

"Well, our brides report very positive guest responses to our short ribs. They aren't Paul-level..."

"Nobody's are," said Travis, keeping it real as Aaron's marketing effort trailed off. The cool kids doggedly held the awkward pause, however, until Aaron, encouraged (threatened?) by a more forceful nudge, restated his pitch.

"...unfortuately, Paul works in another state," Aaron continued with a tiny bit more volume, "but everyone likes how well his (mother's) recipe travels..."

"Well, we wouldn't want you cooking for crazy people," responded Fran, finding a camera to interject some much-needed conviction. "Hear that Detroit? You too can bring the Paul Standard to your next event."

Ding!

Ding!

Ding, ding, ding, ding, ding, ding...

Troy released Aaron's shoulder to let him fumble around for his phone's ringer, and Rhonda took advantage of the distraction to get back on script. She quickly turned the audience's attention to B-roll of Oliver all sexy-craggy out at sea. It did make much better TV than watching Aaron poke at beef in a stewpan, but his business needed far less of the limited Reunion Show promotional spotlight. America discovered, when invited back after two minutes of words from the show's sponsors, that business at Catch as Catch Can Café was booming. Oliver used his plug time to instead ask for continued fan support in convincing Paul to give up being a rich Philadelphia lawyer, ignore any catering opportunities in Motown and move to Gloucester to be his poor sous chef.

"Everybody knows you would be happier abandoning materialistic, non-culinary pursuits while learning how to sing a decent sea chanty," Oliver insisted, forcefully reiterating with his best head shake the argument all of America had been having on Twitter once Paul devastated the dining public by announcing that working less and just having more dinner parties was the right balance in his food journey. "When was the last time you had snapper, and don't even pretend you can get a decent lobster roll where you live. America has voted."

"Not a chance," Paul responded. "My husband likes money and doesn't like fish."

A collective sigh went out across the land. Fans both at home and in the live audience recognized the same finality and commitment that got him sent home for making Spaghetti Bolognese during Thai Me a River! Week. Always painful to watch real time, they knew to cook the Paul Standard their boy had to live the Paul Standard, whatever the cost.

"Now everybody, we have a special surprise!" Rhonda interjected with an added layer of bright enthusiasm, which might have been fear, when a new series of commands sounded in her ear. "It wasn't certain whether our satellite link would work at this altitude, but our tech guys have really outdone themselves. Please welcome, all the way from Seoul, fan favorite Chloe joining us via Zoom, along with Guest Judge for Gimme Some Sugar! Week, you know that wasn't his mad face, Chef Ji Kyung-ho!"

"Hi guys!!!" Chloe said, waving at the camera as she came up on what the audience at home now saw was a large screen set up on the other side of Rhonda that allowed the contestants to see, or hide from, the clips being highlighted.

"Where's my Troy?" she asked.

"KHS!" came the answering cry from the tiers, while Rhonda pointed her microphone at the newcomer and braced for the segment she had not rehearsed, and one contestant hid his bandaged arm behind Ajiz.

It was late morning in Seoul, and Chloe and Kyung-ho were seen seated outside at a metal table with a brick wall behind them topped by a heavy vine of purple wisteria. Kyung-ho looked remarkably less austere with his arm around Chloe's shoulders than he ever had standing in front of her. Suddenly, in the middle of their hello's, a large crash was heard off screen.

Hoping for a breaking news segment to take back to Poughkeepsie, Rhonda quickly asked,

"Is everything okay there, Chloe?"

Chloe turned her head slightly to listen to the noise.

"Oh yeah, that isn't us, Beer Cream is getting a delivery."

"Beer Cream? What's a Beer Cream?"

Chloe nodded knowingly at Rhonda's confusion.

"No idea, but their business model is indestrucible. They're having, like, their seventh blowout sale."

"Okay, moving on!" said Rhonda, unknowingly losing her promotion to co-host *Good Morning Albany* by failing to report out such an enduring mystery when it landed in her lap. Doggedly pointing her giant microphone at the giant screen, she stuck to asking the tough questions from people contractually required to answer them.

"Chloe, the first thing on everybody's mind is, how are you feeling?"

"Chef just gave me this garden, isn't it nice?" she responded, flashing the audience at home her characteristic, bright smile. "Who knew heaven came with bees, plated desserts, and a whole platoon of sous chefs to chop things for me. The US Army loves them some Marsden Sweet & Sassy to bring them a taste of home. I kinda feel like I'm in the USO."

"She gives them advice, condiments, and sings 80's classics," reported Kyung-ho. "I think they may want to send her to the DMZ."

"Aren't you ever coming home?" asked Fran. "The Carnival needs you more than North Korea."

"Oh, yeah. Soon. Maybe. Love to be there for the premiere of *Zombie Killer Dolphins Are Coming for You!*, there's a cult classic waiting for a release date. Hi Al!" she said waving at the cameraman behind the camera.

"Getting back to today's news," she continued, "congrats to Fran and Travis!! I knew you could do it!!!"

"I didn't win," reminded the ever-laconic runner-up, "Fran did."

"It was probably the strawberries," added Rhonda.

"Don't be silly, Linus. We all did. You showed up, and did the next right thing and oh look, started a new, worldwide phenomenon in food delivery. There's representing for the cool kids. Plus, you won the extra, secret bonus prize – finding all of us – and we love you just as much as we love Paul. That's a lot. I don't know how much more of an overachiever you expect yourself to be."

"None of that comes with a title. Or a quarter of a million dollars."

"True, right, of course you're right, but anybody can have one of those."

Anybody could also see he remained unconvinced and deeply unhappy with his performance.

"I know you didn't get the outcome you thought you needed to change your life, Linus, but you are mistaken. Which is great news, because you thought you had to be perfect. Nope. You thought you had to "win". Nope. Now that that reveal is behind us, now we get to see all the infinite ways God can bless you that don't involve a giant, cardboard check."

"Today it sucks. Yes. It's scary and embarrassing and it sucks, and it sucks to live through the sucky part of a story. But it's not the end of the story. It's just the listen to Lee Ann Womack part. Can I get an amen, Big A?"

"Her department," Ajiz immediately concurred. "Name one time she has ever been wrong about these things."

"You can't, no one can. The woman knows," said Chloe. "Listen, trust and believe, Linus."

In a low, clear voice, she began to sing.

"I hope you still feel small when you stand beside the ocean...,"

"I know I do," said Oliver.

"Whenever one door closes, I hope one more opens..."

"Feel it, you know she's right," counseled Ajiz, and added his low, backup tenor. Behind him the contestants – the one's with a soul – started to bob and sway along with finger snaps.

Despite Rhonda pointing her giant microphone with full Fran-level conviction towards Red Shirt Ronnie – as if anyone dumb enough to think Chef Parker ate food plated off the floor had something more to contribute to the culinary world – Al trained his camera on the giant screen, and their Linus, the rest of the contestants, the audience at home, the crew, Chloe's husband, and the thousands of next year's hopefuls tuning in listened to her serenade. By the chorus, even the great pumpkin farmer gave in to a higher authority and the convicting elbow from his new business partner. He raised his workworn hand to join the others waving their arms over their heads, and together the cool kids brought the *Yes, Chef! America* dance party one more time to close out the legendary Season 14. Slow jam style.

I hope you never fear those mountains in the distance
Never settle for the path of least resistance
Livin' might mean takin' chances, but they're worth takin'
Lovin' might be a mistake, but it's worth makin'
Don't let some Hell-bent heart leave you bitter
When you come close to sellin' out, reconsider
Give the Heavens above more than just a passing glance
And when you get the choice to sit it out or dance

Dance
I hope you dance.

about the author

Judith F. Kennedy is a writer, ancient historian, and Historic Preservation policy wonk who was born in the Berkshires and grew up on the North Shore of Boston. She has been known to run off to Paris because it was a Thursday, and has a special place in her heart for social media posts of cockatiels dancing to K-pop. She sends this book out to the people doing the work with love, a mustard seed of courage and no available parachute. It has been the author's great privilege to travel the country and halfway around the world recording your adventures, supporting your efforts, and celebrating the impact you may have never known you had.